BETH BOLDEN

Prologue

The flashbulbs going off again and again were nearly blinding as Micah faced the cluster of photographers.

"Get closer, and let's take one more picture of you two," someone insisted.

Micah glanced over at Beck, who'd just been hugging his agent, celebrating that he'd been taken in the first round in the NFL draft.

Micah had been taken a few picks before, the Miami Piranhas hat sitting on his head making everything more real than it had been only an hour before, when his future had been totally up in the air.

It wasn't anymore. Now it was set in stone. He was going to play football for the Piranhas and Miami would be his new home. He'd never have to worry about money ever again.

He'd just have to worry about everything else.

"Yeah, one more picture?" Beck said, turning back to him with a bright, infectious grin. He was wearing his own Charleston Condors hat tilted to the side, his curly brown hair peeking out from underneath it.

Tonight was supposed to be all about beginnings, but Micah was surprisingly stuck on the one thing that was ending: his partnership with Beck.

Beck slung his arm around Micah and tugged him close, with zero hesitation, the way Beck had never once hesitated to touch him.

It was like the prickles that had started out as a mere annoyance, then turned into daggers, insistently digging into him, reminding Micah of all the things he still refused to acknowledge, didn't bother Beck at all.

Maybe they didn't.

Maybe touching him wasn't like when he touched Beck and it was heaven and hell combined into one bitterly sweet moment.

Beck's arm, thick with muscle, tightened. "You alright?" he asked under his breath, after the photographer had gotten his shots, but Beck still didn't let him go.

Micah shrugged, not sure if he was okay or not.

Maybe in time these burning feelings—all the yearnings he didn't want to have—would pass. He wouldn't see Beck every day anymore.

Beck wouldn't be a stranger, because he wasn't designed like that. He was quiet and easygoing, the foil to Micah's high intensity. He was someone Micah could always go to, no matter what, and he could trust him to be exactly what he needed, even though he never said it. But it wouldn't be the same. Not ever again.

"It's gonna be weird," Beck said. "Not seeing you all the time."

Micah knew, and suddenly, he wasn't prepared for it.

Nothing about the draft had felt real until the Piranhas had called his name and then half an hour later Roger Goodell had announced Beck's.

"But don't worry," Beck continued, "you're not getting rid of me that easily."

Beck released him then, and for a second, all Micah wanted was to get lost in that prickly, uncomfortable, stomach-swooping feeling again.

He reached up and tugged Beck's hat, trying to fix it, but finally giving it up as a lost cause. "We should go out after this."

"Don't you have to fly to Miami first thing in the morning?" Like Beck wasn't headed to Charleston equally as early. Rookie camps wouldn't be starting for a month or two but before that, teams always liked to bring in their new players to visit, to talk to the media, and to get the lay of the land.

"Yeah, but still." Micah shrugged awkwardly. "We're in New York. We can find a bar, get a few drinks, celebrate . . .well, celebrate. One last night."

The funny thing was he'd anticipated feeling so differently in this moment. After all those years of hellish hard work, expectations, and unbelievable pressure, he should be elated. Joyous. Full of relief.

But all he felt was regret, and it tasted bitter at the back of his throat.

Beck tucked his head in close.

"Yeah, we can do that," Beck said. He glanced behind him, where a whole table of his family was sitting. His family was huge and diverse. Micah's table had only contained his mother and his uncle. Beck had probably needed *two* tables. "But I gotta deal with the fam first, okay?"

Beck was so much more than the sum of his parts. Hazel eyes. Dark brown hair, which he never cut properly, and too many days of scruff on his chin, still. He wasn't even close to the most handsome guy on the planet. In fact, he was just like every other fit white guy, and yet he was the one Micah couldn't help but look at twice.

He'd stopped asking himself why that was, and started asking when it would finally end.

Maybe *this* was the end.

Maybe that was what they were actually celebrating: the final death of the most unfortunate crush in existence.

A crush so persistent and insidious and inappropriate, it had snuck up on him slowly, when he wasn't paying attention. He'd been half in his feelings before he'd even realized what was happening.

This was Beck. He was his goddamned best friend. And even though Beck had confessed a few years back that he was gay, he'd never given a single hint he was into Micah.

They'd been friends, *only*.

Up until now, Micah would've said that was a great thing, the *best* thing, but now, he felt torn apart by the possibility that there *were* no more possibilities. It was only six hundred miles between Charleston and Miami—he'd looked, the first second he could, which was an extra level of ridiculous, even for him—and yet it felt like a million.

"Yeah, sure, take care of whatever you need. Text me when you're free." He would go over and see his mother. Make sure she got back to her hotel alright. Avoid talking to his uncle if he could.

He hadn't wanted Josiah to come tonight, but his mother had insisted, claiming that his uncle wanted to support Micah.

But he knew, better than anyone else, including his mother, what Josiah really wanted was for Micah to support *him*.

Hell was gonna freeze over before that ever happened.

"You're staying at the Hilton, right?" Beck asked, putting a hand on his arm.

"Yeah," Micah said with a sharp nod.

"Good," Beck said. "Same as me."

Was it just Micah and all this sudden inexplicable regret, or was Beck touching him more now than he'd ever done? Beck was normally a pretty touchy-feely guy. Always reassuring, always with a friendly smile, a nice pat on the back, anything to make Micah feel like he was part of something.

Not just part of the team they'd played on for Northwestern, but a team of the two of them. It was why they'd been nicknamed the Wall. They were so much bigger than the sum of their parts.

It was the Wall against the world.

But tonight, it felt like Beck was touching him whenever he could, like he had Micah's same reluctance to let go.

Like he didn't want to let *him* go.

"Well, I'll see you soon, then," Beck said and then turned away, heading back to where his family sat in the green room.

Micah posed for three more pictures and signed two Piranhas hats before he made it over to where Sheila, his mother, sat with Josiah.

She was holding herself stiffly upright, like she was nervous, which she didn't have to be anymore. He'd taken care of it. Tomorrow she wouldn't have bills. Tomorrow she wouldn't have a house payment.

He'd be the one to handle that for her now, the same way she'd handled everything for him when he'd been growing up, not letting him worry or stress about where their rent was coming from, or if there'd be a meal on the table when he got home from practice. She'd refused to let him shoulder that burden, and now he would finally be able to repay her.

"Oh, good, there you are," Josiah said. "Your momma's tired. She needs to get back to the hotel. It's been a long night."

"No, no, no need. We can stay and celebrate a little longer." Sheila tilted her chin up, in defiance of Josiah's edict. Sometimes Micah thought *she* didn't even like him, her own brother, and yet he not only continued to be invited to things, she often did the inviting herself.

Like tonight.

"Actually, I've got plans, so we can go whenever you want," Micah said awkwardly.

"With who?" Sheila asked as she gathered her purse together, and Micah reached over to give her a hand to help her stand in her heels.

"Beck," Micah said, refusing to hesitate when he spoke his friend's name.

Sheila loved Beck.

But not surprisingly Josiah had never warmed up to him.

Probably because the first time they'd met, Beck had casually mentioned seeing a guy, romantically.

That was all it took for Josiah Rose.

It wasn't like Micah agreed with him. He didn't. He *wouldn't*. Especially when it came to someone who was not only a great friend, but a fucking amazing football player.

"Ah," Josiah said knowingly. "That guy."

"*That guy* got me to the NFL," Micah argued, even though he'd told himself that he wouldn't argue. That it wasn't worth it.

Josiah didn't say anything back.

He didn't need to. Micah knew the score with him.

"Come on," Sheila said soothingly, playing the peacemaker like she always did. "Let's head back to the hotel."

As they walked out the exit, Micah couldn't help the rogue thought.

She should be standing up for Beck, too. She knows what a good guy he is. How much he's helped me.

But she didn't, because these were their parts.

Josiah would pick on Micah, fucking pick him apart, and then Micah would blow up and then Sheila would soothe.

It was all they knew how to do, apparently.

One thing Micah wouldn't miss when he was in Miami was this dynamic.

This wasn't a thought he allowed himself to have very often, but every once in awhile he wondered what his life would've been like if his father hadn't died young, in a bad car accident on a wet road, leaving his mother to raise him on her own. Sheila had ended up leaning on her brother, because that was the family *she* had. And the only family Micah had inherited.

He would blame her a lot more for letting Josiah hang around, if he didn't know how tough her life had been as a young widow with a three-year-old kid to raise.

He finally got his mother and Josiah settled into the hotel, told her that if she needed anything, she could call the front desk. When Josiah had asked him where he and Beck were going, he'd ignored him.

His mood already questionable enough, he didn't need Josiah making it worse.

Or assuming Beck was somehow going to corrupt him by taking him to a gay bar—even if Micah secretly, deep down, probably in a place not even Beck suspected, wanted to know what that might be like.

When he finally left his mom's room, he headed to his own, changing out of the sharp purple pinstripe suit he'd worn for the Draft ceremony and throwing on a T-shirt and jeans. Then he grabbed his phone, texting Beck that he'd be downstairs in the hotel bar.

He was nursing a few fingers of whiskey when Beck slid onto the barstool next to him.

"You should be way too happy to look this glum," Beck said, elbowing him, as he motioned to the bartender to bring him a beer. "You're literally angsting into that glass."

"I am not," Micah retorted. Except he had been.

He'd been sitting here thinking that this might be the last time in a long time he and Beck would meet up like this, even though they'd done it on the regular for the last four years.

And he'd been thinking, *God, that fucking sucks.*

"I told you," Beck said confidently, "you're not getting rid of me that easily. After all, what is it, only six hundred or so miles from Charleston to Miami?"

Micah stared at his friend. Surprised that Beck had looked too.

"What?" Beck laughed a little self-consciously.

"You looked too," Micah said reflexively. Couldn't help himself.

"Well, *yeah*, you think I don't give a shit about you?" Beck asked, the question clearly rhetorical. He slung an arm around Micah, loose and happy and easy in a way Micah couldn't help but envy.

That he'd *always* envied.

But then, Beck didn't have any reason not to be loose and happy and easy.

He had a huge family who adored him, who'd never even blinked when he'd come out to them, who owned a huge rambling house on the outskirts of Chicago, in one of the more affluent suburbs, and their future wasn't resting exclusively on Beck's prospects in the NFL.

He could afford to fuck up. He could afford to do whatever the hell he wanted.

And yet, Micah had loved him anyway, when with anyone else, he'd have been bitter and resentful as hell.

"It's just gonna be . . .weird," Micah said. *Awful. Terrible. I'm gonna be all alone, nobody to trust, to lean on, the way I do with you. And after you, I don't know how to be alone anymore.*

"Hey, you even have the best freaking corner in the world to teach you," Beck said brightly. "You're gonna learn so fucking much from Sebastian Howard."

Or Sebastian Howard would take one look at him and see right through his act.

"Yeah. Well. Gonna be interesting."

"Not as interesting as me existing in the same space as Tom fucking Taylor," Beck retorted, sounding, for the first time all evening, not completely thrilled he'd been drafted in the first round.

"You make sure to hand his ass to him on the regular, okay? I know you can do it." Like Beck, Micah wasn't a fan of anyone who decided women were a convenient punching bag.

"Sure," Beck said with a bittersweet smile. He knocked back the rest of his beer. "You have anywhere in particular you wanna go?"

Micah shook his head. New York was overwhelming, in a good way mostly, but also just plain staggering. And he'd lived in Chicago for four years.

"There's this bar a friend recommended," Beck said. He pulled out his phone and typed the name in.

"A friend?" Micah couldn't help the question.

Beck did date. Not much. But frequently enough Micah occasionally heard about his partners.

Had to quell the insistent surge of jealousy that rolled through him every single time, even though Beck never seemed to be serious about any of them.

"Okay, you caught me. It was a guy I hooked up with a few months back." Beck shot him a look. "Are you really okay? You seem . . .off."

He was fucking freaking out, that was what he was doing.

Micah had known, of course, that this was all ending. His college life. The Wall. The super-close friendship with Beck. But none of it had seemed real, not until his name had been called and then Beck's.

And now he couldn't shake just how fucking real it felt.

"I'm just gonna . . ." Micah swallowed hard, then tipped the rest of the glass into his mouth, letting the burn of the alcohol give him more courage to admit the truth than he might've before. "Just gonna miss you, that's all."

Beck *glowed*. He shouldn't look this goddamn happy they were being forcibly separated, Micah thought morosely, but then Beck teased, "Awwww, you love me, Rose. I knew it!"

"Yeah, yeah," Micah retorted. "Come on, find that bar. I wanna get drunk."

He wanted to remember every moment, every single time Beck looked at him, every glance he returned, and he didn't want to remember any of them, at the exact same goddamn time.

It would be easier, maybe, with booze dulling the thoughts that wouldn't quit.

"Alright, I got it," Beck said.

Micah shoved a few twenties under a paper coaster, and they slid off their barstools. He couldn't remember the last time his wallet had been this full. The last time he hadn't had a budget for a night out. The idea was intoxicating.

They could go out and do anything.

Anything.

Outside the hotel, the valet attendant waved a cab down and they slid in, Beck giving the address.

Beck, who was annoyingly a few inches taller, stretched out his legs in the back seat, his thigh brushing Micah's, and normally, he might've moved away.

But how many more times would they touch like this?

Before tonight, the number had felt infinite.

Now it felt like it had a beginning, and also a very concrete end.

He shifted, letting his leg rest a bit more purposefully against Beck's as the cab pulled out into traffic.

Beck didn't move, just looked over at him, a quiet, assessing look in his light eyes, but he didn't say anything.

"How far is it?" Micah asked awkwardly into the silence that had fallen between them.

"Not sure, but it comes highly recommended, at least," Beck said wryly.

The want that lived inside him, that rose and fell with unsurprising regularity, spiked and then didn't relent, just with the feel of Beck's muscular leg against his own.

Casually, Beck set his hand on his knee, the back of it brushing Micah's. It could've been inadvertent, but then he didn't move it.

It turned out the drive wasn't far. But the whole ten minutes was chaotic, the cab moving in starts and stops, the horn blaring out more than once. When they finally came to a stop in front of a low brick building on a side street, Micah's heartbeat hadn't slowed one bit.

He told himself as they climbed out that crazy New York drivers were the reason why, but he knew deep down that it wasn't true.

Was it possible that Beck . . .?

No way, Micah insisted to himself.

But it was undeniable Beck was standing closer to him, his hand a ghost touch on the small of Micah's back as they approached the door.

Glancing up at one of the small dingy windows, Micah stopped in his tracks, Beck so close to him that he nearly plowed into him, the impact of his big, broad body tempered by his soft, gentle touch.

Beck saw immediately what he'd noticed.

A big rainbow flag spread across the window.

Every muscle in Beck's body stiffened, like he was bracing for something.

For Micah to tell him no fucking way would he go in there?

For Micah to say something derogatory even though he never had before?

Maybe...Micah wondered...Beck was waiting for him to tell the truth.

That he'd always wanted to go to a gay bar, but he'd never found the courage to do it before.

"If you don't . . ." Beck trailed off. Like he didn't want to actually vocalize the thought—or the question.

But this was Beck.

Surely he had to know Micah wouldn't.

Maybe he's guessed about you, too.

It was weird because at any point before this, Micah would've shied away from the truth in Beck's touch. Even as he strained toward it.

But not tonight.

"No," Micah said, surprising even himself with the vehemence in his tone. "No, let's go. I've always wanted . . ." He couldn't finish the sentence. It would've left him naked. Exposed.

Beck was suddenly next to him, a wealth of reassurance in the brush of his hand against Micah's waist. "Yeah, okay," he said. "Let's go."

Beck was the one who pushed open the door, the heavy bass thundering through the club echoing the fierce thumping of Micah's heartbeat.

They paid the cover, the bouncer checking their IDs, and then they ventured farther into the smoky darkness.

The bar was lit up with neon pink and purple lights around the edges, beckoning like a beacon, and Micah led them there, because liquid courage was going to be necessary.

"Whiskey," he demanded the moment the young, cute bartender with the trendy haircut, blond hair streaked with blue, appeared in front of them. "Shots. And keep them coming."

Beck raised his eyebrow, but he didn't say a word as the guy poured two shots and left the bottle within easy reach.

Maybe he was used to seeing guys trying to pretend they belonged by ingesting tons and tons of booze.

Micah had never wanted to believe he was a cliche, but it seemed he was, anyway.

He picked up the first shot and tossed it back, the liquor burning his throat as he swallowed.

Beck licked the edge of his shot glass first, pink tongue darting out, and Micah knew he was staring.

Knew, maybe for the first time, that it didn't matter if he was.

"That's shitty," Beck said, laughing a little as he swallowed his liquor.

"More," Micah said, raising his voice to the bartender.

The blue-haired guy eyed them, but he poured the shots anyway.

They took two more rounds, and by then Beck was leaning against the bar, looking loose and happy.

"I'm worried about you," he said, after they took the third round. "I wasn't. But now . . ."

"Now what?" Micah retorted. He knew Beck never would've tried to talk to him like this, not if they were sober.

They both pretended like Micah had his shit together.

"You should be happier. You just got everything you wanted."

Oh, if only that was true.

The funny thing was that Micah had believed—or rather, he'd *wanted* so goddamn hard to believe—that he'd done it. That having his name called during the first round of the NFL draft was the peak achievement he'd been looking for this whole time.

But hearing it had proven that wasn't true.

He still felt empty.

Still felt like nobody really saw him.

Except, of course, the man who was looking at him now.

Beck had always seen him. Maybe even a little too clearly.

"Not everything," Micah muttered.

"I know," Beck said, and his hip nudged Micah's. "We knew it couldn't happen. Just like we wouldn't win the Heisman."

"We got there, though," Micah said, like he was trying to remind both of them.

"And we got this, too." Beck hesitated. "I told you, you're not getting rid of me that easily, Rose."

"You keep sayin' that, and I don't even know what it means," Micah griped. Though he wanted to believe he did.

That it meant no matter where they were, what they were doing, what team they were playing for, they were ride-or-die for each other. That they'd always have each other's backs.

But it *would* be different, not having Beck on the field next to him. Would be different not seeing his calm smile in the locker room before practice.

Beck motioned for the bartender to pour another round. Yep, they were in this now.

Maybe what they needed was half a dozen shots each to be really honest about this.

About this desire crawling under his skin that he'd never been able to banish entirely.

"You do know," Beck said matter-of-factly, "you're my best friend. That isn't going to change."

But what if I want it to change?

It was insane, to even think it.

Six hundred miles.

That was the first and last reason it was insane and then there were a ton of other reasons in between.

Micah nursed his next shot, sipping it. Feeling Beck's eyes on him.

For once not flinching away from the warmth in his gaze.

The way it was tracing the edges of him.

Beck didn't do it very often. In fact, Micah couldn't remember the last time. He'd believed, because it had been easier and a hell of a lot more convenient, that it didn't mean what he knew it did.

"You need to get your hair cut more often, and by someone who knows what the fuck they're doing," Micah said instead, reaching up and brushing one of Beck's curls aside. He had great hair. Micah wanted to bury his hands in it as he leaned in and . . .

You're not gonna think about that. You're not gonna go there.

"Motivation to see me more often," Beck said with a grin. "You can drag me to some barber who charges more than a cup of coffee."

He turned away and picked up his shot and downed it in one swallow, throat working, and Micah stared, mesmerized even though he didn't want to be.

A guy approached Beck's side of the bar and the way Beck tilted his head down to hear him, a frisson of something raced up Micah's spine.

It wasn't jealousy. It couldn't be.

But this was *their* night.

He couldn't go as far as to say Beck was his, because he knew that wasn't true, but tonight, just for the space of a night, he wanted to pretend they weren't going their separate ways in the morning.

"Sorry," Beck said, raising his voice a little. Like he wanted Micah to know he'd turned the guy down.

The guy, who was undeniably cute, shrugged, and went off to look for easier prey.

Beck shifted his weight back, and the look in his eyes was suddenly too clear, too blunt.

Micah wasn't proud of it, but he panicked.

What are you doing?

He didn't fucking know.

"You could've—"

Beck stared at him in disbelief. "You wanted me to go with him," he interrupted before Micah could even finish his sentence.

"No. *No.*" He could say that much.

"Then what *do* you want?" Beck asked, like this wasn't the most loaded question in fucking history.

Like Micah could actually vocalize what it was he did want.

"I want things to not change. I want everything to stay how it is, now. I want to be here, with you. I want you to not leave tomorrow. I want to stay, too. I want . . ." Micah's voice cracked.

God, he must be drunk.

He was definitely getting there, but he couldn't say he didn't know what he was saying.

His filter, totally demolished by the alcohol and the desperation swelling inside him at the thought of flying to Miami while Beck flew to Charleston, told the truth for him.

Beck didn't say anything for a long minute. "You never told me," he said softly.

There was a part of Micah that wanted to cry. Another to yell at him that he *couldn't, wasn't he smart enough to know that?*

But he didn't do either.

"It wouldn't have changed anything," he said bitterly.

"It could've," Beck insisted. "God, come 'ere, I thought maybe, but I wasn't sure. You never said." Then suddenly he was being pulled into Beck's big, strong body, and Beck was hugging him for all he was worth.

It wasn't the same as Beck telling him that he felt the same, but it was good enough.

For one endless moment, he hung onto Beck's bigger frame, enjoying the feel of his body pressed against his own.

Feeling his love and his acceptance. Even if it was platonic, it was going to have to be enough.

It *would* be enough.

It was Beck who moved away first. Micah didn't know if he could've.

"Come on," Beck said, reaching out and touching his arm, like he didn't really want to let go. "You wanna dance?"

"You don't dance," Micah teased. It turned out just by telling Beck, the burden of his secret felt lighter.

"Yeah, but I don't know, the music's pretty good. Even I probably can't mess that up."

"I'm not sure," Micah drew out the last syllable. "Maybe I don't want any of these guys to know I'm slumming it."

Beck elbowed him in the side, but he was smiling. "Maybe," he said, leaning in a fraction, his breath brushing Micah's cheek, "I don't care. Maybe I only care about you. And I think you care about me."

Trust Beck to cut right to the quick, right to the truth, deep down where it burned inside Micah.

Micah didn't answer. He just took his last shot and then, before he could overthink it, reached for Beck's hand.

It was warm and big and callused and felt so goddamn right, Micah found himself squeezing it. Felt Beck squeeze right back as they wandered over to where a few dozen guys and girls were moving under the pulsating lights.

Beck *couldn't* dance. He sort of flailed around without a single fucking shred of rhythm, and it was probably good Micah had had a few drinks by this point because he could only smile and then laugh out loud as Beck wiggled his hips and then his eyebrows suggestively.

On the other hand, Micah knew he *could* dance, but while he'd done it plenty of times over the years in front of Beck—at parties, in bars, after practice in the locker room, in the end zone a handful of times after he'd picked off an opposing player—it had never felt like this before.

Beck's gaze never left Micah's body as he twisted and turned it, grooving along to the intense beat of the music.

They had a few feet in between them, but as one song segued into the next, Micah found himself drifting closer, like they were magnets and it was impossible for them to stay apart any longer.

Maybe it wasn't actually his last chance, but it *felt* like it. The last possible moment, frozen in time, before everything changed for good.

He reached out, and his hand, oh so casually, brushed Beck's hip.

Micah felt rather than heard Beck's sharp intake of breath.

His pulse was beating unevenly, echoing in his head, and then he took a step closer.

"Like this," Micah said, raising his voice so Beck would hear him over the music. It was a completely transparent reason to touch him, to set his hands on Beck's waist, and pull him in closer, showing him the rhythm, but Beck came easily. Tilting his head like he was wondering how far Micah was prepared to take this.

The problem was Micah didn't know how far that was.

He only knew he wanted more, and Beck was willingly giving it to him.

"Yeah?" Beck's voice cracked.

There was no denying it now. He felt lit up inside, more aroused touching Beck's toned waist over his cotton T-shirt than he'd ever been with a woman, when she was completely naked.

He'd never gone even this far before because of the fear it would prove something he hadn't wanted to know about himself, but there was no denying it now as Beck moved into the circle of his arms.

Then Beck turned and he was so close, that even in the dim light, Micah could pick out the hundred different colors in his eyes.

Could practically feel how soft his scruff might be against his hand. Against his cheek. Against his mouth.

You only feel this free cause you're drunk.

That was true and yet it didn't matter.

Beck took a deep breath and put a hand on Micah's shoulder. Was he going to kiss him, finally?

Oh, God.

Panic surged through Micah that Beck would do it—and that he wouldn't, at all.

How could he want both things, so desperately, so entirely?

But Beck came so far and didn't move any closer.

Was he waiting for Micah?

Panic roared through him, and even though he'd had too much whiskey, it wasn't enough.

"I'm thirsty," he announced instead.

He wasn't, not really.

They certainly didn't need more booze, and yet Micah still grabbed Beck and led him back to the bar.

But right before they got there, the sight in front of him stopped Micah in his tracks.

A very young, very fit guy hopped up on the bar and then pulled his T-shirt off to a cacophony of cheers, caging the other, bigger, guy between his legs as he pulled him in for what looked to Micah's eyes to be a completely filthy kiss.

You will not squirm. You will not think about what you want.

Or that what you want, more than anything, is . . .

"You okay?" It was Beck, leaning down, his lips practically brushing the shell of Micah's ear.

Was he okay?

He was not okay.

But he couldn't look away either. His eyes were practically glued to the pair in front of them, the heat of Beck at his back unmistakable.

They finally stopped kissing, and for a second, Micah thought he could breathe again.

But it was too soon.

Beck's hand, impossibly hotter than the rest of him, settled at his waist. He tugged him back, and *oh God*, he was just as aroused as Micah was. He could *feel* it, Beck's cock, pressed into him.

He'd thought he knew exactly what he craved, but he was wrong.

"Watch," Beck said, voice rough and low, and that was his mouth at Micah's ear again. "Just watch."

Micah's mouth went dry.

The younger guy on the bar had grabbed a saltshaker and was leaning back, sprinkling a stripe of it right down his abs.

Then the taller guy leaned in, and he was licking right up the salt, tongue lingering on the rippled golden skin.

Micah panted.

He didn't know what that felt like, what that *tasted* like. But he couldn't deny anymore that he needed it.

The guy took the shot of tequila with a dramatic flourish and then leaned in, plucking the lime from the other man's mouth, turning around to cheers.

"Hot, wasn't it?" Beck's voice rumbled against his neck.

Micah felt it deep down.

He couldn't do anything else but nod helplessly, arousal and all the booze they'd drunk burning right through any hesitation and any regret he'd ever felt.

Later, he wouldn't be able to say why he'd spoken up.

It was like the voice wasn't even his, like it came from someone else he'd buried in a bottomless pit, so far down he'd never really expected to see the light of day.

"We should do that," he said.

Beck froze behind him, his fingers tightening on his waist.

"Seriously?" Beck sounded incredulous.

And okay, it was crazy. It was totally, impossibly nuts.

Yet, Micah turned and nodded emphatically. Suddenly, it was absolutely fucking imperative they do this right now.

Right now.

He pushed through the crowd, lifting himself onto the bar in a single, hopefully graceful, movement before he could change his mind.

Beck was right there, his olive-toned skin flushed with heat and something else entirely different. Micah had never seen him look like that before.

Like he could *devour* him.

Beck's hand moved to his thigh, then higher, tugging up his T-shirt, and Micah let him, the catcalling of the guys surrounding them fading into the background as Micah practically knelt at the altar of his body.

The saltshaker was cold in his hand, and his fingers shook as he sprinkled the salt onto his skin, right above the waistband of his jeans.

Beck's eyes didn't darken, they fucking *glowed*, as Micah set the lime wedge between his teeth.

He leaned in and Micah hissed as Beck's lips touched his skin.

They were soft and warm, and probably everyone in this entire bar could see the hard line of Micah's cock in his jeans, could know much having Beck between his legs, Beck's mouth on his skin, turned him on.

Beck didn't linger though. He lifted his head and then took the shot, lifting himself up to take the lime wedge from Micah's mouth.

For a split second, he could almost imagine if the sour fruit wasn't between them, if it was just his lips and Beck's, pressing together, sweetly—even innocently—at first.

But it wouldn't stay sweet *or* innocent for long.

Hiding it forever meant that when he gave it freedom now, the desire tore at him with an insistence that scared the fuck out of him.

Beck's eyes fluttered open, so close to his own.

His hand found Micah's and squeezed, then helped him down from the bar.

"Well," Beck said, after he'd discarded the lime wedge in his empty shot glass.

"Well, *what?*" Micah demanded to know, even though he was pretty sure what Beck was saying—or *not* saying.

"You think you know a guy," Beck teased now. "But no, it was fun. It was—" Beck stopped right in the middle of his sentence.

He was staring right at Micah's mouth.

Like he was thinking about it too.

Micah got it.

He couldn't think about anything else either.

You can't kiss. If you do, you're never gonna be able to take it back. Not ever.

Then, even worse: *you won't even want to, not anymore.*

"Let's go dance," Micah blurted out.

"Oh, singing a different tune now, are we?" Beck questioned.

"Yes," Micah said, reaching around Beck and grabbing the shot the bartender had poured for him, downing it without the salt or the lime or any of the performative aspects. Maybe if he got drunk enough, he could stop worrying about what tomorrow would bring.

The dance floor was more crowded than it had been before, though Micah hadn't needed the excuse to get close—*closer*—to Beck.

Beck was still flailing around but it didn't matter. Micah just grabbed his shoulders and went along for the ride.

Looking into his eyes, into the free and easy smile, Beck thought he saw a different Micah.

A Micah he wanted so badly to be real.

Beck was riding the very fine line between perfectly drunk and *too* drunk.

It wasn't just the booze he'd drunk, but seeing Micah in this new light.

Seeing how he *could* be, if he laid down all those burdens he insisted on carrying around with him.

He'd always wondered if Micah was bi-curious, but the more he'd seen him tonight, the way he'd grabbed and embraced this part of him Beck had only vaguely suspected existed, it was becoming clear it wasn't just bi-curiosity.

Micah had buried himself so far in the closet, it was like the closet didn't even exist.

But it did, and he was banging on the door now.

Or, maybe a better way to phrase it was, he was *banging* on Beck.

Beck shouldn't have liked it. He hadn't even dreamed he'd felt this way about Micah before. Hadn't let himself even think about it. But now that the idea and all the liquor he'd drunk had taken over his brain—more like taken over his dick—he couldn't stop.

He'd always loved Micah.

Maybe he *loved* loved Micah.

He certainly fucking loved the way Micah was moving his hips now, head thrown back, his handsome face thrown into light and shadow from the neon pulses scattered across the dance floor.

It felt like they'd been dancing forever, and he was hot, almost unbearably, so he pulled his T-shirt off, tucking the tail of it into the waistband of his jeans, and he couldn't miss the way Micah's eyes darkened at the sight.

The way he lifted his palms to press against Beck's pecs.

Beck swore that they'd been naked around each other a hundred, a *thousand*, times before, and it had never felt like this, like a live wire was running right under his skin, and Micah wanted nothing more than to grab it with his bare hands.

Would he do it?

Would Beck let him?

It would be a memorable end to a memorable night, for sure. But something kept holding Beck back from making a move.

If Micah had been any other guy in this club, he'd have done it, no question.

But this was Micah. This was his *best friend*.

Beck couldn't help but think this might be more than sex. More than any other hookup he'd ever enjoyed.

But it could also be just that. Just sex. Something Micah wanted that he'd denied himself for a very long time.

Even as Beck thought it, even as the thought skittered across his fragmented, drunk brain, he knew it couldn't be that, could it?

"I need some air," Micah announced suddenly, and Beck was helpless not to follow him wherever he led, so he trailed behind him as they crossed the crowded bar towards the exit.

The air was cool outside as they leaned against the brick of the building.

Sweat dried on Beck's skin and he shivered.

"How late is it?" he asked when Micah didn't say anything, just stared up at the dark New York sky.

"Late," Micah said.

"Maybe we should be getting back," Beck said, not entirely sure what he was saying. Should he invite Micah back to his room? Lean in now and kiss him? Make it clear that if Micah was interested in exploring this side of him, then Beck was one hundred and ten percent on board?

Six hundred miles, after all, was only six hundred miles.

Lots of NFL players played in cities their loved ones didn't live in.

They had all the money to do anything they wanted. Including figure out what this brand-new thing was between them.

Beck, who hadn't even known it existed before tonight, suddenly wanted that so badly it hurt. Even if it was just sex, he could give Micah that. Something he'd remember forever.

"You wanna go back to the hotel?" Micah raised an eyebrow.

They were both definitely drunk. But not so drunk they didn't know what they were doing.

"Actually, yeah," Beck said. "Come on. Let's go."

He stepped out onto the sidewalk and hailed a cab moving by. It pulled up to the curb and they slid inside.

This time when they fell into the back seat in a tangle of legs, Micah didn't move away. In fact, he scooted closer, until he was practically in Beck's lap.

Come on, Beck nearly said, *I know you want to. And trust me, I want you to. It's where you belong.*

But that was crazy, wasn't it?

Maybe it didn't feel nearly as crazy as it should, Micah's shoulder pressed to his, his leg draped over Beck's.

"I don't want to go tomorrow," Micah said, his head falling against Beck's shoulder. "I don't want this to . . ." He stammered over the words. "I don't want this to end."

Beck reached out and tucked Micah against him. He was only an inch shorter than him, and hardly much smaller in terms of his build, but it felt right to do this. *The rightest thing you've ever felt. Second only to when you're on the field together and the game slows and then stops and it's just you two against the world, and you keep winning, and you're never gonna lose.*

"Imagine, someday we're on the same team," Beck said. Because it was what he'd been thinking about. How he'd want Micah behind him forever. Micah next to him forever. "Imagine we're going to the same place tomorrow."

"But we're not." Micah pouted.

"But what if we were? What if . . .what if we played for the same team again? Someday?"

If that fantasy came true, then this would happen again. And again. And again, in a thousand different variations. Beck could see it, as he laid his head back on the ripped taxi seat and imagined the future playing out so differently.

"We should promise that we will," Micah said earnestly. "Play together again. *Be* together again."

Beck knew what he should say. *It's not gonna happen. Not anytime soon.* But it wasn't what came out of his mouth. "We will," he vowed. "And when that happens . . ."

"What?" Micah asked when he didn't say immediately what they'd do.

"I don't know, we'll do this again." Beck wanted to say more. But he also didn't want to scare Micah away.

"This, and more," Micah said sleepily. Sounding happier and more relaxed than Beck could ever remember. Enough that he did swear to himself that he'd make this happen again. As soon as possible. Even if they didn't, in fact, end up on the same team, someday.

"More?"

"Yeah, a whole thing," Micah said, waving abstractly in the air. "Like the whole fucking nine yards."

"A . . .a *relationship*?" Beck murmured.

"Yeah," Micah said firmly. "You and me."

"I'll do you one better," Beck said, Micah's honesty making him suddenly reckless. "We end up playing for the same team, I'll fucking marry you. We can do that now, you know, not just two guys legally, but in the NFL. It's happened before. It could happen again. Spencer Evans married that agent guy, didn't he? Heath Harris is gonna marry his QB boyfriend. Colin O'Connor's fucking married. *We* could get married."

Micah didn't say anything for a long time.

So long, Beck was terrified he'd pushed too hard. Too far. They hadn't even kissed yet, and here he was drunkenly proposing.

But when he chanced a look down at Micah's face, he was staring at him with something like wonder. "You'd promise that?"

"For you?" Beck felt himself drifting closer. "Yeah. I'd promise it."

"Then I'd promise it too." Micah stared at him expectantly, his chin tilted up, his mouth wet and irresistible and right there.

Kiss him, Beck's brain screamed at him.

Or maybe it was his dick.

Or maybe they were both on the same page, right along with his heart, and he couldn't deny them any longer, not when what he wanted, what he *needed*, was right there.

"Micah," he murmured and leaned down, but before he could, everything came to a screaming, horrible stop.

Nope.

That wasn't him. That wasn't Micah.

That was the fucking cab.

Pulling up to the curb and stopping, throwing both of them nearly off the seat.

"Out," the driver barked. "I don't care if you fuck, but if you're gonna, don't do it in this cab."

Before they . . .*what?*

It took a second for Beck to even realize what he was saying.

Oh.

Before they kissed.

Before they had sex.

Micah pulled out his wallet, yanking out bill after bill, finally throwing them at the driver with a cackle of delight, and they fell out of the cab in the same sort of mess that they'd fallen into it.

Before, Beck hadn't been sure he should invite himself to Micah's room instead of going back to his own.

But now he was sure.

It didn't matter what happened tomorrow.

They both wanted the same goddamn thing.

Each other.

Micah was fucking floating.

This had to be a dream.

It felt like a dream, anyway.

Beck was hanging all over him, laughing as they stumbled towards the hotel entrance, drunk and happy, and they'd nearly kissed.

Beck had nearly kissed him. Had told him he wanted everything Micah held so close and secret.

Then he glanced up at the hotel door, and everything inside him went cold and still and awful.

Josiah was standing by the door, near the valet stand and its nearby outdoor ashtray, smoking a cigarette, the glow from the end lighting up his face.

He was staring right at Micah.

Right at where he and Beck were intertwined together, like one person and not two.

He could probably see the way Beck was looking at him. The way Micah had been looking back.

The way that had, only a few seconds before, seemed wonderful and perfect and glorious. But now, exposed every single one of his closely held truths. Josiah knew now. The look on his face made it unmistakable.

"What is it?" Beck asked, because he'd certainly felt Micah stop. Felt him freeze.

"Nothing, nothing," Micah mumbled, because he couldn't say it. "Just. . .uh, tired."

"All of a sudden?" Beck sounded disappointed and confused.

But Micah was seeing clearly for the first time in what felt like hours.

What are we doing? We can't do this.

"Yeah," Micah said with finality, watching as Josiah put out his cigarette and turned on his heel, walking into the hotel.

"You're really gonna go to bed . . .alone?" Beck asked, waggling his eyebrows.

Normally that look of his would've made Micah laugh ten out of ten times. But he couldn't. Right now, he just felt nauseated.

"Uh, yeah, probably. Feelin' a little sick." It wasn't what he'd intended only a little while ago, what he'd been hoping and praying and dreaming might happen, but now, that was impossible. It was all fucking over.

It wasn't that he gave a shit about Josiah and his stupid-ass opinions. He didn't. He absolutely fucking did not. It didn't matter what Josiah thought of him.

But even though he told himself it didn't, he couldn't help the feeling as he walked into the hotel lobby, Beck trailing behind, that he did.

Somehow, he did.

"Ah, okay." Beck sounded hesitant. Like he never did. Like Micah had taken something from him. Like he'd *stolen* something.

As if Micah didn't feel bad enough.

Now he felt like he was really, truly going to be sick. No faking about it.

"Sorry," Micah said. He was too good of a liar now, because that even sounded real, like a casual regret was all he carried for turning Beck down.

"Right, it's fine," Beck said as they walked towards the elevator. He pressed the button and the doors opened with a cheery chime the opposite of his current mood. "Just . . .drink some water, okay? It'll be an early morning and you don't need to be hungover on your first day in Miami."

God, even now Beck was being a friend. When all Micah had been was . . .what? A coward and a liar.

"Yeah," Micah mumbled under his breath as the numbers ticked by on the screen.

His floor came both way too soon and not soon enough.

"Well, thanks for a great night?" Beck said, as Micah turned to look at him before he walked out.

But Micah couldn't find the words.

They were stuck inside him.

So he didn't say anything, just walked out as the doors shut in Beck's face.

He went to his room, which was thankfully fucking empty, threw his clothes off, paced around a little, and finally collapsed into bed, but didn't sleep.

Instead he lay on the bed and stared, gritty-eyed, at the ceiling as dawn crept closer and he slowly, horribly, sobered up.

The problem with sobering up wasn't the actual sobering-up part but the fact that he hadn't been drunk enough not to remember, in technicolor, every single thing he'd done and said with Beck.

He'd never be able to forget. Not now.

His flight *was* early, so he dragged himself out of bed, took a long cold shower to try to wake up, and dressed quickly. Packed up the rest of his stuff. He'd left for the draft the night before with the understanding that he'd be flying to the city of whatever team picked him early this morning.

He only checked his phone when he was in the elevator heading downstairs.

Josiah hadn't sent anything.

But then, Micah hadn't expected he would.

What would he even say?

I knew about you, boy, before you even did?

Beck, on the other hand, had sent one.

You okay?

Ha.

Beck should know better than to ask that. Should know *him* better than that.

The timestamp read only a few hours ago, which meant Beck hadn't slept either.

Micah supposed that should make him feel better, but it didn't. Not at all.

The valet hailed him a cab, and he collapsed into it, rubbing his eyes behind his sunglasses. He felt like hell, and not just because of his hangover.

He didn't know what to say to Beck.

Especially because while Beck had every fucking reason to be angry with him, he wasn't. Instead, he was *concerned*.

He didn't want to call him on his bullshit. Instead, he wanted to make sure Micah was okay.

The sick feeling he was pretty goddamn sure was guilt followed him all through the drive to the airport and through security.

He found an empty row by his gate and closed his eyes, belatedly wishing he'd grabbed coffee before he'd found this chair and then never wanted to leave it. But it was too late for that, and even caffeine didn't have the motivational power to force him upright.

"Oh good, you're not dead."

Micah squeezed his eyes shut behind his sunglasses, that yes, like a real asshole, he had not taken off inside. That was not Beck's voice. He would not have tracked him down in the airport.

Great, now I'm hallucinating.

Except instead of going away, the voice continued. "You're really gonna ignore me? Mature, Rose."

A body dropped down in the seat next to his.

Micah peeked out one eye. Yep, it was definitely Beck and not a hallucination. After all, he hadn't had *that* much tequila.

"No, I'm not dead." *But I kinda wish I was.*

"Listen, we should talk," Beck started, leaning in, looking way too good considering what they'd gotten up to last night—what they'd *almost* done.

"No," Micah said before he could get any further.

"No?" Beck looked mystified.

Clearly, he was still laboring under the terrible misapprehension that Micah was a good guy. A good, brave guy, who tackled things he wasn't sure he could handle.

But that wasn't him.

It hadn't ever been.

Maybe in another history, in another version of his life, things could've been different—but they weren't.

"No," Micah repeated.

"I know this shit isn't easy," Beck said, "but I don't think pretending it didn't happen is the right call. You told me—"

"I was drunk," Micah said bluntly. *Lied* bluntly. When he'd told Beck his secret, he'd been almost entirely sober.

"You were *not*," Beck said, a confused crease forming between his dark brown brows. "What is wrong with you? It's *me*, you know I'm not gonna—"

"You're imagining things," Micah interrupted. "I don't know what you want to talk about, because nothing happened."

He stood, because even though the lure of coffee hadn't been enough to leverage him upright, the idea of getting away from this conversation with his heart at least mostly intact was much more appealing.

Before he said something he would truly regret later.

"Nothing happened?" Beck gaped at him, and unfortunately, *followed him* as Micah attempted to stomp off. "A *lot* fucking happened. I was there. And I know you. I know you weren't that drunk."

God, why wouldn't he just let it go?

Because he was Beck. That was why.

Micah stopped a few feet from the busy Starbucks line. Turned.

Don't make me do this.

But Beck would, because he was Beck.

You're not getting rid of me.

It's only six hundred miles.

We end up playing for the same team, I'll fucking marry you.

Like *that* would ever happen. It had been a pipe dream, but even as impossible as the dream had been, that didn't mean deep down, it hadn't been real.

Even as Micah kept trying to kill it dead.

"I was drunk, we were both drunk. That's the only reason it happened."

"No, no," Beck insisted, shaking his head. "No, it happened because—"

Micah was no stranger to hating himself. And yet he'd never felt this much self-loathing before. "Because you're in love with me? I was tryin' to be nice, but I can't. Not anymore. Not now that I'm sure."

Beck's face went white.

"You're not—"

He didn't finish his sentence. Just stared at Micah like he'd never really seen him before.

Micah had always believed Beck had seen deep down, to the real Micah under all the posturing and all the bullshit, but now, it was like he was *really* seeing, and Micah was nearly sick all over this airport carpet.

"I have to go." It was a lie. His flight wouldn't be boarding for another twenty minutes.

"You're lying," Beck said bluntly.

"No, I'm not. I'm not the one lying to themselves."

But I am, some part of him screamed.

He just didn't know how else to make Beck go. How to make Beck *stop.*

He pushed, as easy as breathing. It was ironically one of the things he'd always loved about the guy. You could push him down. Tackle him. But he just kept getting up and still coming. He'd never quit.

Not unless Micah made him.

He turned and walked away, but not before he saw a glimpse of all-too-familiar bitterness on Beck's face.

All the way down to the next bathroom, Micah walked, not turning around, not *letting* himself see if Beck had followed, even though he knew with a growing despair that he hadn't.

He went in, shut himself into a stall, puked his guts out, and somehow, even after emptying his stomach, he didn't feel any better.

When he came out of the bathroom, they were calling his flight to Miami, and Beck was gone.

For a month, then two, there'd been silence. There were so many times Micah wanted to text. To call. To just get in his car and drive to Charleston. It was, after all, only six hundred miles away.

But he didn't.

Micah didn't like to think it was cowardice stopping him, but the more he pretended it was something other than raw fear, the more he tried to not even *think* about Beck.

If sometimes, late at night, he opened that last text conversation with Beck, fingers ghosting over the screen, wanting to tell him, *No, I'm not okay. I've never been and I'm not okay now, not even fucking close*, then that was between him and the dark ceiling.

But he never did tell him the truth and Beck took the hint, and never reached out either.

You're not getting rid of me that easily, Beck had claimed more than once.

And yet, Micah thought, he had.

So easily.

Then, early one morning he woke up to a single text from the one person he kept trying to forget.

Thought you might want to know before I do it, it read. **I'm coming out this afternoon. Just a video we're posting to social media. Hopefully not a big deal.**

Before Micah could even consider responding, a second text came through.

I hate that we've come to this.

Micah hated it too.

But he didn't know what to say.

Congrats, I hope you're not throwing your career away? I hope you get what you want out of this?

And even though it wasn't right, Micah felt a surge of bitter resentment. *I hope you're not expecting me to do the same.*

He typed out a reply. Then deleted it. Then another one. Deleted that one, too.

You'll think of something to say; just give it time.

He gave it a day. Then two. Then a week.

Everything he tried to say to Beck reeked of his own fucking fear, and how could he say anything like that to Beck, who'd discarded his own entirely?

He couldn't.

Beck wouldn't respect him anymore, and somehow that seemed worse than Beck hating him.

Worse than them ghosting each other.

In the end, Micah realized, as he headed back to Miami for the beginning of training camp, they'd gotten rid of each other.

And it had been way too fucking easy.

Chapter 1

Beckett West knew this was coming.

He'd seen this trade coming from the moment he'd heard the Condors' old corner, Rex, confess to betting on NFL games in front of their owner, Grant Green.

But seeing it coming didn't necessarily mean he was ready for it. Ready for *him*.

Micah Rose.

Or that he wasn't pissed off and annoyed and frustrated now that what he'd both wanted and dreaded had finally come to pass.

There, his uncooperative brain announced, *you got what you wanted, in the end. You're on the same team, now, again.*

Beck had always imagined if this finally happened, in some faraway hazy future, he'd be happy about it.

But now, he couldn't be happy, because instead, he was too numb. Too angry.

He'd imagined that in some undetermined amount of time, he'd learn to forgive the lies Micah had told to push him away.

It turned out that day was still not *this* day.

Still, this wasn't a confrontation—or a conversation—he could put off any longer.

Together, they'd been a force to be reckoned with at Northwestern, and he knew the expectations now that they were reunited. Even if they were never close again, even if Beck never trusted Micah again, in the same way he had a year and a half ago, they were going to have to find a way to co-exist.

Step one: see each other again.

Beck forced himself to push open the cafeteria door and headed into the room.

Of course, Micah was the first person he saw—truthfully, the *only* person he could see—and just like he'd dreaded, there was that flare of . . .something . . .deep inside.

Maybe he wasn't all that numb, because if he was guessing, it sure felt like pure, undeniable happiness.

He'd intended to march right over to where Micah sat without a single ounce of hesitation.

But instead, he hovered in the doorway as Micah looked up and their gazes caught.

It was funny. *Ironic kind of funny.* Because two years ago, even right in the lead-up to the draft, he'd only thought he'd be losing a friend and teammate. He'd never imagined he'd had feelings for Micah other than squeaky-clean platonic ones.

But now, he knew that was all bullshit.

The night they'd shared had destroyed that lie forever.

He'd never be able to look at Micah now and believe that some part of him, buried deep, didn't want him.

Didn't care about him more than he should.

You're in love with me.

Maybe he hadn't been before.

But he'd mourned the loss of his friend and the hazy sweet possibilities of the future with a kind of regret so painful he'd wondered more than once if Micah hadn't actually been right.

He took a deep breath and walked across the room.

It wasn't the hardest thing he'd ever done.

That had been to walk away in the airport, after Micah had lied to him, again and again.

But this was a close second.

"Rose," he said, stopping in front of the table where Micah sat with a few of the other players. Deacon was there, Riley and Landry, too.

He ignored the pain in Micah's eyes.

Felt wretched for doing it.

But did it anyway.

"West," Micah said. "Good to see you again. But even better to play with you again."

Beck heard the unspoken question in his statement. *Can we do it again? Go on the field and work together like none of this shit ever happened?*

He wanted it.

Wanted it so badly he ached.

"Yeah," he said. "That was always the dream, wasn't it?"

It was a low blow, because there was no question Micah would remember the reference. Micah hadn't been drunk enough that night to forget what they'd said.

No matter what he'd said the next morning, Beck knew the truth.

They'd both meant every single fucking thing.

Now the universe was playing a cruel prank on them, calling them on every promise they'd ever made to each other.

"Yeah. Yeah, it was." Micah's voice was full of regret. Full of apologies he wasn't saying.

Apologies he'd never made.

Apologies he'd never made, Beck reminded himself.

There. He'd done it. He'd come over. He'd made nice, whatever the fuck that meant. That was where his obligation ended.

"Gonna grab some lunch," he said, turning away from the table, "then head to a meeting."

Out of the corner of his eye, he saw Micah open his mouth and then snap it shut again.

He was not running away.

He just didn't have anything in particular to say to Micah. And Micah sure as fuck wasn't going to say anything to him that he had any interest hearing.

After picking up his lunch, Beck took it to one of the defensive film rooms. He didn't have a meeting—not in the official sense—but he had tape he wanted to watch on the Toronto Thunder. They were playing them this week, and even though Riley *was* the smaller of the two brothers, the elder, Aidan, was just as wily, just as skilled a quarterback. And he had several more years of NFL experience under his belt.

The defense needed every bit of edge they could find to beat Aidan Flynn and the Thunder.

He was just finishing reviewing tape of Aidan throwing downfield—his favorite thing to do, which meant he and Micah would have their work cut out for them when it came to coverage—when the door opened.

Deacon walked in and leaned against the opposite wall, regarding Beck with consideration.

Not anger. Not happiness either.

He was clearly something in between. Something conflicted.

"Is this gonna be a problem?" he asked when he'd let Beck squirm for long enough.

"No," Beck said.

"I'm not blind you know. Or deaf. I saw you two at lunch today."

Beck really liked Deacon. He'd held this team together when it had been in acute danger of falling apart, two opposing forces attempting to rip it to pieces.

When he'd shown up in Charleston, it had been pretty obvious he had to choose a side, and he'd done it and never doubted Deacon once. He'd also taken Beck under his wing during his rookie year, a clusterfuck if he'd ever seen one, and made it mostly bearable.

Between Deacon and Jem, he'd come out better on the other side.

"And?"

"You two have an issue." Deacon paused. "Is it the same issue that you were having when you showed up here before your rookie year?"

He'd been quieter then. Hurting. Missing Micah so much sometimes it felt like he couldn't breathe. So angry with him that he'd considered, more than once, flying to Miami and giving him a piece of his mind.

Or kissing him.

Sometimes in his mind they melded into the same goddamn thing.

"Yes. No. I don't know." Beck shot to his feet. Began to pace back and forth even though that would definitely tip Deacon off that things were not okay. He didn't want to talk about this. He didn't need anyone to know what had *almost* happened between them.

There was some part of him that still wanted to protect Micah and therefore didn't want to tell Deacon what he'd done to piss Beck off.

It's okay to be afraid.

That was what he should have said.

That was what he still wanted to say.

"I'm serious. This can't be a problem." Deacon said it gravely, like Beck didn't already fucking know that. "But I don't want you to think I don't give a shit about your feelings. You're free to feel them, just—"

"Off the field. Out of this facility," Beck finished for him. Hearing the bitterness in his voice. "Message received."

Deacon sighed. "That's not what I mean. I mean, *you're ours,* Beck. But he's also ours, now."

"Noted," Beck said. He'd never wanted anyone to choose, but even if he had, he'd had to know in the end it wouldn't be *either* of them.

Deacon was going to pick the team, over and over again.

It was what he'd always done.

Yes, they were Beckett West and Micah Rose, but they were also the starting safety and starting corner for the Charleston Condors.

"You're really not going to tell me what happened between you," Deacon said in disbelief after a long moment. "Are you protecting him? You *are* protecting him. I heard he had a little trouble fitting in with the Piranhas at first. But after that, they seemed to be fine. Accepting. That why he requested the trade?"

Beck dropped back into his chair.

"I don't know why he requested the trade." That much was the truth, though Beck had a horrible suspicion he knew why Micah had done it.

With thirty-one possible teams, he could hardly be guaranteed to come here, but maybe, the chance had been enough.

"You have a theory though," Deacon said, taking the chair opposite him, settling into it backward, his elbows on the table as he leaned forward. "Talk to me, Beck. You know that's how we made it through last year. We *talked* about this kind of shit."

Beck knew. But this was different. It shouldn't still feel this way, but every time he poked or prodded the wound, it felt raw.

"You know we were close."

Deacon nodded. "I saw you together at the Big Ten Championship game, your senior year. You were thick as thieves. You went to the Heisman ceremony, and there are how many pictures of you two grinning like crazy at the draft a few months later. What the fuck happened?"

The night *of* the draft happened.

Beck tried to unstick his tongue.

How could he even explain?

"Were you in love with him and he rejected you? No—" Deacon answered his own question. "No, if that was it, he wouldn't be looking at you like a kicked puppy, like he'd beg for any shred of your affection."

Beck glared. "That isn't how he looks at me."

"Then *you're* the blind one," Deacon said in his matter-of-fact way.

"If that's open for discussion . . ." Beck trailed off pointedly.

Deacon's flat stare had intimidated offenses for fifteen-plus years. Beck could get through it with only a minor amount of squirming.

"Okay, point received. No, I wasn't in love with him. No, he wasn't in love with me. We just . . ."

"Fucked."

Beck shot Deacon a look of his own. "No."

"No? Okay, I was thinkin' I was gonna need to send Carter in for this conversation, instead, if that was all it was."

"The night of the draft we went out, got drunk, said a lot of stuff I didn't think either of us would regret. I *didn't* think I loved him. I didn't think he loved me, either. Not like that. But then . . ."

"God bless booze," Deacon said with a grin.

"Fuck you." Beck paused. "Do you want to hear this story or not?"

Deacon nodded, so he continued.

"Anyway, *yes* it opened my eyes a little. We drank. We danced. We, well, *I* sure thought something was gonna happen on the cab ride back to the hotel." Beck could still remember the feel of Micah pressed against him. The shock and awe in his dark eyes when he'd leaned in and they'd nearly kissed. Like he couldn't fucking believe that Beck would ever want him like that. More than once, Beck wished he'd drunk enough that he *didn't* remember every moment of that night so goddamn clearly. It would make things a lot easier. "Then, he just clammed up. Freaked out. Couldn't get away from me fast enough."

"You're not fighting like this because he had a gay freak out," Deacon said bluntly. "You're not that much of an asshole."

"Thanks, I think," Beck retorted dryly. "No. I was worried as fuck about him. I texted him. He didn't text me back. So the next morning, I found him at the airport, when he was on the way to Miami and I was headed here. He tried to pretend I'd imagined the whole thing. He lied and lied and *lied*. To *me*. I was his best friend and he lied to me."

That was the thing that had hurt the worst.

The lies.

If Micah had just patted him on the shoulder and said something like, *it's not gonna happen, we can't be like that,* yes, it would've stung. Yes, he would've needed time to shift Micah back to the friend zone, because yes, that night *had* irrevocably changed some things for him. But he'd have done it, because that was what Micah wanted. What he'd needed was a friend. Not a lover. Beck would've made his peace with it, even though he'd have mourned the death of that possibility.

But no, Micah had gotten belligerent. He'd gotten angry. He'd lied, over and over. And then he'd gotten aggressive and tried to claim that Beck had made *him* uncomfortable. When Micah had been with him every goddamn step of the way. Pushing them, even.

How many times had he woken up with the taste of Micah's skin, salty and sweet, in his mouth? That had been *all* Micah.

"So, he freaked out."

Beck shot Deacon a look. "It was more than that. A few months later, I tried again. Right before I came out, I told him I was going to, and you know what I got? Fucking nothing. He *ghosted* me."

"You of all people know how hard it is to come to terms with this sport and queerness," Deacon said.

Goddamn it. Was Deacon kindly, but firmly, reproaching him? For being angry? For walking away?

As far as Beck was concerned, Micah had walked away first. *Twice.*

He hadn't been able to get far enough from him, like he'd wanted to forget the whole thing.

"I know exactly how hard it is," Beck said. Except, did he? He'd never had any real pushback, other than a handful of teammates over the years. His family had always known the truth about him, and always supported him. The head coach at Northwestern had, too. He'd never had a weird look or a shitty word from one of his teammates there.

Beck knew how lucky that was. How the guys who'd come before him had paved the way for the kind of freedom he enjoyed now.

"Do you? You told me your family was with you every step of the way. Maybe Micah knew his wouldn't be. You ever met them?"

"It's just his mom, and his uncle, who he doesn't like, who . . ." He trailed off, thinking of how much Micah didn't like his uncle, though he hadn't ever specifically said *why.*

But now the why seemed painfully obvious.

It wasn't like that possibility hadn't occurred to Beck before. In the wake of their fight, he'd spent probably way too much time thinking of every angle, every reason Micah could have had to behave the way he had.

"Exactly." Deacon reached out, patted him on the arm reassuringly. "I'm not saying you don't have the right to be pissed, because what he did *was* shitty, no question about that. And I'm guessing he never apologized either."

"That was the last time we talked until . . .well, until today."

No, Micah had never apologized. Never reached out. Not after Beck knew he'd come back home for the summer, before rookie minicamp started. And not when he'd come out, in June. Not a single message of support or anything else.

It was like he was a dead branch, and Micah had simply excised him out of his life, like it was easy. Like he and their friendship had meant nothing to him.

Deacon winced. "Ouch."

"Yeah." Maybe it wouldn't have hurt so much if Micah had reached out before this, or tried to apologize. Attempted, at least, to fix things between them. But he never had.

But neither did you.

That was true, but it hadn't been Beck's fault. He'd *tried*, hadn't he? Then again, he'd only been a friend as long as his own pride wasn't bruised.

"You know what he told Riley, Coach K, and Grant this morning?" Deacon asked.

Beck shook his head.

"He told them he was gay. He came right out with it, no secrets, no hiding. I'm not saying he's always been perfect—God knows none of us are—but he's trying. And maybe you should too. That's all I came to say." Deacon rose.

Beck didn't know what to say. Micah had come out? Not *publicly*, necessarily, though that was less of an issue now than it had been in the past, now that nearly two dozen NFL players had come out of the closet in the last few years. But he'd told the truth to the people who really mattered. The leaders of this team.

"Really, I do hope you work it out," Deacon said.

Beck looked up at him, confused.

"No, no," Deacon said with a sudden grin, "not like that. Though if you did, I don't think anyone would hate *that*, either."

"I don't think that's gonna be happening," Beck said slowly.

He figured if they could learn how to be civil to each other again—and effective on the field—that was probably the most anyone could hope for.

On the field, Beck knew they'd be fine.

They'd always been fine the moment their feet hit the turf.

Today would be no exception.

Beck told himself firmly he was gonna leave all his anger, all that baggage, on the sideline, where it belonged.

But Coach Kelley clearly wanted to see what he had in his new defensive backfield, and after warmups, he set the first team offense against the first team defense.

Micah was as good as he'd been at Northwestern—or maybe even better, Beck realized. He watched as Micah covered Carter aggressively, shadowing his movements with an impeccable sense of timing, until at the perfect moment, he leapt up, half a second before Carter, and knocked the ball away before he could catch it.

"Goddamnit," Carter muttered, ripping his gloves off and spiking them after the play was over.

Sometimes it was easy to forget Carter had a temper, but then, moments like this made it painfully obvious.

"You're good at that," Riley said to Micah as they regrouped between plays, his voice easy, the opposite of Carter's belligerent frustration at being so well covered.

"Yeah," Beck said before he could force his mouth shut. He didn't need to be part of this conversation. And yet he was, anyway. An inevitability? "Your timing was good before, but it didn't used to be *that* good."

It was true; Micah's timing had been pretty decent at Northwestern. But it was impeccable now, a masterclass in coverage.

Micah looked over at him, undeniable heat in his gaze at the compliment.

Damn it, he hadn't meant to praise him that easily.

But it was deserved. How could they go back to normal, to a partnership that felt like a worn glove, fit perfectly to his hand, if he kept censoring himself?

He couldn't.

They couldn't.

"Howard gave me a bunch of pointers," Micah admitted. He was still looking at Beck. Maybe he was remembering that night too, when Beck had observed who he'd get the chance to learn from.

The memory of that night—and so many others, *too* many others—clogged up Beck's throat before he could force them away.

Goddamn it, he'd done this to them. He'd ruined them.

They'd ruined each other.

"Surprised you were willing to listen," Beck said. It wasn't right to fight pain with more pain, but he didn't know what else to do.

He'd promised Deacon they could handle it.

But when that hurt boiled over inside him, it was impossible to contain.

Micah didn't even look surprised.

Please tell me this will get easier.

But there wasn't anyone to tell him that.

Not even himself.

They lined up for the next play and Coach Kelley blew the whistle, setting the players in motion.

Beck dropped back, moving confidently across the turf as he took in the offense's formation, decided that Landry was probably Riley's most obvious target, and even though he'd tried to run a quick fake route to the left, it was clear where Riley was going to throw the ball.

But instead of seeing through the fake, like Beck had, Micah bit to the left, crossing over, and Landry caught Riley's pass before Beck could compensate, running past both of them for an easy touchdown.

"What the fuck was that?" Beck bellowed, before he could hold the words back. Temper them, somehow, to make them less angry.

Micah should've seen that coming. Landry hadn't been particularly subtle about it, and instead of even hesitating for a second, he'd committed, full-on, even though it had been wrong.

He's so fucking quick to commit to an angle on a play, Beck thought miserably, *but he couldn't fucking commit to you. To your friendship.*

It was a shitty excuse, but Beck couldn't help it. He was beyond furious, even though he kept trying to hide it or bury it or ignore it. That feeling wasn't just going to go away.

He took a step closer and then another. Micah was breathing hard, but probably not from running. He was still in amazing shape, the muscles rippling along his chest even under his practice jersey.

That was the problem: they'd unpacked that particular box with a drunken carelessness and now it wouldn't all go back. They were stuck lugging some of this shit around with them.

Beck didn't see Deacon coming over until he was practically on top of them.

"Hey, it's cool, Landry's tough to cover in the best of circumstances," Deacon said. "You'll get there. It's what practice is for."

He patted Micah on the back before shooting Beck a pointed look—no doubt a reminder of the conversation they'd had earlier.

When Beck had promised no matter how he felt off the field, he'd make sure his feelings didn't intrude here.

Well, they had.

"*I'm* not the one who's worried about it," Micah said with a quiet, determined confidence.

Micah hadn't had that before, Beck realized as he headed towards the sideline. To cool down, yes, but ostensibly to grab his bottle of Gatorade as they took five between plays.

Micah had been brash and a little overconfident, even if it was mostly earned and deserved. He'd run his mouth sometimes.

But now he just glowed with the certainty that he'd get it right.

That shouldn't be pushing Beck's buttons, but it was.

Where was this fucking confidence when it came to you? that uncooperative part of him bellowed.

But there wasn't an answer.

There wouldn't be an answer.

Beck was just going to have to learn to live with it, as painful as the unknown was.

CHAPTER 2

Micah had known this would be hard.

When he'd told the Piranhas he wanted a trade, he'd never imagined he'd end up in Charleston. Back with Beck.

If he was being one hundred percent totally honest with himself, it might have been what he'd desperately hoped might happen but hadn't even allowed himself to seriously consider.

But even though he hadn't even let himself hope, here he was anyway.

In Charleston. With Beck.

Scott had warned him way back in Miami, before the trade had gone through, that no amount of running was going to fix the mistakes he'd made.

"Trust me on this," the older man had said in his deep, gruff voice, "pretending something didn't happen isn't a good way to forget it."

"You alright?" Riley dropped down next to him.

The last person he'd expected to befriend him once he'd arrived in Charleston had been the Condors' brand-new quarterback, Riley Flynn. But from the moment they'd met, he'd felt like a kindred spirit. It was the way Riley had met his eyes, man-to-man, when he'd come out to him. Like it had actually *raised* him in Riley's opinion, not made him lesser.

"Yeah," Micah said, and to his surprise he meant it. He *was* okay.

Maybe it would hurt, guilt surging through him, mixed with an undeniable longing, every time he saw Beck. But seeing him, even with the inevitable wave of pain, was better than not seeing him.

He knew that now.

"Good, we're really fucking glad you're here, you know?" Riley said. Relaxing into the seat next to him. Like he fully intended to sit here during the entire flight. With Micah. Not even with Landry, to whom he seemed to be attached at the hip.

They were on their way to Toronto, to play Riley's older brother Aidan. He'd never met the guy, but he'd heard rumors. Then there was the way Riley's face grew tight and contained every time he came up.

Never mind the promise they'd made to each other, the day Micah had arrived in Charleston. Riley had confessed about his overprotective brother, also a renowned quarterback in the NFL, who apparently didn't think he was good enough or big enough or strong enough to play the same position.

So how about this, Riley had said, *we make a pact with each other. You messed up, but you made it right. Then you came here and wanted more than anything to start this new experience with honesty and transparency, and so far, you've done it. So let yourself off the hook, okay? And I'll try to work up the nerve to tell my brother to fuck off. Or at least mind his own business.*

Micah hadn't known he'd needed this, but the way Riley—and the rest of the team—had welcomed him helped erase some of the regrets he'd carried with him from Miami.

Maybe he'd never be able to erase the single worst moment of his life, but he'd come to realize erasing it wasn't possible. Maybe he could only learn to live with it.

"I'm happy to be here, honestly," Micah said.

Riley shot him a look. And okay, there was a big reason he might not be.

Not just Beck, but Beck's anger. He practically fucking vibrated with it.

"Really," Micah said. Meaning it.

Living with Beck, no matter how much he hated him now, was worth it for *Beck*.

"I missed him," Micah added when Riley still didn't say anything. "Maybe he didn't miss me the same way, but . . ."

"But maybe that's why he's so angry," Riley said quietly. "'Cause he missed you too."

"I guess we'll see." Micah knew there was more to Beck's anger than merely the distance that had separated them.

"I know you might think we'd be on his side, but there are no sides," Riley said. "Not with us."

He was familiar with that attitude from his time with the Piranhas, but he'd not necessarily expected to find it here, too. Or for it to ever be directed towards him.

But then, he'd never really expected to come out either.

"Doesn't take bravery or courage or any of that shit they say," Scott had told him once, "it just takes fucking guts to say what's in your heart. To tell people who you really are."

It was true.

He hadn't felt particularly noble, sweating under his arms, palms damp, as he'd confessed his truth to the Condors' owner, head coach, and Riley.

But he'd done it, hadn't he?

"Everyone's been great so far." That was the truth, no embellishments required. He'd felt it. Coach Dawson had pulled him aside once the trade had gone through and told him he'd worked hard with the new owner of the Condors to make sure the culture was better. *Different*, Coach had said. *More like here.*

Like everything else Coach said, Micah discovered it was the truth.

"And," Riley continued, "if you ever want to talk about what happened—or not talk about what happened, but anything else—I'm here. Landry's here. Deacon and Jem, too. God knows, even Carter might be willing to listen."

He'd been included, eventually, in the Piranhas. But only after he'd gone out of his way to express contrition and show just how much he was trying to change.

But here, none of that mattered.

He was accepted, mistakes and warts and all, without anyone batting an eyelash.

It was the fresh start he'd so desperately wanted.

Now he just had to shake that annoyingly pervasive thought that he didn't really deserve it.

Even now, he could look up and see Beck's head, his messy-as-fuck hair that needed a decent cut more than ever, rising above his seat.

He'd sat as far away from him as possible, but Micah could still see him.

Maybe Micah had been accepted here. But that didn't mean he'd finished making amends.

Not by a long shot.

"I got a lot of apologies to make," Micah admitted.

"And you'll make them," Riley said, sounding confident.

Micah couldn't deny that he *wanted* to tell Riley the truth about what had happened with Beck—*you ever want something, someone, so bad, you feel like you might die if you don't get it?*—but he still believed it wasn't entirely his story to tell.

He might've been the one who fucked it all up, but it was Beck's story, too. He'd been right there, right next to Micah, that night.

So instead of sharing, he asked Riley something else. "What made you realize you weren't straight?" he asked.

Riley raised an eyebrow. He didn't look unhappy or uncomfortable, but he was clearly surprised. "Nick Parsons, in seventh grade," Riley said. "We were in gym, playing flag football, and he tackled me to the ground. And I realized, later, I never wanted him to let me up."

"You ever do anything about Nick Parsons?" Micah asked.

Riley hummed to himself. "Not then. But later, a lot later. High school. My sophomore year. He kissed me under the bleachers, and I knew. But—" Riley paused. "But I knew before that. Before I ever touched a guy or a guy touched me."

Micah nodded. He got exactly what Riley was saying.

He hadn't needed the proof during that night, with Beck. He'd felt it, deep down, even as he'd tried to hide it. Tried to pretend he didn't feel it.

"I thought maybe if I never did it, if I never made a move, or touched him—" Micah mentally smacked himself. He'd meant to say 'any guy' but then he'd said 'him' and there was no way Riley wouldn't figure out what that meant. But Riley only smiled that gentle supportive smile of his. "Or touched a guy, I could pretend that it wasn't real. That I wasn't . . .that I wasn't gay." The word still didn't come as easily to him as Micah would've liked, but he was trying, goddamn it. "But I was. No matter what."

"Yeah. I get that. My brother thought if I didn't tell anyone, that meant we—and the NFL—could pretend that I just liked women. Guess what, it doesn't work that way."

"Is your brother . . ." Micah trailed off, almost afraid to ask. *Is he like my uncle? Does he think you're just a piece of garbage lying on the side of the road because of who you are?*

"No, actually." Riley sighed. "He can be an ass, sometimes. No question of that. But he's not *that* kind of ass. He supports me. But that didn't mean he thought everyone else would be that supportive. He was afraid I was painting a target on my back. Another one, to go with all my others." Riley chuckled. "He didn't want me to play football at all. Thought I was too small."

Riley wasn't your typical quarterback, that was for sure. But he had moves on him, moves that had already forced Micah to take him very, very seriously in practice.

Pax Kelly, the quarterback of the Piranhas, was a great player.

But he wasn't quick like Riley. Couldn't just take off and run the moment a play fell apart.

"Seriously? But you're really fucking good."

"Thanks," Riley said dryly. "I'm planning on making him see it once and for all tomorrow. If I—if *we*—beat the Thunder, then he can't ever say I'm not meant to do this."

"We're gonna make it happen," Micah promised.

"Yeah?" Riley looked pleased. "That's what Beck said."

Micah knew he'd dropped his name on purpose. Probably half the team had explicitly told Riley they wanted to help him beat his brother. The rest of the team might not have said it in words, but they were all-in, anyway.

But Riley had said Beck's name.

"You gonna keep looking like that, every time he comes up?" Riley challenged.

"Like what?" But Micah knew.

He knew how it felt, and no matter what, he'd never really been able to have much of a poker face. Not when it came to Beckett West.

"Like he's a nightmare and a dream wrapped up in the same guy," Riley said kindly.

"Someday, maybe." Micah chuckled, even though it wasn't particularly funny. "I'm workin' on it."

"Good. 'Cause I'm rooting for you, you know." Riley leaned back in his seat and closed his eyes. "We're *all* rooting for you."

And for the first time since that draft night, two years ago, Micah believed it. Really, truly believed it.

Micah knew he'd been good at Northwestern.

Back then, he'd also been an unbearably cocky asshole. He hadn't wanted to learn anything new. When he'd been drafted by the Piranhas, he hadn't thought there was anything that anyone could teach him. Then Sebastian Howard had come along, annoyingly gorgeous and annoying confident, and way too fucking good at being a corner, and proved that not only did Micah have something to learn, he had a *lot* to learn.

That stung.

Sebastian had taken his overconfidence and slowly, inexorably, destroyed it piece by piece.

He'd needed it, Micah thought as he jogged out onto the field. The echoes of the Thunder's theme song, courtesy of AC/DC, were still fading away, the smoke clearing out of the air from the fireworks announcing the entrance of the Toronto players.

"You good?" Jem asked, coming by and checking in as they finished their final warmup.

"Yep," Micah said. He felt ready.

Thanks to Sebastian.

Sure, he'd only had a few days of practice with the Condors' defense, but the scheme wasn't so different from the one the Piranhas employed, and it wasn't like Beck being in the backfield with him didn't feel more natural than anything else.

But in the end, Micah knew his adaptability and his newfound skill were thanks to Sebastian.

He hadn't been ready to play in the NFL, and Sebastian had known it.

"Don't let Aidan throw behind you," Jem reminded.

Micah grinned. "Oh, he's gonna want to. But he won't. It's not gonna happen. Not with me covering Lucas, and Beck in the middle." Lucas was the Thunder's best receiver, and Micah had been really pleased to find out that even though he was brand-new to the team, Coach Rufus, the defensive coordinator, had assigned him to cover Lucas.

Without Sebastian's one-on-one tutoring, Micah knew that never would've happened.

Instead of being touted as one of the most exciting second-year players in the NFL, he'd be languishing on the bench, just another guy who'd been good in college who hadn't panned out when he'd turned pro.

There was no doubt in Micah's mind he'd needed to learn *how* to improve before he ever could. Because he'd shown up in Miami with a chip on his shoulder, anger and regret boiling inside him in a toxic stew, missing Beck more than he'd ever imagined was possible.

Maybe Micah never would've handled any of it well, but feeling attracted to Sebastian had not only been humiliating and embarrassing, it had felt like a final nail in the coffin with whatever hadn't happened with Beck.

"Feelin' cocky, huh, Rose?" Jem teased, his smile bright. They watched as the Condors' kicker sent the ball soaring towards the Thunders' offense, beginning the game.

In a moment, he'd take the field as a Condor for the first time.

Next to Beck again.

"A little, yeah," Micah said, and Jem gave him a thumbs-up before he wandered away.

Micah looked down the sideline and there Beck was. Holding his helmet, his hair even messier than usual, tossed around by his warmup and the breeze in the stadium.

Beck was still not the hottest guy he'd ever seen. But somehow it was possible that he was still the only man Micah had ever wanted with an intense kind of burn that never seemed to fade.

Being attracted to Sebastian, who *might* be the hottest guy he'd ever seen, had felt like a betrayal, especially when he'd already been hurting from his fight with Beck.

Of course, Sebastian hadn't ever been interested in Micah. In fact, he'd been falling for the coach's son and assistant, Beau.

The anger and confusion and frustration boiling away inside of him had eventually overflowed and he'd called Beau the one word he'd promised himself he'd never say—especially not after Josiah had never hesitated to use it around him.

But once it was out of his mouth, he couldn't take it back.

You might not be able to take it back, Micah promised himself, *but you can prove it wasn't true. You can prove you're not that guy.*

Today.

Right fucking now.

When he'd learned where he was being traded, it had felt like a blessing and benediction and also an opportunity to set things right, and there was no time like the present.

Micah didn't hesitate.

Even though he'd been giving Beck space, respecting the distance he'd put between them, now he walked right over to where Beck stood.

They'd started every single game the same way at Northwestern, and when he'd begun playing in the NFL without Beck, it had felt so fucking weird to not have him there.

Like he'd lost a limb.

But now they were back together again, and no matter how much Beck hated him off the field, they were partners again.

The Wall, reunited.

Beck glanced over at him as he approached.

His face was closed. Opaque.

Micah might've never managed to perfect his poker face around Beck, but Beck was an entirely different story.

"Hey," Micah said.

"Hey." Beck turned, but not away. He turned towards Micah. "You know what? I thought maybe it would be weird to have you on the field again, but, truthfully, it was weirder not having you there."

It was the nicest thing Beck had said to him since he'd arrived.

Maybe it wasn't an olive branch, but it was *something*.

"Yeah," Micah agreed. "It never felt right."

"I had to deal with that asshole, Rex. But you? You had *Sebastian Howard* with you," Beck said.

There was something about the way he said the name that pinged Micah's brain. Was he jealous? He couldn't possibly be. First, because Sebastian had been in the NFL for over ten years, and Beck was just starting out, and comparing himself to a legend was just plain stupid, and second, because Beck couldn't possibly know he'd been attracted to Sebastian.

Nobody knew that, except Scott.

"Yeah, but maybe I didn't want him," Micah retorted. That was undeniably true.

Beck looked over at him. "I know why you're here."

"To play in this game?" Micah tried to play it off, but Beck wasn't stupid, and he shot him a look that said exactly that.

"Okay, fine, yeah, I'm here 'cause we *should* do it."

"It's not the same."

"It's exactly the fucking same," Micah argued. "Am I me? Are you *you*? We on the same side? We playin' together? Then it's the same."

He didn't want to know what would happen—how he would feel—if Beck refused to participate in their pre-game ritual.

"I guess you're right," Beck said slowly.

Micah realized that Beck didn't think it was any different. He just didn't *want* it to be the same. He wanted to pretend everything had changed.

Micah stuck his hand out, wondering if Beck would ultimately leave him hanging.

Knowing he deserved it if he did. Ultimately, it was his fault they'd had this falling out. It was *him* who'd ghosted Beck, who'd only tried to be a friend to him.

And more, that uncooperative voice reminded him. *For a minute, he wanted to be way more than just your friend.*

Beck sighed. "You're gonna insist on this, aren't you?"

"Yep." He said it optimistically, because he didn't want Beck to know how much it would hurt if he turned him down.

"You're impossible," Beck said, but his expression had morphed from frustrated to fond and affectionate.

"So I've heard." Micah grinned.

Beck reached out and took his hand, clasping it in his own, tugging him closer.

Their gazes met.

"Sixty minutes," Beck said. He was smiling now too, like he'd missed this as much as Micah had.

"No more, no less," Micah chanted back.

He'd come over here for exactly this, but when they pulled closer, layers of pads and fabric between them, Micah still felt the impact of Beck's body, just for a second, pressed against his own.

Micah tapped Beck's shoulder just as Beck put a hand on his.

For a second, neither of them moved.

Micah, out of Beck's line of vision, squeezed his eyes shut, emotion clogging his throat.

He'd never thought he'd ever have this again.

Beck pulled away, dropping his grip on Micah, and he couldn't do anything but follow suit.

It had been less than thirty seconds, but it had rocked him.

"Sixty minutes," Beck repeated, nodding.

Micah nodded back.

Beck looked like he wanted to say something else, the words right on the tip of his tongue, but then the defense was taking the field, and he turned away to grab his helmet and the moment was over.

"Come on!" Deacon's voice rose above the crowd noise, and he led them onto the field for the Thunder's first series.

From the first play, it was obvious Aidan was desperate to throw down the field.

Deacon and Jem pushed hard against the offensive line, trying to break through and pressure Flynn hard enough he was forced to throw the ball away.

Micah had studied plenty of film of Aidan Flynn and his incomparable arm. Couldn't miss the way he could throw touchdowns on a dime from fifty yards away.

But he wasn't going to do that today.

He and Beck, as well as the rest of the secondary defensive unit, were going to make sure he didn't. That he *couldn't*.

Lucas was fast—but not as fast as Tristan Nicholson was, and Micah had spent a season and a half practicing against him—and while it wasn't easy for Micah to keep up with him, he did, running an aggressive route against him as Flynn dropped back.

Out of the corner of his eye, Micah saw Beck coming across the middle of the zone, sticking to the other side, mostly, because it *would* be stupid to throw to Lucas. He wasn't open, and if Micah had anything to say about it, gaze narrowing as Flynn pulled back to throw, he wasn't *going* to be open.

This was why they'd been nicknamed the Wall in college.

Most teams had one good cornerback. That had been true at Northwestern; Micah had been heads and tails better than the other guy. But other teams didn't have a safety like Beck, who was tall *and* fast and could cover the middle so thoroughly, assisting the corner on the other side to lock down the deep ball. It was a dynamite combination that meant almost nobody could throw on them.

Together, they were an unstoppable force.

Today was no exception.

Flynn threw and Micah tracked the ball across the sky. It never came even close to being received as it sailed past the sideline.

He'd thrown the ball away, and Micah could see from the frustrated look on the older Flynn's face as they returned to the line of scrimmage that he wasn't happy about it.

Waiting for the whistle, Micah glanced over at Beck.

His smile was unmistakable, even behind the visor on his helmet, hunger in his eyes for another play.

Yeah, that *had* been fun.

Of course Sebastian Howard, the safety he'd played with in Miami, *was* an unbelievably good player, especially since he'd switched over to safety from corner, but there was nothing, no experience in the universe, like playing with Beckett West.

He was hungrier than anyone else. Pushed harder, ran faster, played tougher.

He made an entire defense want to give everything.

The ref whistled the next play, the Thunder's center snapped the ball, and this time Micah watched, feet moving back into the zone as Beck shifted up, tackling the Thunder's running back as he came through the defensive line.

Jumping up after his tackle, it was obvious how fired up Beck was.

He was jumping around, one fist beating his chest as he celebrated the Thunder gaining only a single yard so far.

The defense huddled up loosely, as the Thunder tried to regroup for a third and long.

"Come on," Deacon called out, "let's take care of them *now*, okay? No deep passes, got it?"

Micah felt Beck's eyes on him. Couldn't help the need inside him to look back.

"Got it, boss," Micah said. "We've got this."

Deacon nodded, confidence in every line of his body as the huddle broke up and they took their places on the line.

Lucas looked jumpy, skittish almost, and then, almost at the last second, he changed sides. Micah followed him, and after the whistle blew, sprinted across the line after him just as the ball was snapped.

Sure enough, Flynn was still hoping for a deep pass. Something that would not only get them a first down but would move the chains further into Condors' territory.

Not today, Micah chanted to himself, as he tracked Lucas down.

Lucas was a very good receiver. He was no Mo Jeffries, who the Thunder hadn't been able to afford to keep, much to Aidan Flynn's very vocal disappointment, but he was still fast as hell, and could run a competent route.

Too bad Micah was better.

One glance behind told Micah Flynn was still hoping to throw.

A second glance, five seconds later, told him it was happening now.

Flynn wasn't going to wait until Lucas was open. He was going to throw it anyway.

Challenge accepted.

Some quarterbacks could throw a wide receiver open by adjusting their route on the fly. Aidan Flynn was one of those quarterbacks. In fact, he was one of the best in the NFL at it. Deacon had warned him about Flynn's skill, but that was why he wasn't alone out here.

Lucas shifted to the right, cutting suddenly to try to lose Micah, but it didn't matter.

Because it wasn't just Micah.

He had a partner.

His equal in every single fucking way.

Beck saw the move coming, because Beck always saw it coming, and shifted over too, and was right there to bat the ball down with his larger frame before Lucas could hope to catch it.

"Yes!" Micah let out a primal scream, and he was right there, in Beck's face, hands all over the other guy as the defense came together to celebrate the incredible play.

"Goddamn," Jem yelled. "Y'all are something else together."

They were.

Micah felt it in every molecule of his body. He didn't know if Beck felt it too. He could only hope.

They were on the way back to the sideline when Beck caught up with him, jogging in tandem as they crossed towards the bench. Beck pulled off his helmet. His expression was wild, eyes lit up with an inner glow Micah remembered all too well.

Nothing could be like Beck when he was fired up like this.

"Fuck, that was awesome," Beck said, panting, not because he wasn't in the best shape of his life, but likely because of the adrenaline coursing through him.

"You're the one who did it," Micah said.

"Only because you forced him to do it." Beck raised his hand and Micah didn't hesitate, not for a second.

"Sixty minutes," Micah chanted, and Beck chanted it right back.

Beck released his hand and flopped down on the bench.

"That felt fucking awesome," Micah said, not holding back.

"What, like Howard couldn't pull that play off in his sleep?" Beck teased.

"Not like you."

Sebastian was *very* good. There was no discounting that.

But nobody had a fire like Beck.

Nobody could communicate with him with only a single glance, and Micah knew exactly what he needed to do.

It was like they always found a new gear when they were together.

"Damn straight," Beck said, sounding very satisfied with Micah's answer.

"Aw," Jem said, dropping down next to Beck. "You two are adorable. And like, fucking otherworldly out there."

"They've got some kind of weird psychic bullshit," Deacon agreed. He crouched in front of the bench. "But you know Flynn's gonna try it again and again. He's like a freaking surgeon. If we let him, he'll pick us apart."

"Then we won't let him," Micah said.

And they didn't.

When the game ended, it was 21 to 3, and the only reason the Thunder had scored at all was when Beck had bitten a little too hard on a fake and Aidan, clearly desperate, had thrown towards Eric, the other corner. The receiver had barely caught it, and that had finally put them far enough into field goal territory that when the drive stalled out three plays later, they'd scored three points on a field goal try.

"Absolute brutal defense today, guys," Coach Rufus said, high-fiving each and every one of the players as they walked into the locker room after the game had ended. "I love to see it. Just awesome."

Coach Kelley gave a speech too, about perseverance, and Micah decided, listening to him, that he might not be Coach Dawson, but he was pretty good all the same.

He couldn't even disagree when Coach Kelley tossed Riley the game ball.

It had felt to Micah like he and Beck had finally rediscovered their connection, and maybe begun to put some of their problems behind them, but then when Beck climbed onto the bus to take them to the airport, Micah couldn't deny he felt a pulse of disappointment when Beck walked right past him.

Didn't bother sitting down.

Didn't even acknowledge he was there.

Well. Maybe they still had some progress to make.

And you have a long overdue apology to give, a voice inside Micah's head reminded him. It sounded suspiciously like Scott, and Micah couldn't deny it.

His apology *was* long overdue.

He'd just have to figure out a way to get Beck alone, even though he kept avoiding it.

CHAPTER 3

BECK WASN'T STUPID.

He knew Micah had deliberately left a seat open next to him on the bus as the team headed to the airport.

Probably hoping that even without an apology—even without a *single fucking word* over the last year and a half—Beck would just give in and his anger would simply evaporate.

Had it felt good playing together again?

Beck couldn't deny that it had felt really fucking amazing.

There was nothing like the high of knowing Micah was behind him. And his skills, already fantastic before he'd been drafted, had improved significantly, just as Beck's had. No question about it: together they could be the backbone of a secondary defense the NFL would be talking about this year and for years to come.

But that was on the field.

Off the field was a different story.

Beck still felt raw around the edges from all Micah's silence, and so far, nothing he'd said or done had come even remotely close to healing the gaping wound.

So he'd avoided the seat next to Micah on the bus, and also on the plane back to Charleston.

He'd just pulled his truck into the drive when his phone buzzed.

It was from Carter. **Victory party at my place, tomorrow night.** An address followed the first text.

Beck's fingers hesitated on the screen.

He wanted to go. He *should* go. But he had a feeling Carter wasn't going to leave Micah out. Did he really want to join in, if Micah was going to be there?

You can't avoid him forever.

It was ironic, considering the promise he'd made when they'd both been drafted. *You aren't getting rid of me that easily.*

And Micah had.

He'd torched all of Beck's good intentions, until there was nothing left.

On purpose, that uncooperative part of his brain added, *he did it on purpose and you* let *him do it.*

Okay, maybe that hadn't been his best moment, but Beck also thought nobody would blame him.

Still, by the time he'd woken up the next morning, he was no closer to a decision about whether he'd show up.

He'd slept in, not setting an alarm, and then, after making himself breakfast—which was actually more like lunch—sat down at the kitchen table, scrolling through the messages he'd gotten on his phone last night. Tons of friends and family had sent him congrats for their victory in Toronto, and it felt good.

Beck knew he'd be lying to himself if it didn't mean more because he'd done it with Micah behind him, the way he'd always meant to be.

He pulled up the text convo with Carter. He should tell him something, but before he could decide what excuse he was going to make—or if he was actually going to swallow his pride and *go*, Carter texted him again.

You coming, or are you gonna be a big, fat chicken?

Beck rolled his eyes.

Maybe I'm busy and I'm not being a chicken at all. *That* was an easy answer to type out and send.

Carter's reply came back almost immediately. **You're gonna have to face him at some point.**

Beck made a scoffing noise at his coffee mug, like it could hear him or it actually *cared*.

And not on the field. But in real life.

Carter giving him life advice was truly evidence of how far he'd sunk.

Before he started talking to the silverware, Beck decided he had to take action.

He dialed a familiar phone number.

"Congrats, honey," his mom answered on the third ring, her voice warm and welcoming. "What a great win yesterday."

"Thanks," he said.

"And I saw it wasn't just you in the backfield," she said, a little slyly.

"Of course it wasn't just me. I play with ten other guys," Beck argued. But he knew what she was saying. What he hadn't been able to tell her since last week, when the trade had officially come through.

"I saw he was traded to the Condors, and I kept expecting you to call me," Jolie West said reproachfully.

He hadn't ever intended to tell her about the night when everything had changed between them. Telling her meant that it was real, that it had happened and that he couldn't change it.

But then he'd come home for a few weeks, wrapping himself up in the warmth and acceptance of his family while he prepared to drop the statement that revealed his sexuality to the public, and she'd immediately picked up that something was bothering him.

When Micah hadn't answered his text, sent the morning before the video came out, it had been impossible to hide his disappointment and the inevitable hurt from her.

Jolie West knew him too well. She'd confronted him that night, and the whole story had come tumbling out.

Maybe not the part where he'd been *so sure* they were going back to the hotel to have sex—she *was* his mom, after all—but how he'd hoped everything was changing between them.

"I didn't want to talk about it," Beck told her now, and it wasn't a lie. He *hadn't* wanted to talk about it. With Deacon or Jem or even his mother.

He'd wanted to hide away and lick his wounds in private.

"Honey, you can't pretend it's not happening."

"Thanks, Mom. I'm aware of that."

"Beckett," she warned him. "You called *me*."

That was also true; he *had*.

"I don't know what to do with him."

"Do you have to *do* anything with him?" she asked archly.

"I mean, he's around. We're working together. In practice. In the film room. He's just . . .he's there. It's not like I can pretend he's not."

"Is he pretending like you don't exist, still?"

"No," Beck said reluctantly. "He's . . .he seems happy to see me. He's happy to be here, with us, generally. With *me,* specifically. He made that clear."

Jolie sighed. "And you're not ready to forgive him." She phrased it as a statement, not a question. Like she already knew.

"Well, how could I? He hasn't apologized."

Beck might be angry about what had happened, but at least there, he was justified. Micah *hadn't* apologized.

"Have you given him a chance?"

Beck froze.

Of course he hadn't. He'd been avoiding the guy, whenever he could.

"You have to actually give him a chance, Beckett," she continued when he didn't say anything.

"What if I don't want to give him a chance?" It terrified him actually, how much he wanted Micah to do the right thing. Give them both another shot at renewing their friendship—and God, as much as he hated the painful truth of this, maybe even *more.*

He'd had his eyes opened that night, and he hadn't been able to close them since. On top of that, now he knew when Micah had looked at him before, with a mixture of desire and fear in his eyes, what that meant. What he wanted.

Because what if he didn't do the right thing? What if he took Beck's chance to make an apology and just didn't say anything? What if he panicked again? What if he broke Beck again?

"I know you're just saying that because you're scared," his mother said very frankly.

Like he wasn't one of the most feared defenders in the NFL. Like being afraid was *acceptable*.

"That's okay, you know," Jolie continued, her tone softening. "It's okay to be worried that he won't do what you need him to do. That he'll let you down again."

"It's funny." Beck hated the way his voice cracked. "I didn't even think about him in a romantic way, really, before that night. And then after, that was all I could think about. Were we friends, or were we really more, and I just pretended because it was easier?"

"You were being Micah's friend, there's no crime in that," she reassured him.

"Even when we could've been more?"

"Maybe you should start with the friendship for now."

"That wasn't—"

"What you meant?" Jolie chuckled. "Yes, I know. But you could try just being his friend, at the very least. Give him a chance. He's a good man. Good men make mistakes sometimes. You know that."

He did. He was hardly perfect either.

"And," she added, "I think he might've not had the easiest road to this realization. Maybe remember that, when you approach him, or he approaches you. He's probably even more scared than you are."

His mom's advice wasn't all that different from Deacon's. But still, Beck knew how hard it was going to be to open himself up to Micah as a friend, again. Never mind anything else.

"Okay."

"This is where you say, *Thanks, Mom, I'll keep that in mind. And I won't be a stranger, either.*"

Beck laughed. It felt rusty, like he hadn't done it enough in the last few days.

Maybe he hadn't.

He'd been too busy obsessing over Micah.

What he *should* do was go to Carter's.

"Thanks, Mom," he repeated, word for word. "I'll keep that in mind. And I won't be a stranger, either."

"Good. I know you hate change, but this sounds like a good one, okay?" Jolie sounded very satisfied.

After telling his mom he loved her, he hung up, but still hesitated when it came to Carter's text.

He could go to Carter's.

Or he could hang out here and worry about dealing with Micah later.

When it might be easier.

Of course, who was he kidding? It wasn't ever going to get easier.

His mom was right; he *hated* change. But maybe she was right a second time too. Maybe it would be a good kind of change, to have Micah back in his life again. Even as a friend.

He finally picked up his phone again and told Carter that he'd be there, but late.

Maybe he'd be lucky and by the time he arrived, Micah would've already cleared out.

Better not be too late, Carter texted back.

Like he already knew why Beck wasn't going to be there on time.

Beck groaned as he leaned back in his chair.

Nothing about this was going to be easy.

By the time Beck got to Carter's, the party was in full swing.

The circular drive in front of the refreshingly normal looking house was full of cars Beck recognized.

He caught a glimpse of Riley and Landry, tucked into each other on the far end of the house's wraparound porch, but before he could greet them, the front door opened and there was Carter, arms crossed over his chest, giving Beck a chastising look.

Carter.

Okay, if Carter was thinking he was out of line, then he might really need to reconsider how he was making his decisions.

"Finally showed up, huh?" Carter asked, leaning against the jamb, his foot propping open the screen door.

"It's our day off. I had a lot to catch up on," Beck argued, which was basically untrue.

He'd not done jack shit today.

Except agonize over how he was going to face Micah.

"He's inside," Carter said, his voice growing softer as Beck stopped in front of him. "Don't be an ass, okay?"

"Seriously?" Beck couldn't believe Carter Maxwell—*Carter Maxwell*—was telling him not to be an ass.

"I know he probably fucked up," Carter acknowledged, "but it's just hard to watch him whenever you come up. He's like a kicked puppy."

"That's ridiculous," Beck argued. Micah had ghosted *him*.

"Is it? You should've seen his face when I told him I hit on you."

Beck rolled his eyes. "You didn't even mean that, not really."

"I didn't?" Carter eyed him up and down. "I don't know if that's true. We could still—"

"Don't even think about it," Beck said, laughing in spite of himself.

Carter's expression turned smug. "You know I'm totally responsible for Landry and Riley hooking up."

"They were always going to figure their shit out," Beck claimed.

"Yeah, maybe. But a little jealousy . . .a little envy . . .sometimes it can be very motivational."

Beck shot Carter a look. "What are you saying, you want to hit on me *again*?"

Carter just shrugged. "If it works?"

"Next, you're gonna say it wouldn't be such a hardship, hitting on me."

"What?" Carter raised his hands in mock innocence. "Most people, and I repeat *most people*, think it's pretty damn awesome when I hit on them. They even take it as a compliment."

"I resent the implication that I'm most people," Beck retorted, but Carter just laughed.

It wasn't that Carter Maxwell wasn't attractive.

Oh, he was.

His blond-streaked brown hair was a little too long, his honey brown eyes just a little too sweet, his body just a little too much, and then there was his attitude, which was a study in overindulgence.

If you hooked up with Carter, you'd never regret it.

It would probably be a night you'd never forget.

Too bad you already had one of those.

Yeah, he had, and it hadn't happened with Carter.

Even worse, he and Micah had never made it as far as a single kiss.

Beck sighed.

"There's the good guy I know you are," Carter said approvingly, patting him on the back. "Go in there and do your good guy shit."

Why did everyone think he was so good, so noble? Wasn't he allowed to want things he wasn't supposed to? Do things he wasn't supposed to?

No, he'd apparently become the upstanding gentleman of the Condors, which was totally unfair. Wasn't that supposed to be Deacon? Who seemingly lived like a monk?

"Oh, look who showed up." Jem grinned at Beck as he walked through the door. "I guess you owe me ten bucks." He nudged Deacon, who set down his beer and met Beck's look with one of his own.

Yes, it was shitty to show up late.

But hey, he was here now, wasn't he?

"Oh, you came."

Beck's head whipped around and there was Micah, standing in the doorway, making his T-shirt and jeans look like a million bucks.

How did he always look straight off the cover of *GQ*, while Beck always felt like such a scruffy mess?

Apparently, nothing was fair today.

"Yeah," Beck said.

"Food's in the kitchen. Beer and soda, too," Carter said, chiming in, his welcoming smile turning into something more like an invitational leer. "And anything else you want, just let me know."

"Are you hitting on Beck *again*?" Deacon sounded incredulous.

Micah's smile never wavered.

Maybe jealousy wasn't the magic bullet Carter was convinced it was.

Beck told himself he wasn't disappointed at all, but even he couldn't deny he felt a tiny pulse of regret.

Maybe Micah had gotten over him, just as he was discovering how much he'd always wanted the guy.

"There's nothing wrong with repeating something 'til you get what you want," Carter said with a grin and a wild look in Beck's direction. "He's all repressed and shit, I'm sure he'd be a monster in bed. In fact, I'm counting on it."

That was what it took. Micah's expression froze.

"What," Carter continued, gazing intently at Micah, "don't tell me you never thought about West here in the sack? 'Cause *I* have, lots of times."

It turned out that as disappointed as Beck had been at Micah's non-reaction, the way he was struggling to contain his feelings now was just as goddamn hard.

Maybe he *was* that noble guy, the good guy Carter insisted he was, because he couldn't help but take pity on Micah.

Or maybe he just didn't want their dirty laundry exposed to all their teammates.

Because from what had happened on draft night, Micah had *definitely* thought about it. And while Beck hadn't necessarily thought about the two of them together before, after, he hadn't been able to help himself.

He'd thought about it plenty.

"Stop it, Carter," Beck said gruffly. "I'm not going to sleep with you. So quit fantasizing about it."

"I'll crack one of you, someday," Carter said lightly.

"A cold day in hell, maybe," Deacon retorted in a dry voice.

"Aw," Carter cooed. "I'm hurt. My ego is permanently damaged."

But while Carter was busy being overdramatic, Beck hadn't looked away from Micah. Not once.

He'd gotten his face back under control, but there was a burning fire in his gaze Beck recognized all too well.

Micah might not have said it, but he'd *felt* it.

He felt it, still.

Well, that answered *that* question. Micah's attraction hadn't changed after all.

"I'll show you the food," Micah said shortly. Turned and Beck was helpless not to follow as he led him into the kitchen.

It was a big farmhouse kitchen, with white and bright blue cabinets, a huge sink, and enormous expanses of countertop, all shining and clean.

"Not what I expected from our resident sex addict," Beck observed as he found a paper plate and loaded it up with a few pieces of pizza from the boxes spread across the island.

"No," Micah said.

He'd shoved his hands in his pockets, and for the first time since Beck had arrived, he looked uneasy.

Plate loaded up, Beck turned to the fridge and grabbed a beer from it, popping the top off with a twist of his wrist.

"Forgot how good you were at that," Micah said.

"It's everyone's favorite party trick." Beck leaned against the counter, making it clear he wasn't going anywhere.

They were going to need to talk. Beck knew it, even though he'd avoided it before now.

But avoiding it had only prolonged the inevitable, and it was time to face this head-on.

Beck took a drink of his beer and waited for Micah to speak.

"I didn't think you'd come today," Micah finally said.

"I didn't think I was going to come, either," Beck admitted.

"These are *your* friends—"

"And they could be yours, too, if you don't decide to randomly ghost them."

It wasn't necessarily fair, because they both knew Micah hadn't *randomly* ghosted him. He'd abandoned their friendship because Beck—and what Beck represented—had terrified him.

Well, it was Beck's turn to be scared shitless.

But fear wasn't going to solve anything. He knew that now, even if the thought of it still made him squirm.

Micah stared at him.

Beck finished the first piece of pizza and started on the second. It tasted like ash in his mouth. He'd never assumed that given the opportunity, Micah *wouldn't* apologize. But apparently that was a step too far for him.

Why had Beck believed anything different? Micah had had plenty of time to apologize before this and had never bothered.

"Don't worry," Beck said bluntly. "I think we can co-exist in a vaguely friendly space."

"Is that what you want?"

God, he wanted so many things he couldn't even separate them all out anymore. But he did know that co-existing in a vaguely friendly space was definitely not one of them.

"Sure," Beck said.

Even if Micah never apologized, he could live with it. Hadn't he been living with it, already?

He wasn't *happy* about it. But he could live with it.

At least he knew now Micah regretted it, and at last he was done denying himself, if what Deacon had told him was true.

Maybe it shouldn't have mattered to Beck, but it did.

Goddamn it, he was just as fucking noble as Carter had said. Beck made a face.

"What if that isn't what I want?" Micah asked, sounding like he was afraid to even identify what that might be.

Well, nothing was new, then.

"I don't know what you want, 'cause you've never fucking said." Beck finished the last piece of pizza. Threw the paper plate in the trash. Took a long drink of his beer.

Still, Micah didn't speak.

Fuck this.

He'd told himself he could come here and pretend like everything was okay. But he'd also anticipated that once he gave Micah the chance to apologize, he wouldn't waste it.

He was wasting it, and it cut at Beck in a way he hadn't expected at all.

He *should* have, though, because he'd come to way too many inconvenient and painful conclusions during the last year and a half.

"That's it," Beck said. He was halfway out of the kitchen when Micah's voice, low and bitter and full of self-recrimination, stopped him.

"This isn't easy for me, you know," Micah said. "I thought it would be. Coming here. Starting over. Even easier because you were here, but then you *were* here, and all I feel when I look at you is . . ."

But he still didn't fucking say. He just stopped, right in the middle of the sentence, like Beck wasn't hanging on every single word.

"When all you feel when you look at me is *what*?" Beck retorted, turning back.

He'd imagined his anger would be enough. Micah would slink off, licking his wounds, like *he* was the freaking wounded one.

Like he hadn't ghosted Beck *twice*.

But surprisingly, *finally*, Micah held his ground.

"You're right, you deserve to hear the words. And I should've said it ages ago. I should've said it that morning, the moment you left. Should've chased after you and made you hear it, even if you didn't want to."

Beck knew it was coming, and he'd had time to prepare himself for it, at least. But still he hadn't anticipated the effect the words would have on him.

"I'm sorry," Micah continued. "I'm so fucking sorry."

Breaking his heart and repairing it, in the same moment.

"For what?"

The surprise in Micah's eyes surprised Beck. Didn't the guy know how to apologize? Didn't he realize how many times Beck had imagined this apology? How about all those times when Beck could've used a friend, and had *wanted* Micah, more than anyone else, to be that friend, but he hadn't been?

Even if they had left behind everything else, all those hazy possibilities they'd just begun to explore that night, and *only* had that solid friendship, it would've been better than silence.

He didn't get to just come back here now, say he was sorry, and all that shit went away.

"You know exactly what I'm apologizing for."

Beck rested his hip against the corner of the kitchen table. Hoped he looked unbothered, even though he was very, very bothered.

"I don't know, do I? Is it that you totally freaked out and wouldn't talk to me? Is it that you never told me why? Is it that apparently I *imagined* everything we did together that night? Are you apologizing for accusing me of being crazy in love with you and pushing *you* so hard I apparently made you uncomfortable?"

Beck hadn't meant to sound so frustrated.

He'd wanted to be cool and calm and collected. Feathers unruffled.

But it turned out that it was impossible to even pretend all of this wasn't killing him inside.

Impossible to look at Micah, more handsome, more together than he'd ever been when they'd been in college, and pretend that he didn't want him desperately, *still*.

How was it possible that for years he'd managed to compartmentalize his attraction, but now he just couldn't? It was just one more unfair thing in a long list of them.

"Am I allowed to say all of the above?" Micah cracked a smile.

Beck didn't smile back, even though it felt like the most natural thing in the world to meet him halfway.

"I guess not," Micah said, voice full of regret. "I *am* sorry. I should've told you how much a long time ago. I never should've taken my freak-out out on you. I should have told you the truth. And I never, ever should have insinuated that you were . . . well, you know." *In love with me.*

Micah didn't say the words, but they existed, in the air between them.

"That was you freaking out, then?" Beck asked, before he could bite his tongue and keep the question from escaping. It didn't matter. He kept telling himself that, and yet, he still wasn't convinced. He'd needed Micah to admit it, in blunt black and white.

Micah nodded. "My uncle . . ."

"All I knew was you didn't like him. I didn't know he was that much of an asshole."

Micah shrugged. Not only did he not go into detail, he didn't say anything at all.

Were they really back to this?

Beck didn't want to pry this apology and explanation out of him, but what else could he do?

The words needed to be said. Otherwise, the pain of their separation would keep cutting at both of them until they were both bloody and exhausted.

"I guess you're still not talking about it," Beck said. Maybe it was too harsh, but it was also the truth. They could both use a little more truth right now.

"What do you want me to say? I didn't think I could ever do this. I didn't think I *should*," Micah argued. "I thought it was some kind of dirty secret I should pretend didn't exist."

Beck opened his mouth, so *he* could apologize, but Micah kept going, determination practically vibrating in the curve of his jaw, the tilt of his head, in his dark eyes, like if he didn't say it now, he wouldn't ever. "And after, I hated myself so much. Hated everyone who pretended like it was easy."

"Even me?" Beck remembered how he'd texted Micah before he'd come out.

Thought you might want to know before I do it.

At the time, Micah ignoring that text had felt like the worst thing he could imagine.

A rejection of everything he was trying to do.

Everything Beck was. Everything *Micah* was, even if it was buried so deeply almost nobody ever saw it.

Nobody except you.

"No, not you," Micah admitted. "But everyone else. *Me*, most of all. By the time I arrived in Miami for training camp, I was a mess. Angry. Bitter. Full of regret."

"God, that must've been terrible. I'm so sorry."

Beck hadn't even meant to apologize, but it had come out before he could stop it.

Micah looked shocked.

"You shouldn't be apologizing to *me*," Micah insisted.

"Yeah, I should," Beck said. "I knew what was wrong. Or I suspected, anyway. And I let you walk away. Twice. I should've pushed. I told you that you wouldn't get rid of me that easily, and you did."

"Except I tried to get rid of you. Like you not being around changed anything," Micah said ruefully.

Beck thought he understood what Micah was saying.

Maybe if Beck wasn't around to remind Micah that he was into guys, he wouldn't be anymore.

But that wasn't the way it worked, and it sounded like Micah had discovered that the hard way.

"I wish you'd talked to me," Beck said.

"I wish I had too. I had others . . .Coach's husband, Scott, he helped me a lot. But I sorta . . ." Micah took a deep breath, let it out. "I still wish it had been you."

"Well, is it over?"

"Is what over?"

Beck waved around. "Your whole existential crisis, I guess. 'Cause in my experience, coming out isn't something you do once and you forget it. You do it a lot. Over and over again. Sometimes every day of the rest of your life."

"Don't make it sound so great," Micah said wryly.

"I'm not. I'm trying to be honest. I'm trying to say . . .goddamn it. I'm trying to say maybe I wasn't there for you before, but I want to be there for you now."

"You do?" Micah looked downright shocked.

That made two of them.

Beck had not expected this was how this conversation was going to go, but maybe he should have. Maybe he should have remembered how close they'd been, and how close he wanted to be again.

"Yeah."

It had been tough enough living without Micah, with Micah six hundred miles away physically and a million mentally. But now that he was right here, practically in Beck's pocket, there was no way he was going to be able to preserve that kind of vaguely polite distance.

He didn't even want to.

If the happiness blooming across Micah's handsome face was any indication, he felt the same way.

"You really mean that," Micah said, marveling. "Except I don't think I really deserve it."

"Do we ever deserve anything? You apologized. I forgave you. End of story."

"Alright." Hesitation mingled with the joy in his dark eyes. "So . . .friends?"

Beck looked at him. It wasn't going to be easy to be *just* friends.

But he had a feeling Micah wasn't ready for anything else. And his own heart certainly wasn't.

It was still battered and bruised from the last time they'd ventured, even a few steps, out of the friend zone.

"Friends."

Micah held his hand out, awkwardly, no doubt wanting to shake on it.

God, and when had they ever hesitated to touch each other before this?

Sure, they'd done it during the Toronto game—the same kind of casual touches Beck would exchange with a couple dozen other Condors players—but they hadn't touched each other with purpose since Micah had been traded.

Not since that night.

And those touches had hardly been casual.

They'd been loaded with meaning. With purpose.

Beck hesitated for only a moment, then took Micah's outstretched hand and tugged him into a quick hug.

He felt the gentle collision of their bodies, from their shoulders brushing, to their chests bumping, to the briefest impression of Micah's hard, muscular thighs, the zing of connecting again undeniable.

Well, Micah not even bothering to attempt hiding the pleasure in his face as they broke apart, that answered *that* question.

Yep, they were definitely still attracted to each other.

If he'd had his way, they'd have stayed like that for a hell of a lot longer than a moment—and then he'd have leaned down, closing that scant inch between them and finally, inevitably, kissed Micah Rose.

But he didn't.

Because they were trying to be *friends*. And friends did not kiss their friends. No matter how much they wanted to, *still*.

"Oh, good."

Beck looked over in the doorway to the living room, and Carter was standing there, a triumphant grin on his face.

Micah raised a questioning eyebrow.

"You two finally made up," Carter continued. "Deacon owes me fifty bucks."

"You really put *two* bets on us?" Beck asked incredulously.

"Oh, sweetie, just two? There's a lot more than that," Carter said, patting him affectionately on the back. "And let's not start on the one where you finally give in to my many, many seductive talents."

"That's not happening," Micah muttered under his breath, just loud enough that Beck, still standing close enough, couldn't help but hear.

It shouldn't have felt so damn good he was a little jealous.

But it did.

Chapter 4

He'd done it.

He'd apologized.

And Beck, because he was a kind, generous, *amazing* soul, hadn't spit in his face.

No, he'd encouraged him. Offered to be there for him. Even *hugged* him, like Micah hadn't been a complete asshole.

It was easy to remember why they'd gravitated together in college. Why Micah had been so gone for him back then. He was a wonderful fucking person.

But Beckett West wasn't entirely noble.

Micah could still remember the incredibly dirty, incredibly hot way he'd whispered in his ear, on that night.

Watch. Just watch.

Hot, wasn't it?

Carter was no doubt right about one thing and one thing only—when Beck let his good guy persona go, it was going to be in bed, and it would be overwhelming in the best kind of way.

Satisfying, in every single way.

You aren't gonna be learning anything about that, Micah told himself firmly.

Beck had said it, after all.

They were gonna be *friends*.

Just friends.

That had always been enough for Micah before, and it was going to have to be enough again.

"Rose!" Coach Rufus, the defensive coordinator, bellowed. "Focus!"

He *had* been focusing.

Well, not on the thing Coach wanted him to focus on.

Beck just looked particularly hot today, his too-long hair flopping around as he ran drills, a shadow of dark scruff on the curve of his cheek. He'd cut the sleeves off his practice jersey, exposing his powerful arms, and every once in a while, the light material would bunch up in the afternoon breeze, and Micah would catch a glimpse of his muscled stomach and the trail of dark hair, damp with sweat, disappearing under the waistband of his shorts.

Micah couldn't stop thinking of what else it might lead to, and how his body had felt yesterday against Micah's own.

Strong and warm and perfect.

"Yeah, Coach," Micah returned with a sharp nod. He forced himself to re-focus, this time on where Carter was doing his final stretches.

"Maxwell's gonna keep you on your toes today," Deacon said, grinning as he passed behind him, ready to get set up for the first play of practice.

"When doesn't he?" Micah retorted.

He'd had a feeling that was what Carter had been doing yesterday, trying to provoke a jealous reaction out of him, when he'd brought up more than once how he'd hit on Beck—and that he'd like to do it again.

Over Micah's dead body.

After they got set in formation, Coach Rufus blew the whistle, and Micah tracked Carter with his body and his brain, a lifetime of lessons from coaches echoing in his thoughts, *and* pretty much everything Sebastian had ever said to him.

Watch his eyes, Sebastian reminded him. *He's gonna curl off, and you wanna know which way he's gonna go.*

Sure enough, Carter telegraphed his direction a half second before he broke off to the right, and Micah followed, legs covering acres of turf in a moment, as they sprinted together down the field.

"Damn it," Carter panted. "You're like a fucking *shark*."

"Blood in the water, baby," Micah retorted, his own breath uneven.

Carter was *fast*.

But then Micah'd cut his NFL teeth covering Tristan Nicholson, who was one of the fastest receivers in the league.

He stuck his hand out at the last moment, just when Riley tossed the ball in, and batted it away.

Sebastian would be proud, Micah thought, coming to a breathless halt.

He glanced over, and Beck was standing there, on his side of the field, like he hadn't been entirely sure Micah could handle Carter on his own.

But the approving look on Beck's face made it clear he'd handled him just fine.

"Good coverage, good coverage," Coach Rufus called out. "Strong work, Rose."

"No fucking joke," Carter muttered as they walked back towards the huddle. "You got a problem, Rose?"

"No." Micah shrugged. "If I had a problem, I'd have tripped you up, instead."

"That was just Rex," Carter complained.

"Let's try it again," Coach announced.

"Did he really?" God, even in the middle of his inner mess and insecurity, he'd never, ever been tempted to trip a receiver on purpose in practice.

"Lots of times," Carter admitted as he headed back to where Riley was standing.

"Rex really pulled that crap?" Micah asked Beck when he came up to stand next to him.

"It was bullshit," Beck murmured.

He'd wondered lots of times last year, because he hadn't been able to help himself, how Beck, one of the most loyal and upstanding guys in the world, had handled being on a team that didn't know the meaning of either of those two words.

The two times the Piranhas had played the Condors last year, he'd steered way clear of Beck, because he hadn't been nearly ready to face him yet. Not even close to being ready to apologize for fucking everything up.

But he'd seen him from a distance, wearing the particularly stoic look that told Micah he'd been hanging in there, because that was the only choice he had.

Neither of their rookie years had been particularly pleasant, though Micah admitted most of his problems were his own fault, and he'd gone out of his way to fix things as the season had come to an end.

But Beck hadn't had a Scott to guide him, to nudge him in the right direction.

He'd only had himself.

"I guess it goes without saying *you* wouldn't," Deacon said, his voice light, but Micah would have to be deaf not to hear the steel under it.

"Would I be here if I thought that was a fucking good idea?" Micah pointed out.

Mr. G, the Condors' new owner, had cleaned house when he'd bought the team during the offseason.

"Rex was still here," Deacon said. "He'd still be here if he hadn't been a total moron."

It was a good point.

Micah set himself on the line again. He looked over at Deacon, who was still looking at him like he was trying to figure him out.

It occurred to him that as far as Deacon's approval was concerned, the jury was still out. The guy didn't trust *anyone*. But then, if Micah had been through what this team had, then he supposed he wouldn't either.

"I just want to get ready to face Adams next game," Micah promised. "Carter's the best chance I've got to practice covering him."

Deacon nodded, then he broke into a smile. "Well, shut him down, Rose."

"Yes, sir."

Behind him, Micah could hear Beck chuckling.

They ran the route again, then again, and half a dozen more times, until sweat was dripping down Micah's forehead, and Carter looked like he was about to throttle him.

"Goddamn," he panted after Micah dug down and found the strength to leap up, batting the ball away for the third time in their ten attempts at this play.

Carter had only caught the ball once, and Micah could see how his normally easy-going attitude had morphed into frustration.

"Let's break it up," Coach said, clapping in approval. "Rose—you're looking great."

"Fuck," Carter yelled, spiking his helmet on the ground as the team started to head towards the sideline and the locker room to clean up.

"You okay?" Micah asked, glancing over at the guy.

He'd learned covering a receiver for that many plays, that intently, could teach him something about the guy.

He'd discovered Carter was more meticulous in his preparation than anyone gave him credit for, carefully shifting his routes, trying one thing and then discarding it when it didn't work for something else the next play. But he did not have the patience of a saint.

Carter shot him a look full of heated exasperation, but Micah just shrugged his anger off. Maybe he'd owned him today, in practice, but he wouldn't be surprised if tomorrow, Carter came back twice as determined to get by him.

"You just—*ugh*." Carter kicked the turf.

"Here I just thought you were just some laid-back guy who just liked to party and hit on his teammates," Micah said wryly.

Carter grinned at that, the anger disappearing from his expression. "Still hung up on that, huh?"

"Of course not."

But he'd be damned if he'd stand by and watch Carter offer to have sex with Beck again.

It wasn't happening.

Micah picked up his Gatorade from the bench and sucked down half the bottle. Damn, he was thirsty. It was hot here, just as hot as it had been in Miami, or maybe more so, because without the ocean breezes, the humidity was a constant thorn in his side.

"You asking me not to do it again?" Carter leaned against the bench.

"It's hardly my place to ask you to do anything or *not* do anything with Beck," Micah pointed out. *But yeah, could you just quit it, please? I'm having trouble not reacting anymore. Not when I want it to be me.*

"It's alright," Carter said. "I'll consider it." Like he *had* asked him to stop it, even though Micah was damn sure he hadn't. "As for practice tomorrow . . ." He straightened and shot Micah another one of those knowing smiles. "Watch yourself."

"He's insane," Micah muttered to himself as he picked up his helmet and started to walk towards the locker room.

"Everything okay?" Beck asked, jogging over to join him.

He'd pulled his practice jersey off, in anticipation of showering, and Micah didn't know where to look.

Okay, that was a lie.

He wanted to look *everywhere*.

Beck's broad shoulders and his firm pecs. His curved biceps. The ridges of abs.

The drop of sweat winding its way down his chest.

Be cool. Be normal. You've just said you're going to be friends.

After the shit you pulled, that's more than enough. More than you could've hoped for.

"It's fine," Micah said, but his voice came out high-pitched and squeaky. "Everything's fine."

"Carter giving you a hard time?"

Oh, he was.

But not about practice.

"It's good. He doesn't bother me."

Carter had clearly guessed that whatever had gone down between him and Beck hadn't been *only* friendly in nature, and was now trying to prod him to act by pretending that he might be interested in Beck.

But Micah had been forged in a much hotter fire than this. He could handle himself.

He could handle *this*.

It was funny, because he'd thought Beck was irresistible before, but now that he'd finally begun to embrace who he was—enjoy his differences instead of constantly hiding from them—it was even tougher to stop all those not-so-just-friendly thoughts.

"He doesn't mean it, you know," Beck said, pausing by the entrance to the locker room.

"Doesn't mean what?"

Beck grinned. "All the times he's offered to have sex with me."

It wasn't like he and Beck hadn't ever discussed sex before.

It had come up, a handful of times, over the years.

Most recently, on draft night, when you thought you might actually have it with him.

"Uh, yeah," Micah said.

"Not to say he wouldn't have sex with *you*, if you asked him real nice," Beck teased.

"I . . .uh . . .I think I'm good," Micah said.

He didn't say there was only one person he really wanted to have sex with—and it was Beck.

Surely Beck realized that by now.

"What is his deal, actually?" Micah asked, because changing the subject seemed like a better idea than pulling Beck to the side and confessing all the inconvenient and completely, utterly not platonic ways he'd fantasized about them re-connecting again.

"Oh, the sex?"

Micah wanted to shake him. *Stop saying sex. Stop it right now.*

But he nodded, because maybe this torture would end sooner rather than later.

"He says he uses it to control his temper."

"Temper?" Micah knew he looked confused.

"Yeah, well, that's the deal, right? You don't know he has it, until you *know* he has it. I saw a few glimpses of it today, when you shut him down."

"He manages his temper with . . .sex?"

Beck just shrugged. "He claims it works."

"Oh."

Micah was hardly a saint. He'd had sex before. Of course it hadn't been anything to write home about, probably because he'd been having it with a person he wasn't really attracted to. A gender that didn't particularly fire him up.

He'd never taken what he *really* wanted, because he'd been terrified of what it would say about him if he did. That he might not be able to deny the truth about himself any longer if he took that step.

Of course, then when he'd been ready, when he'd finally acknowledged what he wanted and who he really was, it turned out the person he still wanted, more than any other, was Beckett West.

He'd been attracted to Sebastian, but even before he'd realized Sebastian wasn't interested, he'd known he hadn't wanted to get him into bed.

Same thing with Julian, one of the reporters in Miami, and it turned out, the Piranhas' running back's boyfriend. He'd hit on him, more because he *could*, than because he'd actually wanted to do it.

For him, it had always been Beck.

"I know," Beck said with a dark chuckle, "it's a *choice*."

"Hey, whatever works for him, right?"

Micah was trying this new thing, the last six or so months, where he attempted not to judge others for the way they lived their lives, because he didn't want to be judged in return.

He hadn't been perfect, but he was trying, and Scott kept telling him that in the end, the effort was all that mattered.

"You better hope he hooks up with someone tonight, or else he's gonna be coming for us tomorrow," Beck joked.

"I'm ready. You're ready. Let him come for us." Micah had struggled with overconfidence compensating for his insecurities, and now he was learning how to just be sure in what he *could* do. And he could do this.

He could cover Carter Maxwell, and on Sunday, he knew he could take Davante Adams, too.

Especially with Beck beside him, supporting him, smothering the Raiders' defense one play at a time.

"Damn straight," Beck agreed, slapping him on the back. "We'll be ready."

But the one thing Micah knew he wouldn't ever be ready for was the white-hot supernova of desire that exploded in him whenever Beck touched him.

He should be used to it by now. But he wasn't.

"You're bein' a stranger." Scott answered the phone with a wry chuckle. "You promised me when you left Miami you wouldn't be."

"There's been a lot going on," Micah retorted. He settled back on the couch in the impersonal apartment the Condors had offered him when he'd been traded.

At some point he was going to have to find more permanent housing, but he'd barely been home.

Barely had any time to himself.

Definitely hadn't had any time to talk to his mentor and one of his best friends, the new defensive coordinator for the Miami Piranhas, Scott Callaway.

But the first real moment he'd had, tonight, he'd picked up his phone and called him, because nothing settled him like talking to Scott.

"Not like we aren't busy here," Scott agreed gently. "Everything going alright there? You settlin' in okay?"

When he'd decided he needed to get out of Miami, Scott had been the first person he'd told, and to his shock, Scott hadn't immediately told him he was stupid or crazy or full of wishful thinking.

No, he'd told him he understood.

That was why they were close. Why they'd become friends, even though Scott was thirty years older, though, as he liked to say, not really any wiser.

But that was a lie, because while he'd stuck himself in the closet for so long, Micah didn't think there was anyone smarter or more observant than Scott Callaway.

After all, he'd taken one look at Micah and realized exactly why he hated himself so fucking much—and even more than that, Scott had helped him pull himself out of it, when Micah had despaired of being stuck in that black hole of agonizing desperation forever.

"It's going pretty good," Micah said.

He might not have thought so, only a few days ago, but the Toronto game and Beck's reaction to his apology had made a world of difference. He was finally beginning to settle in here, and could see a future, stretching out in front of him, that looked bright and clean.

Even if he and Beck were never anything but friends, Micah knew he'd made the right decision leaving Miami and coming here.

"You finally talk to that guy you didn't want to tell me about?" Scott asked archly.

Micah chuckled. He *had* told Scott some of what had happened with Beck. Enough, but not everything. He hadn't told him who it was, but then Scott wasn't stupid. He'd clearly guessed who it was, or else he wouldn't have asked if Micah had talked to him.

"You knew it was Beck," Micah said. He'd very deliberately not told Scott who the guy was.

"It wasn't that hard to guess," Scott retorted dryly. "You played with him in college. You were friends. You weren't friends any longer. I'm fairly sure I wasn't the only one who noticed when the Condors played us in January, you and West stayed far away from each other. Not like two guys who'd been close in college. So, you talk to him or not?"

"Yeah," Micah said. "Yeah, I . . .we cleared the air."

"Am I gonna be coming to *your* wedding now?" Scott teased.

Shortly after he'd reunited with Coach Dawson in Miami, after too many years believing they couldn't be together the way he'd wanted them to be, Scott and Coach had actually gotten married.

Micah laughed. "Don't hold your breath. He's just stopped avoiding me whenever he can."

"Hey, you'd be surprised what a slippery slope that is."

"We aren't you and Coach," Micah said. Feeling a pulse of regret and melancholy that they weren't.

Their love wasn't epic or written in the stars. It wasn't love at all. It was just something that had begun to grow, that Micah had crushed before it could be anything at all.

"God, I sure hope not," Scott said. "Maybe you won't waste your lives pretendin' you're just friends, like we did."

"Maybe." But Micah wasn't going to count on it. He had a lot of work to do, to prove he was worthy now of Beck's friendship.

"What did we say?" Scott asked archly. "What did you promise? And didn't you promise Riley too?"

Micah *had* texted Scott that first day in Charleston, telling him how the Condors' new quarterback had reached out, and they'd already begun to bond over their mutual promises to each other—that Riley would tell his older, overbearing brother off, and that Micah would stop punishing himself.

Scott had replied almost immediately with, **Well, then you're gonna have to actually do it.**

And that was the problem, wasn't it?

Actually doing it.

Scott knew it, too, which meant he wouldn't ever let it lie.

"Yeah, you know I did," Micah grumbled.

"Then, you'd better actually do it. Riley Flynn doesn't strike me as the kinda guy who'd just let a promise go."

Micah rolled his eyes. "You don't even know him."

"Yeah, but I know *of* him, and let me tell you, you don't make it in the NFL being undersized and underappreciated with the kind of results he's had the first few weeks of the season without working your ass off."

"Okay, fine, you want me to say he'd kick my ass? He'd try."

"There you go." Scott sounded smug. "So you're gonna let yourself have this. You've made amends. You've apologized to Beck. You're gonna be his friend."

"Yeah."

What if I want to be more than just his friend?

But he didn't say it. He probably didn't need to, the way Scott kept hinting that there might be something more between them.

"Listen, you're a good friend, so just be that guy I know who's under those ridiculous suits, and you're gonna be just fine."

"My suits aren't ridiculous."

They were *extra* not ridiculous, especially after he'd worn his new camel plaid suit the other day, on the way to Toronto, and he'd been far too aware of Beck's eyes skimming over him when they'd been boarding the plane.

He looked good, he *knew* he looked good, and it had felt satisfying that Beck had been forced to acknowledge just how good.

Especially when he was still so caught on how *Beck* looked.

"Son, they're ridiculous, but it's alright. It's your thing. I'm just glad you're expressing yourself now."

Scott didn't have to say it bluntly because Micah already knew what he really meant: *you're not too afraid to express yourself anymore.*

"Thanks."

"So you're gonna fix things, huh?" Scott continued.

"I apologized, yeah. And he said he wanted to be friends again."

"What're you gonna do about that?"

"Geez, *Dad*, ask an easier question," Micah retorted.

Scott laughed. "And here Asa thinks our only kid is Beau."

"You've got an entire team of kids," Micah pointed out.

"Plus one more." Scott's voice was warm.

And while Micah had known he wouldn't lose Scott's friendship—or Asa's respect—when he left Miami, it felt good to hear it, too.

Clearing his throat, Micah tried to change the subject. "What do you mean, what am I gonna do about it? We're friends."

"Friends spend time with each other, Micah. You gonna invite him over? Meet him out for a drink? How about what you're gonna tell him? He's going to want to know why you left Miami."

"I don't know. Some of those, I guess." Micah could admit he hadn't thought that far. He'd been pretty stuck on just getting the apology out—and hoping Beck listened to it.

"You should tell him." Scott's voice was knowing.

"About what happened with Sebastian? Hell no."

He knew how he'd feel if Beck told *him* about some guy he'd been attracted to. Because it had happened more than once, and Micah had hated it every single time, even though he'd refused to do anything about it.

"You can't just talk to me, no matter how much it warms my heart to know you don't think I'm some old, washed-up, uncool dude," Scott teased.

"Fine, fine, I'll talk to him about some of it." *Not about Sebastian, and why we didn't get along. That's way too far.*

"Invite him over for a beer," Scott suggested, "and then when he's there, get close on the couch—"

"Enough!" Micah yelped. He stood and started pacing. How had being *just* friends with Beck been so easy before and now felt impossible? "You're supposed to be helping me be his *friend.*"

"Come on, Rose, we both know that's not what you really want."

"It's all I'm gonna get."

"It's all you're gonna get if you don't make it clear you're crazy about him."

"Maybe I'm not." He knew how stubborn he sounded.

Scott scoffed. "Don't lie to me. Especially not when it's so freaking obvious. You're absolutely head over heels for that guy. Don't do either of you the disservice of pretending otherwise."

"He probably doesn't—"

But Micah didn't get the rest of it out.

"You're never gonna know if you don't say anything. But, that said," Scott said with a chuckle, "maybe try to be friends for a little while first. Get used to each other again."

"Thanks, Dad."

"You keep calling me that like I'm gonna hate it, and so far, not so much," Scott teased.

"Ugh," Micah complained.

"Text him. Ask him to hang out. Go to dinner. Get a beer. *Talk* to the guy. But what am I even sayin'? You know how to be friends. You were friends before, for a long time."

"Four years," Micah said.

But he didn't need to explain to Scott how that one night they'd shared had changed everything about their friendship.

How it didn't want to fit so neatly back into its *friendship only* box any longer.

Scott would be all-too familiar with that particular situation, since it had happened between him and Coach Dawson.

"There you go, you know how to do this," Scott soothed.

It wasn't that Micah didn't appreciate Scott's confidence in him. He *did*. More than Scott probably knew, because not a lot of people had ever really believed he was anything other than an athlete. In so many minds, he started and ended as a football player.

But Scott had always seen him.

And so had Beck.

"You're telling me you knew how to be friends with Coach again, after you came back?"

"That was different," Scott claimed. "We fought. He wanted something I wasn't prepared to give, and I walked away."

"Yeah, don't know anything about that," Micah retorted dryly.

Scott sighed.

"It was hard, okay? It was like we'd let the cat out of the bag. I didn't know if the cat still existed. Or the bag, even. But I had to try. So I did. And so will you."

"What's the cat? And what's the bag?" Micah asked. "I'm not sure I'm following this very *clear* metaphor."

He could practically hear Scott's eye roll over the phone line. "You know what I mean."

"I'm not sure I do, but I'm not gonna ask you to go into details, 'cause I know Beau's still scarred from what *he's* seen, and also, 'cause I don't want you to sprain any brain cells tryin' to explain it to me."

"Fine, fine," Scott retorted.

"But thanks. Really." Micah said it like he meant it because he did.

He didn't know where he'd be without Scott's guidance, and his friendship.

You'd be figuring out your shit pretty dang well on your own, he could imagine Scott would say but Micah wasn't sure that was true at all.

Scott was the first to not only hold up the mirror so he could see his own behavior, but to hold his hand while he'd done it, so he'd known he wasn't alone.

"'Course," Scott said. "I told you not to be a stranger."

"Not that you'd let me be," Micah said.

Scott laughed. "Stubborn meets bullheaded."

"Sounds about accurate."

"Well, don't do anything stupid. Where are you at next?" Micah could hear Scott pause as he looked up the schedule on his phone. "God, Vegas. It's like I knew it before I even said it. Don't do anything stupid in Vegas, alright?"

"You don't have to worry. I'm done doing stupid things," Micah promised.

CHAPTER 5

He and Micah might've agreed to be friends, but Beck was still surprised that after practice on Friday, as he finished getting dressed, Micah approached him.

"Hey," he said. To anyone else, he might look calm and composed, but Beck knew him too well to miss the slight hesitation in his voice, the tightness of his jaw as he met Beck's eyes.

This wasn't easy for him.

Well, it's not easy for you, either.

The only problem with that was Beck didn't know if it was hard for them for the same reason—or a different one.

"Hey," Beck said, turning towards him.

Felt Micah's eyes snag on his bare chest as he tugged his T-shirt over his head.

Okay, it was *probably* the same reason.

"I was wondering, you want to grab some dinner? Maybe a beer?" Micah shifted from one foot to the other. There was no way he wasn't nervous, and maybe Beck shouldn't have felt a surge of fondness at the realization, but he did. "You know, friends stuff."

It was Friday, which was usually a lighter day, and after practice was over they were done, with an evening free.

Of course, Riley and Charlie were probably heading to the quarterback room to review the practice tape, and there were occasionally meetings or charity obligations to fill the time.

But tonight, Beck didn't have anything on the calendar.

He'd imagined going home, picking up takeout on the way there, and maybe relaxing on his back patio. Having one of those beers Micah had suggested.

There was no reason he couldn't invite Micah to tag along.

That was what friends did, wasn't it?

"Friends stuff?"

Micah chuckled self-consciously. "Yeah, that's what we're doing, right? Being friends?"

"We are." Beck picked up his bag. "Well, I was going to grab some takeout on the way home and eat it out on my patio. You should join me."

"You want me to come to your house?" Micah sounded surprised, like he'd been anticipating Beck would continue to keep him at an arm's length, even though he'd done what he could to show him that he'd accepted his apology.

"Yeah, that would be cool. You haven't been there."

How could he have? Beck mentally whacked himself. They'd just made up. How would Micah have been to his house?

"I'd like that. A lot," Micah said.

Beck realized he would, too.

"I was gonna pick up Thai; you got a preference?"

Micah shot him one of his charming, completely disarming smiles. Before, those had never given him butterflies, but after that night, it was like they'd set up permanent residence in his stomach.

Maybe this wasn't a good idea, after all.

"You know what I like," he said, his voice dropping lower. It scraped roughly over Beck's nerves.

Yeah, he did—and he didn't, all at the same time.

Chicken pad Thai, extra spicy, with shrimp salad rolls and peanut dipping sauce on the side.

But otherwise? Maybe Beck had only imagined the shiver up Micah's spine during that night, when they'd watched the other couple taking tequila shots. Maybe he hadn't liked him talking dirty to him, overwhelming him, caging his slightly smaller body with Beck's slightly bigger one.

Or maybe he loved it as much as Beck had.

"Yeah." Beck cleared his throat. "Pad Thai, yeah?"

"Make sure they make it spicy. I like it real hot."

I just bet you do.

How Beck had managed to not think about Micah and sex before that night was a miracle, because now, afterwards, he couldn't stop thinking about it.

"Got it," Beck said, hearing the restraint in his voice.

"Good." Micah nodded approvingly.

Beck rubbed his neck. "I'll text you my address. Say in about an hour we'll meet up?"

"I'm looking forward to it," Micah said, and Beck knew that he wasn't the only one who was looking forward to it.

He watched as Beck pulled his phone out.

Beck knew what the last thing he'd texted Micah was.

I hate that we've come to this.

He had, and Beck imagined as he typed out his address and then pressed send that he was doing his part to fix this. If he lingered on those last words he'd sent, this would never get fixed.

And goddamn it, he wanted to fix it.

"Got it," Micah said.

If he saw all of Beck's old messages, the ones he'd never answered, Beck couldn't see it in his face as he glanced up, with a smile, looking pleased with himself that he'd made the effort and pleased that Beck hadn't rejected him.

"Well, see you soon," Beck said.

Micah nodded.

As Beck left the practice facility and headed to his favorite Thai place to pick up the food, Beck couldn't forget the undeniable eagerness in Micah's voice. In his eyes.

Beck couldn't deny it assuaged some of the hurt he'd felt over the last eighteen months. It hadn't been only him who'd missed the close friendship they'd used to share. Hadn't been only him who'd spent too many lonely nights staring at his phone, wondering if he'd ever hear back from his ex-best friend again.

It definitely hadn't been only him who'd felt the sparks between them that night. Micah hadn't straight out said he'd lied, but the implication was clear enough.

He'd felt it, just the same as Beck, and instead of feeling galvanized by the possibilities, he'd panicked at what they could mean.

It was hard for Beck to blame Micah for that entirely.

Beck's first serious crush, back in eighth grade, had sent him to his room for way too many long, angsty afternoons and evenings, agonizing about what those feelings might mean. He'd continued for weeks until one night, his mom had shown up, just after dinner, and told him it didn't matter who he liked, as long as he liked himself.

But Micah probably had never had that kind of acceptance gifted to him.

He'd had to fight for every single fucking inch.

Beck still didn't know if he'd ever told his mom—even though Beck knew they were close—and he couldn't imagine that Micah had ever decided to tell his uncle, considering what he'd insinuated about his homophobia.

He parked in front of the little Thai place in the strip mall by his house, jogged in, placed his order, and only a few minutes later, was on his way back home.

He'd told Micah an hour, and he had precisely twelve minutes to do a quick run through his house, making sure that his dirty socks were picked up off his bedroom floor—though *why* they'd be in his bedroom, he wasn't sure—and that the dirty dishes he'd made this morning were packed away into the dishwasher.

It wasn't like he believed Micah would care, but Beck wanted to put his best foot forward. He wanted Micah to like his house, because *he* liked his house.

It was an updated mid-century modern house and a split-level, remodeled with an entirely open floor plan.

But what had won him over wasn't just the crown moldings and the beautifully restored wood floor, but the extensive landscaped backyard with over an acre of property.

There was a long overhang across the entire back of the house, with a stamped concrete patio, complete with outdoor kitchen, a built-in fire pit, and a wide expanse of green lawn that he'd used as an excuse to buy the riding lawn mower of his dreams.

He set the takeout bag on the low coffee table in the screened-in section of the porch, and looked around, making sure everything was in its place.

Should he get plates? They'd never eaten on plates in college—it hadn't ever even occurred to them—but Beck was trying to be a grownup, with this house. His mom had come out to help him furnish it, and now he not only had proper furniture he hadn't found on Craigslist or on the side of the road, but dishes and glasses and real silverware, and even serving dishes and platters he'd never actually used.

But before Beck could decide if it was better to grab the plates, his phone dinged with the alert for his front door camera.

Micah was here.

"Wow," he said when Beck opened the door. "You don't fuck around, do you? You bought a real house and everything. You even got those big pots with flowers in the front." He gestured to the ceramic planters his mother had insisted he buy, for "front door appeal." Beck didn't even know what that was, but he couldn't deny they looked nice, the flowers overflowing the sides, carefully tended now not by him, but by the gardener he was probably paying too much for.

"Didn't you have a place in Miami?" Beck asked as he opened the door wider and Micah walked in.

"Well, yeah, but it was an apartment in this big tower, you know? I thought it looked cool when I bought it and then the more I lived in it . . . well, I didn't really live in it," Micah admitted.

"That sucks." Beck hated the thought of Micah miserable during his rookie year—even living in a place he didn't like.

"Well, it just sold, so good riddance," Micah said.

"Where's all your stuff?" Beck led him down the entrance hall through the kitchen and out the back door, onto the patio.

"In storage, still." Micah paused, looking out at Beck's yard. "Honestly, this is awesome. Do you really take care of all of this?"

"Ah, well, not exactly." Beck rubbed the back of his neck. "*Sort of*, I guess. The gardener comes a few days a week, and on Mondays, I like to ride around on the mower, pretend I know what I'm doing."

Micah laughed, and Beck couldn't help but join in.

"You're an idiot," Micah told him, but fondly. Like he'd missed Beck being an idiot.

The more he laughed, the looser he felt, something he didn't recognize unwinding inside of him.

Something that had been coiled too tightly since the morning they'd walked away from each other.

Maybe they could do this friendship thing after all.

"And here I thought you'd be impressed," Beck said.

Micah shot him a look. "I think this is one of those times when *both* things are true. Yeah, it's impressive, and looks like it's actually a pretty damn comfortable house to live in. Good job there. But yeah, you're also an idiot, West."

"Takes one to know one, Rose," Beck teased as he stepped over to the mini fridge built into the rock ledge. He pulled out two beers, popped the tops off, and handed one to Micah.

"Cheers," Micah said, clinking his bottle against Beck's.

"What should we toast to?" Beck asked.

"Friendship," Micah said confidently. He raised his glass. "And the Wall, reunited again."

"Together again," Beck agreed.

Maybe it was better for both of them to focus on what mattered, what had *always* mattered, which was their friendship, and the fierce skill they'd always brought to the field.

Maybe anything else was just a distraction.

Micah had imagined way too many times what it would feel like if he left Miami and went to a city and a team where he could be himself *and* stop worrying about all the shit he'd said and done in the past.

He'd *hoped*, of course, that he might get a chance at rekindling his friendship with Beck again.

But he'd not asked for the trade because he'd assumed that would happen.

So many other teams could have wanted him. Thirty-one of them to be precise. Or he could have ended up staying on the Piranhas, if the owner and general manager hadn't gotten the kind of compensation offer they'd been looking for.

But in spite of all that uncertainty, all of that doubt, he'd ended up here. Back with Beck.

Friendship was all he could hope for.

Yet, as they settled in to eat Thai food, the way they had so many times in college, Beck's fork finding his container and stealing a few bites, his face flushed at the level of spice he preferred, what had always felt like enough no longer did.

"You're gonna regret that later," Micah teased as Beck reached for his beer and gulped half of it down.

"Probably," Beck admitted, but he was grinning. Like he'd missed this, too.

The Thai food was the same, maybe, but everything else felt different.

For one, they weren't sitting on Micah's thrifted couch in that shithole apartment. This view was a hell of a lot better. He'd never imagined Beck living in a place like this, but Micah realized it suited him.

And second, the truth of that night existed between them, an endless electric charge in the air.

No matter how much they ignored it, what had happened between them that night existed.

Maybe Micah might've been able to pretend better before, but now that he had an inkling what Beck felt like, and sounded like, and looked like, when they weren't trying to be only friends, it was a lot tougher.

"Eat the shrimp rolls. They won't exact revenge," Micah suggested, gesturing towards the container they were sharing, set on the coffee table between them.

"Always lookin' out for me, huh?" Beck asked lightly.

He'd done a shit job of it, but he could do better. *Be* better.

"I'd like to," he admitted. He didn't mind if Beck knew how serious he was; in fact, he kinda welcomed the idea he did.

He'd screwed all of this up, and he wanted to make it right. *Needed* to make it right.

Scott's voice popped into his head, reminding him that he'd apologized, he'd done his penance, and there was no need to continue punishing himself.

But this wasn't that, either.

It was . . .he wanted to be the best version of Micah Rose he could be.

It turned out his best version was the one sitting here, right next to Beck.

Beck picked up a shrimp roll, dipped it into the peanut sauce, and chewed half of it, before repeating the motion.

Micah was sure he was avoiding what he'd said, maybe pretending he hadn't said it at all because that was easier than listening and believing what Micah said was the truth.

But then, just as Micah was searching for a less difficult topic to bring up, Beck said, as he stood and went back to the fridge, grabbing them another pair of beers, "I think we should talk about it."

Micah nearly choked on his bite of pad Thai. "You think so?"

Beck set a bottle in front of him. Gave him a frank look. "Yeah, I do."

God, where to even begin?

I'm sorry, I only had a crush on you forever. You weren't only my friend, but so much more, and I know I screwed up that reveal, but I can do better. I want to do better.

If you'll let me.

But before Micah could open his mouth and any of those uncomfortable truths could spill out, Beck spoke first.

"So, why did you leave Miami?"

Micah choked again.

"You alright?" Beck looked at him with concern as he sat back down again.

"Oh, yeah, um, great. Really great." He was not great. He was both relieved and disappointed Beck had been talking about the *other* elephant in the room.

"You don't have to tell me, of course, but if we're going to be friends again?" Beck shrugged. "This is the kinda shit we should talk about. I want you to know you can talk to me, if you need someone."

Beck sounded so caring. So confident he wanted to hear whatever Micah had to say.

So of course, what he said was the worst possible thing in the world.

"You ever meet Sebastian Howard?"

Beck's forehead creased in confusion. "I don't think so. Why?"

Shit.

That had not been what Micah had intended to lead with.

He'd never wanted Beck to know how he'd felt about Sebastian.

"Uh." Micah hesitated.

"What about him?" Beck grinned. "You cheating on me with another safety, huh?"

"You could probably teach *him* something, since he's still figuring out the position," Micah said, hoping that changing the subject would distract Beck enough.

But it didn't.

"Doubtful. And that's what you're going with? You wanted to leave Miami because Sebastian wasn't the safety I was? He's still *Sebastian Howard*." Beck raised an eyebrow. This was ridiculous, even by Micah Rose standards.

Maybe there was nothing to do about it but just *say* it.

"He's hot, okay? He's so hot." Micah felt a flush rise up his neck. It wasn't that warm out here—there was a nice evening breeze and Beck had turned the porch ceiling fan on earlier—but he was suddenly sweating.

"Okay," Beck said, nodding. Not looking upset in the least. Or else he was a lot better at hiding shit than Micah was. He felt a flame of white-hot rage whenever Carter talked about hitting on Beck. "I can see it. So Howard's your type, huh?"

You're my type.

But he didn't say it, because the words kept getting stuck in his throat.

"No, actually no. I didn't want him like that."

Beck laughed. "You just wanted to fuck him, huh? So is that why you wanted to leave? Things go wrong with you and Howard? But wait, isn't he dating the coach's son?"

"He is." Micah felt ridiculous. "It wasn't like that, not really. It just . . .it made me angry. I was already so angry. So bitter. Full of regret."

Beck leaned back against the couch, his expression softening.

"And yeah," Micah continued, "I might've been an asshole. Especially to Howard. Definitely to Beau. He's Coach Dawson's son. He's a good guy. He and Howard are good together. But it was like that word vomit shit. It just came up and up and I couldn't stop it. I wanted . . ." *I wanted you. More than I could handle.* "I wanted a lot of things I couldn't have. Back then. Maybe still. I don't know. But I didn't deal with any of it well."

"I know how you can get when you get backed into a corner." Beck's voice was soft. Understanding.

"I said some shit. Something I swore to myself I'd never say. I said it anyway." Micah reached for the fresh bottle of beer Beck had given him. Took a sip. It didn't help, but then maybe nothing would. "That was the low point. Things eventually got better after that, but it took awhile. Though Scott showing up helped."

"Scott?" Beck was frowning now, and that was the craziest thing, because he wasn't pissed at Micah thinking Sebastian was hot. He was pissed because *Scott* had arrived on the scene?

Maybe it wasn't just Micah who got jealous, after all.

"Scott is Coach Dawson's husband. Well, he wasn't when he showed up. They were just old friends. Got into a fight once, a bad one, and they weren't for awhile, because of it, but when Coach Dawson had that heart trouble, Beau brought Scott in, to help, and they fixed things."

"Guess they did, if they ended up married."

Micah didn't want to think Beck's relief, quickly crossing over his face, meant anything.

"Yeah. But he's a friend. He encouraged me to be . . .well, to be me."

"I always liked you, so I'm glad," Beck said seriously. "Everyone needs to know the Micah Rose I know."

And like it was nothing, like he *deserved it*, Beck put his arm around Micah and tugged him into a hug.

"Thanks," Micah said, his voice muffled against Beck's big, broad shoulder.

How easy would it be to just turn his head and press his lips against Beck's cheek? Go a little farther and kiss his mouth?

Way too easy.

And not at all why he'd come here tonight.

Micah moved away.

"That still doesn't explain why you wanted to leave," Beck pointed out. "They're probably going to win a Super Bowl. Did they not let you off the hook? Did they stay mad? *Seriously?*" Beck looked like he wanted to go fight someone if that was the case.

"No, no, they forgave me for the bullshit I pulled early. That wasn't the problem."

"Then what was? Seeing Sebastian and Beau together?"

"God, no. *No.* It wasn't ever like that between us. He ended up being a pretty good mentor, more of one than I deserved, anyway. But . . . you ever really fuck up?" Micah shook his head, answering his own question. "I know you haven't. Not like that; you'd never pull that crap. I know you. Anyway, it's like I was carrying the weight of all those choices behind me. I couldn't let them go. I couldn't move on. Even if everyone else had. It was like I was a hundred pounds heavier, having to face those choices every day."

"I'm not perfect," Beck argued.

"Close enough," Micah said.

But Beck shook his head emphatically. "Fuck no. I let you go, didn't I? I knew, *I knew,* maybe not the details, but the problem, and I didn't help you. I was your friend and I just let you go."

"I wanted you to," Micah said wryly. "I said everything I could so you would."

"Still," Beck insisted.

For a long moment, he stayed quiet and Beck didn't speak again, either. They just stared at each other.

It was like that night, except so much *more*.

They both knew how much the other meant now, because they'd had to live without their friendship. Micah had already sworn to himself he wasn't going to do anything to lose it ever again. If he could just control himself, appreciate Beck as just a friend, maybe he'd eventually earn the right to ask for more. To tell Beckett just how much he craved not only his friendship, but his love, too.

Beck looked away first. Cleared his throat. "I'm really sorry you felt that way. But also selfishly glad you came here, too."

"I didn't think there was much chance it would happen," Micah admitted. "But did I hope it might? Yeah, I did. And then that shit went down with Rex, and I thought, maybe there's hope, after all."

"I wasn't happy about it at first," Beck admitted.

Micah wasn't surprised. He'd ghosted Beck. He'd rejected him with silence, even when he'd reached out during one of the most important moments of his life.

"Then I realized it wasn't that I wasn't happy. I *was*. I wanted to see you again. Play with you again. Figure out if we could have this again. What I wasn't happy about was just how much I wanted it, still," Beck confessed. "Just sitting here, chilling, and eating Thai food."

"You mean stealing *my* Thai food," Micah teased.

If Beck kept being this sweet and heartfelt, so irresistible, it was going to be hard to hold back.

Hard not to say what was in his heart: that while Beck's friendship had been one of the most important in his life, it wasn't all he wanted.

That he believed they could be so much more.

"Hey, I *missed* stealing your Thai food. I never have the balls to get it that spicy."

"Exactly."

"Hey," Beck cried in mock-outrage, elbowing him in the side.

"Not my fault you got a weak stomach," Micah said.

"Not mine either," Beck retorted, flopping back on the couch. "You know, you should take some of the help Coach Rufus wants to give you on Adams."

Micah raised an eyebrow. "You don't think I can handle Davante Adams on my own?"

"I think you can, but I think there's no shame in taking the help. Not many corners can take him one-on-one."

"So, what you're saying is let *you* help."

"Yeah."

"Would I be able to stop you?" Micah asked dryly. "You got your own shit to handle, but I'll have my hands full with Adams. Can't exactly control you, too."

"Exactly." Beck grinned. "What I'm sayin' is don't get all wounded and butthurt if I help you out."

"I don't get butthurt," Micah claimed even though that was not technically true. When they'd played Ohio State their senior year, even though Micah had *told* Beck not to help him cover Chris Olave, he'd done it anyway, and Micah hadn't talked to him for *days* after.

Of course, between the two of them, they'd held Olave to career low yards.

"Fine, fine, if you think I could use the assist on a play or two, I'm not gonna be mad at you after."

"I'm holding you to that," Beck said.

Micah raised an eyebrow. "What are you gonna do to me if I don't?"

Beck grinned at him. "Exact my revenge."

He didn't tell the guy, *nothing could be as bad as before, when we weren't friends anymore, and you know it.*

But he had a feeling Beck already knew that.

Chapter 6

Beck was running behind.

He'd woken up late, apparently having turned off his alarm in his sleep, and as a result he was late.

Late to board the plane to Vegas.

He skidded to a stop in front of the stairs up to the plane sitting on the tarmac, his suitcase falling over the moment he let go of the handle.

Right in front of Micah.

God, he looked gorgeous, dressed in one of his perfectly pressed three-piece suits, this one the light blue of a flawless summer sky, his white shirt open at the collar, Beck able to see a little more of his gorgeous light brown skin.

He'd been gorgeous last night too, in a T-shirt and jeans.

On his screen porch.

In his living room.

And glowing under the light of a streetlight as they'd said good-bye.

"Hey," Micah said, leaning over and picking it up. "You alright? You seem . . .frazzled. Even for you."

He was.

He wasn't proud of the fact, but after one last hug, Micah's arms curling around him like he wanted to keep him, like he wanted to *stay*, he'd felt buzzed, even though he wasn't even remotely drunk.

After he'd left, he hadn't been able to settle. Instead, he'd wandered around, cleaning up, the arousal lighting him up finally driving him to the shower.

It wasn't the first time he'd groaned out Micah's name as he'd fisted his cock, imagining what might've happened if he'd invited the guy to stay.

"Yeah, yeah. It's just . . ." Beck waved his hands around.

"It's just what? You know, you can tell me anything, right?" Micah leaned closer. He smelled amazing, like salt water and his mother's garden, and Beck wanted nothing but to close the distance between them and take a bite out of him, right on that exposed collarbone.

Not this. Not right now.

While Micah looked calm and relaxed, totally unbothered, Beck knew his own forehead was damp with sweat, and his hair was a total mess.

After the shower he'd taken, he'd tossed and turned, trying to not let regret and guilt build up inside him, too many thoughts and questions taking too strong a root inside him to be easily dismissed. Starting and ending with: *was this how Micah felt all the time, before?*

This morning there'd been no time to shower again, only to throw his clothes on and make sure he made it to the airport on time so the plane didn't leave without him.

"I slept in," Beck admitted. "Turned the alarm off without even trying to."

"I guess you stayed up too late," Micah teased, joy lighting up his eyes.

Maybe he was thinking about how much fun they'd had last night.

How much more fun they could *have.*

"Don't regret it," Beck said wryly. "Even though I'm a mess."

They climbed up the stairs into the plane. This time when Micah slid into a row, Beck followed, dropping his bag down and pushing it under the seat.

Micah arranged himself, all those long limbs so fucking elegant under acres of blue fabric. "Now, I can't do anything about *that*," he said, gesturing towards Beck's rumpled T-shirt and sweatpants, "but I can fix the rest of you."

"You can?"

"Yeah," Micah said, but when he went to stand up, a voice came over the plane's loudspeaker, announcing for everyone on the plane to take their seats and buckle up. "Well, I *will*, when we're free to move around the cabin again," he added with that particularly lopsided smile that Beck had always loved.

He loved it a little bit more than he had before.

"I'm looking forward to it."

"What are you looking forward to?" Jem leaned over the seat in front of them. "Going to Vegas? Letting loose?"

"You're staying?"

Coach had given them the option of staying in Vegas after their game, because the next week was their bye and practices wouldn't be starting up on Tuesday. They'd get a whole week off.

"Hadn't decided," Beck said.

"I thought I might as well," Micah said, and he glanced over at Beck.

What the hell. He was probably going to stay now.

If he got to spend more time with Micah?

He'd take it.

Now that he'd finally heard the whole story, knew where Micah's head had been at, it was safe to say he was no longer holding any kind of grudge.

"Well, don't do anything I wouldn't do," Jem pronounced.

"That's fucking terrible advice." Deacon's voice drifted over the seats. "You'd do a lot of shit we don't want them touching with a ten-foot pole."

"True," Jem said, laughing.

"I told Coach it was a mistake to let the team loose on Vegas, but he told me we'd earned it." Even though Beck couldn't see it, he could *feel* Deacon make a face. "But he said it was actually Grant's idea."

"Grant?" Micah looked confused.

"You've met Mr. G, right?" Beck said. "That's what Deacon calls him."

"It's his *name*," Deacon retorted.

"You call the owner of the team *Grant*?" Micah looked incredulous and Beck couldn't blame him. He hadn't known what to think ever since Grant Green had bought the Condors during the offseason.

On one hand, it made sense that Mr. G and Deacon were close. Deacon had essentially been his liaison to bring about the kind of change the NFL commissioner had insisted on.

On the other hand, Beck was seeing a whole new side to Deacon.

One who didn't look one hundred and ten percent sure of himself, every single second of the day.

"He does. Maybe he'll explain it to you 'cause he's never explained it to me," Jem grumbled good-naturedly.

"Bullshit." Deacon's voice was blunt. "I told you we were close because we're trying to fix this goddamn team."

"Right," Jem teased. He slipped back over the seat, and Beck could hear them still bickering as the plane readied for takeoff.

"They're not—" Micah asked him under his breath after the plane was in the air.

"Not as far as anyone knows. Besides, Mr. G bought the team to root out problems and trouble. Do you really think he'd get involved with a player?"

Micah shook his head.

"Yeah, I don't think so either. But I think . . .I think Deacon's got a crush, anyway."

He wouldn't have said that to anyone else—he definitely wouldn't have admitted to his theory in front of Deacon—but it felt right to tell Micah.

"Yeah? That kinda sucks for him."

"I don't know, maybe it'll be good for him. Push him out of his comfort zone. He spends so much time taking care of everyone. Making sure everyone's okay."

"Is Deacon the one who showed you the ropes last year?"

Beck nodded. "He's been a friend. A really good friend." He brushed his hair back, suddenly, way too aware again of how messy it was. How he felt like a rumpled disaster in front of Micah.

Finally the flight attendant announced over the intercom that they could move around.

"Come on," Micah said, standing and grabbing Beck's hand, leading him through the aisle towards the bathroom.

It was not any bigger than any airplane bathroom Beck had ever been in, but somehow, Micah managed to fold them both into the tiny space.

"What are you doing?" Beck squeaked with surprise as Micah crowded in even closer, his thigh splitting Beck's legs in half.

If he moved even an inch, even a *fraction* of an inch, they'd practically be humping.

Micah's eyes were full of amusement.

"Told you already; I'm fixing you," he murmured and leaned in.

Beck's heart rate felt like it doubled.

They'd been alone in his house last night. More than once he'd imagined closing the distance between them and kissing him. But he hadn't been sure. Their friendship, newly resurrected, was so important to him. Too important to risk. So he hadn't done it.

Surely if Micah had wanted to kiss him, he wouldn't be doing it in an airplane bathroom, with the whole team outside the door.

Even though it was an insane thought, Beck wanted it anyway—and was inevitably disappointed when Micah wet his hands in the sink and then raised them to Beck's head and began to fix his hair.

"What do I always have to tell you about getting a decent haircut?" Micah murmured under his breath as he worked.

Maybe the question was rhetorical, but Beck couldn't help but answer it anyway, in a breathless, rough voice that probably gave all his feelings away. "Maybe I just like you telling me." *Maybe I just like you touching me.*

"Maybe I like it too." Micah's hands were deft and careful, pressing and twirling chunks of his hair. "You have great hair. I always tell you that."

"Yeah."

Micah's gaze was level with his. He hadn't moved his hips, but if he felt anything like Beck did, it was a herculean effort.

Why am I even trying so goddamn hard?

"There," Micah finally said, when Beck was sure that any second now he'd lose his war with self-control and push his hips against Beck's with purpose. That he'd forget why it was probably a bad idea and lean in and take a bite out of his glorious bottom lip.

Beck took a breath and then a second one.

He still felt like a mess, but at least his hair looked good now.

"Better?" His voice came out in a rough gasp.

A corner of Micah's mouth turned up. "Yeah. You'll do. After all, I said I'd marry you, and I still would."

The point filtered sluggishly through all the arousal clouding up Beck's brain.

"You remember?"

He'd been so drunk that night. On booze, yes. That was undeniable. But on Micah, too. Blood singing with the inevitability of them getting together. The way he'd flipped in Beck's mind, the new angle showing him all kinds of possibilities.

Possibilities he'd never gotten to explore, and for a long time, had been sure he never would.

Micah shot him a look. "You think it's every day that I get a proposal like that? Of course I remember."

"I . . . uh . . ."

"It's alright," Micah said, reaching up and patting him on the cheek. His hand was still damp with water and so warm. So familiar. And yet so different.

Beck sucked in a breath.

"It's not alright," he said. "I didn't think you remembered. We were both so drunk and so . . ."

Micah stared at him as he hesitated.

Oh God, it's gonna happen.

But instead of leaning in that half an inch, Micah finished his sentence. "I was so torn up about you. But I didn't think you felt that way about me."

Beck opened his mouth to say, *I didn't then, but now I do, and I don't know what the fuck to do about it,* but before he could, a loud banging on the door jerked both of them back to reality.

"What's going on in there?" It was Deacon. He sounded concerned.

Like he'd break down the door if they didn't answer in the next five seconds.

He probably would too. There was no doubt in Beck's mind that he was one hundred percent capable of it.

"Just a second," Micah said, calmly. Like his own heart wasn't racing a million beats per minute, but when Beck touched him, palm against Micah's warm chest, he could feel it, even through three layers of cloth.

Whatever this was, they were both feeling it.

Goddamn Deacon, shoving his nose into a place where it didn't belong.

"I guess we should—" Beck swallowed hard.

"Yeah," Micah agreed reluctantly. He reached over and pushed the door open. Moved away from Beck.

He was hard in his sweatpants. Micah had probably felt it. Hadn't exactly moved away from it, either. But Beck didn't need Deacon to see his hard-on, and know what it was for. *Who* it was for. He was not even remotely ready to have *that* conversation yet. He adjusted himself, tugged his T-shirt down, and hoped Deacon wouldn't be looking.

"Everything okay?" Deacon asked in a hushed tone as Beck followed Micah into the narrow aisle next to the bathroom.

"We're fine," Beck said in a clipped voice.

"I was just fixing him . . .you know . . .the hair," Micah said, gesturing towards Beck's head. "It needed fixed."

"Right." Deacon didn't look particularly convinced. "Well, if you're done, get back to your seats, alright?"

That was fair, though Beck didn't feel particularly fixed. He felt blown to pieces.

But he nodded anyway.

Micah remembered their pact.

He barely remembered their pact.

Was it true he'd been talking a little bit out of his ass because he'd never imagined they'd end up back on the same team again, playing together like nothing had changed?

Yes.

But he *had* meant it. Every word of it.

He would never have said it otherwise.

We end up playing for the same team, I'll fucking marry you.

He hadn't even thought it was something he wanted until he'd said the words, and then he'd wanted it so badly it hurt.

Probably because he hadn't thought it could really happen.

But now, it had.

They took their seats again, and Beck glanced over at him.

Really, they *should* talk about it.

Clearly, despite the fact that they *should've,* Micah's feelings hadn't changed. And while Beck's *had* changed—they'd actually only become stronger and more insistent. Because once he'd let himself see Micah in a romantic light, he couldn't stop. Couldn't stop thinking that maybe, just maybe, the guy he'd wanted by his side was the one who'd been there first and was now back again.

"You good?" Micah asked, the corner of his mouth tilting up irresistibly.

You should have kissed him when you had the chance. Every single goddamn time you had a chance. That night. Last night. Just now.

"Uh, yeah. *Yeah.* Actually." Beck smiled.

Micah not only remembered, he'd meant it.

He *still* meant it.

"That's not gonna make things weird between us?" Micah sounded concerned now, like he really thought bringing up Beck's—*Beck's*—drunken marriage proposal was going to freak Beck out.

He'd been the one to say it, hadn't he?

"Not even close," Beck promised. "This time, I mean it. You're not getting rid of me."

Their friendship, Beck realized, wasn't just resurrected. It *was*, but it had changed. Morphed into something else.

It was friendship *and* more.

If he was brave enough to reach out and take it.

Next time, you will be, he promised to himself.

"Maybe now it's *me* that's not letting *you* go," Micah said.

Beck thought he liked that a hell of a lot.

"It's a promise," he said, and reached out, grasping Micah's hand with his own and squeezing.

For you? Yeah, I'd promise it.

Micah's eyes softened even more.

"Same," he said.

God, why were they on a plane? Couldn't they have done this last night? Beck was in the middle of lecturing himself with endless recriminations for not taking what was essentially the *third* opportunity he'd been presented with, when Micah said, "You wanna watch a movie?"

Beck stopped thinking.

Or really, he stopped *overthinking*.

What if last night hadn't actually been a wasted chance?

No time he spent with Micah could be a waste.

"Yeah. Yeah, actually."

Maybe it was okay that they hadn't taken that step during draft night, or last night, or just now. Maybe it was okay to take their time. Be cautious about it.

Because you meant it. You'd marry him tomorrow. This is it, for you.

Beck was suddenly very sure that it wasn't just a matter of *if*, but a matter of *when*.

"Great." Micah's face broke into a wide smile. "I got *White Men Can't Jump* and—"

"The remake?" Beck asked.

Micah shot him a look. "Hell no."

"I don't know if I should be insulted or what," Beck stated, but he was smiling. He couldn't help it. Micah had brought that movie—one of his favorite movies, Beck remembered that much from college—on the plane, with the hope Beck would watch it with him.

"What, suddenly unsure if you can jump?" Micah teased, nudging him with an elbow.

"Oh, I know I can." He stretched out his long legs. "Come on, put it on."

"You don't want to know what else I've got?"

"It's your favorite movie, isn't it?" When Micah looked surprised, Beck just shrugged. "I remembered. That and *more*," he teased, lowering his voice.

Micah shot him a look as he reached down and grabbed his laptop, setting it up on the tray table. "I guess you think you got moves."

"I know I do," Beck said. Hoped that maybe after the game was over on Sunday, he'd get a chance to show Micah just how good they were. Just how good they could be together.

"Guess we'll see," Micah said. He handed Beck a pair of earbuds.

"You came prepared." His favorite movie—one they'd always teased each other over, and a second set of earbuds. Maybe Beck wasn't the only one with moves.

Then there was Micah's flawless suit. The way his shirt opened at the neck, drawing Beck's gaze effortlessly.

Was he showing off? Was he making the moves on Beck without Beck even realizing it?

He remembered hands in his hair, a hard thigh between his own, almost no room to even *breathe* in that tiny airplane bathroom.

Yeah, it was definitely possible.

Micah flashed him one of those irresistible grins. "Yeah, guess I did."

Micah took one shuddering breath and another, lifting his gloved hands to his shoulders as he paced back and forth on the sideline, trying to magically find more lung capacity.

"Hey, you good?" Beck was there when he turned, ready to make another pass.

It was deep in the third quarter, and he was way fucking tired of covering Adams.

"Is Adams getting out there next play?" Micah asked, rhetorically. Of course he fucking was.

Beck nodded.

He'd been sprinting up and down the field for the whole game.

If he'd had the energy to be mad at Beck for helping cover, he still wouldn't be, because *one*, he'd promised him he wouldn't be, and *two*, they'd needed every bit of help they could get.

Riley and the offense were keeping up with the Raiders, but it wasn't an easy task.

At some point, the defense was going to need a big stop.

"Deacon sent me to check on you."

"I'm fine," Micah retorted.

"Oh, I told him that." Beck put a hand on his shoulder. His face was streaked with sweat, his hair plastered to his head. It shouldn't have been appealing, but then this was Beck, and they'd have to both be dead or dying to not feel the burn whenever they were close enough to touch. "But I thought I'd come over anyway. You know, you're holding him."

"Not well enough," Micah said, breath gusting out of him in one long sigh.

"We're in this game, aren't we?" Beck demanded, getting even closer. "You're doing it."

"We're doing it. Together."

"Exactly," Beck said, nodding in approval. "You're not alone out there. You've got me. And we've got the rest of the defense, too. Deacon. Jem. They're doing their job, pressuring the quarterback. It's all adding up. It doesn't have to just be on you, Rose."

He knew it. It hadn't been just him at Northwestern.

It sure hadn't been just him in Miami. He'd learned that the hard way, then.

Then why had he come to Charleston expecting that he'd need to take the whole burden?

Scott would tell him he was being stupid.

And Scott would be right.

"Yeah," Micah agreed.

"Hey, seriously, though," Beck's voice dropped, "*are* you alright?"

"Yeah, yeah, I'm fine. I'm solid."

Beck nodded, believing what he said, and Micah realized he *had* meant it.

In some ways—in the ways that truly mattered—he'd never been better. He and Beck had hung out on the plane. Had sat together during the team dinner and the walkthrough.

Had stood on the sideline together before the game had begun and done their chant.

And Beck had been a fucking beast on the field today, everywhere at once, it seemed, batting balls down, before they could get even remotely close to Adams and become Micah's problem, defending passes like his life depended on it. Even moving up to tackle the Raiders' running back a handful of times.

But more than anything else, he'd been right there, crossing over the field to help Micah cover Davante Adams, one of the best, and *fastest*, receivers in the NFL.

It was mostly because of Beck—and Micah had to admit, the way the defense was working so well together—that it was 14 to 10, the Condors having a slight advantage heading into the fourth quarter.

"We got this," Beck said, and they clasped hands again. "*You* got this."

"Yeah."

And when the defense took the field a few minutes later, after Ethan, the Condors' kicker, sent the ball through the uprights for another field goal, Micah felt his own confidence growing, but it wasn't just him.

As the defensive unit jogged out, Micah met their eyes, one by one, and it seemed every single one of them had found a new well of confidence and determination.

We can do this was the unspoken agreement as they huddled up.

"One more quarter," Deacon announced as they all leaned in. Micah felt Beck's hand on his back, brushing him briefly.

His touch might've been fleeting, but it gave Micah power and a fire he knew he'd missed in Miami.

They were the Wall. He *dared* even Davante Adams to score on them.

"Yeah," Jem agreed with his friend. "Everyone good?"

Micah gave a nod.

"Good." Deacon clapped his hands, and the huddle broke up, everyone taking their spots opposite the Raiders' offense.

"Watch the roll out," Jem called out as they took their places. Which meant they'd be pressuring the quarterback and the chances were high he'd take off, trying to run for the first down.

Micah braced his foot behind him, ready to take off the moment Adams started sprinting downfield again.

Infuriatingly, the receiver was barely breathing hard, still.

Of course, his work was a hell of a lot easier than Micah's.

He just needed to catch the ball.

Micah had to not only prevent him from doing that, but also get into a position where he had a chance at the ball himself.

So far he hadn't had any interceptions while in a Condors uniform, but every play was a new chance for him to make that happen.

The whistle blew and the Raiders' quarterback called out the snap count, and everything went very still inside Micah.

Out of the corner of his eye, he could see just the edge of Beck, his gaze narrowed.

The ball snapped.

The problem wasn't just that Adams was fast—there were plenty of guys in the NFL who were fast, like Nicholson back in Miami—but Adams was sneaky, too. Clever.

On this particular play, Adams crossed over the zone, lingering long enough so that Micah knew he was trying to lull him into a state of complacency. But instead of letting that overconfidence bite him in the ass, Micah pushed off and followed him closely, step for step. Micah had a feeling he knew what was coming.

All of a sudden, Adams twisted and sprinted down the sideline, Micah's lungs *and* legs pumping as he focused both on keeping up with him and making sure his angle was the best angle.

He caught a single glimpse of Beck, dropping back and sprinting over to where they were running down the sideline.

The quarterback hesitated for a second, but Micah tracked his eyes.

He was going to throw it to Adams, anyway. Even though he was—at least Micah *hoped*—mostly covered, not just by him, but by Beck.

But even if they tackled Adams right after his catch, it would still be a big chunk of yards.

Too many.

The timing on this had to be flawless, and luckily for Micah, he not only had a natural gift for it, but Sebastian Howard, who'd arguably been one of the best corners in the NFL, had taught him how to time his jump even better.

The quarterback threw the ball.

A moment later, Micah made a move to the inside of Adams, and then jumped, the ball landing right in his hands.

He came down hard—no chance for a return on this particular interception—but that was okay.

A second later, Beck was leaning over him, laughing and yelling.

"You crazy fucker," he shouted as he stuck out a hand for Micah, who took it with one, cradling the ball in the other.

"Hey, I was right, wasn't I?"

"If you hadn't been . . ." But Beck was smiling. Looking like they'd both just won the jackpot.

"If I hadn't been, you'd have got him. I knew you would." *I trusted you would.*

It was the kind of trust, the unshakeable belief in each other, plus all the skill they'd worked so hard to hone, that had made the Wall so effective in the first place.

"Damn straight," Beck said.

"God, what a fucking awesome catch," Jem said, patting him on the back as Micah tossed the ball to the ref, and they jogged back to the sideline together.

"Awesome work, Rose," Coach Kelley told him, slapping him where Jem's hand had been only a moment before. "Take a rest, you've earned it."

Micah dropped down to the bench. Hoping that maybe the offense could move the ball down the field and give him a long breather. It would be even better if they could score, not completely putting the game out of reach of the Raiders, but close.

Riley looked like he intended to make it happen, taking the first snap of the drive, moving fast through the line, dodging defenders.

"God, am I glad I don't have to keep up with *him*," Beck said, taking a seat next to him. He shoved a hand through his sweaty hair.

"Seriously," Micah agreed. Riley Flynn might've been the quarterback nobody had seen coming, but *Riley* had known it. Sometimes that was all that mattered.

Micah's hands itched as Beck continued to push his hair out of his face. He wanted to touch him. He wanted to touch him all over.

Beck was always sexy as hell. But sweaty, working hard, and in his uniform? He was an irresistible temptation.

His lack of street clothes stripped away the cool, calm, affable smokescreen and revealed the intensity of the man beneath.

God, Micah wanted all of that focused not on the game, but on *him*.

Maybe it would actually happen now. Beck had miraculously *seemed* interested earlier. Not just in hanging out, but in more. When they'd been wedged together in the bathroom—not one of his finer moments, honestly—he'd definitely felt Beck's cock, hard and interested, against his own.

There'd been chances before this one for Micah to have the kind of sex he really, truly craved—sex with a man—but he'd never done it. Had never taken that irrevocable step, yet.

But even if all Beck was willing to give him was friendship and sex, Micah would take it, willingly.

Anything he'd give him.

"Great moves," Deacon said as he passed by where they were sitting. "How did you know he'd throw?"

"His eyes."

"He was forty yards away," Deacon retorted incredulously.

"Yeah, he sorta tilts his head when he glances where the ball's going," Micah said. "I saw it on some film. Confirmed it earlier. I knew he was gonna throw it my way, and even if I mistimed the catch, Beck was right there."

Deacon raised an eyebrow. "You were willing to give up a forty-yard pass to grab that ball?"

Micah didn't shrink from his hard stare. Hadn't he been forged in far hotter fires than this? Josiah could give Deacon—or anyone else—a run for his money when it came to a confrontation.

"I play to win. But we would've stopped them, no matter what."

Deacon nodded slowly. "That's the attitude I like to see, Rose. You played lights out today. Hard and close when it mattered, and then when you saw your chance, you took it. No hesitation."

"That's Rose for you," Beck said smugly. Micah picked up a bottle of Gatorade to cover how fucking pleased he was at Beck's words.

They meant so much.

More than Deacon's.

More than anyone else's.

Deacon shot Beck a look. "Yeah, yeah, we know you love him, West."

Micah's insides froze, but Beck just replied to Deacon's words with a careless smile and a shrug. "Yeah, I do," he said. "The Wall's back and it's better than ever."

Jem slapped Deacon on the shoulder. "Calm down, old man. They got it done, didn't they?"

"We all did," Micah said, and then, suddenly, a roar went up, and they turned towards the field, watching as Carter plucked one of Riley's passes out of the air and kept his feet when he came down, sprinting down the field like it was a playground and the rest of the guys around him didn't even exist.

"Shit," Beck cried out. "He's gonna go . . .all . . . the . . .way!"

And Carter did, leaping into the end zone, throwing his hands up in the air in triumph.

"Well, I guess that was definitely the right call, huh, Rose?" Deacon said and patted him on the shoulder. "One more good drive like that one and we should have this one all sewn up."

Deacon's words proved to be true.

After Ethan kicked off, Deacon and Jem smothered the Raiders' quarterback on the next play. Then they started just running the ball, even Adams giving up the attempt to make something miraculous happen as the rest of the fourth quarter ticked down.

"Great game," Carter said, throwing an arm around him as they stood on the sideline and watched the clock hit zero.

"You're tellin' me," Micah joked. "That catch was pretty damn brilliant."

"No less than yours," Carter said graciously. "I like to think I gave you that little extra somethin'-somethin' today. Lining up against me in practice all week."

It was ridiculous, but Micah laughed anyway. "And so did I."

Carter conceded with a grin. "Yeah, probably. Now . . .it's Vegas, baby, so it's time to celebrate!"

CHAPTER 7

To Micah's surprise, before he could approach Beck in the locker room, he was there, standing in front of him as he buttoned up his shirt.

"Hey," he said.

Beck rarely looked uneasy. But he looked nervous now.

"Hey," Micah said.

"You said you were staying, right?"

"Uh, yeah, I am." Should he ask if Beck wanted to stay too, hang out? Was that even right? Or was it just a poorly concealed euphemism for what *he* was definitely thinking about and maybe Beck was too?

He could still feel the phantom pressure of Beck's legs against his own.

"Cool." Beck shifted from one leg to the other.

He'd changed into dark gray slacks and a blue polo shirt that clung to his chest, still damp from a shower, outlining all his muscles. He'd even done something with his hair.

It was a really good look.

Bullshit, Micah thought to himself, *it's a fucking amazing look. But honestly, all of that would look better on the floor.*

On my *floor.*

"Would—"

"You could—"

They'd spoken at exactly the same time, and Beck burst out laughing. God, he was so gorgeous like this. Micah's fingers slipped on the final button of his shirt.

Beck waved at him. "You go first."

"Do you want to stay too? Hang out? I've got a suite at the Wynn."

"You didn't have any plans?"

Even if he had, he would've dropped them immediately, just for the chance to spend time with Beck.

He shook his head.

"Well, that works out then." Beck smiled. "You wanna grab dinner? Maybe a few drinks?"

"That sounds great," Micah said, only realizing after Beck stepped away, saying he was going to get some transportation and a dinner reservation, just how much this sounded like a date.

But that didn't mean Beck had meant it like that.

It wasn't until they were in the back of the car, the lights of Vegas flashing by them as the Uber driver took them down the Strip, that Micah began to realize maybe Beck *had.*

"This is kinda like that night," Beck said, looking at him.

Micah froze. "That night? You mean *that* night?"

Beck nodded.

"Ah, yeah." Micah swallowed hard. Beck was sprawled against the leather seat, his legs endless, his teeth flashing white in the dim light of the car.

"You *said* you remembered it," Beck teased in a low voice.

Like he could ever forget it.

"I don't remember us going to dinner that night."

"Oh, I don't know," Beck said. "I *nearly* had a mighty fine meal, there, at the end."

Micah's jaw dropped open. He was not used to this Beck. This Beck, who was smiling at him like he had a secret. Like he couldn't wait to share it.

"Don't tell me you haven't thought about it," Beck said. He was still relaxed against the seat. Like none of this conversation was full of atomic bombs they could accidentally trip over.

After all, they'd tripped *and* fallen over them that night.

Of course, Micah knew he was better now than he'd ever been then. He'd admitted who he truly was. To himself. To others. He'd come out to his coach and one of his teammates. He'd told the truth to everyone who mattered, regardless of the consequences.

He was ready to take that inevitable step of being with someone. Maybe he shouldn't have wanted it to be Beck, but he did, more than ever.

"I . . ." Micah took a deep breath. It was time for honesty, not for fear. "Every single fucking day."

"Good." Beck sounded very satisfied.

"You tryin' to drive me crazy?" Micah demanded.

But Beck was still staring at him, expression smug and a little possessive.

"Maybe both of us, a little," Beck admitted. "But don't tell me you weren't tryin' to do the same yesterday."

Okay, that was fair.

He'd seen the chance, and he hadn't been able to resist taking it.

Seemed like he wasn't the only one.

"Where are we heading?" Micah asked, clearing his throat. Was he nervous? Was he nervous and as a result changing the subject? Maybe.

Definitely.

"I got us a table at this steakhouse at the Wynn. Came highly recommended when I called the concierge. Dropped your name." He grinned. "Hope that was okay."

"What, like dropping your name wouldn't get you the same exact thing?" Micah grumbled.

"Yeah, but I'm not staying there, officially. I'm just crashing on your fun weekend," Beck pointed out, elbowing him gently.

"It isn't crashing if I want you here."

Beck's gaze softened. Oh, they were in deep shit. Micah knew it, and it was hard to even care anymore. "Yeah?"

"Yeah," Micah repeated with certainty.

"I haven't said—" Beck hesitated. "I'm so glad you're here. I missed you so damn much."

"You sap," Micah teased. But he felt warm with the confession. Let himself scoot closer on the seat, until their thighs were nearly touching.

He remembered a time when touching Beck had been overwhelming, like too much honesty banging against a door he desperately wanted to stay closed. But now, it felt *good*. So goddamn good he didn't want to stop.

"You like it," Beck retorted fondly.

He did. He really, really did. Only in his dreams had he ever imagined Beck like this.

Sweet and charming and seductive.

Micah was pretty sure now that was what this was.

Beck was trying to woo him.

"Yeah," he echoed. It was the truth. He didn't just like it; he *loved* it. He wanted to see Beck like this all the time. He never wanted this night to end.

Micah's heart was still racing from his sudden realization when the car pulled up to the Wynn.

"Alright, gentlemen," the driver said. "We're here."

Beck shot him an utterly devastating lopsided smile as he slid out behind Micah.

"Doesn't that feel a little like déjà vu?" he asked as they stood outside the front awning of the Wynn, waiting for the driver to grab their bags from the trunk.

A bellhop came up to them and took their bags and a folded-up twenty Micah handed him. He'd already checked in with the concierge last night, so the room he'd reserved should be ready. "Rose," he told the bellhop. "Suite under Rose."

"Sounds good, sir," the man answered, grinning at them. "Great game today."

"It really was, wasn't it?" Beck slung an arm across Micah's shoulders, tugging him close. "This guy played lights out."

"I think you're talking about you," Micah pointed out as they headed inside the Wynn lobby. "You were unreal today."

"Ah, you a number one Beckett West fanboy, now?" Beck asked as they took the corridor that directed them towards the steakhouse.

The lights were turned down, the gold trim everywhere glowing softly, and Micah couldn't deny that if this wasn't a date, it was still the most romantic non-date he'd ever been on.

Plus there was Beck's arm, which was still tucking him into his side. Micah could feel the pressure of every single one of his fingertips, burning like brands into his shoulder.

Way too soon they reached the restaurant entrance.

"West," Beck told the hostess, who smiled at them.

"Right this way, sir," she said and led them deeper inside the room, all the way to the back, to a fairly dark corner.

"Oh good, this is perfect," Beck said, slipping her a bill Micah didn't get a good glance at.

He'd asked for this privacy, Micah realized. He'd wanted them to be alone.

They sat, Micah's fingers trembling a little as he picked up his menu.

This felt the same as the other night, when they'd companionably shared takeout, and also radically, wildly different. He'd thought if he ever took this step, he wouldn't be nervous anymore, but he was.

Not because he thought he wouldn't like it. Or he'd be ashamed of it. But because he'd never wanted anything this badly in his whole goddamn life.

The waiter appeared, and without Micah even saying a word, Beck ordered them two double whiskeys on the rocks—specifically an expensive brand he must have remembered Micah liked.

"Hope that's okay," Beck said, as the waiter left them to peruse the rest of the menu.

"It's totally fine. I just didn't realize you remembered."

"How could I forget?" Beck answered wryly, leaning back in his chair, his whole body practically on display.

Micah wanted to fall to his knees and worship him, the way he was meant to be worshipped. Tug that way-too-tight polo out of his slim-cut slacks and then open his belt. Discover exactly what he'd felt yesterday, pressed against him in the airplane bathroom.

"You alright? You look flushed," Beck said, their drinks arriving. He took a sip of his whiskey. "Damn, that's good."

How to even broach the subject? Beck definitely looked into this. But Micah was in so deep he didn't know if he ever wanted to find the surface again.

He latched onto his drink like a lifeline. He didn't want to be so drunk he didn't remember every single technicolor moment, but he could use something to settle his nerves. He took a long sip, letting the whiskey drain down his throat.

It *was* good.

"I'm fine." *Just thinking about you naked is making me sweat. Isn't it like a hundred degrees in here?*

"Just checking." Beck's gaze on him was warm. Affectionate.

The waiter returned. They ordered. Got a second round. Then a third, as they finished their steaks.

The heat inside him intensified, but this time, he didn't flinch from it. Let himself bask in the idea of what might happen after dinner.

What were they going to do? They could do *anything*. The idea was intoxicating, exacerbated both by the excellent whiskey and the way Beck was staring at him over the rim of his glass.

"I was thinking," Beck said, as they finished up and he grabbed the check, throwing down his credit card. God, this totally *was* a date. "It's not too late, and I got the concierge to get us on some VIP lists. You wanna go out? Go dancing?"

It wasn't too much of a stretch to assume what Beck was doing. The path he was leading them on.

They were re-creating that night. Was Beck hoping it might end differently? Or was this just like every other evening they'd spent together? Just two friends—two completely platonic bros—hanging out?

Micah's skin felt too hot. Too tight.

"Uh, yeah. Sure."

"Don't sound so enthusiastic," Beck teased. "I thought you liked to dance. Or maybe it's *my* dancing you'd rather avoid?"

"You're not *so* bad," Micah admitted.

He'd willingly let Beck flail around him forever, as long as he got to touch him again.

He'd eaten—a side salad, followed by a big, delicious steak, with some crispy potatoes on the side—but the liquor he'd drunk hit him when he stood up.

He'd been sticking to beer since before the season, and the particular brand of whiskey Beck had ordered was potent.

Or maybe it was just Beck and the crackling in the air whenever their eyes met that was making him so much tipsier than he had any right to be.

"You wanna go to the club now?" Beck asked him as they walked through the lobby.

He did. But he also didn't want to give up this hushed intimacy between them.

"Maybe a quiet drink, first?"

Beck nodded, a soft smile blooming across his features. Like he didn't want to give up just the two of them either. "I'll ask what the right place is," he said, touching Micah on the shoulder before he walked over to the concierge desk.

A minute later he was back. "Down this way," he said, gesturing. "The concierge said there's a nice quiet bar. He's called ahead, made sure they reserve a table for us."

"Is this the Beckett West VIP experience?" Micah wondered as they headed in the direction Beck had pointed.

God, in college, they'd shared shitty booze and cheap beer in the worst kind of bars, not worried about dirty tables or sticky floors. And now the moment Beck approached the hostess, she was already nodding to him deferentially, walking them to an empty table, the low light and candles scattered across the tables reflecting off rows of sparkling glassware lined up on the bar and the antiqued mirrors on the walls.

"Don't tell me you didn't go to nice places in Miami," Beck retorted with a grin.

"I did. I mean, *we* did. But . . .it's just different with you."

It *felt* different. Not just because what they'd been used to was so drastically different, but because of the care Beck was taking.

Was this what dating Beck would be like?

"Good kinda different, I hope," Beck said, taking a seat. Micah dropped down into the soft plush club chair opposite.

"It's not even a question." If he had to choose, he'd choose Beck over anyone else.

That had never changed.

The waitress approached, and this time Micah spoke up first, ordering two glasses of *very* expensive bourbon.

Beck raised an eyebrow as she left. "We celebrating something?" he asked.

It felt like the last few months had all been a celebration. One milestone after another falling.

There was only one real one left.

Tonight, if Beck was on board, he was going to touch a man and let a man touch him in return, and he'd finally understand why anyone obsessed about sex.

'Course, it wasn't like Beck didn't already own him in every way that mattered.

"Yeah," he said. "Did Riley tell you?"

"Did Riley tell me what?"

The waitress arrived with their drinks, then disappeared, clearly sensing they wanted to be alone.

"I told him the truth. Him and Coach Kelley and Mr. G." Micah picked up the glass, lifted it, and shot Beck a wry smile. "I told them the truth. I'm gay."

Beck reached out and clasped his free hand. "I'm proud of you."

"You were the first one who knew," Micah said. "Feels right that you know I'm telling other people, now."

"Anyone else?"

Micah nodded. "My mom, of course."

"Right. That go okay?"

It had gone about as well as he'd expected, but he didn't want to go into details—not tonight. "Yeah."

"Telling people isn't always easy, but it's worth it, in the end," Beck promised.

"Agreed." Micah raised his glass. "To telling the truth." *To telling the whole truth, all the truth, tonight.*

Beck clinked his drink against Micah's. "To the truth."

They drank. The liquor went down, smooth and dark and setting fire to something that it felt like had been simmering between them for days.

How long was he going to stay on his side of the table?

He already wanted the whole goddamn thing to disappear. Maybe he should've suggested they go to the club instead. There, he wouldn't have needed much excuse to get close to Beck. Maybe he wouldn't be touching him the way he really wanted to, but it would be better than nothing.

"I can see it in you, you know. How much . . .more *you*, you are," Beck said.

"I feel it," Micah said honestly.

He'd never imagined that embracing this part of himself would feel so good—so good it was worth all the fear and un-certainty he'd experienced.

And now, *yeah*, he was a little bit nervous about taking this last, final step, but he also knew that he'd been waiting for it to be with Beck. Just a few weeks ago, he'd never imagined they'd be reunited, but now that they were, he *knew* why he'd never done this with another guy before.

Beck was who he wanted, more than anything else. More than *anyone* else.

He just hoped tonight they were finally on the same page.

Micah drained the rest of his drink. He felt loose and relaxed and *happy*.

Had he ever felt this way before?

There was no question being with Beck, even platonically, had always felt really fucking great. But then that night had opened his eyes to what they *could* be.

"I'm happy too, you know. I . . .never felt like I could be, like this, but I am."

"Oh, I think you could be a little happier," Beck teased. He drained the rest of his glass. "Come on, you wanna head over to the club?"

It seemed Beck, too, was tired of pretending he didn't want to touch.

Micah tossed some money on the table and then they were walking out, following the signs to the club at the Wynn, where Beck said he'd gotten them on the VIP list.

It was closer to midnight now, and the club was beginning to fill with a long line of beautiful people, all dressed to the nines, but the bouncer didn't even check their names, just waved them inside.

"I guess you're more famous than you realize," Micah teased as they walked in, heading towards the bar.

"Maybe that's you. Or maybe he just thought you were hot as hell . . .which . . .accurate," Beck said, leaning against the bar.

Micah took in the long lines of Beck's body, all that muscle outlined in the clingy fabric of his slacks and polo.

"Uh-huh," Micah retorted. "Just me, huh?"

"Just you." Beck grinned. "You want a drink?"

Yes—but also, *no*.

"Come on," Micah said, reaching for Beck's hand and grabbing it before he could overthink. "Let's dance."

But Beck came easily, letting Micah lead him to the edge of the floor, more than half full already of writhing bodies, the deep thump of the bass resonating through him.

He slid his hand from Beck's grasp but didn't go far—instead he placed it on Beck's hip, making it clear he didn't want Beck going anywhere.

Micah wanted him right here, where he could touch him any way he wanted to and watch his eyes darken with unmistakable desire.

"Yeah," Beck agreeing with a question Micah hadn't even asked, his voice rough and gravelly over the loud pulse of the music.

His fingertips curled into Beck's hip, and it was hard and warm and glorious as they began to move together to the beat.

One song bled into the next, Micah sweating under his shirt collar, not just because of the heat of the people around them, and the exertion, but also how intent Beck's gaze was on him.

It was possessive and confident and lit Micah up in places he hadn't even known existed.

No—that was a lie. He'd discovered them eighteen or so months ago. When they'd done this the last time. But tonight, he wasn't going to let anything interfere with what they both wanted.

Beck must've been on the same page, because after a few songs, he tugged Micah closer and then leaned in, his skin damp with sweat and smelling better than anything Micah could ever imagine.

"I wanna drink," Beck murmured into his ear.

It seemed like the drink Beck wanted was *him*. The idea made his throat so dry Micah couldn't even reply. He could only nod.

The bar was busier than it had been when they arrived, but Beck pushed them through the crowd effortlessly and motioned to the bartender.

A minute later, he was pouring them each a double shot of tequila.

"For old times' sake," Beck said with a glint to his eye that told Micah he wouldn't mind if he stripped his shirt off and repeated what they'd done the *last* time they'd shared tequila together.

But tonight, they just downed the shots, Beck smiling around the lime wedge. Micah wasn't drunk—not on booze, anyway—but he wasn't sober either. So it wasn't *exactly* the booze talking when he said, "I wanna take you somewhere."

Beck leaned in, his hazel eyes twinkling. "Yeah?" he asked. "Where?"

But Micah just shook his head. "Trust me," he said.

"Anywhere you want," Beck said, and Micah had no reason to doubt the promise in his words.

Chapter 8

When Micah and Beck got outside, the air was shockingly warm, even though it was the middle of the night, and the sweet fogginess in his head didn't clear one bit.

Though maybe even an ice-cold blast wouldn't have been enough. Not with Beck casually setting a palm against the small of his back as they walked out onto the sidewalk.

Micah raised his hand, flagging down a taxi, and he pulled the door open, gesturing for Beck to get inside.

They collapsed into the back seat, Beck nearly tripping over his own feet, and Micah falling into the seat next to him.

Practically on top of him.

"Hey," Beck said, staring up at him as Micah froze, wondering if he should move away. He was practically on Beck's lap; just the way they'd been that night.

Beck's hand reached up, cupped his cheek, the touch way too fleeting, before it fell away again.

Micah's stomach clenched with anticipation. What would it feel like when *it* finally happened? Would he feel like drowning and flying, all at the same time?

"Where you goin'?" the driver asked, clearly bored and not like two guys all over each other was anything he hadn't seen a thousand times before.

"Paris," Micah said. He shifted a little, but he could still feel the heat of Beck's thigh under him.

"Ah, you wanna go to France?" Beck teased. "You gonna romance me in the City of Light?"

Micah squirmed. Was he that obvious? Yes, he probably was, and he told himself that didn't matter. They were *doing* this. Maybe they hadn't talked about it, but it was becoming increasingly obvious they'd ended up on this path, together, and neither of them was going to turn back now.

"You're not the only one who can do it," he retorted lightly, glancing over at Beck, who was grinning at him like the cat who'd just lapped up every single bit of cream.

"Well, *I* like it," Beck said, patting him on the shoulder.

It only took a few minutes to make it to Paris and the big lit-up Eiffel Tower standing guard over the casino.

"I've always wanted to go up this," Micah said, as they craned their necks up towards the top. "Imagine the real one is twice as big."

"Is it really?" Beck's voice was a murmur, right against his neck, sending prickles down his skin.

"Yeah. Someday I'll see that one too."

"You could've done that already. You *do* get time off, you know," Beck pointed out as they walked over towards the ticket counter.

"Yeah, but—" Micah hesitated. *I wanted to see it with someone I loved. Who loved me back. I wanted it to be the thrill of a lifetime.* "I'll do it at some point. Maybe when this season's over."

Maybe this wasn't the thrill of a lifetime—*yet*—but as they paid for their tickets and headed towards the elevator, it seemed possible that they might be headed that way now.

The elevator was empty and Micah fell against the back wall, Beck joining him, their thighs brushing together, his pulse racing as they watched the building slowly falling away, revealing a technicolor landscape lighting up the Las Vegas sky.

"Wow," Micah said as the glass door opened to let them onto the observation deck.

The man selling the tickets had said they were one of the last groups up, so unsurprisingly, there was only a handful of other tourists around.

And nobody, Micah realized, was looking at them.

He felt drunk on the good booze they'd drunk.

But mostly he felt drunk—entirely, deliriously, utterly drunk—on the way it felt as Beck stood next to him, pressed close as they took in the skyline, the heat from his body leaking into Micah's own.

"So?" Beck asked after he'd taken a good look. "What do you think? Plenty romantic, huh?"

He was leaning against the wire cage that prevented people from doing stupid shit like throwing anything or leaping off the platform themselves, and his hazel eyes glittered with purpose.

Micah swallowed hard. He wanted to do some *real* stupid shit.

"Yeah. Real romantic." *Find your words, Rose. And then fucking use them.* His hand found Beck's and squeezed it. All he'd have to do was lean in another few inches, and they'd be kissing. He wanted it so much, wanted *Beck* so much, he was lightheaded with it.

"I told myself—actually, I *promised* myself—that if we ever ended up here again, I wouldn't hesitate."

Micah heard the elevator doors ding closed behind them, but it wouldn't have mattered if a thousand people were here on this platform with them, nobody mattered except Beck, and the intent look in his hazel eyes.

"Yeah? Me too." Micah heard how rough his voice sounded. How desperate. "How long?"

He drifted another inch closer. Raised his other hand to the back of Beck's neck. The skin there was warm and soft, so much softer than he'd ever thought to imagine it being, and the question of where else he might be soft drifted across Micah's mind.

"How long?" Beck questioned, tilting his head. "Um, yesterday. In the airplane. After we sat down. I wanted to pummel Deacon into his seat for interrupting us."

"Not gonna be interrupted now."

Beck smiled a little. "Nope."

It seemed, then, that Beck wanted him to do it. To make the move. Was it proof? Or was it more than that? Maybe it was actually an *invitation. Here*, Beck was saying, *I want you to get a chance to take exactly what you want.*

And *oh*, he wanted it.

"Not as long as me, then." Micah could be honest about this, *finally*. "I've only wanted to do this for real, *again*, since it happened the first time."

Micah leaned in, and *finally* took what he craved.

For a second, Beck's mouth was soft, almost hesitant on his. His beard, already growing in after shaving, was slightly prickly. It wasn't anything like kissing a woman.

He'd wondered for so long, *way too long*, what kissing a guy would be like.

Would it be weird or different or would it be the best thing he'd ever felt?

Well, Micah couldn't say what it was like kissing any guy.

But he *could* say what kissing Beckett West was like.

Micah heard a questioning noise in the back of his own throat. Had he made that sound? He must have. But then he was shifting, tugging Beck closer, and they were falling into each other, into each other's mouths like they'd never belonged anywhere else.

The pressure of Beck's lips on his was beautiful and sweet and warm and also unbelievably sexy.

When Micah broke off the kiss, he realized he was actually panting.

Panting.

Then there was the state of his dick. It was rock-hard in his pants, pressing against the zipper, and just because he'd shared a relatively tame kiss with Beck.

Beck's lips tilted into a smile.

I kissed that mouth. The thought was like a lightning bolt.

Suddenly he couldn't wait another moment to do it again.

He pulled Beck back and this time they fell on each other like they were starving. Like they'd waited so long, their hunger was undeniable.

Beck's lips were firm and confident against his own, his tongue slipping into Micah's mouth, his hands digging into Micah's waist, dragging him even closer.

Before he could even stop himself, Micah pressed his cock against Beck's hard thigh, and it was the best pressure he'd ever felt.

This time Beck was the one who pulled back.

"Can't say that wasn't a really long time coming," Beck said into the silence.

Micah's hand was still curled around Beck's neck. He tangled his fingers higher, into the soft hair at the back of his skull. "First time we met," he confessed.

"What?" Beck looked surprised. But he didn't pull away. Didn't seem to mind, in fact, when Micah's fingers dug into his hair more insistently. In fact, he actually leaned into it.

"You remember, right?"

"How could I forget?" Beck's smile was wry, and it was all Micah could do not to kiss him again. And again. And again. This might be a serious problem. Or the best problem in the whole goddamn world.

"It was summer. June, I think? We showed up to the campus for the first time. It was warm."

"Hot as hell and muggy as all get-out," Beck inserted with a lopsided grin.

"And you smiled at me and said, 'God, I could go for a cherry Icee,' and that was it."

"Cherry Icee was the way to your heart?" Beck teased. "If it was that easy, I'd have won you over with bouquets of them."

Micah shook his head. "It was just . . .*you.* How you talked to me. How you looked at me. How you smiled. I just . . .I couldn't even look away. I don't think you probably remember. Then you showed up the next day before practice and you'd gotten us cherry Icees and I threw mine up all over the side of the field midway through conditioning, and I didn't even care. I was yours, ride or die, for life."

"You looked so uncertain. And I wanted you to look. . .I don't know. *Certain.*" Beck's voice was reverent, almost nostalgic. Like he was remembering, too. "Of you. Of me. Of what we were doing out there on the field, because I knew you could bring it. I saw it. I just wanted you to relax and see it, too."

"Playing with you, second favorite thing in the world," Micah said and meant it.

Beck raised an eyebrow. "Second favorite?"

"Five minutes ago, it would've been the first, but not anymore." He leaned in and it was so easy to fall into yet another kiss. And to kiss and kiss like the world would wait for them forever. After all, hadn't it already? They'd taken their time to get here, but now they'd finally come together, and Micah didn't think he could possibly be happier about it.

He was so goddamn happy, he might explode with it.

Someone cleared their throat behind them.

"Platform's closing," the security guard said when Micah looked behind him in surprise.

"Come on," Beck said, and Micah was helpless to do anything but follow.

It felt natural and right to take his hand, the way Micah had wanted to so many times before but hadn't because he'd been too goddamn afraid.

But he wasn't afraid anymore.

Beck squeezed it, and they walked onto the elevator.

"Well," Beck said, grinning at him. "What should we do? It's not that late."

"What about . . ." Micah hesitated. Yeah, they'd kissed. Yeah, they might've spent the next hour making out at the Eiffel Tower if the security guard hadn't interrupted them, but that didn't necessarily mean they were going to have sex.

Even though Micah—and surely Beck, too, after those kisses—were *dying* to have sex.

"Listen," Beck said, pressing a kiss to his forehead. "We've got all night; there's no need to rush anything. I love hanging out with you. I love doing anything with you, even that."

"Especially that?" Micah grinned.

"Well, *yeah*," Beck said, rolling his eyes playfully. "But like I said, it's not that late and we've got all the time in the world. I'm not going anywhere."

"Me either."

The elevator dinged open.

"Yeah?" Beck grinned. "I didn't think so, not anymore."

Micah shook his head. "No way."

"Good." They took the escalator down to the main floor of the bustling Paris casino. "Hey, you wanna play something?" Beck asked, still not letting go of his hand, like it was not only totally normal for them to hold hands, but acceptable.

It is, Micah realized. *I can do this now. We can do this. We can do anything.*

"Blackjack?" he asked. Back in college, they'd taken a statistics class together that had done a deep dive on blackjack odds and how to beat the house, and they'd spent more than a few late Saturday nights at several of the beat-up riverboat casinos around Chicago.

"Yeah. Let's win some money," Beck said with a suddenly fierce grin. "You think we still got it?"

"Not even a question."

After heading to the cashier to get some chips, they beelined to one of the empty blackjack tables.

"Not the high roller section," Beck said under his breath as they were eyeing the dealers one by one.

Micah rolled his eyes. "We can afford it," he said, glancing over at the much nicer section, filled with all the higher stakes tables.

"Yeah, but I'm not sure we *do* have it," Beck teased. "Let's test it out first."

Maybe on a day when he hadn't finally taken a metaphorical leap off the Eiffel Tower and his blood wasn't still buzzing with the way Beck's lips had felt on his and the way their bodies pressed close together, they *might* have had it.

But it turned out they were having too much fun to take it seriously enough to win consistently.

Instead, they passed another hour betting haphazardly and drinking several Manhattans each, Beck using his tongue to tie the stem of one of the maraschino cherries into a knot, sending Micah's insides into an equally twisted knot.

He shoved the rest of his chips onto the felt, feeling reckless—not even giving a shit.

Beck's smirk was knowing. "In a hurry?" he teased.

"Guess you're gonna have to find out for yourself."

There was no denying he'd had a great time tonight. From beginning to end, this had been an absolutely perfect night. But now Micah was ready to end it the way that *other* perfect night should've ended.

"Aw," Beck said as he lost to the dealer again.

"I think," Micah said, tossing back the rest of his drink, Beck handing the dealer the rest of his chips as a tip, "we should go back to the Wynn and you should lick my wounds."

Beck raised an eyebrow. "I like the sound of that."

"Thought you might."

Micah knew there was no denying it as they walked out onto the wide sidewalks that lined the Strip—he was drunk.

On booze.

But also on Beck.

They'd headed to the curb right when they fell into the bridal party—or did the bridal party run into them? Micah was never quite sure. They'd both had more than a few drinks, and it was undeniable these two had as well.

The two guys were young and attractive—one with light brown skin and closely shaved head, the same as Micah's, and the other with blond hair styled away from his glitter-dusted face—and they were wearing shirts that proclaimed them "Husbands to Be."

But it wasn't just the booze lighting them up. Micah could tell. Joy was practically oozing from their pores. A smug kind of joy, like they *knew* they'd found the person they wanted to spend the rest of their life with.

Before tonight, Micah wouldn't have even allowed himself to think anything close to that, but now he couldn't help but embrace it.

I know what that feels like.

"Hey, sorry," Beck said, shooting them an apologetic look.

"No big deal," the blond guy said after Micah apologized for bumping into them. Then he did a double take. "Hey, you're Beckett West, aren't you?" He glanced over at Micah. "And *ohmigod*, you're Micah Rose." He whacked the arm of his "husband to be" insistently. "Blake, it's *the Wall*."

"Yeah, that's us." Beck was clearly relaxed and feeling himself—Micah could always tell, because they'd had enough of these encounters to know when Beck was just being nice and when he was genuinely okay being recognized.

"I went to Northwestern," the blond said, eyes glazing over with the expression Micah had always privately referred to as nirvana. He'd seen it way too many times, when they'd been in college. "I was always hoping I might run into you, convince you to go on a date."

Beck had the nerve to look surprised by this. He'd never realized how attractive he was, which Micah thought was seriously ridiculous.

"Ah, well . . ." He trailed off, shooting Micah a lopsided grin.

He and Beck definitely hadn't been together in college—no matter how much he'd wanted it to be true—and there'd been probably dozens of times when a guy had hit on Beck, and he'd just had to stand by and *watch*.

Eating his heart out with jealousy and bitterness, believing that could never be him.

But tonight, he could break the pattern.

Destroy it with only a few words.

"That would've been awkward," Micah said with a confidence he didn't exactly feel but was trying to embrace anyway. He tucked himself into Beck's side, wrapping a possessive arm around his waist. Leaned in and pressed a kiss against Beck's stubble-covered cheek.

The man actually squealed with delight. "No, no, no, *no*, this is even better. Blake, can you believe this? They were actually together *together*, just like I told you that one night I thought they were." His voice dropped. "Honestly, you two were just *so* close, you know? Too close to just be bros."

"Right," Micah said.

Beck was holding back laughter; Micah could *feel* it, even if he couldn't hear it.

"That old bro excuse," Beck said in a strangled voice, shaking his head.

"God, this is just the best night ever," the blond said. "I'm Rick and this is Blake and well, it was *great* before this, but now it's even better."

Blake gestured to his shirt, a fond smile on his face as he gazed over at Rick. "We're getting married tonight."

"Congratulations," Micah said.

"Guess it's good I never asked for that date, for *multiple* reasons," Rick said with a grin. "Hey, would you two take a selfie with us? Commemorate the moment?"

"'Course," Beck said, nodding. He glanced over at Micah. And the fondness in his expression impossibly matched even the way Blake was looking at Rick.

Had Beck always looked at him that way and he'd somehow missed it because he was too caught up in that horrible cycle of guilt and denial?

Beck nudged him a moment later. Oh, *right*. He was the designated selfie taker because of the two of them, his arms were longer.

"Aw, you two really *are* adorable," Rick cooed as they gathered into a group, Rick handing Micah his phone, and then he clicked away half a dozen shots.

"Hey, send one of those to me," Beck said after Micah handed Rick his phone back.

Rick looked up, his smile glowing as he scrolled through the shots. "Oh, of course, God, *of course*. I'm just . . .so fucking flattered, honestly."

Beck put a hand on his shoulder. "Don't be. We're just two guys out, celebrating, just like you two."

Both Blake's and Rick's eyes widened. "Oh, not like that," Beck said quickly. "But uh . . .yeah."

"Why shouldn't you?" Blake said slyly.

Micah thought but didn't say, *because that would be crazy.*

But Beck didn't answer Blake's question at all, just gave his phone number to Rick so he could text the pictures to him.

A few minutes later, Beck was even promising them tickets to a Condors game if they ever made it to Charleston.

"Maybe for our honeymoon, huh, Blake? Wouldn't that be amazing?"

Blake nodded. "We just decided to . . .do it. We haven't been together all that long, but it felt right, you know? And we didn't want to waste any more time."

Micah nodded, feeling the weight of all the years of their *own* wasted time.

"This is going to sound crazy . . ." Rick grinned. "But would you two come along with us? Stand up with us at the wedding?"

Beck glanced over at Micah.

It hadn't been in their plans to be best men at a gay wedding that no doubt featured a rainbow-jumpsuit-clad Elvis impersonator, but well, they hadn't planned any of this, had they?

And what was another hour before they could finally, *finally* be alone?

Micah nodded and then Beck did too. He'd noticed Beck was taking all his cues from him.

Making sure he was comfortable, and that dissolved his already wobbly heart into a gooey, charmed, *fond* mess.

"When's the wedding?" Micah asked, clearing his suddenly dry throat. Maybe they *had* had too much to drink when, after peeling away all the layers of thoughts back, he realized what he truly felt for them was *envy*.

Which was ridiculous, wasn't it? They'd just been about to catch a cab and head back to the Wynn. To Micah's suite.

Where hopefully they spent the next couple of days in bed together.

There was absolutely no reason to be jealous of these two.

"Oh, in about an hour? Or sooner?" Blake said. "Whenever we get our asses down to the chapel. What do you guys say? You in? It won't take too long if we head there now."

"It's a fine ass, too, if I may say so," Rick teased, reaching out to cup Blake's ass, giggling.

Totally drunk.

But also totally drunk on each other.

"Yeah, let's do it," Micah said and only realized, after they'd flagged down a cab, what that sounded like.

The whole way to the chapel, he was pressed right up against Beck, and next to him, Blake and Rick were making out.

Micah squirmed in the miniscule amount of seat underneath him.

"You alright?" Beck asked, leaning in, his voice rumbling deep and affectionate in Micah's ear.

He nodded.

The truth was, with the place they were headed, he couldn't help but think about it. He didn't think *Beck* was, but then that was the story of their friendship, wasn't it? Micah thinking all of the things Beck hadn't even considered before.

Blake had been right; the trip to the chapel, right off the Strip, was fast.

Before Micah had managed to regain his equilibrium, they were standing in front of the rainbow-festooned doorway.

"Isn't it amazing?" Rick enthused as they walked through.

They'd made reservations, so it was painfully simple to pay the fee and head right down the aisle. Who knew marriage was so easy?

No, he reminded himself, *marriage isn't easy. But getting married sure is.*

Standing across from Beck, his gaze glued to Micah's face, as Elvis had Blake and Rick repeat their vows, Micah discovered his heart was racing.

I'll do you one better, Beck had said. *We end up playing for the same team, I'll fucking marry you.*

It was Beck's words echoing in his head.

It was Blake talking about not wasting any more time.

It was the booze.

It was the way Rick and Blake kissed like they just *knew*—and how from Micah's vantage point as they both applauded, along with Elvis, at the conclusion on the ceremony, it wasn't all that different from how he'd kissed Beck on the Eiffel Tower.

How Beck had kissed him right back.

"Congrats," Beck said, returning Rick's phone after he'd finished shooting a few more pictures of the happy couple. "You two are adorable."

"Like knows like," Rick teased as they walked towards the chapel door. They were already chattering about heading back to their hotel, where they'd booked the honeymoon suite. "Complete with heart-shaped rotating bed!" Blake confided proudly.

"Well, thanks again for coming with us. Being our witnesses," Rick said, as the cab pulled up to the curb next to the chapel. "It means so fucking much."

"Have a great night, and uh . . .a great life," Micah stuttered.

"You should do it too," Rick called out as he slid into the cab. "Trust me, you won't regret it."

Micah stared at the cab as it drove away.

Beck was staring too, Micah realized a second later, and not at them, but at *him*.

"What?" Micah said, suddenly feeling self-conscious. Had his envy been written all over his face? Oh God, if it *had* been . . .that was only slightly humiliating.

But then, it hadn't been him who'd brought up marriage in the first place.

That had been Beck. Eighteen months ago.

"We should do that."

"Do what?" Micah was so sure he wouldn't even consider it that he missed Beck *actually fucking suggesting it*.

But Beck's expression was intent and affectionate and one hundred percent certain.

"Do *that*," he said, gesturing towards the chapel. "Get married. After all, I said we would. And *you* said you still would."

Micah's jaw dropped even as his heart accelerated wildly with the knowledge he'd never wanted anything more.

Beck and him, together for life.

The thought felt right and true and perfect, clanging inside of him like a bell. He'd thought it was just him. Just him who'd been desperate to switch Blake and Rick's positions with their own.

You're crazy, he meant to say.

But that wasn't what he said at all.

Instead, he looked Beck straight in the eye, opened his mouth, and said, "Yeah. We should."

CHAPTER 9

Beck woke up with one agonizing blink and then another, the pounding on the door painfully matching the pounding in his head.

He groaned and rolled over.

Sunlight was streaming in the windows, and Beck gasped and regretted every decision he'd made his whole life, mid-blink.

"What are you doing?" The voice next to him was gruff and confused. Slurred from sleep.

He'd know that voice anywhere.

It belonged to Micah Rose.

Okay, they'd ended up in bed together.

He could remember that part. Sharing dinner with him. Dancing with him. Drinking with him. *Kissing* him.

More than once.

Memories were filtering back through his mind, and they flashed by in a nauseating blur.

Dinner. Dancing. Drinks. So many drinks.

Then the kiss.

The Kiss.

It had been one of the top five moments of his life, hands down, finally knowing what Micah tasted like.

He remembered heading down from the Eiffel Tower. Playing blackjack. *Losing* at blackjack, and not even giving a shit.

Feeling on top of the world. Running into those guys, the *husbands*.

Everything went still in a sickening lurch.

He'd proposed, *again*, and this time Micah had not only accepted, but *oh God*, they'd . . .

Beck let out a soft sigh and opened one eye, risking the pain shooting through his head. He had to know.

Sure enough, there the ring was, on the fourth finger of his left hand, glowing gold in the bright morning light like it freaking belonged there.

"Micah," Beck said, reaching a hand back and trying to shake him. "*Micah*."

"What?" Micah still sounded half-asleep.

"You need to wake up *now*."

The person at the door was still insistently knocking, and if the increased impact and decreased time in between sounds was any indication, they were getting annoyed.

"I really don't wanna," Micah slurred.

"Yeah, me either," Beck said honestly. But they were gonna have to face this thing.

What did it say about him that his first thought, the one that overrode all the thoughts, on discovering they'd gone and gotten married last night, was that he was absolutely fucking thrilled? And that his second wasn't even close to the terror-tinged regret that most anyone else would feel in this situation?

There was terror, sure, but terror that they'd messed this up before they'd even begun it.

He knew the moment Micah opened his eyes because he yelped, and he had a feeling it wasn't because the sun was way too fucking bright, and they'd been obviously far too preoccupied with the bed when they'd finally returned to Micah's suite to bother with closing the blinds.

Nope, it was almost certainly because Micah, too, had spotted the ring on his fourth finger.

"We . . .we . . ."

Beck rolled over. Grinned, even though it hurt. "Yeah."

Micah's eyes were wide and shocked.

He glanced down at his clothes. And yeah, they were both still mostly clothed. Beck had lost his shirt, but he was still in his pants and even his socks, and Micah was similarly attired.

"Did we—" Micah asked hesitantly.

Beck wasn't sure which he was asking. Had they gotten married? Had they had sex?

He was pretty sure that if he ever got Micah into bed—and now that was looking like a pretty damn sure thing, unless this whole marriage thing freaked him or both of them out—they'd both be completely naked, without a stitch of clothing.

"Wedding, yes," Beck said. They could deal with the rest later.

"Ah." Micah scrubbed a hand over his face. "And that person at the door . . ."

"Probably someone coming to kill us for getting drunk and married in Vegas."

"We were . . ." Micah hesitated. "We weren't all that drunk. I feel like that happened . . .after."

Beck's mind was still piecing the evening's events together, but that seemed fairly accurate. They had definitely been drinking when he'd proposed *again*, and when they'd . . .*oh my God* . . .walked down the aisle. But it wasn't until after that the *really* intense drinking had begun. He remembered tossing back shot after shot. He remembered kissing Micah, over and *over*. He remembered being as happy as he'd ever been in his whole goddamn life.

Happy and wildly, completely, utterly in love.

Well, *shit*.

This was not the time nor the place to be having that realization. Though, Beck could concede, last night had definitely not been the time or the place to have it either, because having it had clearly led to him pushing them both down the aisle.

"Yeah," Beck agreed. "I think it *was* after."

"You don't sound unhappy about this."

No, he did not.

There was only one thing he *could* say. "I do know my mom's gonna kill me."

Micah stared at him, mystified.

"We—*I*—got married and she wasn't here. None of my family was." *And I can't imagine ever getting married again. Not now. Not when it's you.*

"Right." Micah still looked confused, but that was okay, because Beck definitely was not up for having that particular conversation now.

"I guess we should . . .get the door," Beck said reluctantly. No doubt whoever was on the other side of it knew what they'd done, and chances were good they weren't exactly happy about it.

"Yeah." Micah didn't sound any more excited than Beck felt.

The pounding continued as he swallowed a gulp of water from the bottle on the table next to the bed and grabbed for his shirt, lying next to it. After shrugging it on, definitely smelling booze on it as it passed over his head, there was nothing else to be done but face the music.

But first.

"Before I deal with that," Beck said, waving a hand towards the door, "I want to just say, for the record. . .I'm not mad about this."

It was not even remotely close to how he *really* felt about what had happened last night, but he didn't think Micah, who still looked decidedly uneasy, was ready to hear just how ready for marital bliss Beck felt.

"You're not?" Micah's jaw dropped. "But we—"

"I know," Beck said. Reached for his hand and squeezed it briefly, before letting go again. "But I meant what I said. You're not getting rid of me again. Not for this. Not ever."

For a long, horrible moment, Micah didn't blink and didn't say a word.

Was he going to bolt now? He kinda looked like he wanted to, which Beck couldn't even be mad about, because they'd gotten fucking *married* last night.

They hadn't even dated yet, and now they were together, *forever*.

But then Micah smiled, and it was like the first time they'd met all over again. Like falling in love all over again.

"Yeah. *Yeah.*" Micah nodded emphatically. "It's . . .well, it's crazy, but I wasn't . . .we weren't . . ."

"We weren't that drunk," Beck agreed, understanding what Micah was trying and failing to say.

"No, we weren't," Micah said wryly. "Might be easier if we were."

This was true. Everyone understood if you got drunk and married in Vegas. Sympathy was probably less standard if you got tipsy and got married just because you wanted each other too goddamn bad.

"Probably, but . . .we'll figure it out, okay?"

"You don't mean—" Micah frowned.

But Beck wasn't even going to let him say the word. "No," he said emphatically. "No, we're not getting divorced or annulled or any of that shit, okay?"

Micah's face relaxed. "Okay." He paused. "You better answer the door before they have an aneurysm."

"Probably," Beck said, chuckling.

He headed out of the bedroom and after bracing himself, opened the door.

Nicole, the public relations liaison for the Charleston Condors, was standing on the other side, looking pretty fucking pissed off.

"Did you fall in a hole?" she demanded, pushing her way into the room. "I've been knocking forever."

"Uh, we were asleep." Beck ran a hand through his very uncooperative hair. He had a feeling that what had led to this particular style was not sleeping on it, but Micah's hands in it.

"Micah is here too then."

"I'm here."

Beck looked up as Micah walked into the room.

He looked about as ready to puke as Beck did.

"Oh good," Nicole said, "two birds, one lecture. What the ever-living fuck were you thinking last night? And don't say you weren't thinking, because from what I can piece together, you were still pretty sober when you left Paris after playing blackjack."

Beck didn't know what time it was, but he supposed he shouldn't be surprised Nicole would be on top of this or already have all the pertinent information. She'd been one of Mr. G's first hires after he'd bought the Condors, and she'd shepherded them through a hell of a lot of bad press.

"This is . . .true," Beck said hesitantly.

"So then you just walked outside, after losing a few hundred bucks and thought, oh hell, why don't we just get married?" Nicole's voice reached near-hysteria levels. "And not just that, because people get married in Vegas *every freaking day*, but you decided to wander around *telling* everyone? And not just telling everyone, but taking pictures and selfies, and signing autographs? Buying way too many people shots to celebrate?"

"I guess so," Micah said.

Nicole threw up her hands. "This is a disaster."

"I don't know," Beck said mildly. "I don't think it's so bad."

But Nicole ignored him and instead turned her gaze, which currently resembled a nail gun, to pin Micah in place. "You realize you're out of the closet now, right? You married a guy. You married *him*." She pointed at Beck. "And while he was out, you weren't."

"I realize," Micah said softly.

Regret speared through Beck. He hadn't put two and two together, but now he couldn't help but do the math.

Before today, if he'd married a man, nobody would've really blinked twice.

But Micah?

Nicole was right. He hadn't been out of the closet yet.

And now he was.

"Now *everyone* knows. You made damn sure of that."

Beck didn't know if Micah had thought that through. *He* certainly hadn't thought it through. But then, they'd both been so freaking happy. Riding on a wave built from pure fucking joy. He hadn't had time to even consider it.

But Micah didn't look particularly perturbed by the way Nicole was laying out the consequences, so maybe he *had*.

Beck didn't know who was more surprised—him or Nicole—as Micah moved closer to him and then took his hand.

"Yeah," Micah said. "Yeah, they do."

Nicole stared at their intertwined hands. "You . . .you *meant* this. I didn't even know you were dating!"

"We weren't," Beck said firmly. But Micah's hand in his gave him strength. Resolve. *Purpose*. "But we're married now."

"That's not news," Nicole retorted lightly. She paused. "So . . .no divorce? No annulment?"

"We're staying married," Beck said firmly, and Micah nodded along with his pronouncement.

It seemed that particular confession took the wind right out of Nicole's sails. She didn't know how to take the news. No doubt she'd come up here with a whole crisis plan already in her head, and they'd already destroyed it, because the first thing they were going to do *wasn't* to figure out how to undo this.

"We've known each other a long time," Micah said softly, "and I guess you could say this has been a long time coming."

Nicole took a deep breath. "*Well*," she said, "I guess it has."

"If we're staying married, do we have to do anything about it?" Beck asked.

Obviously there would be no more need for a crisis plan. At least not the flavor she'd been concocting since the news had hit her phone.

"No, I . . .uh . . ." Nicole didn't typically hesitate, not in Beck's experience, but she was floundering now. "We'll just put out a statement. Succinct. Please respect your private lives, etc, and you're looking forward to continuing to play together at a high level." She turned to Micah. "Did you want to add anything specifically?"

"Not at this time." Micah said it quietly, but resolutely.

"That's one hundred percent your right," Nicole said. "Good news is you have a bye week to figure out how to be married. Though now that I think about it, I can see it. You kinda were, back at Northwestern." She laughed. "But not as much as you're gonna be now."

Beck squirmed. He'd barely had time to come to grips with what they'd done, and now he was already thinking of *everything else*. All the other adjustments and changes. He loved Micah but he couldn't deny he hated change.

"I'll go ahead," she continued, "and let Mr. G know the details. But I can't say he'll be pissed. Who knows, he'll probably enjoy it. He likes a feel-good story, and you know what, so do I. And this is such a great one."

"Great," Beck said weakly.

He didn't know how to be a feel-good story. He didn't know how to be married, either. He barely knew how to date.

And now he and Micah were committed. For life.

"Well, you two enjoy Vegas. Don't get married again, okay?" Nicole chuckled. "Or if you decide to, call me first, okay?"

"Sure thing," Beck said.

A minute later, she was gone. The moment the door was closed, Micah let go of his hand and five seconds later, Beck could hear him retching in the adjoining restroom.

"Well," Beck said.

It seemed like there was no time like the present to learn how to be a husband.

Micah was wiping his mouth, still half leaning over the toilet as Beck rested his hip against the doorjamb.

"You okay?"

Micah took a deep breath and then another. "We drank a *lot* of tequila last night."

"That was probably my fault," Beck said. "Sorry."

"Yeah, it was." Micah flashed him an uneasy smile. "You and your nostalgia are gonna end up getting both of us into deep shit."

"Seems likely," Beck said. He stepped forward and helped Micah up, even though he was no doubt very capable of rising on his own.

Micah turned the sink on and began to brush his teeth, which, frankly, seemed like a *great* idea, once he saw Micah doing it.

It wasn't the *most* domestic thing they'd ever done—brushing their teeth side by side at a sink—which really, probably said it all.

"I'm taking a shower," Micah said, as they finished up. He shot Beck a hesitant look.

"I need food. And coffee. A *lot* of coffee." Beck leaned against the doorjamb again. He still didn't feel *good*, but he didn't feel as bad as he had, either.

Micah flipped on the water. Eyed him again.

Beck realized then that maybe Micah wanted privacy before stripping down and getting in the shower.

Sure, they'd showered in front of each other dozens of times before, but that had been different.

All those times had been before they'd ever touched each other.

But now they'd kissed and at least *talked* about having sex, though Beck was still pretty sure they hadn't actually done anything past passing out in the same bed, and getting naked in front of each other definitely wasn't the same.

"Alright," Beck said. "I, uh . . .well, I'll leave you to it."

He turned and just caught, out of the corner of his eye, as he walked away, a glimpse of light brown skin, glowing under the fluorescent bathroom lights.

He was unquestionably hungover, but even the thought of Micah getting naked under the water had him half-hard in his pants.

God.

If things had been even slightly more certain between them, he'd have asked if he could stay. He'd have pinned Micah to the wall, kissed him, and asked if he could *join* him in the shower.

But there was no way they were ready for that.

Okay, that was a lie.

He was ready. He'd married the guy after only a handful of kisses, hadn't he? But he was Micah's first guy, and there was no reason to rush things.

Now that they were married.

He took the time to find his phone. It was nearly dead, but after he plugged in, he scrolled through the photos.

Yep, there was the wedding. There they were, kissing, in a crooked selfie.

They looked way too happy—and like Beck had already guessed, not very drunk.

After flipping through the last twenty-four hours of photos, Beck moved onto the text messages. Sure enough there were a *lot* of them from Nicole. Almost a dozen, in fact, each growing more frustrated and annoyed as Beck didn't reply.

There were others.

Two from Coach Kelley. The first was a vague congratulations, and the second was a directive to contact Nicole ASAP.

Then there were a handful from teammates.

Deacon's text read: **You did WHAT? You need to fucking call me right now.**

Carter had texted too. **I can't believe you married Micah and didn't invite any of us :(**

And then a second text. **If you think you're getting out of a totally kick-ass bachelor party, think again.**

Beck groaned out loud.

His agent had texted too. **Anything you want to tell me?** Kevin asked. It was a pretty mild question, all things considered.

Thankfully there was nothing yet from his mom or his family, but Beck knew it would only be a matter of time. He would have to call them today. Definitely sooner rather than later, but first, he needed that shower and then food. And *caffeine*.

"You alright?"

Beck looked up, and Micah was standing there, a towel wrapped around his waist. His color was better, and he was smiling.

"Oh, yeah, just . . . dealing with everything we didn't last night."

"You groaned," Micah said.

"Oh, just 'cause Carter was texting about a bachelor party."

Micah sat down on the bed next to him. Closer than he'd gotten since they'd woken up, but not as close as Beck wanted to be.

"Shower's all yours," he said.

"You look better."

Micah smiled ruefully. "Nowhere to go but up."

"You wanna get breakfast after I'm done?" Beck asked, standing up and stretching.

"Yeah, we can do that." He hesitated. "You want to plan to take off or should we stay . . ."

"In Vegas?" Beck hadn't gotten that far, but he supposed they were married now. This was the kind of thing they should be discussing.

Micah nodded.

"When were you planning to leave? I didn't have a ticket back to Charleston yet."

"Tomorrow morning."

"Then let's stay til then. I'll get a ticket on your flight home."

"Or, I could just take care of it," Micah said. He drummed his fingers against his towel-covered thigh. "Get us set up in first class and everything."

Beck was not used to other people wanting to take care of things. He was definitely not used to *trusting* someone else to take care of anything, but that was the bare minimum in a marriage, wasn't it?

"That'd be great," he said.

Micah was nervous.

Not normal kind of nervous.

Not nervous, buzzy kind of anticipation nervous.

But really fucking, sick-to-stomach nervous. He hadn't been lying when he'd told Beck this morning that his vomiting had been tequila-related. It was everything else too.

What could he say? He'd never even dated a guy before, and now he was *married* to one.

And not just any guy, but *Beckett*.

The man he'd always wanted.

Beck sat across from him, practically inhaling cup after cup of coffee. The waitress had taken a single look at them and said, "I'll leave the pot."

They'd ordered too, a ton of food between them, and even though he *was* hungry, Micah wasn't sure he could actually stomach a bite of it.

But that was a problem for ten minutes from now.

"So," Beck said, leaning back in the booth. "What should we do for the rest of the day?"

He'd hopped in the shower after Micah had finished, and the T-shirt he'd thrown on after was tight across his chest and around his biceps.

It was one thing to recognize these things before, when Beck had been a faraway unattainable fantasy.

But now they were fucking *married*.

There was nothing stopping them from eating breakfast and then going back to the hotel room and not leaving again until they had to for their flight the next morning.

That, more than anything else, was making Micah jittery with nerves. Sure, it was strange to be sitting here and know *anyone* looking at them knew the truth now. Not only that they were married, but that Micah liked guys.

Specifically, *his* guy.

But it was the sex that was making him the jumpiest.

"I don't even know what time it is," Micah confessed. After texting his agent to book Beck's flight, he'd left his phone in the room, charging, and even then he hadn't taken more than a glance at all the many, *many* notifications he had.

"After one," Beck said.

"The concierge at the Wynn emailed me a list of VIP options," Micah said. Of course he didn't remember most of them off the top of his head. "The pool club, of course, and a few other spots. The spa, I think? Some restaurants?"

Beck wrinkled his nose.

Yeah, Micah wasn't into the idea of going to the pool club either, though he might've been at any other point. Floating around in the water *would* feel good, but he wasn't sure he'd be into all the loud music and the booze and all those inquisitive eyes. Not today, anyway.

"But there was another place, I think. A private pool attached to the spa."

"I could go for a massage," Beck said, finishing another cup of coffee.

Micah eyed him. "You hurt after yesterday's game?"

"No, just a little sore, but—" Beck shot him a disarming smile. "I have a feeling that has more to do with all the dancing and running around we did last night than the game we played in."

What they had and *hadn't* done once they'd stumbled back to the suite lay between them like a live wire, and Micah was too afraid to touch it. Maybe he wouldn't always, but right now, he skirted right around it.

"Yeah," he agreed. "But we can book some massages. Hang out in the private pool after."

"That sounds great, actually," Beck agreed.

"I'll call when we get back to the room. Maybe she can book us something for dinner. And a show after?"

Beck nodded in agreement, and Micah squirmed in his seat. At some point, it was *going* to come up.

At some point, *he* was probably going to be the one to bring it up. But for now, they could at least stay busy so he could attempt to ignore the fact they had a perfectly nice wide, comfortable, *empty* bed in their suite.

God, *their* suite. Would he ever get used to that? Probably not.

The waitress showed up with food then, and Micah discovered that deciding on a plan for the day had actually settled his stomach.

The plate in front of him steamed, stacked with eggs and bacon and a ridiculous pile of crispy hash brown potatoes.

"Looks good," Beck said, refilling both of their coffee cups. Surely he'd done that at some other point during their friendship, but Micah had to wonder if it was because Beck wasn't just his friend anymore, but his *husband*.

Maybe he didn't feel just obligated to take care of him. Maybe he wanted to do it.

"Thanks," Micah said, shooting him a grateful smile.

After setting down the carafe, Beck stole a fragment of bacon from his plate.

"Hey," Micah retorted. "That's *mine*."

"I don't know, is it anymore?" Beck teased. "Maybe consider it a trade for more coffee."

"You'd have given me that anyway," Micah blustered. He was *pretty* sure Beck would've.

"Yeah." Beck's gaze went serious. Intent. Lit a fire inside him. "Yeah, I probably would've. Anything you want, you just tell me, okay?"

Micah bit into his toast, using the excuse of chewing and swallowing to delay his question. "That 'cause we're married now? Is this the Beckett West Husband Experience?"

Beck stared at him. "You think I've got any fucking clue what I'm doing?"

"Well . . .uh . . ."

"I don't," Beck said, shooting him a lopsided grin.

"Oh."

"But, if it makes you happy, if you're happy, then that's good enough for me."

Micah swallowed. "Are you around?"

"I'd sure hope so."

"Then I'm happy," Micah admitted. "I'm not very difficult, I promise. I just want . . ." *I just want you. However I can get you.*

"Hey," Beck said, reaching over and tucking Micah's free hand into his own. "You got me, okay? I told you I'm not going anywhere, and I meant it. I promise. Maybe this isn't how I thought it would go, or how you thought it would go, but we're here now."

Beck's words didn't completely relax him, but they did set a lot of his anxiety to rest.

Maybe neither of them knew what they were doing, but what was most important was that they were gonna figure this whole marriage thing out together.

Two hours later, Micah felt they had a pretty good grip on this whole marriage thing.

They'd managed to pay for breakfast without arguing who was going to pick up the bill, and then, back at the room, Micah had approved Beck's plane ticket for the next morning, while Beck called down and took care of the VIP pool passes and booking two massages.

Now, post-massage, they were floating in the private lagoon pool attached to the spa. Unlike the club pool, there was no loud music, no screaming drunk idiots, just a lot of peace and quiet.

Of course, this now meant Micah had nothing to distract him from Beck's body.

He was floating along the edge of the pool, arms stretched onto the sides of the deck, head tipped back, his eyes closed.

He'd also really not wanted to know that while Micah's spare swimsuit had fit him, it was tight on both Beck's thighs and ass. But now he had a prime front-row seat to all of that.

You can touch him now; it's allowed and everything, Micah reminded himself.

After all, Beck had been a full participant in their kisses last night, and those had definitely been *pre-wedding*.

Micah drifted a little closer.

"I can feel you staring," Beck teased, not even opening his eyes to double check he was right.

"Yeah?" Micah joined him at the edge of the pool, not quite tucking himself into Beck's side, but close enough. Beck's fingers drifted down, touching his shoulder.

Touching just to touch. That was new, and Micah would be lying if he said he didn't like it.

If he tried to claim he didn't *love* it.

"Yeah, it's nice. Makes me feel . . .I don't know . . .*wanted*, I guess."

"I married you," Micah pointed out dryly.

"Yeah, but I sort of pushed you into it."

Micah stared at him, not sure he understood what Beck was saying. "Are you trying to say it was *your* idea?"

"It was," Beck insisted. His eyes fluttered open now, and they were sharp, bright green, the color echoing the foliage around them. "I brought it up the first time, and then I was the one who suggested it last night."

"No, no, *definitely* no," Micah said. And suddenly he was laughing and couldn't stop because this was all so ridiculous he could barely stand it. They were both tiptoeing around each other, terrified they'd pushed the other too far—when in reality they'd done it because being crazy about someone apparently made you do crazy things.

Beck frowned. "Is this hungover-inspired hysteria?"

Micah shook his head emphatically. "Just . . .we are just so fucking bad at this."

"Oh?" Beck tilted his head, not looking particularly offended by Micah's blunt words—only curious what they meant.

"I want you. I *wanted* to marry you. I want to be married to you. I just want you." It felt like the most natural thing to slide the rest of the way into Beck's side, his arm curling around Micah's shoulders like that there was just where he belonged.

This time Micah didn't hesitate but leaned in and kissed Beck.

"God," Beck groaned into his mouth and his fingers tightened into his shoulder. "I thought you didn't . . ."

Micah pulled back. "Are you fucking kidding me?"

Beck's smile was sheepish. "No?"

"This isn't how I intended to do this. I hadn't even gotten that far, but I'm not mad it's done," Micah admitted, which was true. He had been thinking about coming out, of course, in a more public way than he already had.

It wasn't that he hadn't necessarily felt ready—from the conversations he'd had with Scott, Sebastian, and a few others, it seemed that you were *never* really ready to take that step—but he *had* been ready to stop pretending to be someone else.

"You weren't feeling guilty about it, were you?" Micah asked when Beck didn't say anything.

"No, *no*, well. A little." Beck shrugged. "I didn't even think about it! The thought never even crossed my mind that everyone would know after this."

"How about . . .*I wanted* everyone to know," Micah argued.

"I just worried I wasn't being a good friend to you."

Micah swam closer, so he could look Beck directly in the eye. Placed his hands on his shoulders—those awesome, broad shoulders he'd stared at way too many times over the years—and said, "I didn't want you to be *just* a good friend, anymore."

Micah thought he'd said the same thing in half a dozen more obscure ways, but it was like he hadn't said it at all, because Beck had the nerve to look surprised.

"Come on," Micah retorted. "You *knew*."

"I *hoped*, okay? But I wasn't sure, and you were still figuring your shit out and I did not want to assume."

Micah tucked a hand behind Beck's head. Tugged himself closer. Felt every place their bodies touched under the water, each one a mini earthquake exploding through his system. "So what was yesterday then?" he teased. "You assuming?"

Beck's smile was so bright it nearly blinded him. "Yeah," he said. "Yeah, I guess."

"Assume more often, alright?" Micah said.

"Like this?"

Micah knew it was coming, but the moment Beck's mouth touched his, it was like the first time all over again.

He groaned as Beck tilted his mouth, capturing his own more fully, and Micah's fingers tightened on his shoulders, as water sloshed between them.

Why hadn't they been smart enough to do this in the privacy of their hotel room?

"Do you want—"

But Beck didn't have to get the words out before Micah was nodding in agreement.

"Yes, *yes*," he chanted.

CHAPTER 10

If Micah had been nervous before, he was practically vibrating out of his skin now as they took the elevator back up to their suite.

Beck didn't touch him in the elevator, but every time he glanced over, he was staring at him with a gaze that felt as proprietary as a caress.

Neither of them had spoken since Micah had agreed—they'd just picked up their stuff and headed straight to the elevator.

When they finally made it to their floor and down the hall, Micah's hand shook as he pulled out his key card, letting them in.

He fell against the door after it shut behind them.

"We didn't talk about it," he said quietly as Beck just eyed him. "Specifically about what happened last night."

The corner of Beck's mouth tilted up. "I hate to break it to you, but you married me last night."

"Yeah." God, he had.

The man in front of him was *his*. And even though it was just a piece of paper, it confirmed what Micah had hoped and wanted and dreamed of for way too many years.

"But I don't think that was your question," Beck pointed out. "You want to know if we had sex last night."

"Did we do it and I forgot it?" The possibility that they had finally touched each other the way he'd fantasized about, and he'd *forgotten* it, erased in a haze of booze, felt like a loss.

He'd get over it. He had to, because there was nothing to do but move on, and realize that it wasn't the only time. Micah hoped it was just going to be the first of many, many times.

But it would've been his first time with a guy. After so fucking long.

If Micah couldn't mourn for that, then he couldn't mourn anything.

"Listen." Beck took a step closer. Stripped off his damp T-shirt. Micah's swimsuit was still clinging distractingly to his thighs and to his dick. "I don't remember it. And I remember everything. I remember coming back here. We kissed. A lot. And then I think we fell asleep."

"We *were* mostly clothed still," Micah agreed, wetting his lips. If he'd been nervous, anticipation buzzing under his skin, before, he was wild with it now—just from the way Beck was looking at him so intently. Like he intended to take him apart and then put him back together again.

Like he'd wanted to do it for nearly as long as Micah had.

"That's pretty good evidence we didn't," Beck agreed. "If we had sex, you'd be naked. There's no way that wouldn't be true."

"What about you?"

Beck's grin was half-devil, half-angel, and *all* Micah's. "Interested in getting me naked, Rose?"

Micah shot him a look.

"Let me say it another way." Beck moved closer, then closer still. Until his hands were on either side of Micah's head, his gaze dark and purposeful, his lips only a breath away from Micah's. "If I'd had my hands on you—you'd know. You'd remember."

He didn't know if he rose up and kissed Beck—or if Beck leaned down and closed the distance between them, but it didn't matter, because this kiss was wilder, hotter than any they'd shared yet.

Micah groaned into Beck's mouth. He'd never imagined a kiss could feel so good, but Beck's lips were fierce and confident, his tongue slipping against his own.

His thigh pressed up against Beck's. *Please*, he thought he groaned, *oh, please, please please.*

Maybe he'd said it out loud, or maybe Beck just knew.

"I got you," he murmured into Micah's ear, nipping his earlobe with just enough teeth to make Micah tremble with the mixed pain and pleasure of it. Then Beck's hands were stripping away his T-shirt, and then they were at his waist, big and warm and sure, tugging down his swim trunks.

His cock bobbed out, as hard as he'd ever been in his whole goddamned life.

He would've tried to return the favor, but Beck was pressing him so intently into the door, with the perfect kind of pressure.

"Yeah," Beck ground out, as Micah's fingertips traced his dick. "God, yes, sweetheart, just enjoy it, okay? I'm gonna make you feel so good."

"Yeah?" Micah's voice cracked, because it was already so good. Better than any sex he'd ever had.

Then Beck sank to his knees, one of his hands still pressing into Micah's chest.

"So fucking long I've wanted to get my mouth on you," he said.

Micah trembled as Beck's tongue flicked out, licking a stripe up the underside of his cock.

Then he couldn't watch any longer. Because if he did, if he watched as Beck slid his length into his hot mouth, he'd lose it immediately. And there was nothing he wanted more than for this to go on and on forever.

It was unlike any blowjob Micah had ever experienced, and not just because Beck was damn good at it, confident and sure, swallowing around him like he'd been born to do it, but because he kept teasing him. Kept talking to him.

Kept up a litany of the dirtiest talk Micah could ever imagine—and not because it was necessarily all *that* dirty, but because it was Beck, and it was his mouth saying those words. His mouth unraveling him one lick, one suck, one brush of his fingers against his balls at a time.

"Yeah, sweetheart, moan for me, okay? Yeah, just like that. God, I could listen to you forever. Could do this forever. You taste so goddamn good."

Micah couldn't tamp back the cry of pleasure as he sucked him particularly hard.

"Oh yeah, just like that," Beck encouraged. "Oh, baby, you're gonna lose it, but next time, you're gonna fuck my face just like that. Like you can't even control yourself anymore."

He couldn't.

Micah's mind was one haze of *more, please,* and *feels so fucking good.*

Then Beck's fingers trailed up his inner thigh, the skin so sensitive there, and brushed up behind his balls, right in the place where he'd spent way too many secretive nights with his fingers buried inside himself and his moans muffled by his pillow.

And every single one of those nights, it had been Beck's name on his lips as he'd come.

Beck pulled back a little, and the grin he wore was so filthy, his eyes so full of joy that he could give this to him, Micah lost his war with control.

"God, yes, give it to me," Beck moaned, and for the next few moments, Micah didn't think at all, just lost himself to the orgasm, stripes of his come falling across Beck's broad shoulders, across his cheek, in his hair.

But Beck didn't seem to care. He just worked him through the orgasm of a fucking lifetime, crooning to him the whole way that he was so hot, so perfect, so unbelievable that Beck was lucky to touch him.

Micah finally slumped back against the door, panting.

Beck leaned back on his heels and grinned.

"Well, how was that?" he said.

Micah started to laugh, and this time he couldn't stop.

He laughed, the sound coming from deep inside him, in a place that had always been dark and hopeless, but that with each round of laughter, lightened.

When he finally stopped, Beck had used his T-shirt to wipe himself off, but otherwise, he hadn't moved.

It felt the most natural thing to reach for Beck. To attempt to give him a fraction of the pleasure—and the pure fucking lightness—he'd just experienced.

Beck didn't say anything, just let him tug down his shorts.

His cock was long and thick, and if Micah's was perfect, then Beck's was a fucking masterpiece.

"I don't—" he started to say, figuring that considering this was his first time, he better offer some kind of blanket apology for his lack of skill, but before he could finish, Beck was shushing him.

"No, just . . ." Beck arched against Micah's hand as he began to stroke. Just the way he liked it. A little hard and tight. Teasing strokes in between. "Just like that," he finished breathlessly. "And kiss me."

That was easy enough. So easy to fall into Beck's mouth, like they'd been doing this forever, when that had only ever been in Micah's imagination.

"Shit," Beck groaned as Micah worked his hand faster.

Micah swallowed his noises with his own mouth. A minute later, Beck went still and tense and then began to come over his hand, and Micah took every single one of those incredible noises, stealing them away for any time he felt wrong or weird or unsure.

Beck had always made him feel like a better version of himself, but there was no question now he'd make sure, with every fiber of his being, that Micah was worthy of him.

Worthy of being his friend, his lover, and his husband.

After a very rudimentary cleanup job, it made perfect sense to stumble to the bed and collapse into it together.

Beck had never imagined that Micah Rose would be so touchy-feely, so goddamn cuddly, but he was going to soak up every bit of it he could.

"I think," Micah said sleepily, not bothering to turn his head to meet Beck's eyes, his cheek currently pressed to Beck's pectoral muscle, "you were right."

"Yeah?" Beck smiled again. He couldn't help it.

"Don't rub it in or anything," Micah grumbled.

"Oh, I'll rub it—"

Micah made a sleepy outraged sound.

"You love it," Beck retorted lightly.

"I do." Micah shifted, and his gaze was soft as it met Beck's. "But yeah, we didn't have sex. I wouldn't have ever forgotten that."

It was hard not to preen under the inherent praise in that statement.

He'd been pretty sure it was Micah's first time with a guy, and he'd wanted so badly to make it good. To make it *memorable*.

"Me either," Beck agreed. He hesitated. If he was wrong, he didn't want Micah to think he was mad he'd found someone else to experiment with. "So there wasn't anyone in Miami?"

Micah's stare was unnerving—even though Beck knew how much he cared for the guy. How prepared he was to be married to him for the rest of their lives. "How could I have found someone else?" he asked.

Beck thought that must be a rhetorical question.

"It was always going to be you or no one," Micah continued with a wry twist of his lips. "You were the one I wanted, and I wasn't ready to settle. I guess I hadn't given up on us yet, even though I probably should've."

Beck's arm tightened around Micah before he could even help it. "No, you shouldn't have. We talked about this."

"Yeah." Micah re-settled on his chest. He sounded more at peace now. Maybe he'd eventually be able to forgive himself. Beck hoped so, because *Beck* had forgiven him.

"You know," Beck said after a few minutes of lazy silence, "I'm gonna have to call my mom and tell her about this."

"Hmmm," Micah agreed.

"You tell yours yet?" Beck asked.

"She knows," Micah said after a long moment of silence.

The way he'd phrased it was weird, but before Beck could ask, Micah raised his head and after shifting, leaned in and kissed him again.

Beck groaned in the back of his throat. "Yeah?" he asked, when Micah pulled back an inch.

It was undeniable that his cock was already stirring, his blood beginning to heat. He'd wanted Micah Rose for way too long to not fully enjoy himself once he was in his bed.

"God, yes, please," Micah said in a breathless voice.

Beck was just about to put his mouth on his neck, practically already tasting the curve of it under his tongue, and his hand on Micah's cock, when his phone rang.

No, it *blared*.

"Shit," Beck said, falling back against the pillows.

"What is it?"

"There's only a few people who are set up in my phone to ring through, even though it's on silent." He swallowed hard. "My mom is one of them."

"I guess it's likely the news is *really* public, now," Micah said, sounding nervous about this.

It was a good reminder, Beck decided, as he rolled over to grab his phone. Yes, he'd gotten married in Vegas and he hadn't managed to tell his family before they'd found out, but Micah hadn't been out before this.

Not only had he married Beck in Vegas, he'd come out.

Surely with everything Micah was dealing with, Beck could face his mother.

"Hey, Mom," he said, answering the call.

"Don't you *dare* 'hey, Mom' me," Jolie retorted with heat.

Beck winced. "I guess you found out. I was actually *just* about to call you—"

"It's almost five in Vegas!" she exclaimed. "Why was I not your *very first* call, Beckett? You got *married*."

"Guilty as charged," Beck said weakly.

"And to *Micah Rose*," Jolie said reproachfully.

"Yep, that's the guy."

Beck met Micah's eyes and they both smiled.

"Is this something you're gonna be undoing sooner rather than later?" she asked after a long moment. Obviously, this wasn't how she'd thought this conversation would go.

"There're no plans to do that right now," Beck said.

There was a long silence on the other end of the line. "You're serious, aren't you? You're not joking. This isn't one big joke."

"Would I joke about this? You know I wouldn't." Next to him, Micah tensed. Beck reached out and put a hand on Micah's knee. Squeezed it reassuringly.

"You also wouldn't get drunk and get married in Vegas either," Jolie pointed out dryly. "But you did."

"Actually . . ." This had been more information than he'd wanted to tell his mother, but maybe she'd accept the truth more easily if she knew.

"You were *sober*?" Jolie sounded incredulous.

"Well, not exactly. But not drunk either. Not . . .not like that."

"Beckett." She sighed. "You could've just *dated* him. You didn't have to marry the man."

"Maybe I wanted to."

Micah's eyes were wide. There was no way he didn't hear everything his mother was saying—and no question he heard everything Beck was saying in response.

And it *was* true. He'd wanted to. He'd wanted to make sure they couldn't have any more misunderstandings. Make sure Micah couldn't push him away again.

He'd also known, with a bone-deep certainty that he hadn't even been able to put into words until the next morning, that Micah was the guy for him. The only guy he'd want to spend the rest of his life with.

Jolie was silent for a long moment. "You're really very serious about this, aren't you?"

"I told you I was."

"I'm seeing that now. Well, you are still coming to Chicago this weekend? For the game? I'm assuming you'll be bringing Micah with you now. Bring him around. It won't be the same as being *at your wedding*, but we'll want to congratulate you properly."

"Sure, we can do that." He'd actually totally forgotten that in a few days he was due to fly to Illinois to spend the weekend at Northwestern.

It would make sense if Micah came with him.

Frankly, Beck would be surprised if he hadn't been invited, too—but before they'd made up, he'd actively been hoping Micah had turned down their offer so they wouldn't run into each other on the Northwestern sideline.

Now unless Micah had other plans. . .well, they were going to be taking their first official trip as a married couple.

"I'm excited to see you both." Jolie's tone left no room for doubt that was true.

"I'm not sure he's coming yet, Mom," Beck reminded her. "But yeah, hopefully."

"Beckett West, you make sure he's with you," Jolie said firmly. "I didn't get to be at your wedding. The least you can give me is this."

Beck chuckled. He shouldn't be surprised. After all, one of his first thoughts waking up this morning had been: *oh, my mom's gonna be pissed.*

"We'll see. I'll let you know."

"Beckett," she said quietly, "I know how much capacity for love you carry with you. You're going to do just fine at this thing. Yes, it's a change but this is one of those good changes we talked about. Just in case you were worried."

How had she known?

Well, she *was* his mother.

"Thanks, Mom."

"I mean it, Beckett. You'll do just fine at this. Just don't forget that it doesn't come easy, always. But it's still worth it, in the end."

"Yeah, he is." Beck glanced over at where Micah lay.

"Good. I thought so."

"Mom, I gotta go," he said. "But I'll text when I know more about my schedule."

"You make sure you do," she ordered.

"Love you."

She repeated his words back and then hung up.

Micah was watching him, eyes narrowed.

"What was that about?" he asked casually, his tone at odds with the tense way he was holding himself.

"You're not going to Northwestern this weekend? I was sure they'd invited you." Beck frowned, immediately wondering how he was going to make that right. It wasn't okay at all for him to be honored at halftime if Micah wasn't as well.

"No, I am. They invited me after the trade." Micah frowned. "We're . . .we're going to have to go together now, aren't we?"

Beck nodded slowly, and Micah let out a breath.

"Guess I hadn't really gotten that far."

"We've been married for less than twenty-four hours," Beck joked weakly. "It's hard to know which life-changing circumstance to deal with first."

"I was kinda enjoying *not* dealin' with any of it," Micah admitted.

"Honestly? Me too. We could go back to that. Where were we?" Beck ran a hand down Micah's back, feeling the muscles ripple under his touch. Would he ever get used to the idea that he could touch now, whenever he wanted to?

"First," Micah said. "Tell me what you promised your mom."

"Well, you're going, right? To Chicago?" Micah nodded. "Okay, well, she just wants us to come around for dinner one night. I was already planning on doing it. But now you're coming with me so it's . . .it's not a big deal, I hope? You've met them all before."

Micah wet his lips. "Not as your husband, I haven't."

"Right." Beck sighed. "If you don't want to—"

"No," Micah interrupted before he could finish his sentence. "No, I want to. I just . . .I didn't expect it, that's all." He shot Beck a wry smile. "That *was* one of the first things you said. That your mom was gonna kill you."

"I can't say she won't make some big party thing out of it," Beck warned. "But I can run interference if you hate that."

"No, I don't mind. I'm not ashamed. Not of this. Not of you."

Beck wanted to ask if he was still ashamed of who he was, too, but that seemed right on the edge of pushing too far. After all, he'd been Micah's husband for not even a whole day. There was plenty of time to ask that—and to make sure Micah had whatever he needed to banish that self-hatred forever.

"Alright." Beck leaned down and kissed him. Just because he could. Because he wanted to.

But before he could really lean into it and get right back to where they'd been before his mother had interrupted them, Micah pulled back.

"You're really okay with this." He said it, a puzzled crease forming between his brows.

Yeah, you darling idiot. I'm crazy in love with you.

But it was *way* too soon to say that. Ironically. Beck would have to have almost no sense of humor to not see the hilarious twist in this whole situation.

"Yeah, I am."

"Me too," Micah said, and leaned in, kissed him again.

It felt like a miracle every time Micah reached for *him*. Like he was slowly, inexorably blasting away those thoughts of, *I'm not right, he's not for me, I can't have anything I want*, one kiss at a time.

And *God*, they were good kisses.

Micah's mouth was lush and wet underneath his own, and it didn't take long for Beck to climb over him, grinding their cocks together, Beck's breath coming in uneven pants as Micah drove them both towards another sweaty, unsteady, fucking perfect orgasm.

When the aftershocks finally finished rocketing through him, Micah collapsed on his chest, laughing again.

He could listen to that laugh for the rest of his life, and if he was very, very lucky, he *would* be able to.

"What's so funny?" he asked breathlessly. Micah had stolen his breath, his sanity, his self-control, his *heart*.

"You, me, *us*," Micah said, between hysterical gasps. "I can't believe we haven't been doing *that* this whole goddamn time."

"I'd say it seems like a waste," Beck agreed, nodding, "but then I can't say we didn't have plenty of great times before this, too."

"Yeah. *Yeah.*" Micah hesitated. "You're right. We did have a lot of good times. You're my best friend, you know?" He seemed suddenly shy, admitting it, which in turn made *Beck* laugh, because God, they were actually married now. Weren't you supposed to marry your best friend?

And they'd done it.

"You're mine. And my husband, too." Beck couldn't help the pride and smug satisfaction that stole over him when he thought it.

Micah crinkled his nose. "Still seems unreal. Like it didn't really happen."

"Oh, it happened." Beck grinned. "Even though I promised Nicole we'd stay away from any wedding chapels and Elvis officiants, I'd happily do it again, if you wanted."

"No, I'm good." Micah settled his cheek against where Beck's heart thumped away, unaware of just how much it was currently beating *solely* for him. "We should really take a shower."

"Soon," Beck said. He stroked the long line of Micah's back.

He'd wondered if they ever did this, if it would feel weird or awkward, but the truth was, it only felt like the rightest thing in the universe.

Like coming home.

CHAPTER 11

"So is this the next chapter in the Beckett West Husband Experience?"

Micah gazed out at the Bellagio fountains, taking in the incredible view of the water fountains Beck had secured them when he'd called ahead to the restaurant.

"Well, I just said I wanted a good table," Beckett said, shooting him a crooked smile that twisted Micah's insides.

"*And* you gave them your name and a pretty healthy tip when we showed up," Micah pointed out.

Beck was so adorably charming when he shrugged, like it was no big deal that he'd gone out of his way to make sure they had a great view of the fountains.

Like it didn't mean fucking everything that he wanted Micah to have an unforgettable evening. Like just spending time with Beck like this—on a date, because while last night that had been unspoken between them, tonight it was explicit, 'cause, *oh yeah*, they were married now—wasn't already special.

"Maybe I did, maybe I didn't," Beck retorted, gazing fondly at Micah from across the table.

When they'd sat down, Beck had ordered a bottle of wine, and it sat in the ice bucket between them. He hadn't missed when Beck had poured him a glass, the twinkle in his eye that said *yes,* he'd remembered this was one of his favorite kinds. Or the fact that the food here at Yellowfin was just what Micah liked too. Apparently there was a real advantage to dating someone who knew him as well as Beck did.

"Well, it was worth it, no matter what it cost," Micah said. "This view is pretty awesome."

"And we've got over an hour to enjoy it," Beck confirmed after checking his watch.

He was wearing another one of those gloriously clingy polos, outlining his pecs and abs and biceps, but this time as Micah gazed at him, he knew what Beck looked and tasted and smelled like.

Somehow that made Beck even more addictive than he'd been before, when Micah had been mostly in the dark.

He wondered what Beck would say if he suggested they skip the show and just head back to the room.

What he'd say if he asked Beck to stretch him open with one, then two, then three, of those wide, blunt fingers and then bend him over the bed and fuck him like the world was coming to an end tonight.

Micah shifted in his chair. He shouldn't even be thinking about having even *more* sex. He'd already had more pleasure today than he'd had in his whole life. And speaking of his whole life, he had *forever* to ask Beck to do that.

But he couldn't deny he wanted it.

He'd *always* wanted it.

"So, were you really going to go to Chicago next weekend? Even though you knew I'd be there?"

Micah shot him a look. "You were frankly the biggest reason I was going," he admitted.

Beck actually had the nerve to look surprised. "But—"

"But you were still pissed at me when they reached out? Yeah, I know." His wine was tart and cool on his tongue. But it didn't really make the nauseating roll of guilt in his gut feel any less.

He wasn't sure he deserved Beck—or his careful consideration or his friendship or his forever.

But he was taking them anyway, because he'd lost the ability to turn any of them down.

"*You* ghosted *me*." Beck didn't even look angry about this anymore, though he probably should be.

Micah didn't want to talk about this. They were nearing their 24-hour anniversary; shouldn't they be celebrating that, improbably, they were actually still married, instead of revisiting all the terrible things he'd done? But Beck weirdly didn't look very perturbed by the subject; he'd even been the one to bring it up. Like it didn't bother him anymore.

"Doesn't mean I didn't want to make it right," Micah said.

Though it wasn't like he'd had much hope. Scott had told him, when they'd talked about Micah going to Chicago, that Beck might not be happy about it.

Micah had told himself he'd been prepared for it—just as he'd been prepared for Beck to continue to be pissed when he'd arrived in Charleston.

Micah was still marveling over the fact that Beck hadn't immediately wanted to get a divorce.

But he hadn't even considered it.

"Aw, you were planning on wooing me?" Beck grinned.

"I was planning on *apologizing*. The wooing was much later on down the line. Didn't know if you even wanted to be my friend anymore, after what I'd done."

"You're kinda irresistible," Beck admitted. Under the table, he knocked one foot against Micah's. "I don't think I could've held out, to be honest."

"Maybe both of us are a lost cause," Micah admitted.

It was as close as he'd ever come to spilling the truth: that he'd been in love with Beckett West practically since that first cherry Icee.

"Yeah?" The corner of Beck's mouth tilted up, and he looked completely delighted by this. "Knew I was right to lock you down."

"Hey, *I'm* the one who brought up that stuff you said . . .well, that you said, that one night . . ."

"True." Beck leaned in and captured his mouth in a kiss that was not only completely addicting but *allowed* now. "Guess we weren't so stupid after all, huh?"

Micah could think of a lot of people who no doubt believed they'd been incredibly stupid.

But he couldn't find even a single shred of regret inside him that they'd finally decided they belonged together.

"Guess we weren't," he said. And this time, he reached over, and captured Beck's chin in his hand, kissing him long and slow. Not giving a shit who saw.

By the time they headed to the show, Micah was closer to losing his self-control than he'd ever expected. After all, he'd already had two spectacular orgasms today.

But Beck kept touching him—with casual touches like he'd always craved, but never had, before—and every time his hand brushed his back or his arm or his knee or, God forbid, his thigh, he felt like he was going to vibrate out of his skin.

"You alright?" Beck glanced over at him, his fingertips brushing the small of Micah's back as they walked towards the theater entrance.

A humorless chuckle escaped him. "You ever think about this?"

"About going to Vegas with you?" Beck shrugged. "Not specifically."

"No, I mean *this*." Micah slowed and Beck's hand, warm and sure, collided with his back more firmly.

This hallway was dimly lit—no doubt the designer would've called it *atmospheric*—but he could still see Beck's eyes dilate, just from the single touch.

But before Beck could answer, Micah was word vomiting it all out.

"I did, all the time. For years. I thought I knew what I wanted. Thought I knew what it would feel like, if it ever happened. But—" He shook his head. "It's nothing like I imagined. I . . .I can barely stand sitting across from you at dinner. I want to touch you all the time. I can't think, I can't focus, I can't do *anything*, except . . ."

"Except?" Beck's voice was low and intense.

"Except think about the next time you're gonna touch me. The next time I'm gonna touch you." It was a ridiculous confession.

Micah knew it. But if he was going to be able to admit it to anyone, the only person on earth he could say it to was Beck.

Beck stared at him. "You can't say shit like that."

It had been a mistake; Micah knew it now. He turned, ready to go into the theater and maybe lick his wounds, but then Beck's hand caught his, squeezed it. Then Micah found himself being dragged back the way they'd come. "Where are we going?"

Beck shot him a look. "Seriously?"

"*Seriously*," Micah said, and he was just as strong as Beck was, but apparently he wasn't as determined as the other guy, because Beck just kept dragging him along, like he hadn't even given him a fight.

Beck only gave him a sharp shake of his head as they headed out of the hotel and was silent all the way to the entrance, where he pulled open the door of a taxi lingering under the portico.

"Get in," he said.

"The Wynn," he told the driver after sliding in after Micah.

He didn't know what the fuck this was, but the chances were good he might be getting what he really, desperately craved, because Beck's hand moved from his own, to his knee, and his thigh.

His touch was hot even through the fabric of his pants, Beck staring at him the whole way.

It was late at night on the Strip, so the drive wasn't as short as it could've been, but by the time they reached the Wynn, Beck still hadn't said anything.

When the cab stopped in front of the hotel, Beck tossed him some cash and didn't wait for the valet to open the door, he just shoved it open, and Micah couldn't do anything else but follow.

"What *is* this?" Micah finally broke the silence when they walked into the empty elevator and the doors shut behind them.

Beck shot him a dark look. A dark, *hungry* look.

A thrill shot up Micah's spine.

He still remembered what Carter had said about Beck. *I'm sure he'd be a monster in bed. In fact, I'm counting on it.* How could he forget it? Carter made him half-crazy with how intently he flirted with Beck but didn't really want him. Not the way Micah did—with a deep intensity borne of way too many late nights and back-breaking practices and glorious wins and unspoken words.

Had he just unleashed the monster?

The elevator doors dinged open, and Beck stalked down the hallway, stopping in front of their door. Micah fumbled for the key, shoved it in the slot, and they fell into the room, Beck on him the instant the door closed.

His back hit the wood, and Beck's hands were cradling his face, kissing him more fiercely than he ever had before—simply devouring him.

Micah's knees were already weak; like it was only Beck's hard thigh, shoved between his own, that kept him upright.

"You can't say shit like that, because *God*," Beck murmured, pulling away. His light eyes had been entirely taken over by his huge pupils. "I *didn't* think about it before. I thought I was being smart and some shit, putting you in the friend zone and keeping you there. But then that night happened, and I couldn't pretend anymore. You were gone and I could only go through every single fucking moment we'd spent together, and how much I regretted not doing anything. Not until it was too late. It was all I could think about, until I was crazy and going out of my head with how much I wanted you. How much I *want* you. How much I . . ." Beck's voice cracked. His palm was warm and gentle on Micah's cheek, the polar opposite of the wildness in his gaze. "How much I love you."

Micah's jaw dropped.

Probably not the way you should be reactin' to this man tellin' you he loves you, Scott's voice echoed in his head. *Don't make my mistakes. Tell him back. 'Cause I know you feel it.*

He'd never felt anything more.

"Remember the cherry Icee?"

Beck nodded.

"I loved you then. I've never . . .not until you."

"And never again," Beck said with satisfaction, his face lit with joy. "This is it."

Micah kissed him again. It was softer and a little sweeter, but then Beck groaned and they were attacking each other's mouths again, like they didn't have a whole lifetime to do this. Like they might internally combust if they didn't do this right the fuck *now*.

"Bed, *now*," Micah gasped as he shoved Beck off him, stripping off his jacket.

Beck's fingers ripped open his shirt, buttons flying everywhere, and then they hit the edge of the bed, nearly falling over on top of it.

"Shit," Beck said, and then he laughed. Micah couldn't help but join in.

"Hey, can I ask you for something?" Micah hadn't intended to say it, but Beck's confession—and then his own—had unlocked his tongue.

He'd always trusted Beck, more than anyone else he knew, but this was a new kind of trust. Like if he leapt off the edge of a cliff, Beck would be right there with him, strapping on a parachute.

"Anything." Beck pushed Micah's shirt off his shoulders, then after tugging up his own, tossed them both on the floor.

"I want you to fuck me."

Beck's fingers froze on his belt.

"You know, we don't have to . . .I'm into that too, if you wanted. Or we can just . . ." Beck waved his hands around, like that was supposed to mean something concrete.

It was cute, Micah decided, watching Beck squirm.

He was clearly not against the idea—he just worried Micah wasn't totally, completely, one hundred percent on board. But he was.

"I know," Micah said, steadily. "But I *want* to. I've wanted to for a long, long time. Do you wanna know how many nights I fucked myself with my fingers and imagined it was you?"

Beck whined low in his throat. "Are you trying to kill me?"

"Maybe I'm just tryin' to get *you* to destroy *me*," Micah teased.

"That's really what you want." Beck sounded incredulous. Hot and bothered, yes, but also shocked.

"Tonight, *yeah*."

Micah scooted up onto the bed, shedding his shoes and socks as he went. They hit the floor with a satisfying thump, and as he lay back on the bed, he palmed his hard cock. Licked his lips as he groaned into his own touch.

"Anything you want, but you save *that* for me," Beck said. He pinned Micah's wrists over his head, leaning into the grip. Micah squirmed, not sure if he'd like being held down, but as Beck leaned over him, pressing a hot kiss against his mouth, he realized he didn't just like it. He freaking loved it.

Then Beck's lips drifted lower as he worked open Micah's pants, only brushing his cock with teasing little touches, no matter how he tried to buck against Beck's hands.

"Patience," Beck murmured against his skin.

"I'm—" Micah swore. "There's lube. And condoms in my bag."

Beck pulled back. "Did you *plan* this?"

"Hope's a terrible thing," Micah tried to joke. "I didn't *plan* it, but I . . .well, I sure fucking hoped you might stay. That we might do this."

"Jesus. I was right. You're gonna kill me." Beck rocked back on his heels after he finished stripping the rest of Micah's clothes off. Stared at him, his eyes tracing every bit of his naked body. Every inch of his cock, hard and brushing against his lower abs. Even though Beck had released the grip he'd had on his hands, Micah hadn't moved them.

Turned out he didn't even want to.

"Yeah?"

"But I'm gonna die a happy man, that's for fucking sure."

Beck slipped off the bed.

Micah heard him rummaging around in his bag, and when he came back, he had the bottle of lube and the box of condoms in one hand and the other was shedding his pants.

Leaving him in only a pair of midnight blue briefs, his dick straining against the fabric. Micah's mouth went dry. Beck was so big. So powerful. Muscles tensed. And all of that was for *him*.

Beck took his time settling between his legs, slicking up his fingers. "You may have done this before," he said bluntly, "but we're gonna go slow, and I don't wanna hear a single word of complaint." His face broke into a shit-eating grin. "But begging? You can do that all fucking day."

"I can do that," Micah said, his tongue feeling thick and heavy in his mouth. Uncooperative. Because every bit of his body was primed to feel the touch of Beck's fingers on him.

"Then let me hear you, sweetheart," Beck said softly. A fingertip brushed against his hole right as Beck dipped his head and licked Micah's cock, pleasure spearing him through in a dual assault.

He'd always liked this a lot. Like he'd told Beck, he'd fingered himself so many times he'd lost count. Even when he'd been most ashamed of this part of him, the part that wanted it, that *enjoyed* it, he still hadn't been able to stop himself from doing it.

Or from the terrible hope that one day it wouldn't be just him and his own two hands.

That someday, it might be Beck.

Still, he'd never imagined they'd be *married*, or that Beck would be gazing at him with love as he began to split him open with those big callused fingers.

"I said, *let me hear you*," Beck said, raising his head. His eyes pinned Micah to the bed and his mouth was red and wet, and Micah felt frozen in a constant clench of pleasure and pressure. Caught between all the best parts of the man he loved.

"Give me another, *please*," Micah pleaded.

"That's right," Beck crooned.

To Micah's surprise, he didn't hold out longer, but a few strokes later, another finger joined the first, gliding home in a slick slide that felt a hundred times better than every single time he'd done this to himself, a *thousand*. God, if he'd known it could be this good, he'd have ditched every bit of fear and begged for it ages ago.

It was almost too much to watch Beck fucking him, but he couldn't help but look.

And not just glance at him briefly, but look his fill. File it all away to remember later. Beck's eyes were so dark as they flicked up to meet Micah's gaze.

"More," Micah begged.

"I don't know," Beck said, pulling off his cock. "I like this. I love this, in fact. You squirming in my hands and against my mouth."

"Cocky asshole."

Beck grinned. "Yeah, you love it, sweetheart."

There was no denying that he did.

Or stopping the babbling nonsense that came out of his mouth when Beck added another finger, the third sliding up the other two, stretching him out in a steady, inexorable movement. They brushed up against that spot that lit him on fire, right as Beck swallowed him down, and Micah wasn't proud but he wailed with the fierce pleasure of it.

"That's it, take it." Even Beck's voice wasn't quite steady as he pushed him further and further.

So far Micah wasn't sure he could take it, but he *had* to, because he wanted so much more than this. He wanted Beck inside him, just the way he'd fantasized about so many goddamn times.

"Come on, come on, *come on*." Micah was only half-aware of how much he was moaning for it. And he knew later he wouldn't feel even a second of shame. This felt too good to be ashamed of, too *right*.

"How do you want it?" Beck asked as he finally took pity on Micah and slowly slid his fingers out, spreading and stretching him as he went, so Micah felt every single fucking inch.

"Just like this," Micah insisted.

Beck raised an eyebrow. "But—"

"I don't fucking care."

Beck laughed unsteadily at the demand in his words, but Micah didn't miss how his fingers shook when he grabbed the box of condoms and pulled one out. He swore as he tore the package, and it wouldn't open, Beck finally resorting to using his teeth. He rolled on the condom, eyes gleaming as Micah raised his hips.

Yeah, they were both right on the edge.

When he went over, he wanted Beck there with him, the two of them clinging together.

"I love you," he said, as Beck lined himself up, right before he slid home. "I love you so fucking much."

Beck squeezed his eyes shut for a minute. "You can't say that shit right now," he ground out, his voice rough and deep, fingers digging into Micah's skin. "I'm hangin' on by a thread here."

"You could just say you love me too," Micah said.

"Goddamn it, I do," Beck said, and slowly, carefully pushed his way inside.

With how many times he'd fingered himself over the years, Micah hadn't expected this would feel so much different, but it did. So much different. So much *better*.

"Shit," he cried as Beck bottomed out, Micah tight in his grip.

"Too much?" Beck frowned. "Cause Jesus, sweetheart, you're tight. So good, so tight. So . . .*ugh*."

"I'm good. It's . . ." Micah's voice broke. "It's *amazing*."

"Good." Beck smiled smugly. "'Cause I think you're gonna love this."

He didn't lie. In fact, he delivered better than Micah could've ever dreamed, all those years ago.

Beck's thrusts were powerful but steady, his control honed from so many years training his body to do whatever he needed it to do. He found the spot that made Micah swear and wail, clenching up, and then hit it over and over, until Micah was delirious with it.

Until he couldn't bear to take it anymore. Then Beck slowed down, gazing down at him, so much love in his eyes, and asked him to feel it a little more, and what else could he do, but nod?

"Just a little more," Beck swore to him, "God, sweetheart, you feel so good, I don't wanna stop."

Micah groaned, and finally, reaching the end of his control, let his hand drift down his stomach, towards where his cock bobbed, hard and leaking steadily at the tip.

He knew if he just touched himself, he was going to come harder than he ever had in his life.

"Yeah," Beck encouraged him. "You want it? Tell me how much you want it."

"So fucking much," Micah cried out. "Let me, *please*." Beck hadn't told him he couldn't come, but in this moment, it made perfect sense to let him decide.

After all, all his other ideas had turned out really fucking great, hadn't they?

Beck batted his hand away and the moment his fist closed around Micah's dick, he was coming so hard he nearly blacked out, in pulse after dizzying pulse.

He heard Beck's bellow as he followed after him, and then for a very long moment, he just *floated* on a sea of bliss as he came down, Beck collapsing onto the bed next to him.

"For the record, that was a very good idea, and I feel stupid I even *tried* to protest," Beck said as he tucked Micah into his side. It was hard to believe there'd been a time when Micah had hated that extra inch or two Beck had on him, but now it just felt like serendipity. So he could hold Micah just like this.

Micah laughed. "And here I thought *you* were the one with all the good ideas."

"Nope, that one was all you. Here I just thought we might make out, and hump like we had no fucking control at all, but no, your idea was way better."

"Thanks?" Micah nuzzled into Beck's pectoral muscle.

"We should clean up," Beck said after a long moment.

"Yeah, we should."

But then neither of them moved, and that felt just right, too.

Chapter 12

"I GUESS WE SHOULD'VE thought about this."

Beck shaded his eyes from the intensely hot sunshine streaming onto the sidewalk just outside the main terminal of the Charleston airport.

Micah looked over at him. "Thought about what?"

Beck felt a pulse of shame that he *hadn't* thought this through ahead of time, so they wouldn't be having this uncomfortable discussion outside the airport. Their first semi-big test as a married couple, as any kind of couple at all, and he'd let himself be completely distracted by sex.

He wasn't proud, but there was no denying it. His brain had been in his cock for the last forty-eight hours. And who could blame him when the man reaching for that cock looked like Micah Rose? Tasted like him? Groaned like him? Was completely, utterly irresistible like Micah Rose was?

"Did you end up getting a place here yet?" Beck asked. "I don't know where to tell the Uber driver to drop us off. Together or—" He hesitated, watched as comprehension dawned in Micah's eyes.

"We don't have to do anything you're not comfortable with," Beck added. "You don't *have* to come home with me. I mean . . .I guess it's *our* home, now."

Micah rolled his eyes. "It's not," he said bluntly. "It's *yours*. Honestly, I don't know, I didn't think about it." He shrugged. "I'm still staying at the short-term condo the Condors found for me after the trade. I can still stay there, if you want. Get my own place, eventually."

"Those places aren't great. They're so fucking impersonal. We both know it. You should come home with me," Beck said, when he hadn't really been intending to say that at all. He'd been intending to be a lot more reasoned with the situation. After all, there was already a shit ton of change going on, and some of it was undeniably making him itch underneath the collar, even though what he had said *was* true. Those places were terribly impersonal. He just hadn't left for Vegas thinking he'd return with a roommate—or a husband.

Micah just stared at him. Like he'd shocked him with the suggestion. Well, okay, he'd shocked both of them.

Maybe he should be honest about this. Maybe they should *both* be honest.

"Beck, we didn't even live together in college."

That was true.

They hadn't even roomed together in college because both of them had seen too many friendships fall apart with the pressure of a hundred stupid, petty disagreements. *We're better than that*, they'd always said. *We're not gonna do that shit.*

Well, it wasn't just a friendship now.

The stakes were so much higher.

"I know, but—"

"But what?" Micah questioned.

Beck started to pace.

What were the facts?

He had plenty of room. They didn't necessarily have to share a bed—or a life—even if Beck was beginning to figure out that was *exactly* what he wanted most.

Still, it was a lot, going from best friends to nothing to friends again and then to lovers and so much goddamn more.

"Come on," Micah said. "It's hot as hell right here. Let's go inside so you can have a meltdown there."

"What?" Beck yelped as Micah grabbed his arm and dragged him back through the big doors.

"You're having a meltdown, and I'm not going to have it with you in the heat," Micah said to him once the air conditioning hit them both like a blast to the face. Very patiently, Beck could add.

Very much like he was not freaking out, even though Beck was aware enough to know *he* was.

"I'm not having a meltdown." Beck tried to match Micah's reasonable voice, but he knew he didn't. It came out all high-pitched and wonky instead.

"This is a lot of change, and we know how you are with change. What did you say yesterday? You didn't know what life-altering situation to deal with first? Well, here we go. First big one."

"I thought that was where we should go to dinner last night." Beck was aware his joke was not only badly timed, but it wasn't going to help them.

Micah obviously knew it too, because he shot him a look. "You're only saying any of this about me moving in because you think you should. Because I don't have my own place here."

"Yeah, but also . . ." Beck hesitated, because it turned out both things *could* be true. He could be totally freaking out about this level of change—how when they'd left for Vegas they were still trying to even be friends and now they were *married*—and also really happy about it at the same goddamn time.

Micah raised a questioning eyebrow.

"Okay, here's the facts. I'm not lying when I say I *do* want you to. I just know it's a lot. I don't want to pressure you. I don't want to pressure myself. I've got a few guest rooms. It doesn't have to be . . .it doesn't have to be like it was in Vegas."

No, it didn't *right now*, but the moment he said it, even during his freak-out, Beck realized he had every intention of working up to that.

The end goal, at least for him, was crystal fucking clear. It was the two of them, a unified front together against the world, the way they'd always faced off against opposing defenses. The Wall on the field, and off it. But if it took time to get there, that was okay. Good things couldn't always be rushed.

The corner of Micah's mouth tilted up, and Beck's heart kicked into overdrive. "And if I want it to be like that?"

Beck felt a surge of unexpected relief. For both of them. Maybe this wouldn't be as difficult as he'd worried it might be. Maybe his meltdown had actually been a good way for them to clear the air. Make sure they were on the same page.

"Then it'll be like that," Beck said. He sounded—and *felt*, actually—a lot more confident than he'd assumed he would.

Okay, so they hadn't lived together in college. Maybe that was for the best. They'd have either ended up having sex before Micah was ready, or their friendship would've fallen apart in the middle of too many arguments about who cleaned the bathroom last.

Now, nobody had to clean a bathroom, because he absolutely loved *and* depended on his cleaning lady *and* Micah was definitely very enthusiastically on board the gay sex train.

See? Beck told himself, you've already avoided both problems.

"You're not going to freak out again?" Micah questioned.

Beck shook his head. "Nope. That's done. Freak-out over. I'm happy we decided about this."

"I don't know if *we* decided. You offered and I couldn't really resist accepting," Micah teased.

"Is that how it's gonna be?" Beck found himself relaxing into the normal rhythm of their friendship again. Thankfully.

"Absolutely."

"Guess we should get ourselves a ride home, then."

Micah raised his phone. "Before you panicked at the thought, I'd already ordered an Uber and it's on its way," he said. He shoved his hands into his pockets as they went outside.

"I know I don't have the best record for not panicking about shit," Micah said as they waited for the Uber to arrive, "but I didn't today. Guess you shouldn't have assumed I would either."

Beck elbowed him in the side. "I didn't think you were gonna freak out."

"Listen, I don't know what kind of husbands you've had before me, but *this* husband doesn't go for that separate beds bullshit."

Beck laughed.

Okay, Micah was not wrong. He had been a little preoccupied worrying about Micah panicking, and not even thinking about his own adjustment period.

"How about this?" Beck asked. "We'll get home, grab a car, and head over to your temp place, get your stuff packed up."

"There's not much," Micah said. "Most of it is in Miami, in storage."

"I guess we'll deal with that next." It was daunting, the thought of combining their two lives into one, even just logistically. Never mind everything else.

How were they going to do this?

Slowly, carefully, and with some really blunt honesty. The answer was simple, but Beck didn't know if the execution was going to be.

They were going to have lots more moments like this one.

We just have to get through this in one piece, Beck reminded himself, *because there's only one thing I can't handle and it's losing him again.*

"I guess we could've done the easy things first, and dated like normal people," Micah teased, but Beck heard the deep satisfaction in his voice. Saw the smile on his face.

He wasn't unhappy about this.

And no matter how difficult it was, ultimately Beck wasn't either.

"We'll figure it out as it comes," Beck said, leaning in and giving him a kiss. Micah's hand reached up, to his shoulder, and held him fast when he tried to make it a quick peck.

"You gotta promise me you'll be honest, even if you're worried," Micah said bluntly, his dark eyes very serious.

"How about *especially* if I'm worried?" Beck questioned.

Micah's suggestion settled something uncertain inside him. No, neither of them knew how to be committed like this. Even Beck, who'd dated more widely than Micah, still hadn't ever met anyone who'd made him want to walk down the aisle before.

His longest relationship had been a few months—and now they were hoping, if they could figure their shit out, to spend the rest of their lives together.

"Perfect." Micah was the one to lean in the rest of the way this time, and there was something miraculous about this. Micah, who'd been terrified to even walk into a gay bar eighteen months ago, feeling free enough to kiss him on a public sidewalk.

But before the kiss could go anywhere serious, Micah's phone chimed, letting them know their Uber had arrived.

The ride from the airport to the house was quiet. They'd both been public figures long enough to learn anything you said in a taxi or an Uber was fair game, at some point.

But after the car dropped them off, and Beck typed in the code to the garage letting them inside, he turned to Micah.

"Someday, you're going to have to tell me what went down in Miami."

Micah shot him a look as they walked from the garage into the house. "I *did* tell you what went down in Miami."

"No," Beck said, setting down his duffel, "you told me how things went bad. You didn't go into much detail about how they got better."

Micah's grin was immediate. "You mean, how I'm not having one gay freak-out after another?"

"That's not what I said," Beck grumbled, even though Micah was right, and it *was* what he meant.

"It's not easy not being afraid," Micah admitted. "I'm still afraid. I guess I thought coming out was the absence of fear, and it's not."

"It's not," Beck agreed. Put his arms around his man and tugged him close. How many times had they hugged like this? A million, and also, zero.

"Here, though," Beck continued after a moment, "you're safe. No fear required."

"Except the fear you're gonna banish me to the guest room," Micah joked.

"Trust me, that's not the plan."

"I guess," Micah added, like he hadn't even spoken, "if you did, I could just seduce you."

"I'm not that easy," Beck scoffed. But he was. So fucking easy.

"You're so easy. I think all I gotta do is say three words," Micah said, leaning in and pressing Beck against the kitchen counter. His breath was irresistibly warm against Beck's lips, his body a solid and reassuring yet arousing weight against Beck's own.

"Yeah?" Beck was aware of just how winded he sounded. "What three words are those?"

"I love you," Micah said and leaned in another inch.

Beck was *pretty* sure they were going to end up fucking on the floor of his kitchen in a minute, which hadn't been something he thought he'd be into, but this was Micah and it turned out he was into *everything* when it came to him—but before Micah could actually kiss him again, his phone rang.

"Ugh," Beck said.

"Turn it off," Micah murmured, nearly into his mouth. Beck felt his cock, hard against his thigh, and wanted nothing more than to reach down and feel it twitch against his palm.

Instead, he reached down and yanked his phone out of his pocket. Fully intending, as Micah had demanded, that he turn it off, and get right back to where they were.

But as he looked at the screen, Beck groaned. And not in the way he'd wanted to, either.

"I *want* to, trust me, but I don't think I can duck this one."

"Who is it?" Micah glanced down at the phone in Beck's hand. "Carter? You have to take *Carter's* call right now? Seriously?"

Beck shot him an apologetic look. "He's been texting me nonstop since well . . .since the wedding."

"And?"

"And, well, I wouldn't be surprised if he just kept calling now. It's totally his MO," Beck said. Also, he knew what Carter wanted and despite his promise with Micah to be honest with each other less than an hour ago, he was already tempted to break it, just so he wouldn't have to confess what Carter kept harping about.

"Let's test that theory," Micah said, plucking the phone from Beck's hands and pressing the decline call button. He tossed the phone on the counter and was just about to lean in again, both of them eager for another kiss, when the phone, unsurprisingly, began to ring again.

"Goddamn it," Micah groaned, dropping his forehead down to Beck's shoulder. "He's the worst."

"Or the best, maybe? He's been pestering me about throwing us a party." Beck hesitated. "A bachelor party."

Micah laughed. "Isn't it a little late for that?"

"Probably. But he's trying to be a friend and I'm thinking we should let him."

"He should be a friend by not cockblocking me," Micah complained.

"How about not cockblocking *us*?" Beck grinned and pressed the answer call button.

"Hey, you're alive," Carter announced matter-of-factly. "Are you still deep in a sex coma or have you finally recovered?"

After all Carter's texts, Beck had finally answered before they'd gone to dinner last night, claiming that he was busy. That they were *both* busy.

In response, Carter had texted back that a sex coma wasn't a good enough reason to go MIA. Which was rich considering that Carter seemingly spent half of his life in a sex coma.

"We're fine," Beck said.

"*We're*," Carter drawled out with exaggerated emphasis.

"Better get used to that."

"Oh, I am. It's already happened. You two are gonna be the super duper cutest couple. Maybe we could host you in a death cage match at the Pirate's Booty against Riley and Landry for most adorable couple of all time. I think we'd give you the edge, though, 'cause you love each other so much, you got *married*."

Beck rolled his eyes. "No death cage matches, please."

"Bummer. What about bachelor parties?"

"About that . . ." Beck exchanged glances with Micah, who just shrugged.

Like it was inevitable, so maybe better to just give in now.

"Are you seriously gonna bail? From your own bachelor party? I even convinced a couple of guys to stick around in town through Thursday, so they could come."

"We're not bailing. We're just setting some parameters," Beck said.

Micah motioned to him, and Beck lowered the phone from his ear and set it on speaker.

"Hey, Carter," Micah said.

"Oh my god, it's the other half of the happy couple!" Carter exclaimed.

"I'm still confused why we need a bachelor party," Micah said. "We're already married."

Beck kept thinking he was going to get used to Micah declaring that so proudly, like it was one of the best things he'd ever done, but each and every time it happened, it felt freaking magical.

Terrifying, also. But first and foremost, it was magical.

"We want to celebrate with you, this is a big deal," Carter said persuasively. "Y'all could've just dated, but you went out there and made the most declarative statement you possibly could. Kudos for that, by the way."

Yeah, they fucking had. *God*, what had they been thinking?

Beck still wasn't sure. He only knew one thing: he loved Micah Rose.

"You told me last year you didn't believe in marriage," Beck inserted before Carter could continue waxing rhapsodic about how amazing their marriage was.

They'd been married less than seventy-two hours. They didn't know how to be married yet, never mind how to make it amazing.

"Not for *me*," Carter said. "But there's nothing wrong with me thinking you guys were already goddamned attached at the hip even before you walked down the aisle."

"We weren't," Micah said weakly.

Beck agreed with him. After all, how could you be attached at the hip if you hadn't spoken to each other for eighteen months?

But, Beck was afraid Carter also had a good point.

Even when they hadn't been speaking, they'd still belonged to each other.

"You just keep tellin' yourself that, but *we* believe differently," Carter said firmly.

"Alright, so when is this super-special party?" Beck said, trying to change the subject.

"Aw, already thinking it's gonna be special! I'm touched," Carter cooed.

"Carter," Beck warned.

"This Thursday night, and I've rented out the whole Pirate's Booty for our pleasure, so anything is gonna go, okay?"

"Carter," Beck warned again.

"And if that means strippers, then that means strippers."

"You realize we're both gay, right?" Micah reminded him.

"Well, duh. I got *male* strippers, okay? I don't discriminate. You know that."

"Unfortunately all too well," Beck said. "We're leaving for Chicago the next morning so it can't get too wild or too crazy. Just remember that when you're trying to rein in your over-the-top impulses, okay?"

"You mean, not too wild or too crazy like . . .I don't know . . .an impromptu Vegas wedding?" Carter asked archly.

"Point taken," Micah retorted dryly.

"I'm still bummed I wasn't there. If I'd known you two were going to go nuts in Vegas, I'd have stayed, too."

"I'm actually surprised you didn't," Beck said.

"I had a date."

"AKA you had an orgy planned." Micah grinned at Beck. "It's alright. We get it."

"You sure do." Carter was smiling; Beck could hear it in his voice. "Anyway, *no*, it will not get too wild and crazy on your end. Just some strippers, and some Kieran signature drink specials and well . . .a few other fun things up my sleeve."

"Carter," Beck warned. He was becoming a broken record.

"No, seriously, I mean it when I said they'd be fun. They will be. I promise. You'll like them. *All* of them."

Beck exchanged another glance with Micah. Maybe they *had* already been sort of married, because he could tell what the guy was thinking without even having to ask.

"Alright," Beck conceded. "We'll see you Thursday."

"And seriously, man," Micah added, "it means a lot you wanted to do this for us."

"Yeah, definitely," Beck echoed.

"Well, show up like you mean that," Carter teased.

After Beck hung up, he glanced over at Micah, who was lean-ing against the edge of the counter, a thoughtful expression on his face. "I could've told him no," Beck said. "If you really didn't want to do this kind of thing."

"What kind of thing?" Micah asked, raising an eyebrow. "The out-and-proud thing? I think that ship sailed when we marched down the aisle and then told the whole world about it after."

"Well, *that*, but also . . . I don't know . . . pushing this marriage thing."

"Aren't you the one who announced you didn't want to get divorced?"

Yes, that had been him. But he'd also seen a future where he lost Micah over this and that was unacceptable—and it was *still* unacceptable.

"I just mean, we don't have to be, like, embracing it. We can go whatever speed you want. Or we want, I guess. We can dial it back, even, and just date, if that works better. There's no pressure. I . . ." Beck hesitated. "I love you, and I want to be with you. But not just for a little while. Not until the pressure gets too intense and we fall apart because we pushed too hard, too fast. I'm in this, and I want you to be in this too. So if that means putting the marriage stuff on hold for now . . ."

"I don't know what any of this means. I don't know what it means to be dating you or married to you. I just know . . ." Micah took a deep breath. "I just know I've wanted to be *with* you forever. So however that works, however *we* work, that's what we're going with. That sound good to you?"

"I guess we're going to the bachelor party then," Beck said, grinning.

Micah's answering smile was slow and devastating, the look in his eyes so affectionate and fond Beck didn't know how he hadn't been aware of his feelings from the beginning.

Scott called when they'd just gotten in the door from grabbing the rest of Micah's stuff.

It was both terrible timing and also really great timing because no matter how good of a game Micah knew he kept talking, he still didn't know what the fuck he was doing.

He didn't even know how to date anyone. He definitely did not know how to be *married*.

Now that they were at Beck's house—Micah knew he wouldn't be thinking of it as *his* for some time, or maybe ever, no matter what Beck claimed—and all the pressing, immediate needs had been taken care of, he had no clue what he was supposed to do now.

He had a feeling Beck didn't either, because the first thing when they got in the door with Micah's stuff, he claimed he had urgent errands to run.

"I'm gonna run to the store, grab some stuff for dinner and the next few days, before we leave for Chicago," Beck said, as Micah glanced down at his ringing phone. He'd put Scott off once before, with a text that he'd explain later, when the news had first broken of their Vegas wedding, but clearly he was not going to be put off again.

And that was a whole other thing he was not prepared to deal with—how were they going to deal with the nitty-gritty of starting a life together?

Because that was what this was, wasn't it?

"Sure," Micah said. "I'm just gonna take this."

"No problem, I'll be back soon. I remember just what you like." Beck's grin was affectionate, if not still a little wary. Micah got it. He was freaking out, too.

He let himself out onto the big screen porch as he answered the call, his palm slick against the back of his phone.

"I thought I told you to *not* to do anything stupid in Vegas," Scott said reproachfully. "You *married* him. I told you to figure out how to be his friend!"

"Like you didn't marry Coach," Micah retorted. "You did it the first chance you got."

Scott sighed, a deep rumble. "Micah."

"I love him, you know." It was getting easier to admit it. Each time he said it to Beck, it was easier to say it to himself. It still wasn't *easy* to say it to anyone else, but Scott wasn't just anyone else, either.

Beck had wanted to know who or what had changed him in Miami.

The answer began and ended with Scott Callaway. He'd seen the prickly defensiveness radiating out of Micah and had somehow known exactly what flavor of pain he'd been trying to hide from and every bit of shame that had threatened to consume him.

Scott had been the first one he'd truly been honest with, and each person he'd confessed the truth to after had been easier.

He'd been telling the truth to Beck earlier: coming out wasn't the absence of fear; it was deciding, one person at a time, that there was something more important than that fear.

Scott had taught him that.

"I know, son," Scott said gently.

"But what the fuck am I doing?" Fear clogged his throat. Leaked into his voice. He'd tried to keep it hidden from Beck, who didn't deserve it, but he didn't care if Scott heard it. "I don't know how to do this. I don't know . . ."

The inventory of things he was suddenly, painfully aware that he didn't know felt far too long to even begin listing.

"I don't think anyone knows how to do this."

"Beck sure does," Micah said. "He's . . . well, the first fucking thing he said to me was he didn't want to get divorced. He *wants* this."

"And so do you," Scott reminded him.

"I *do*. God, that's the problem. What if I fuck it up?"

"Oh, you're gonna do that, *guaranteed*." Scott chuckled. "Trust me on this one."

"I thought you were supposed to be reassuring me," Micah complained.

"Marriage isn't doing everything perfectly. Marriage is promising to do it anyway. Even when you fuck up. *Especially* when you fuck up."

"Is that supposed to make me feel better?" Because it didn't at all. God, he *was* going to fuck this up, and losing Beck, now that he knew what it was like to have him, was basically going to kill him. Staying away before had been the hardest thing he'd ever done, but he'd done it because at the time, he'd believed it was for the best. It was only later he'd figured out that was a big lie he'd told himself just because he'd been too afraid to tell himself the truth.

Too afraid of what admitting the truth to Beck would mean.

Too afraid of anyone ever knowing who he really was.

Now people knew. A *lot* of people knew, and it wasn't as terrible as he'd always imagined. But losing Beck? It would be so much worse than anything his imagination could come up with.

Scott chuckled. "Shit, no. But you love him, right? And he loves you."

"Yeah." Micah paused. "Not sure why, but he does. He actually was the one who said it first."

"That why you dragged him down the aisle?" Scott teased.

"I think we kinda dragged each other. But no. We didn't . . . he didn't . . .not until after."

"Ballsy," Scott observed, chuckling under his breath.

"Don't remind me." Micah stared out at the backyard Beck was so proud of. Beck was building a life here. And now, he'd invited Micah to join him. Not easily. But then, if Beck hadn't struggled with the consequences, hadn't freaked out earlier, Micah wouldn't have thought he really meant it.

Was this the life Micah wanted? He didn't know. He just knew ultimately *Beck* was the life he wanted.

"You're gonna be fine, you know. I know this wasn't how you expected any of this to happen, but it's done now. Nothing to do but embrace it and move forward."

"Right."

"You hear from your mom?" Scott asked.

"She sent a text, but I didn't text her back." He hesitated. "I didn't know what to say."

"She happy for you at least?"

"I think she was more confused than anything else." Micah couldn't even blame his mother for that. After all, the world had been pretty fucking confused right along with her. At least his mother had known he was gay. She hadn't had any idea, just like the rest of the world, that he'd been in love with Beckett West.

That had been brand fucking new.

"You're going to have to talk to her eventually."

"Eventually."

"Does Beck know?"

Micah sighed.

"I take it that's a *no*. No good is gonna come from you keepin' secrets, Micah."

"It's humiliating, okay? His family's awesome and big and accepting. They want to see me while we're there, this weekend. They're over-the-moon. Confused, too, sure, but their first reaction was *happiness*."

He wasn't jealous of Beck's family; he *wasn't*. But only because he didn't let himself. Only because he refused to let that come between them, not when they had so much other shit to overcome.

"I get it." Scott did, too. He'd come from this small-ass town in Alabama, and his family's attitude—frankly from what Scott had told him, the whole town's fucking attitude—had kept him in the closet for most of his adult life.

But one of the first things Scott had ever told him was to not make his mistakes. To not give other people the power to rule his own life.

"I know you do. Doesn't fix it though," Micah said ruefully.

"Nothing fixes it. You know that." Scott's voice was soft. Gentle. Accepting and understanding.

He was the second person, behind Beck, who'd embraced him exactly as he was, even after seeing all the ugliness in front of *and* behind the walls he'd thrown up.

Micah squeezed his eyes shut. He hadn't wanted to leave Scott, who'd become practically the father he'd never had a chance to have, the family that had accepted him wholeheartedly, but he'd had to leave Miami.

He'd known he would miss Scott—and the other guys, too, and of course, Coach. But he hadn't anticipated that he'd end up in Charleston, struggling not to drown under the wave of feelings he had for Beck.

He'd truly believed that it would take ages to earn Beck's forgiveness. Even a place in his life as a friend.

He'd never imagined that a few weeks into his time here that he'd be here, in Beck's house, sleeping next to him in his bed.

It might be a good kind of shock, but it was still a huge fucking shock.

"It'll be good to see you next week," Micah said, changing the subject. He didn't want to talk about his mother. Or think about her. Or wonder what the hell he was going to tell Beck when he figured out the truth.

In a week and a half, the Piranhas were coming to Charleston for their first of two scheduled games this year.

It was funny, before all this, Micah had been sorta dreading the Piranhas coming to town. But now he longed for the feeling of certainty Scott always gave him.

He knew he was going to have to find it in himself. But that didn't mean it was going to be easy.

Progress, Scott would say, *doesn't ever come easy.*

"You gonna introduce me to your husband?" Scott teased. "'Cause I sure wanna meet him."

"Yeah, of course. I want you two to meet. To . . .well, to know each other. That's part of it, right? This whole combining-two-lives-into-one business?"

"It's a start," Scott told him dryly. "But it's a little more than that. You know, it wasn't easy for us, Asa and me. We'd both been alone for too long, too stubborn, too stuck in our own ways."

"And you never just let him get away with his bullshit," Micah pointed out.

Scott sighed. "And then there's that, too. He wouldn't want me to, even when he's pissed as hell at me for calling him out on it."

"That's something I already told Beck. We gotta be honest with each other." Guilt threatened to rise, but Micah swallowed it down.

"Son, you gotta tell him."

"I will. At some point."

"He's gonna figure it out and you wanna do it *before* that. You were close before. He knows you. He knows your family."

"I know." The knowledge lay heavy on him. Inescapable. But things were so good. He wasn't ready to lay this on Beck yet, because knowing Beck, he would want to share some of the load. And Micah loved him too much to let him.

"What I'm saying is that it wasn't easy to do this whole couple thing," Scott said. "Of course, some parts were easier than others . . ."

"Ew, gross. Old man sex."

"Hey, you watch it," Scott retorted with amusement. "But like I was saying, it wasn't easy. Take it slow. You don't have to do it all at once. You at his place now?"

"Yeah, he wanted me to come here. I hadn't really gotten a place in Charleston yet, so it made sense."

"And because you wanted to," Scott added.

It was a reminder that Scott knew him better than just about anyone.

"Yeah," Micah admitted, "because I wanted to."

"It's a good start. You're lucky to not have to worry about money, which is the one thing that stresses most couples out. 'Course, you got a few extra burdens too. You figure out how this is gonna affect you on the field?"

"If I did, I wouldn't tell you," Micah teased.

"Oh, please. I already know you're gonna bring it with everything you got. The Piranhas have a target painted on them this year. I get it."

"I don't think much is gonna change, to be honest," Micah admitted. "We're solid out there. Just because we're together now, officially, I can't see that affecting us much—unless we get even better."

"You played great in the Vegas game, for sure." That was high praise coming from Scott, who was a fantastic defensive coach.

"Thanks, Dad."

He heard Scott's eye roll through the phone. "Still don't hate that," he pointed out.

"Good," Micah said. It was the first time he'd admitted that. Maybe the first time he'd called Scott his father without the ironic twist to his voice. Without pretending it was all just a silly joke.

"You know, if you need anything, anything at all, I'm just a phone call away," Scott reminded him. "Don't let this shit that you play for a different team give you an excuse be a stranger or be miserable even though you don't have to."

"Okay." Micah hadn't imagined Scott would abandon him or their friendship after he'd been traded to the Condors, but it felt unexpectedly good to hear to him say it out loud.

"And we'll see you soon, alright?"

"Yeah." Micah's hand tightened on his phone. Out of nowhere, his throat clogged. "Means a lot. Thanks. For everything," he added.

"Of course." Scott's voice grew soft and gruff. "You're one of us, you know that? No matter what uniform you're wearing."

"I know." Micah wanted to believe it.

When he hung up, he spent a minute still staring out at the pristine stretch of green lawn he had a feeling Beck babied.

He wasn't sure he'd ever give a shit about grass, but he couldn't deny it was nice to have such a gorgeous, comfortable place to hang out.

Maybe next time they had a party, at least *after* Carter's bachelor party, they could host it here.

Micah hadn't thought he'd ever be the host type, but then that was the point, right? He was still figuring out who he was, and what this fresh start looked like.

And that, as Scott had told him a thousand times, was okay—but for the first time, Micah realized he was starting to actually believe it.

Still, he wanted to be mostly unpacked, whatever that meant, by the time Beck got home from the grocery store. Maybe they could avoid more awkwardness that way.

He took his bags up. Beck had told him there was room in the closet in the owner's suite.

Okay, sure, he'd joked plenty of times about how he was the kind of husband who liked to share a bed, but still, it was humbling walking into Beck's private sanctuary and realizing it wasn't just his anymore.

But theirs.

Shit.

Micah's fingers went numb on the handles of his bags as he stood in the doorway.

There was a big bed. The dark green covers were pulled up, a bunch of pillows scattered across the headboard, but none of it was particularly neat.

Micah's heart clenched.

This was the real Beck; it wasn't a picture-perfect, idealized version.

He bypassed the bed, because that was something he'd deal with later, and headed toward the closet.

It was a big closet, but of course, since this was Beck they were talking about, it was only about a third full.

Micah shook his head. He didn't see the point of bringing all his furniture up here, since Beck's house was already fully furnished, but he sure as shit was going to have all his clothes shipped up here, first chance he got. Beck had the room and maybe he could convince him to up his own game while he was at it.

"Doubtful," Micah muttered to himself as he began to unpack his suitcases. No matter how much shit he'd given Beck over the years, he was still only vaguely interested in what he wore.

For someone so ridiculously good-looking, Micah thought it was a waste.

Of course, on the plus side, Beck never wanting to draw attention meant Micah had him all to himself. And he *definitely* could appreciate that.

He finished unpacking his clothes and moved onto the bathroom.

It was huge, tiled in gray and white marble, with a shower that could easily fit the entire Condors defense.

Well, they were one hundred percent taking advantage of that, Micah decided.

There were two sinks on the big vanity, and it was clear Beck only used one side. Micah took the other, realizing as he finished up, sticking his toothbrush in the holder next to Beck's, that maybe this wasn't so scary after all.

They were just things, right? They'd avoided moving in together during college. Micah had claimed it was because he didn't want living together to ruin their friendship but also because he'd known there was no way he could ever keep his big secret if they had.

So they had no practical experience doing this.

Micah could already see the advantages. The shower, the big, comfortable-looking bed. The way his heart beat a little faster when he heard Beck downstairs calling out, "Honey, I'm home."

Micah headed towards the stairs and met Beck at the bottom.

"I thought I was your sweetheart," Micah teased.

Beck leaned and kissed him. Why? Probably just because he could—and Micah could get behind that.

"You're everything," Beck said simply, his eyes glowing as he leaned back. Maybe he hadn't talked to Scott like Micah had, but the time to adjust had helped him. Micah could see it in his face. "You get settled in alright?"

"Yeah, I think so."

"Good. I'm happy you're here, you know?"

Maybe it wasn't easy to be honest about everything, but it *was* easy to be honest about this. "I'm happy too," Micah said.

CHAPTER 13

BECK SHOULD'VE KNOWN THAT warning Carter away from excess when it came to the bachelor party was only going to ensure there was *more* of it.

He got out of the Uber and stared at the enormous balloon banner currently hung across the no longer low-key entrance to the Pirate's Booty.

Happy Fucking, it read, with much smaller letters beneath it, *Plus Marriage.* Clusters of balloons in a dozen rainbow colors sat on either side.

"Well," Beck said, staring at the sign. "*Well.*"

"You did tell him," Micah said. But he didn't sound mad, he just sounded amused.

"I can't believe Kieran let him put this up," Beck said.

"Who's Kieran?"

"He's the bartender and I guess the owner of the bar, too. Part-owner? I'm not sure."

"And he wouldn't want to wish us happy fucking?" Micah raised an eyebrow.

Beck choked on his breath. He was *still* not used to Micah saying shit like that. Especially when they'd woken up this morning, in the lazy, quiet dawn, in the same bed, and it had made every bit of sense in the world to pull him close and kiss him until they were frantically thrusting their bodies together, in too much of a rush to bother with taking their underwear off.

Beck still didn't know how to be married, *still* freaked out every once in awhile, but he could definitely keep doing *that* for the rest of his life.

"What?" Micah laughed. "If we're gonna do it, we can *say* it."

Beck shot him a look, and though he hadn't meant it to, it lingered down Micah's body, the long lines of it clad in a black-and-white checked suit, a white T-shirt underneath that he already knew clung to his chest and abs and left absolutely nothing to the imagination.

He'd already fantasized half a dozen times about removing that shirt with his teeth and Micah hadn't even been wearing it for half an hour yet.

"Don't say shit you can't back up," Beck said in a dark voice. "You know what that does to me."

"Who said I can't back it up?" Micah chuckled. "But that's gonna have to wait. Come on, let's go see Carter." He offered his hand, and it felt so right to reach out and just take it.

Micah's palm was warm and a little damp in his own. Maybe he was nervous too, just the same as Beck.

The last time they'd seen their teammates, they still hadn't figured out if they were just friends, or something more. They hadn't been together like this.

They hadn't been *married*.

Micah pushed open the door and they walked inside.

The Pirate's Booty looked much the same as it had last time he'd been in here—dark and a little grimy, with splashes of green from the plant wall on one side and the trio of palm trees, looking a little worse for the wear, in the corner.

But stretched across the big shiny bar was half the Condors team.

Including Coach Kelley *and* Mr. G, the owner of the team.

Beck really considered hightailing it back out of there, but then Micah's fingers tightened on his. He'd never have guessed, from the easy openness on his face, that he was nervous or anxious, but it was there, in the tight grip of his hand.

Beck squeezed back, and they went to face the music.

Carter bounded up first, unquestionably *thrilled* they'd finally arrived. "Took you long enough!" he crowed. "Kieran, drinks for the happy couple!"

"Carter," Beck said cautiously, but Carter was bouncing on his toes, excitement written clearly across his face, and he wasn't taking anything slowly. Instead, he tugged them both into a big, tight hug.

"Congrats, guys, really."

"On the fucking or the marriage?" Micah asked with a straight face.

"Obviously *both*," Carter exclaimed. He slung an arm around Beck's shoulders and guided them towards the rest of the crowd.

"Congrats," Deacon said dryly, from the spot where he was leaning against the bar. "You know you could've just *dated*."

"Yeah, my thoughts exactly," Jem chimed in, lifting his glass in a mock toast. "And yet, I get it, you know?"

Deacon raised an eyebrow. "You do?"

"I don't know, I think it's kinda cute. Romantic, even." Jem gestured towards their intertwined hands. No doubt it looked like they were hanging onto each other for dear life, because well . . . they *were*.

"Thanks, I think?" Beck said.

"No, seriously, we're thrilled for you two," Jem said, his face crinkling with a big smile. "Deacon's just being Deacon over here. Mr. Doom and Gloom."

Deacon glared at him. "I hate it when you call me that."

"Well, don't be doomy *or* gloomy, then," Jem retorted. He tugged Beck and then Micah into a hug. "Seriously, we're really happy for you. Even Deacon, though he has a funny way of expressing it."

"*Especially* me," Deacon said and set his beer down, putting his hands on Beck's shoulders. "This is gonna be great for both of you."

"That's the idea," Beck said. *That's the hope.*

"And," Deacon added, with a sudden, lopsided smile, "if this brings the Wall back, I'm *especially* good with it."

"Deacon!" Jem said, smacking him on the side of the head. "Not everything is about football."

"Damn straight," Carter said.

It took the next half an hour to go through all the players and coaches who'd shown up to the party. At some point Carter stuck a bottle of beer in Beck's hands, which he took gratefully, and a drink that was bright blue and impossibly sparkly into Micah's. He glanced at it with a perplexed expression, but then drank it anyway.

"I wasn't sure I should come, but then I thought, you might be worried I didn't approve if I didn't show, so here I am," Mr. G said a little awkwardly, after shaking both of their hands.

"So we're not in any trouble?" Micah questioned. They'd known that—mostly, anyway. Nicole had said so, the morning she'd come to see them in Vegas.

"'Course not." Mr. G looked surprised then. "This is a great story. I'm happy for you two. Playing together again must've been a good thing."

"Real good," Beck said, then tried not to look just as uncomfortable as Mr. G had. *Own it*, he decided. *Maybe you weren't happy he traded for Micah, but then he did, and look what happened. It's the best thing that's ever happened to you.* "Actually, about that. I . . .I'm real grateful that you traded for him."

Mr. G's smile was knowing. "Good. I'm glad. Now I'd better be going, before Carter continues with whatever he's got up his sleeve."

"You think there's more?" Micah said.

Beck supposed it was still early, but he'd assumed maybe Carter had decided against hiring any strippers.

But this *was* Carter Maxwell.

Mr. G laughed. "I'm not sure about anything, but whatever he does, I *am* sure I don't want to be present for it, and none of you do either. I'll see you two later." He gestured and a lot of the coaching staff began heading out, too.

"You scare off Mr. G?" Landry asked. He leaned against the bar, Riley tucked under his arm next to him. The two of them looked like they belonged together.

Beck wondered if he and Micah gave off the same vibes—or if they looked unsure, like they were still figuring their shit out.

"He probably decided it was better to bug out before Carter trotted out any of his fun plans," Riley teased. "I'm still waiting to see what they are."

"Who is he kidding? It's totally a stripper. Maybe a couple of strippers. Coming out of a gigantic cake, maybe?"

"I tried to tell him *no* strippers," Beck said, semi-apologetically.

Riley grinned. "Why? It's your bachelor party."

"Yes, but—" Beck tried to argue, but then Micah turned to him and silenced him with a kiss.

It wasn't any kind of quick peck either. It was long and sweet and Beck couldn't help but fall into it, head swimming with desire when Micah finally pulled back.

"Stop arguing," he murmured. "Don't worry, I won't get jealous if you check out the stripper."

"I didn't . . .I wouldn't . . ." Beck stammered. He knew his cheeks were flaming bright red. He wished he hadn't bothered shaving off his scruff this afternoon, thinking he'd wanted to at least attempt looking decently put together. There'd been no hope of looking even a fraction as good as Micah did, but he hadn't wanted him to be ashamed of being seen together either.

"It's alright," Landry said with an easy smile. "I think we all know what you *really* like, Beck. Or should I say *who*?"

"Yeah, not exactly a secret when he kisses you like that," Riley agreed.

"Uh, yeah." God, when was he going to stop going so red and tripping over his own goddamn words?

Landry turned to Riley. "Carter told me they could take us in a cutest couple on the Condors death match, and I thought, absolutely no fucking way. But then . . ."

"Yeah," Riley agreed. His voice was deeper and rougher than Beck could remember. And he saw Riley's hand tightening around Landry's waist, his knuckles glowing white in the dim lighting of the bar.

Had they . . .had they turned Riley and Landry on with that kiss?

Well, it wasn't probably outrageous. He'd caught sight of Landry and Riley making out a few times in corners at the Pirate's Booty that they probably thought were a hell of a lot darker than they actually were. But seeing them together hadn't ever aroused him. Instead, he'd only felt a painful throb of something he probably could've called envy if he hadn't been determined not to look too closely at it.

He'd been hurting so much from losing Micah.

But you haven't lost him now.

"Carter!" He raised his voice, carrying it over the inevitable noise of way too many football players in one small space. "Where's this fun surprise I was promised?"

"Oh, right here, my darling," Carter called back. He appeared in front of them, dangling a rainbow-spangled sparkly garter in one hand. "Who's game?"

A cheer went up through the crowd.

"Do I want to know what we have to do with that?" Beck asked, pouring the rest of his beer down his throat. He was probably going to need it if Carter wanted them to do anything remotely like his imagination was currently conjuring.

"You wanna get creative?" Carter waggled his eyebrows.

But to Beck's surprise, before he could retort that this whole party had been *Carter's idea*, Micah plucked it from Carter's hand and gestured towards Beck. "Come on," he said, "sit on your throne, baby, and let me take it off you."

"Is that the idea?" Beck's heart stuttered at the thought of Micah being so obvious. That around these guys, some of whom he was still getting to know, he felt like he could be his real, true self.

"Do I have to ask you twice?" Micah asked sternly, and that sent a thrill through an entirely different body part.

"No, no," Beck stammered. He took the garter from Micah. It had clearly been meant for a much smaller person, with *much* smaller thighs, because it was tiny. Hopefully it was made with elastic of a decent quality or else it was going to snap before he even got it halfway up his leg. "Where do you want me?"

Carter catcalled as Micah gestured to an open table. "Right here, baby," he cooed.

And okay, he was not typically into PDA, or exhibitionism for that matter, but there was something completely hypnotic and in-credibly fucking arousing about Micah like this. Taking control of the situation—*and* him—and directing both of them exactly where he wanted them.

His cock was already half-hard in his slacks and if Micah did what he imagined . . .well, nothing was going to be left to *anyone's* imagination.

But maybe that was okay.

It is *okay.* The love shining in Micah's dark eyes promised that it would be.

That *they* would be.

Beck's butt hit the edge of the table, and as he lifted himself up, praying the table was made of the same stern stuff as the garter, Carter whooped.

He slid the garter up, debating how far he should put it.

That's just high enough, the angel on one shoulder proclaimed, while the devil on the other crooned that it should go *so much higher.*

He wasn't proud of who he listened to as he took it one inch past the knee and then another and then another until it was nearly at his crotch and the elastic was straining under the sheer circumference of his thigh. But it held.

Micah's gaze, intent on him, darkened as he approached. He slipped his jacket from his shoulders. His broad, gorgeously muscled shoulders. Beck swallowed hard because he'd been right; the t-shirt revealed more than it hid: his hard nipples, the shadows between his pecs, and the ripples of his abs.

Jesus, the man was fucking gorgeous, and Beck knew he wasn't alone in thinking it.

But, *but*, he knew at the end of the night, it would be Beck's bed he would be naked in.

Tonight, and for every night after.

Micah bent down, and wiggled his hips at the enthusiastic applause that greeted him approaching Beck.

"I think he's got this," Carter called out.

"Oh, he's got it alright," Deacon retorted, and everyone laughed.

But the humor was understandably short-lived, because Beck knew he wasn't the only one who could see and identify exactly what that look was in Micah's eyes as he knelt at Beck's feet, his elbows resting on the edge of the table between Beck's legs.

"You ready, baby?" But Micah's words were low and quiet, for Beck alone.

Probably he was asking—*can I do this and you won't lose control completely and hump my face until neither one of us gives a shit who's watching anymore?*

Honestly, Beck wasn't sure. But he nodded anyway.

"Yeah, sweetheart," he said. "Do it."

Every movement of Micah's was sensual grace as he slithered closer, his back a glorious line of muscle under that tight, practically transparent T-shirt.

Jesus, it was a wonder he'd ever let this man out of bed.

Every inch of his body deserved to be worshipped.

His chest brushed against Beck's knee. Then his thigh. His tongue flicked out and Beck went lightheaded at the hot, damp press of it through the light fabric of his slacks.

Which . . .he wished he'd worn jeans. Maybe with the thicker, more constraining fabric, his rock-hard cock might not be quite so obvious.

But Micah saw it—he couldn't help but see it—and probably so did everyone else. But then Micah's face swayed closer, so close Beck could practically feel the warmth of his breath against it. Then he dipped his head and, licking his lips, grasped the edge of the garter with just his teeth.

The entire room was yelling and hooting, but the sound faded away to a muted roar as Micah carefully, gently, insistently tugged the garter down his thigh, hitting his knee and then his calf and then lower as it finally popped over his outstretched foot.

Not once did Micah's eyes leave his.

Beck gripped the edge of the table, and it took every ounce of self-control to not grasp Micah by his shirt and drag him up and kiss him.

"Shots!" Carter yelled, his face appearing next to Micah's. He handed one to Beck and one to Micah.

Beck didn't miss that as Micah tossed the tequila back, his hands were shaking.

Beck's weren't exactly steady.

Then before he could overthink it, he did exactly what he'd dreamed about, and grasping Micah by his shirt collar, hauled him between his legs and kissed him hard and insistent, his tongue brushing against Micah's.

Micah gasped into his mouth as the kiss turned downright dirty.

Distantly, Beck heard Carter whooping loudly, and an even louder round of cheers.

Beck broke the kiss, but Micah didn't pull away, resting his forehead against Beck's, their lips only a breath away still.

Why had he thought it was a good idea to come out here tonight? They should be at his house, in his bed, in *their* bed, so he could cash in on the promise of that kiss.

Beck was half a second away from going total caveman and just dragging Micah outside, when an offended screech he was *pretty* sure could've only originated with Carter forced him to look away from his husband.

From his husband.

He was really not used to that yet.

Maybe the key to the whole adjustment was that he was never getting used to it.

That he never took it for granted.

"This is outrageous," Carter was saying as Beck finally looked up to see what the hell was going on.

"Man, I don't know what to tell you," Deacon said, thumping Carter hard on the back, "but I think we can live without a stripper. Strippers, plural? Whatever you had planned."

"Yeah, we already got a show," Jem teased.

Beck flushed again. "Yeah, we're good," he said, praying he wouldn't stutter over his words. It felt like not only had all his blood left his brain recently but semi-*permanently*.

Carter snapped his fingers. "I got it," he said. He turned towards the bar, where Kieran was pouring drinks. "Turn the music up, baby!"

"I'm confused," Deacon said, glancing from Carter to Kieran. "Did they—"

"No way. Kieran's got better taste than that," Jem teased.

"Hey, I heard that," Carter retorted, head whipping around as he headed towards the bar.

"Besides," Jem continued, "I heard he was already dating someone."

"Really? Who?" Landry wondered.

Jem shrugged. "I just heard him talking on the phone the other night, and it was definitely not how you'd talk to a friend."

"Interesting," Micah said.

"Seems like you two weren't the only couple on the DL," Deacon said with a chuckle, which stopped abruptly as he realized just what Carter had meant when he'd said *I got it.*

Because he was currently standing on top of the bar, Kieran's face behind him looking quasi-murderous—*yep*, Beck decided, *whoever Kieran's mysteriously dating, it's definitely not Carter*—and wiggled to whatever music was playing on the sound system.

"What are you doing?" Deacon called at Carter as he began to lift his T-shirt, exposing what was—no question—a very nice set of abs.

"Providing the entertainment," Carter called back. He turned and shook his ass in a way that Beck could at least admit was very stripper-esque.

Which, really, was not that surprising when it came down to it.

If any of them probably had the ability to moonlight as a stripper, it was Carter.

Deacon and Jem exchanged glances, like they were trying to decide which of them had drawn the metaphorical short straw and would have to get up on the bar and somehow wrestle Carter off it before he decided to take *all* his clothes off.

But before either of them could do anything, Micah was moving towards the bar and before Beck could reach out and ask what the fuck he was doing, he was climbing up too.

The whole bar cheered as he stood up next to Carter.

"Hey," Carter chirped happily. "Look who it is! Half of our happily married couple!"

Micah waved, a little sheepishly.

"What's he doing?" Deacon asked Beck.

But Beck just shrugged. He had no clue what Micah was doing. Was he going to strip right along with Carter? Beck didn't know but whatever happened, he knew Micah well enough to know that he would definitely enjoy it.

Micah didn't know what the fuck he was doing.

Why had he gotten up here on the bar? With *Carter* of all people?

The music was good, though, and it was easy enough to reach out and take Carter's hands. His smile was full of so much of irresistible charm and irrepressible happiness, it was impossible not to smile right back.

Or to start grooving to the music.

Kieran turned it up again, and Carter, not surprisingly, was a pretty good dancer.

He glanced out in the audience below them, finding Beck immediately.

He was dancing too, so badly Micah could only laugh, love squeezing his heart in a vise grip.

"You've got moves," Carter told him, still grinning. "I can see what Beck saw in you."

Micah raised an eyebrow as the song came to a close, and he bowed, right along with Carter, approving shouts growing louder as he jumped down off the bar. Carter followed behind him.

"Honey, that was spectacular," Beck said, hand around his waist, tugging him close. "*And* you kept Carter from taking his clothes off," he murmured into Micah's ear.

"I thought that *was* the spectacular part," Micah teased.

"The happy couple, folks!" Deacon called out, raising Beck's other hand. "Give them one last big congrats, 'cause I'm sure they've got other things they wanna do tonight than just party with us."

Carter whooped at that, but Deacon just shot him a grin. "It's true," he insisted.

It *was* true.

Beck met Micah's questioning glance. "Yeah, it's time," he agreed.

Ten minutes and two shots of tequila later, they were in an Uber, headed back to Beck's house.

It still wasn't *their* house, but . . .Micah was getting used to it being *his* now, too. Mostly because of whose it was. Wherever Beck was, that was home.

"You're quiet," Beck said, nudging him. "That last shot wasn't too much for you, was it?"

"No way," Micah said, chuckling. "But that Kieran guy, at least he stocks top-shelf tequila."

Beck squeezed his knee, and then his hand drifted up higher. "So you're okay?"

"I was thinking of something," Micah confessed.

"Hmmm?"

"Turns out, the Beckett West Husband Experience is actually pretty great." It shouldn't have come out as such a confession. After all, Beck already knew he loved him. Knew he'd loved him for ages before Micah had ever done anything about it.

"Thanks, I think?" Beck grinned. "Being married to me isn't a hardship, at least. Not for me either. Not so far."

"Not at all." It was the opposite actually. Being with Beck felt like the most comfortable, most right thing in the world—but also, on the other side of the coin, the most breathtaking, thrilling, overwhelming turn of events.

The most arousing.

Beck's hand, casually possessive, resting on his thigh, made him want to fly right out of his skin.

"I think I know your favorite part," Beck said, leaning close, his warm breath tickling Micah's ear.

Micah had begun to learn the streets around Beck's house, and he thought they were close.

God, he hoped they were. Because keeping his hands to himself even for this short drive had been an exercise in the kind of self-control he just didn't have where Beck was concerned.

"Yeah?" His voice was low and rough. And God, yeah, Beck *did*.

The sex was amazing. More pleasure than he'd ever imagined he could experience.

He'd always wondered why people lost their minds about sex—but now he got it.

Micah would trade just about anything for Beck's hands on his body, his mouth on his, the two of them intertwined together until he didn't even know who was who anymore.

"Do you know just how much you turn me on?" Beck asked, still murmuring into his ear so the driver wouldn't hear. His hand crept farther up Micah's thigh and he let out a deep, shuddering breath.

Did Beck know how much *he* turned him on?

Probably. Which was why he kept torturing him like this.

Beck didn't wait for an answer, just slid his fingers higher, the brush of them gentle but insistent. "It's the way your eyes get so wide. Like you're shocked it can be this good," he continued. "Like you can barely believe I'm the one touching you. Like you can't wait to touch me, too. Like it's all your dreams and your fantasies, together."

It *was*. How did Beck not already know that?

He was *everything*.

Micah wanted to groan. Wanted to lean into the teasing touch of Beck's fingers. Wanted to pin him to the door and tell him how much kneeling at his feet had turned him on. How the flex of his incredible thighs had been enough to fuel a thousand hot thoughts over the years and now that he got to touch? All those thoughts threatened to go supernova and blow his mind right apart.

The car pulled up in front of Beck's house.

Micah was barely a little tipsy—they'd been too busy fielding questions and congratulations to have too much to drink, no matter how Carter had tried to press shots into their hands—but he felt drunk as they walked up to the front of Beck's house.

It was a warm night, and he hadn't bothered to put his jacket back on, and Beck's hand was hot and firm on the small of his back as he typed in the code and let them in the front door.

Beck opened his mouth to say something—maybe it was important, but whatever it was, it couldn't be more important than *this*—and Micah stopped him short, by turning and pressing his body right back against the door with his own.

Beck's eyes gleamed in the dim light of the entryway.

"Do you know how much you turn *me* on?" Micah asked.

Beck stared at him, wet his lips and even though it was undeniable he probably had some idea—after all, how could he miss Micah's cock pressing hard into his hip?—he shook his head.

"Alright," Micah said smugly. "I'm gonna show you, then."

Beck reached for him, but before he could, Micah took his hand and, circling his wrist, pinned it above his head, against the door.

"Not like that," Micah said. "I'm gonna *show* you." He let go of Beck's wrist, but noted with satisfaction as Beck didn't move it. Just leaned back against the door and watched as Micah ran his hands down his chest, flicking one button of his shirt after another until it was hanging open.

Beck shrugged it off and then sucked in a hard breath as Micah touched his face, letting his fingertips skim across his cheek, already rough with the scruff he'd shaved off only a few hours back, to his broad, sloping shoulders, to the strength in his pecs, Beck hissing as he pinched one nipple. Then he continued lower, following the trail of dark hair that led right down to the belt of his pants.

A hand cradled his head as Micah leaned in, tongue touching Beck's skin. One of them—or maybe it was *both* of them—groaned as Micah tongued his way to Beck's abs as he opened his belt with shaking fingers.

He tasted so good, sweet and salty, his flavor addictive on Micah's tongue.

Beck could touch him all day long and yet he'd still never realize just how much Micah wanted him, craved him, *adored* him. Even this wasn't going to be enough, but it would have to be, because this, *and* his heart, were all he had to give.

"So hot," he murmured. "So fucking hot."

The thing was, Beck *was*. But it didn't matter what he looked like in ten years or twenty or forty. If his stomach wasn't tight anymore, or his thighs weren't solid with muscle.

It wouldn't matter if his brown hair turned gray, or he lost it entirely.

Micah looked up and knew Beck would be looking at him like that for the rest of his life. Awe and affection mingled with an undeniable fondness. When he looked at Micah, it was like he could see all of him and it was still the most beautiful thing he'd ever been honored to witness.

All of that meant Micah would be panting after him for as long as he was able.

Beck's belt and his pants dropped to the floor, and *Jesus Christ,* if he'd known Beck wasn't wearing anything underneath those slacks?

He'd have done so much more than take that garter off. He'd have sat at his feet and begged for a taste.

"Surprise," Beck said, and his hands were gentle on Micah's head, cradling it, but not pushing, not once.

This was all on Micah.

And *God,* how long had he wanted to do this?

He didn't even care anymore if it made him queer. He *hoped* it would.

"Yeah, *God,* please," Beck murmured.

Micah leaned in and his first taste of Beck's cock had him moaning at the back of his throat. It was so good, everything he'd ever imagined it could be, and more.

Maybe he didn't have any experience doing this, but Micah hoped that enthusiasm might make up for any lack of skill, because he *wanted* it.

He wanted Beck's cock to brush the back of his throat. He wanted to be so full of it, he could choke on it.

"Yeah, sweetheart, just like that," Beck crooned to him as Micah took him in, sliding Beck's cock between his lips, letting his tongue caress the underside.

He took his time. Not wanting to rush. Wanting to savor every single fucking moment. Beck let him explore. Not pushing him, not once, his hands always gentle as he touched Micah.

Micah's own skin was burning hot, and between long, endless sucks of Beck's cock, his breath came short and harsh, panting in the silence of the house, so aroused he knew if Beck touched him even once, he'd lose it.

"I want you to do something for me," Beck said, and the rough edge to his voice betrayed how aroused he was.

"Anything." Micah's voice was rough too, from taking Beck as deep as he could, and he'd never thought he'd feel pride and pleasure from the evidence, but it was undeniable.

Beck's fingers trembled on the back of his neck. He was so controlled, so careful, but Micah knew he was close to coming.

He wanted it, because it meant he'd made Beck come apart with his hands and his mouth, but also he didn't, because then that meant this would end.

"Touch yourself," Beck ordered. "I wanna see you."

Micah took a deep breath. "If I do—"

"You won't," Beck said firmly.

Gingerly, he pressed a palm against his hard, aching cock, but before he could rub, before he could figure out just how much pleasure he could take before losing his mind, Beck's fingers tightened against his skull.

"No. Take your pants off. Take everything off. I told you I wanted to see."

God, Micah was never going to survive this.

He wasn't even going to survive the *memories* of this.

With shaking hands, he unbuttoned his pants and shoved them down, along with his underwear.

"Yeah, that's it, sweetheart," Beck murmured. "God, you're so gorgeous. I can't even stand it."

The first touch of Beck's hand against his cock was electric. It was almost too much, and he nearly startled out of his skin at the sudden pleasure of it.

"Give me your hand," Beck said.

He reached up. His fingertips just reached Beck's mouth, and then he took them in his mouth. Micah gasped as he slicked them up with his tongue. He'd never imagined even his hands were sensitive, but when it came to Beck, he was just one big raw nerve.

"All better." Beck released his hand and it shouldn't have been too much to touch himself with Beck's saliva—after all, Beck had had his mouth on his cock, hadn't he? More than once. Both times were definitely in the top five experiences of his whole fucking life.

Micah blocked out the thought, because if he thought that it was like Beck was giving him a blowjob as he leaned in and took Beck's cock into his own mouth, he wasn't going to be able to hold his orgasm at bay any longer.

As it was, it was almost right on the edge of too much as he stroked his cock and sucked Beck's.

Adding to that was the litany of praise falling out of Beck's mouth.

"God, so good. So fucking good. Look at you like this. Like every fantasy I've ever had."

Micah groaned around Beck's cock, his own strokes faster and faster, desperate for release.

Desperate for Beck's.

"Yeah, sweetheart, make me come," Beck groaned, and his fingers tightened hard, and it was all the warning Micah had before Beck's cock twitched and began to unload pulse after pulse of come onto his tongue.

He swallowed, milking Beck's orgasm for everything he could, somehow still holding his own at bay.

Micah didn't know how he did it, only that when he slumped down, Beck's cock slipping out from between his lips, he was on the razor edge of having the best orgasm of his whole life—but he hadn't lost control yet.

He'd wait, gladly, for Beck to give him another incredible release.

Beck reached out for him and dragged him up, Micah's knees weak as he fell against the other man.

Then Beck was kissing him hard and sweet, impossibly both at the same time, and Beck's hand was joining his own, curling possessively around his cock, and it only took one stroke and then another for Micah to fly right over the edge.

When the pleasure finally petered out, Micah slumped against Beck.

"I love you," Beck murmured. "I didn't know . . ."

He didn't say what he didn't know, but Micah had a feeling he hadn't known either.

He'd never imagined, even in his most impossible fantasies, how incredible it could be between them.

"Me either," Micah agreed. He sighed happily, feeling like no matter how much of a mess he'd made and how much they truly did need to clean up, he could lean against Beck's broad chest forever.

CHAPTER 14

"We are *so* excited you two both decided to come for Alumni Weekend," Alice, their Northwestern liaison, said, as she guided them through the bowels of the stadium. Her eyes twinkled as she glanced back at them.

Beck had a feeling he knew why she was so excited they'd come together this weekend: this was their first official appearance after the whole world had discovered they'd tied the knot.

"Bet you are," Micah said, the pleasure in his eyes hidden by a pair of sunglasses, but Beck didn't need to see them to know just how pleased he was.

Not only were they two of Northwestern's most famous football alumni, *and* famous for playing together, so famous they'd actually gotten their own nickname, they'd had to go and top all of that by getting married.

The concierge at their hotel had confessed, when they'd checked in that morning, just how in-demand the tickets were for this game. "Alumni weekend's always popular," he'd said, with a wink, "but I can't imagine why it's extra popular this particular year."

"Must be some big shots coming in," Micah had teased, nudging Beck.

He'd been so cocky in college. Not so much that Beck had ever disliked him for it—though there was no denying he'd frustrated him a time or two—but now, Micah's words didn't feel like he was hiding or overcompensating for something else.

They were just an extension of his own natural confidence. Confidence that had only grown in the last few weeks, since he'd come to Charleston.

Beck liked to think he had something to do with that.

But the truth was, Micah had already begun to find the man inside his own skin long before he'd been traded. Beck was just getting to appreciate the end of a long road of hard work.

"It's great to be back," Beck said. "Yeah?" He nudged Micah.

"Best years of my life," Micah agreed.

"Well," Alice said wryly, "I think you've got some good ones still to come."

Beck chuckled under his breath at her knowing glance back at them. He knew what she was dying to ask—*were you two together this whole time and we just never knew?* "Yeah," he agreed.

"In any case, we're thrilled to be able to honor you."

"Making it in the ring of honor is a big deal," Micah said, and Beck nodded. He'd been surprised when he'd gotten the call. He'd only been in the NFL for a little over a season.

"And it's so cool you two could do it together, during the same game," Alice said. She was still gazing at them with what Carter would call heart eyes. Like she'd already started writing their story in her head.

Beck took pity on her finally. "No," he said.

Alice turned back towards them, frowning. "No, it's not cool?"

"No," Beck corrected gently, "we weren't together when we played here."

"Oh. *Oh.*"

Micah laughed. Beck was still recognizing the changes in him. Cataloging new ones. His laugh now was so much brighter, more open. Less guarded. Less like he might get caught laughing at something he shouldn't be.

Beck thought he'd known him—and he *had*, about as well as anyone—but it was an honor getting a front row seat to all the parts of Micah he'd always imagined existed, but nobody had gotten to see.

"Don't sound so disappointed," Micah teased.

"We just all *assumed*," Alice said apologetically.

"It's alright," Beck said. "I get it."

"I'm gonna have to change all my theories now," she said conspiratorially.

"Well, when you settle on one, let us know, okay?" Micah said.

"Will do," Alice said lightly.

They stopped in front of a door, flanked by two security guards. Down the hall on the left, they'd just passed the locker room for the Northwestern players.

Beck could remember, vividly, every time he'd walked down this hallway.

"I'll come get you just before halftime, so we can get prepped for the ceremony, okay?" Alice said.

Beck liked that the alumni team in charge of their appearances here this weekend had assumed they'd both want to stand on the sideline for the first half of the game.

"Sure thing," Micah said.

"And I'm sure at some point, the announcer will point you out, so you know . . .look extra coupley."

"Do we look coupley?" Beck asked. He didn't know what they looked like.

Alice shot them a look. "There's a reason everyone thought you were together back in college."

"Oh, that's great." Micah's smile had weakened a little.

Beck thought it might have matched his own.

"Hey, you good?" Beck asked under his breath as they approached the door. He wasn't *worried*, exactly, but this was a lot for a first appearance as a married couple. Sure, they'd gone to Carter's bachelor party, but that had been just their friends and teammates.

This was a whole team—a whole *stadium*—full of strangers, who were going to be making a whole ton of assumptions about the two of them, separately *and* together.

It was also Micah's first big appearance not just as a married man, but an *out* man.

"It's The Wall!" the security guard on the left crowed, and he and Micah shook hands, and then the guy turned to Beck. He looked just as thrilled as Alice had. Maybe Beck was worrying for nothing. But could anyone blame him? He loved Micah. He wanted to stand between him and anyone who would ever give him shit about who he was—even though Micah was one hundred and ten percent capable of handling himself.

"So good to have you guys here," the security guard on the right said, and they shook his hand too. "I can't believe—" Beck inhaled a sharp breath, just waiting for him to finish his sentence with *I can't believe you're married, now,* but instead the guard said, "You're playing together again. The Wall, reunited. It's more than any of us could've expected."

"Us, too," Micah said warmly.

Neither of them congratulated them on that *other,* much more personal event, but it was there, hidden between every other word, in both of their gazes, as they opened the door and headed onto Ryan Field, the Northwestern football stadium.

A sea of purple greeted them and a few cheers from fans sitting close to the tunnel.

Beck knew his job. He waved and smiled at as many of them as he could as he and Micah headed down the sideline towards where the team was getting warmed up for the game.

There were only a handful of players he recognized from their time here. That was the problem with college—teams were constantly turning over as students graduated.

But of course, *all* of them recognized the two of them.

Beck felt Micah stiffen and then force himself to relax as they approached their first group, who all exclaimed happily to see them.

All of them said the right things, usually starting with how much they looked up to them, how in awe they were of their NFL careers, and then ending with, wasn't it so freaking cool the Wall had reunited again?

The first time they got this comment, Beck glanced over at Micah.

The sideline of their alma mater was not the right time for PDA, but he also wasn't going to pretend playing together was all they were doing these days.

He'd fought too hard and risked too much to pretend he was straight anymore. No, Beck thought, *they'd* fought too hard and risked too much to pretend they were straight anymore.

"Yeah," Beck said, putting a hand around Micah's waist and tugging him close. Micah relaxed another fraction when he did it, like he'd been waiting for it—maybe even wanting it and dreading it in equal measures. "But," he added, "that's not the only reason it was great."

"Yeah," one of the Northwestern defensive ends said, "is that crazy rumor true? You guys got *married*?"

One of the linebackers shoved an elbow into his side. "It wasn't a rumor, you idiot. They released a statement and everything."

"I thought they just got super drunk or something. That they didn't really mean it."

"Well, that *is* true," Micah said, laughing. "Though that was only *after* it happened."

"Really?" The defensive end stared at them, clearly shocked.

"True story," Beck said, exchanging an easy grin with Micah. "We were a little . . .uh . . .excited, I guess."

"Huh." The defensive end didn't look upset or offended or even pissed off. In fact he looked more surprised than anything else.

Beck couldn't blame him for that, because there was no question it was a surprising story.

No doubt everyone on earth believed they'd gotten married just like every other drunk, impulsive couple in Vegas.

"Hey," Micah said, "he offered and what was I supposed to do? *Not* lock this down forever?" He waved up and down Beck's body.

Warmth and love swamped him.

"Ditto," Beck grinned.

"You two are alright," the linebacker said with an approving nod. They all shook hands again.

"Good luck today."

"Don't let the QB out of your sight, dude," Beck tossed over his shoulder as they headed down the sideline.

By the time they'd had that same conversation in triplicate, with various groups of players and coaches and staff, Beck could sense that Micah was finally really relaxing.

"You still good?" Beck asked as they settled down at one end of the sideline, towards the curved end of the bowl.

Micah shot him a look. "Why do you keep asking me that? You think I'm gonna freak out and run away? Run *where* exactly?"

"I never said you were gonna run away," Beck said, rolling his eyes.

"Then stop worrying I'm gonna." Micah had that stubborn look on his face Beck recognized all too well.

It was the same one he'd worn the night one of their teammates had bet him he couldn't eat two dozen tacos from Taco Bell. The same one he'd worn when he'd insisted he could cover Chris Olave, the best receiver out of Ohio State in ages, by himself their senior season.

"It's okay to be . . .unused to this." Beck had almost said *scared by this*, but he had a feeling that would go over even worse than what he *had* said.

"Are you?" Micah challenged.

"Yeah, you know I am. Change isn't easy for me, but I'm trying. But this is even more for you. I know there are other factors that make it . . .well, that make it even more difficult."

Micah's gaze shifted towards the field. Michigan State was warming up now, a sea of green and white jerseys surrounded by purple.

"Doesn't mean I can't handle it," he said stubbornly after a long silence.

"I get it," Beck said. "You don't need my help. I know that. But maybe I wanna give it anyway. Make sure you're okay. That's what . . ." He cleared his throat. "That's what partners do. And I wanna be a good partner to you. The *best* partner."

Micah shot him a look. "Do you really think you're not gonna be?"

"I don't know," Beck said with a shrug, and it was so much harder to admit than it sounded.

"Wow, you must really think you won't, if you're gonna admit you don't know something," Micah teased. He glanced over at him. He looked less offended now, definitely way less stubborn. More amused.

"Despite prevailing opinion that I know what the hell I'm doing, I don't," Beck admitted. "I don't . . .you know I didn't really date much."

"Well, according to Alison—"

"Alice," Beck corrected.

Micah rolled his eyes. "*Alice*. According to Alice, we were datin' forever."

Beck did not say that according to everything Micah had told him, he'd *wanted* them to be.

But he'd never clued Beck in. Beck had existed for his four years of college and four years of friendship never imagining that they could have *this*.

"I know what I'm doing in bed, but not here. Not like this." Beck hesitated. "I don't want to fuck it up, but I probably will."

"Don't be overprotective, and assume I can handle my shit unless I say otherwise, and you won't fuck up," Micah pointed out frankly.

"Yeah, and don't pretend you're fine, when you're not," Beck retorted. "You forget, I *know* you."

Micah cracked a smile. "Alright, okay. It's a little scary. Hard to know whether someone's gonna congratulate us or say something shitty. That ever change?"

"Uh, sort of? Mostly like you learn to not worry if they're gonna cause trouble."

Micah's eyes traveled up and down his body, checking him out pretty goddamn blatantly. "I'm surprised *anyone* was prepared to start shit with you."

"I didn't say they were particularly smart when they tried it," Beck said with a smile.

The team intros started, Michigan State streaming onto the field in a mass of green, followed by the Northwestern team entrance in a blaze of purple, fireworks, and Willie the Wildcat leading them.

After the national anthem, Micah nudged him with a hip, pointing over to the spot that had always been *theirs*, before games.

Where they'd always done their pre-game chant, almost from the very beginning.

"You ever think we'd be back here?" he asked, just loud enough Beck could hear him.

"Not together," Beck answered honestly.

"Yeah. Me either. I . . .I'm really glad it's with you," Micah said.

Beck tucked an arm around Micah's waist and tugged him close. He wasn't going to start making out on the sideline; that was the kind of distraction their team didn't need, but he wanted to do *something*.

"Love you," Beck said, pressing a kiss against the side of his head.

"Love you too," Micah said, his voice almost smug.

Like whenever he'd imagined they were back here, it was exactly like this, and while he'd never dreamed it might come true, it had, anyway.

"That ceremony was great," Jolie West said, tugging Beck into a tight hug.

Micah told himself he was not nervous—that facing all the Northwestern players and then an entire stadium of people as he and Beck were inducted into the ring of honor was way tougher than facing Beck's family.

But that was a huge fucking lie.

Jolie let go of Beck and turned to Micah.

Every time he'd gone home with Beck, he'd always been welcomed as Beck's best friend, and included as part of the family.

And he'd never, not once, ever believed that he'd deserved their affection or their consideration.

So many things had changed over the last year. He'd made peace with who he was. He'd been traded. Come out. Gotten fucking *married*.

But right now, it was like none of that had happened, and he was back at the beginning. Feeling inferior. Feeling like he'd gotten away with some kind of crime, like he'd stolen Beck away despite every single fucking protest.

Logically, it didn't make sense, because Jolie West was hardly fighting him right now. In fact, she was smiling at him, the same smile Beck wore, and it was lighting up her face. She extended her arms to him without a single moment of hesitation.

"And, Micah," she said, her voice muffled in his shoulder as she pulled him in tight and close. "Welcome to the family."

Micah squeezed his eyes shut.

He wanted to believe it.

Nothing would have made him happier than to reconcile his fears with the truth staring him in the face. But it was hard when his own situation was so different.

When his own mother had made the choice that hadn't been in his favor.

When he'd only had a dad for the first three years of his life and he couldn't really remember anything about him, before he'd been snatched away by fate way too early.

"Thanks, Mrs. West," he said.

She pulled back a fraction and shot him a no-nonsense look he recognized because it was one Beck wore all the time. "You know what I've told you," she said sternly. "It's Jolie, to you. Or Ma. But *not* Mrs. West. That's my mother-in-law and she's terrifying."

"Is she?" He'd never met Beckett's grandmother, but it was hard to believe that any part of the West family was actually terrifying—just terrifying to him, personally.

"You'll meet her tomorrow," Jolie said firmly. "But don't let her freak you out. She's a big softie under that, *yes,* terrifying exterior."

"Micah." Beck's dad was soft-spoken, the opposite of his wife, but there was an undoubtable approval in his eyes as he extended his hand for Micah to take. He shook, making sure to keep his grip firm. He met Patrick West's gaze with his own. "Congratulations. I see you've finally made an honest man out of Beck."

"Dad!" Beck exclaimed, but Patrick just chuckled.

"I did it as soon as I could, sir," Micah said, which was actually the truth. At least, as much truth as he felt comfortable admitting in front of Beck's family.

The whole family was up in one of the guest suites ringing the stadium, the low couches all in various shades of purple, and a large buffet lining one wall, the counters full of food and drink.

"Well, we're real glad, nonetheless," Patrick said, and there was no discounting the ring of truth in his voice.

It wasn't that Micah didn't hear it; it was just a matter of actually *believing* it.

"Tomorrow should be a full house," Jolie told him, drawing him to the side, like she actually wanted to talk to him. "But it shouldn't be too crazy. I promised Beck I wouldn't. There's just so many people who want to congratulate you two and meet *you.*"

"Ah." Micah didn't know what to say to that.

"And your mother, of course, is welcome to join us," Jolie said. "I want to be sure to connect with her."

"I'll let her know." Micah hoped she'd forgive him the lie. He knew he really needed to tell Beck they weren't exactly speaking right now—but he didn't know where to even begin.

Logically, he knew Beck wouldn't judge. That Beck would embrace him, just as he always did. That he'd take his side, because it was *Beck*, and he'd never failed to have his back.

But there was still that ugly voice in the back of his head. The one that kept insisting Beck's family was just putting on a good face, and that Beck was only taking pity on him. Making the best of a bad situation.

He kept hoping the obvious love and affection in Beck's face and eyes and the way he touched him, the way he told him he cared about him, in all those obvious and non-obvious ways, would banish that voice forever. But Micah was beginning to believe that maybe that voice had nothing to do with Beck at all and everything to do with himself.

He was going to have to be the one to get rid of it, once and for all.

"She isn't here today?" Jolie asked.

Micah shook his head. "Last-minute, you know. I wasn't supposed to be here this weekend, but a lot later in the season."

"Ah, but when you were available, I can see why they jumped on the chance to have you both here at the same time." Jolie smiled, a dimple so like her son's emerging on her cheek. "And I'm not just saying that because you're *married*."

"Mom, stop saying it like that," Beck said.

"Like what?"

Beck rolled his eyes. "Like I'm currently in the running for Son of the Year just because of this one thing."

"Oh, sweetheart," Jolie said, patting him on the cheek. "You're in the running just because you're *you*. Don't you agree, Micah?"

Micah could only nod. How could he do anything else? Beck was everything he'd ever wanted, not because he'd ever done anything special. That was the key, wasn't it? To Beck, everything he did and said and *was*, it all came as naturally as breathing.

And Micah loved every bit of it—loved every part of *him*.

"Aw, look at you, you've got such heart eyes for each other," Jolie said, and pulled them both into another tight hug.

"Mom," Beck said, laughing. "You're being ridiculous."

"Yeah, but a mother's allowed when her son gets married," Jolie exclaimed, finally letting them go.

"And there it is again," Beck said, grinning. He turned to Micah, who was still not sure how to react to any of this. He was . . .he was *happy*, too? Happy that Beck's parents were clearly so pleased that they'd finally gotten their shit figured out and gotten together. But there was a thread of caution there, because it wasn't like his own mother hadn't been pleased too, when he'd finally come out to her.

And *that* hadn't lasted.

"Come on," Beck said, tucking an arm around Micah's waist and tugging him towards the front of the suite. "I wanna watch the rest of the game."

They settled out in the front of the suite, Patrick West bringing them a trio of beers as they sat down in the first row of seats.

"Your mother means well," Patrick said quietly during a TV time-out.

Beck raised an eyebrow. "But she's invited half the neighborhood tomorrow?"

If Micah had to guess, Beck wasn't even that upset about it. Resigned, yes, upset, *no*. Secretly kind of relieved his parents hadn't been angry he'd gone and gotten married without them there? Definitely. Micah had known Beck a long time, and he wasn't that hard to read.

Patrick shrugged. "Your brothers and sister are just disappointed they couldn't make it."

"This summer I'll let her plan a big party," Beck promised. "And this time the *whole* neighborhood can come. Invite all our extended family. Invite the team—and your old team." He met Micah's eyes. "Make it a real celebration."

Beck continued, talking out loud about where they could hold it, who could do the catering, even theorizing that maybe they should hire an event planner.

A wedding reception, Micah realized with growing alarm. *He's talking about throwing a wedding reception.*

And that thought *shouldn't* fill him with panic—but it did, because naturally, the West family would assume that the Rose family would come, too.

What could he say? *Sorry, but I don't have the kind of family you do? Sorry, but they're not coming because I don't trust them to be in the same room as us?*

Well not all of them. One person.

But one was enough.

Again, there was that stray thought he tried never to have.

What if my Dad was around to see this? Would he be happy?

But it wasn't really a question, was it? Micah barely remembered anything about him, but he'd known, and *still* knew, instinctively, that Michael Rose had been a good man.

He'd have been thrilled at Micah's achievements. He'd have loved Beck. He'd have laughed at their sudden marriage, but slapped him on the back and told him to be a good husband, no matter the circumstances.

That was probably why this hurt so much. Why he wanted to turn away from it, before it hurt even worse.

But at the same time, there was a part of him that *loved* just how proud Beck was. Micah had never imagined he'd be so into this version of Beck—the smug, happy one, who was all about building castles in the sky—but it was undeniable that he was. It was definitely better than the Beck who panicked every time they tried to combine two parts of their lives into one.

"You good with that?" Beck finished with, glancing over at him.

Micah had so many different feelings about it. On one hand, he was terrified of anyone looking at him and thinking or even worse, *saying,* they didn't belong together. That they'd look at the color of his skin and how long it had taken him to be honest about who he was, and assume he wasn't worthy of being with Beck. He was worried about the inevitable conversation they'd have to have about some of his family.

But, on the other hand, he'd never been prouder in his life to be the one Beck wanted. The one Beck committed to. The one Beck *loved,* more than anyone else. And he'd never ever turn down the chance to stand up next to him and show the world they were together.

"Yeah, I am. That sounds great, actually," Micah said. Took a long sip of beer. Hoped that would banish the doubt lingering in the back of his mind, because once he said it, once Beck had started talking about it, it *had* actually sounded great.

He'd just have to figure out a way to banish the fear.

Baby steps, Scott would tell him. He could already hear his voice in the back of his head, reassuring him that he *would* get there.

But more than anything, reminding him that he *should* be telling Beck about this stuff.

And he would. He *would*. When the right moment came.

This was absolutely *not* the right moment.

Beck tilted the neck of his beer bottle, knocking it against Micah's. "Cheers," he said. "Now let's see if we can hold on to this lead and win the game, huh?"

Chapter 15

"Hey, you okay?"

Beck regretted the words as soon as they were out of his mouth.

Not because he didn't want to ask Micah if he was okay, but it felt like that was all he'd done all freaking day, and if he was Micah, he'd be sick to death of it.

But still, Beck couldn't shake this feeling that something was up with him.

Was there something he wasn't saying?

Something he wasn't telling him?

It felt like it, even though Micah had been the one to suggest they be honest with each other as a way of making this new relationship work.

But Beck didn't want to come right out and *ask*, because what if he was just worrying to worry and there wasn't anything?

Micah shot him a look as he sat down on the edge of their hotel bed. "What the hell," he complained. "You've asked me that a thousand times, and I told you to stop and you're still doing it."

"I know," Beck said apologetically.

Maybe he'd be doing better at this if they were just dating and hadn't decided to skip over all the regular steps and get fucking married.

"Did I do something? Say something?" Micah frowned. "Was it not okay with your family today?"

"No, no, you were fine. You were great. You're going to be great tomorrow too, I just get it's . . .*they're* . . . a lot to handle. Especially with this new development."

"'New development'?" Micah did air quotes around the words. "You mean that we're *married*?"

God, Beck should've known he'd fuck up this conversation.

But Micah had been quiet on the ride back to their hotel, and he hadn't known what to say. Or *if* he should say anything at all.

"I know that we're married." Beck shot him a look as he paused in his pacing in front of the bed.

"Do you regret doing it?" Micah asked carefully.

And God, Beck hated himself right now. He'd made Micah sound like that. He'd made him question if he was happy about it, which . . .nothing could be further from the truth. But also, there was a part of him that squirmed when he thought of how just two weeks ago, Micah hadn't been in his life at all and while he'd missed him, he'd been at least *trying* to make his peace with the fact he wouldn't be back in it.

"No, *no*." Beck made sure to sound very sure. Because he *was* very sure. He was. But his mother had been right. He didn't trust easily. He didn't let people in very easily. Once they lost his friendship, they were typically out of his life.

Micah had always been different, had always meant more, but because of that, his ghosting had cut Beck so much deeper.

"You're sure?"

"Yeah," Beck said and then kissed him. Briefly—but with all the certainty he *did* feel.

He was still getting used to this new situation but that didn't mean he wasn't absolutely fucking thrilled Micah was back in his life, and not just as a friend.

"Alright, 'cause it seemed like you were happy about it but . . ."

"Good, 'cause you were there," Micah teased, trying to lighten both of their moods.

But it didn't really work.

"Are you freaking out about tomorrow? About the plans I mentioned to my mom about this summer? About the . . ." Beck hesitated, because he didn't really want to call it what it was, which was *obviously*, a wedding reception. A second wedding? A re-do?

God, what did you even call that other than what it was?

Maybe he shouldn't have been so afraid to correctly identify it, but there were still his own doubts. The ones that claimed they'd pushed too hard, too fast, and they'd fall apart before making this as permanent as he wanted it to be. Then there were those shadows lingering in Micah's eyes. The ones he tried to pretend didn't exist, but Beck was tired of ignoring.

They were supposed to be really fucking happy right now, and they *were*, but there was still something.

Beck *knew* there was. *Knew* it wasn't just him.

He knew Micah Rose too well to pretend there wasn't.

"You can call it a wedding reception," Micah said frankly.

"Can you?" Beck questioned, and the hurt that bloomed across Micah's face made him immediately regret it.

"Yeah, I can, but I'm not sure you can," Micah's voice was soft, and Beck couldn't help it anymore. He flopped down right next to him and leaned into his shoulder.

"I'm sorry. I know this is a lot. It *should* be a lot. Maybe we should've just . . .I don't know. Pretended it didn't happen. Got an annulment. Just figured out how to date without all this . . .all this *pressure*."

"Too late for that." Micah's tone was wry. "We've definitely consummated the marriage. Multiple times."

They had. Though Beck had a feeling that didn't matter anyway.

Beck didn't know what to say. He'd already stuck his foot in his mouth twice in the last five minutes, so maybe he shouldn't say anything at all.

"We didn't think this was going to be that easy. So no big surprise, it's not," Micah said after a minute or so of silence. "Guess I thought it would be *easier.*"

Beck sighed. "I didn't." He'd known it was going to be hard as hell to do this. And yet here he was doing it anyway, because he knew, more than he'd ever known anything else in his whole life, that the end result would be worth it.

"Really?" Micah sounded surprised. "You wanna talk about it?"

Did he? Not really. Because what was there to say? He was just trying to adjust.

Though hadn't he promised . . .he *had* promised.

"It's just a lot of adjustment, really quickly, and God, I'm so happy we did it, I am, but it's a lot to take in. A lot of changes all at once."

"And you hate change." Micah stated it, didn't even bother making it into a question.

"Yeah, yeah, I do." He did. It was undeniable. "Even if it's good change."

Micah nodded, but Beck could still see those shadows in Micah's eyes.

He wanted to ignore them. But he couldn't.

He had to know.

"I know there's something up with you, and I wish you'd tell me about it."

"Of course you've guessed." Micah sounded full of pain. Pain Beck would do anything to take away, but all he could do was sit here and listen. Be there for him. But maybe, most importantly, remind him that he was loved.

"I *know* you," Beck said and pulled him tightly against him. Tucked his face into Micah's neck and pressed a kiss there. "And I *love* you. Coming here reminded me just how much both are true. How much history we have together."

"Yeah," Micah agreed, his voice sounding raw. He paused. "You know why my mom wasn't here today?"

"You told me, 'cause she found out too late. They moved your induction date to coincide with mine and your new bye week, after you were traded."

"No," Micah said. "She didn't come because I didn't invite her."

Beck couldn't believe it. Micah and his mother had always been so close—especially because it had only ever been the two of them, Micah's dad dying in a freak accident when he was almost too young to remember him. Micah had worked so fucking hard to succeed at Northwestern so he'd be drafted high, and then he'd make enough money to buy her a house and alleviate so many of the financial worries she'd had over the years.

Never in a million years had Beck ever imagined that she might be . . .that she was . . .he'd hardly ever made a secret of his sexuality, even to her, and not once had he ever gotten the feeling that there'd been something she was holding back, any kind of negative feelings she wasn't saying.

"She couldn't be. No. You came out to her and she . . .*no*." Beck rejected the thought. Couldn't even imagine that would be her reaction. Which would've made it so much tougher on Micah, because he never would have dreamed that would be the case either.

But then . . .there had to be a reason he'd denied this part of himself for so long, right?

"No, no, she wasn't horrible about it. Actually, she was happy for me. Everything was fine, but . . ." Micah sighed. "Josiah. My uncle. Her brother. You know they're close."

"Yeah." On the other hand, Beck had never had a good feeling about Micah's Uncle Josiah. Not because he'd done or said anything, but there'd been a look in his eyes, and then there was the way Micah always went out of his way to make sure they barely ever met. That had said more than anything else.

"He was around a lot when I was growing up, because he was all my mom had. I didn't like him, ever, but I couldn't ever figure out why. But then . . .I grew up and I started realizing what some of the shit he liked to spout off about meant. I kept telling my mom I didn't want him around, but . . .she wouldn't listen. And then, after I got her the house, he moved in. I really didn't like it. I knew he was mooching off her—and trying to mooch off *me*—and I warned her, but she told me I was overreacting. I didn't mind giving *her* money, but I didn't want it to go to him. Not ever."

"He's a dick, then?"

Micah nodded, misery turning his mouth downwards. Beck hugged him tighter. "Always has been. But I didn't want to make an issue out of it. I was too busy, anyway, making myself miserable those first few months in Miami, to do anything about it. So I let it go, but then I started to come out of it, and after talking with some friends there, I knew he had to go. So I asked her if she could find another place for him to stay. She refused. We fought about it. But I thought, oh, maybe, it'll still be okay."

Micah was silent so long after this, Beck said, "I guess it wasn't okay."

"No. Well, yes, at first it was. When I came out to her, she was happy. Happy that I was happy. That was all that mattered. But then, when I'd come visit, I asked her to make sure Josiah wasn't around, because I knew he'd say shit. He already *had*. He'd sent me some texts. I sent them to her, and she said he was just 'surprised'. Not that he was a homophobic ass, which he was. She *defended* him. When I said I didn't want him there when I came to see her, she argued with me. We argued a lot, and I hated it, but it was important to me. I thought she must've seen that, because finally, she agreed."

"But then you went to see her and there he was," Beck guessed.

Micah nodded. "She claimed she thought 'exposure' might fix him. Like he could be fixed. He's a fucking cancer. A waste of space. That's all he is, that's all he's gonna be."

"If he treated you that way? Yeah, yeah, he is." Beck heard how hard and unrelenting his voice was. There was nothing he wanted more than to leave this hotel room and kick this guy's ass, for *ever* making Micah feel less than worthy, for making him feel like he didn't belong in his own family and in his own skin.

But if he left now, he'd leave Micah alone, and what was more important than *anything else* was making sure he felt wanted and loved and like he had a home now, because more than ever, no matter how much he was struggling with the nitty-gritty realities of the situation, he knew that Micah's home was wherever Beck was.

They *belonged* together.

"So that's it," Micah finally said. "That's why we're not speaking. She took his side. I still don't know why."

"You know, you tell me my family's awesome all the time—but they're not *all* awesome," Beck admitted. It was hard to say it, hard even to talk about it, but Micah had tackled the subject because he'd asked him to. What else could Beck do but repay the trust Micah had in him?

Micah looked confused. "I don't understand."

"My dad's oldest brother—my uncle—he isn't welcome to our house," Beck said. "Not after he realized that I was gay and proceeded to say enough shit my dad had to kick him out."

He'd felt guilty for that forever. For being the straw that had broken his dad's relationship with his brother. But Patrick had told him over and over again that it wasn't his fault. That his brother's attitudes were his own business, and if he couldn't accept and respect his own son, then he wasn't part of the family any longer.

It hurt, cutting out those people who hurt you. But Beck had learned you had to do it, before they hurt you even worse. Or before you started wondering if they might be right.

"Shit, I had no idea," Micah said, voice sympathetic. "God, I'm sorry."

"Hey, me too," Beck said. "I just thought you should know . . .you're not alone. You're never alone."

Micah's gaze was both sympathetic and understanding. Warm on his face.

It gave Beck the courage to keep going.

"So, you let your mom stay in the house? The house you paid for?" Beck asked, even though he already knew the answer.

"Yeah, of course." Micah shot him a look like he was crazy.

Beck sighed. *Of course.* Like there'd never even been a question in Micah's mind. "You are, without a doubt," he said, wrapping his whole body around Micah best as he could and holding him as tightly as possible, "the *very* best person I know. The person I love more than anyone or anything else. I'm sorry it took us so long to get here. For me to show you that."

"You always showed me that," Micah said, chuckling under his breath. The shadows, they weren't gone, but they were lighter. Like telling Beck had helped him lighten the load just enough. And that was all Beck ever wanted—to share the load.

"I don't—"

"Yeah," Micah said, interrupting him. "Yeah, you did. From the very beginning, I felt seen by you. Cared for by you. You brought me that Icee, didn't you?"

"It was just an Icee," Beck said, rolling his eyes, even though yeah, it had clearly been more to Micah. Not to him, not for a long time, but that was okay, because he'd caught up, and they were here together now. His best friend, his lover, and his partner—for, hopefully, the rest of their lives.

"Well, how 'bout that's one thing we have to have at this wedding reception of yours," Micah suggested, the corner of his mouth quirking into a smile. "Cherry Icees."

Beck didn't flinch—*he did not flinch*—after all, it *had* been his idea, hadn't it?

So what if Micah was calling it what it actually was?

But even though he didn't flinch, Micah still chuckled anyway.

"I guess there's still some stuff we're figurin' out," Beck murmured.

Micah leaned against Beck, head on his shoulder. And this, Beck knew, was the serious advantage of being an inch and a half taller. This right here.

"I love you," Micah said. "And you love me. We're not figuring that out."

"No." No, they were not. That much, they both knew.

For a long moment, they didn't say anything, just held each other.

Sixty minutes, Beck thought. They'd always been in this together. Didn't matter if it was a football game or the rest of their lives.

"Don't tell your mom, okay?" Micah asked, his voice quiet.

"I—" Beck hesitated. "She's going to figure out something's wrong."

"Yeah, 'cause she's smart like you," Micah said wryly.

"Sorry?"

"I'll figure out a way to tell her myself. I just didn't want you to do it. It's . . ." Micah sighed. "It's embarrassing. 'Cause your family loves you and accepts you. Though I guess not all of them do." He didn't *like* that Beck's uncle was a homophobic asshole. In fact, it made him want to kick that guy's ass. But it did help, knowing that maybe the West family wasn't as universally accepting as he'd assumed they were.

"They feel the same about you," Beck said.

"I'm figuring that out. Figuring out how to accept that's true, too."

Before Beck could repeat that it *was*, and that he *should*, Micah continued, "And I don't need you to pep talk me up about it. Just . . .be there, okay?"

"Not going anywhere."

And *that* was the one thing Beck felt very sure of.

"You weren't dating before you got married?"

This question came from one of Beck's many aunts. He'd lost count of how many there were, but more of them kept showing up and hugging Micah and then interrogating both of them.

This was at least the third time he'd been asked why exactly they'd gotten married in Vegas and not in, as the second aunt had said, "in a church or a garden like normal people."

Beck had taken that one, and replied something about how they just weren't very normal.

Well, that's true, she'd said with a knowing smile, patting him on the arm.

Micah exchanged a glance with Beck, who just shrugged and smiled. Apparently it was *his* turn to take the question.

"It was one of those impulsive things," Micah said. *And not very impulsive at all, if you had any idea how long I've wanted him.*

"Well, we are *very* happy for you, regardless," this particular aunt said.

Micah had to give them all credit. Sure, they all asked the question—and frankly he had a feeling *most* people wanted to ask it but didn't; apparently there was an aunt prerogative that meant they could ask the tough questions—but each of them still seemed genuinely glad they'd done it.

"Thanks, Aunt Lily," Beck said, and she tugged him in for another very long hug. Micah braced himself, because based on the pattern, he already knew he'd be next.

They were nearly two hours into this party that Jolie West had put together ostensibly because Beck was home for the weekend but, in reality, to make sure that all their friends and relatives had a chance to see who Beck had married.

At least that was how Micah had thought of it before they'd arrived at the home Beck's parents had owned for his whole life—a big, rambling split-level in a Chicago suburb. But then, to Micah's surprise, it wasn't like that at all.

Instead, everyone he met just seemed more interested in congratulating both of them than checking him out to make sure he was worthy of Beck.

I'm not sure I am, but I'm fucking trying, he'd considered telling some of them, but to his surprise, it had never come up.

Not once.

And now, after several beers and some surprisingly decent potato salad and more hot dogs than he probably should've eaten, Micah discovered he was actually kind of . . .relaxed?

Relaxed enough to tease Beck after Aunt Lily finally departed to do a drive by the dessert table.

"Getting married was your idea. *Twice*. The least you can do is handle all the questions about it," he grumbled at Beck. Beck had spent most of the party with a loose hand slung around Micah's waist. It was reassuring and a little possessive and Micah was not quite ready to admit all that touching was turning him on. Especially not when they were still at Beck's parents' house.

Last night, they'd fallen asleep without sex for the first time since the day after their marriage, both exhausted from the long day and the heavy conversation they'd shared.

And this morning? Micah had reached for Beck, but then before they could share more than a lazy make out session, Beck's phone had rung. And then rung again.

Despite the fact that this party was supposed to be *for* them, Jolie had a list of errands she'd begged Beck to do before showing up at their house.

"I kinda thought . . .equal opportunity," Beck said, shooting him a way-too-charming grin. "If we get another one, I'll take it, alright?"

"You have *another* aunt?" Micah could barely believe it.

Beck laughed. "Nope, you've managed to meet all the aunts. So rest easy there."

"Thank God."

"Don't worry, you're doing great."

"Well, they're making it easy," Micah retorted. Which was true. He'd been prepared to be grilled. To see way more uncertainty lingering in too many of the guests' gazes. But there was none of that.

"You're complaining about that?" Beck teased.

"No way," Micah said.

"Good." Beck pressed a casual kiss to the side of Micah's head.

At least, Micah was sure he'd meant it to be casual, but with desire so close at hand, it didn't exactly feel casual.

"Come on," Beck continued, "let's go find somewhere quiet, to recharge, before a second cousin twice removed decides to ask me why we got married in Vegas."

"A second cousin twice removed wouldn't dare, only an aunt," Micah teased as Beck led him in the back door of the house, through the bustling kitchen.

He saw the look Beck exchanged with his mother before taking Micah up the flight of stairs just off the entry, and down the hall.

Micah had been in Beck's childhood house more than a few times. Always when he'd visited, he'd stayed down the hall, in the guest room, but of course, he'd spent time in Beck's childhood bedroom.

If he was being totally honest, he'd had more than a few fantasies set in this room.

Still, he hadn't ever gotten the vibe from Beck that it had been mutual.

At least not until they reached Beck's room and he closed the door behind them and the next moment, he was kissing Micah like he'd been starving for him.

"God," Beck groaned, gasping for a single breath and then diving back in again.

Micah's back hit the door and it didn't take him long to be a fully enthusiastic participant.

Beck tried to pull back again, but this time, Micah's mouth chased his and they kissed again and again, deeper and deeper, Micah's tongue brushing against Beck's.

The arousal simmering just under his skin was suddenly boiling, and he couldn't help reaching down, palming Beck's cock, already hard, through his jeans.

"Shit, you gotta . . ." Beck gasped.

Micah leaned back, his head hitting the wood with a distinct thump.

He knew how just how hungry he looked, because there was no question that Beck was looking back at him the exact same way.

"I thought it was just me." Someday, he'd realize that it wasn't *ever* just him. That Beck wanted him with the same ferocity that he wanted Beck.

Just another one of those adjustments they were still working on.

"Just you?" Beck laughed. "Hell no. I've only been thinking about getting you up here for at least the last hour."

Micah shot him a look. "Not once before that? I lost count of how many times I dreamed you fucked me beneath your Captain America poster."

Beck's jaw dropped. "Seriously?"

"Oh please. Was I really supposed to think you just had Chris Evans on your wall because you liked Marvel?"

Beck flushed red, the color traveling up his neck. Micah wanted to lick the color right off.

"I didn't think so," Micah said slyly.

Reaching up, Beck cradled his cheek in one of his big warm palms. Any other time, it would've been reassuring, but now all it made Micah think was how much he wanted—no, *craved*—that touch and that hand on his cock.

He'd become addicted to the pleasure they shared together.

He didn't think he was the only one.

Sure enough, when he popped the button on Beck's jeans and then tugged his zipper down, Beck didn't say a word, just flushed brighter.

"Really?" Beck's voice was breathless.

"Tell me you don't want it, and I'll stop," Micah said. But he already knew Beck wouldn't be stopping him—and that in a minute, Beck would be joining him.

"Can't."

Beck's breath was coming faster, in desperate little pants now, as Micah curled a hand around his cock and began stroking it.

"Didn't think so." It was easy to sound smug—to goad Beck into it, especially when he wanted it so much.

When they both wanted it *too* much.

Less than thirty seconds later, his own jeans were around his ankles, and that palm he'd been fantasizing about, callused in all the right places, was stroking him and it felt so damn good, it was all he could do to not groan out loud.

"Yeah, that's right, it's not just me," Micah panted, leaning in and pressing his mouth against Beck's as their hands moved faster and faster.

Beck's grip was so fucking perfect. Tight and a little rough, pleasure shooting right up his spine.

He groaned into Beck's mouth and kissed him, swallowing his moan of reply back.

"Shit, shit," Beck said, tearing his mouth off Micah's, and he was reaching helplessly for a tissue on the nearby dresser, tightening up a moment later, and then coming hard, Micah only a few seconds after him.

"Damn," Micah said, breath still not quite even as they cleaned up as best they could with another handful of tissues. "Never gonna be able to look at Captain America the same way again."

Beck made a face as he tossed the messy tissues into a trashcan next to the dresser. "Yeah, like you never got off to Chris Evans in basically every movie he's ever made."

Micah laughed. "Fair."

"I'm not proud of it, but it's the truth," Beck said, grinning.

"Did you really lure me up here to seduce me?" Micah wondered, wandering through the room, checking out the bookcase full of worn-out paperbacks—the *Hardy Boys*, of fucking course—and the shelves lined with old athletic trophies.

"Hey, I'm not the one who apparently had all these fantasies about fucking in my childhood bedroom," Beck teased. "But uh . . .maybe." He rubbed a hand on the back of his neck. Looking a little sheepish.

"The only question is how I'm gonna face your mother, because she totally knows."

Micah realized now what that set of looks meant that Beck had exchanged with Jolie.

"No way," Beck protested. "I just . . .we needed a minute away. She gets that."

"Uh-huh," Micah teased. "A minute of 'quiet time'. Like the way you think, West."

"I *love* the way *you* think," Beck said, coming up behind him, wrapping his arms around him tightly, and pressing a kiss to his head. "I think we both needed that."

"I wanted it this morning," Micah grumbled. "I wanted you to bend me over the bed and fuck me 'til I couldn't even think straight."

"Didn't think you were thinking straight before this?"

Micah laughed, the sound startled right out of him.

"You and Captain America, both, apparently." Micah turned in Beck's arms, rested his head on Beck's shoulder. He'd never, ever, not in a million years, admit that he liked that he could do this, because Beck was that stupid inch and a half taller. But he did. "I just don't want her eyeing me funny when I talk to her later."

"You gonna?"

"I told you I was going to tell her. Well, maybe not all the truth, but some of it. The most important parts of it."

"You told me the whole truth," Beck said.

"Yeah, 'cause you're *Beck*. You're my husband, you idiot." Micah smacked him in the arm, but he could hear the fondness and the affection in his voice.

"Don't worry, I don't think she's gonna think anything at all about this. After all, she didn't get mad when I snuck Tommy Johnson up here my junior year."

Micah raised an eyebrow. "Should I be jealous of Tommy Johnson?"

"No way. Not even close. Tommy didn't even get his pants off."

"Neither did I."

"But then, I didn't ask Tommy to marry me either."

Micah could still hear the barest hint of hesitation over the word, but Beck had said it.

They were getting used to it.

Slowly but surely, he was beginning to believe that this was real and this was happening—and not just that, but it was forever.

And, he realized, he could get very used to that.

"According to Beck, I'm not allowed to ask if you're okay," Jolie asked Micah as he lugged in three different mostly empty casserole dishes to the kitchen.

Beck was still outside, chatting with his dad and a few of their close neighbors.

The aunts had finally left—taking with them Jolie's terrifying mother-in-law; she had not exaggerated at all, but Micah had still managed to deal with her—and now was his chance, Micah realized.

"Do I not look okay?" He set the casseroles on the big kitchen island.

"You faced Beck's grandmother and barely batted an eyelash. I think you're fine." Jolie put a reassuring hand on his shoulder. "But I know you're not talking about your mom, Micah. I'm a mom, so I know. I can see it."

"It's that obvious?" He frowned. He'd just been thinking that today had gone so much better than he'd ever anticipated. Nobody had seemed upset that he and Beck were together—in fact, they only seemed happy *they* were happy. After the anxiety of worrying about what people might say or do, he'd begun to relax.

To actually enjoy himself.

"Not at all." Jolie tucked a hand into his and led him off the kitchen, to the living room. When she gestured to the couch and sat down next to him, he couldn't help the anxiety spike. Was this finally it? The moment she nicely sat him down and told him he could never be worthy of Beck? That he wasn't what she and Patrick had hoped for for their son?

"Do you want to tell me about it?" she asked quietly.

Micah realized that she'd only pulled him into the other room so they'd have privacy. That the unconditional support in her eyes, so like her son's, wasn't hiding any kind of secret judgment. That she was asking not because she needed an excuse to say, *Oh, well, that Micah Rose, I knew he was no good from the start and now he's proved it*, but because she was genuinely concerned about him.

When he'd told Beck he'd make sure his mother knew the basics of the situation, he hadn't had any intention of telling her the whole truth. Just the bare facts of what had happened, and why they weren't currently speaking.

But instead, Micah found himself confessing the entire story, beginning to end. How he'd come out to his mom, and she'd been accepting. But she hadn't understood—hadn't *wanted* to understand how his uncle wasn't going to feel the same. About their history—his father dying so young, and his mother not having anyone to turn to, and that had allowed Josiah to wiggle his way into their life. How she'd even read Josiah's texts and tried to hand wave them away. Then, their final fight where he'd shown up to have dinner at the house he'd bought Sheila, and there Josiah was, despite all his warnings that he hadn't wanted to see him that night.

Before he'd told Beck—and now Jolie—the only person who knew what had happened was Scott.

He hadn't even intended to tell him, even though he'd been the perfect person to tell, but the night it had happened, Scott had happened to call, and he'd immediately known something was wrong.

The whole story had spilled out, much as it had tonight.

Micah couldn't deny it; he still worried about people hearing the truth and deciding that this reflected on *him*. That he hadn't tried hard enough. That he'd given up on his mother, *his own fucking mother,* for God's sake. Or that this was the kind of messy, dramatic familial bullshit that people avoided like the plague. That *Micah* usually avoided like the plague.

After all, why had he denied it for so long, when it was staring him right in the face? And why else had he waited so long to tell his mom the truth?

Because he'd known something like this was going to happen.

Finally, he ran out of words.

Jolie didn't say anything right away, but the first thing she *did* do was reach over and take his hand into her own and squeeze it hard.

"There isn't anything I can say that fixes this," she said. "There's nothing. I could tell you that Sheila should've sided with you and protected you with the last breath in her body. But I know it's not always that simple, at least to her. Especially not with being alone and needing someone to lean on. But I do know she loves you, and, as a mother, I *can* tell you she's hurting, too."

Micah looked away, tears suddenly gathering at the corners of his eyes and clogging his throat.

This was why he didn't talk about it. This was why he did everything he could not to even *think* about it. Because it hurt so fucking much.

Because he'd hoped—stupidly, *naively*—that if he'd done everything right in his life, it would all work out in the end. He'd tried to be the best son a mother could hope for. Worked his ass off in high school to not only get recruited on the field, but off it, too. He'd gone to a great school. Graduated. Become a rich, successful football player in the NFL. Bought her a house. Taken care of her bills, before he'd even taken care of his own.

All because he loved her, and he hoped, *God he'd hoped*, that when the truth *did* come out, that all that counted for something.

But it hadn't. Not in the end.

"That helps—and it doesn't," Micah croaked. He wiped a tear away.

"I know, I know," Jolie soothed. She wrapped him up in her arms. She was small—Micah had always assumed Beck had gotten all his height and his strength from his father—but it was becoming obvious that the inner strength Beck carried with him, the truth and love that shone inside him like a lamp, he'd also gotten from his mother.

When he finally pulled away, she raised a hand and cupped his cheek. "It doesn't change anything, I know, but now that you and Beck are together, the way you were always meant to be—"

"What?" Micah hadn't wanted to interrupt her, not after she'd comforted him so well. But he hadn't been able to help himself.

"Oh, Micah, you two were so oblivious and so obvious, all at the same time. But now that you *are* together, I know we can't possibly replace your mother or your uncle, but I want you to know, we're here for you."

"Thanks, Mrs. West."

She shot him a look, and Micah didn't even have to listen to her next words to know what it meant, because it was yet another thing Beckett had gotten from his mother.

"I told you," she said. "It's either Jolie or it's Ma. Either one. But *not* Mrs. West." She shuddered.

"Ma, then," Micah said and knew he'd made the right choice because of the smile that bloomed across her face.

"I'm sure Beck's told you that not *all* our family's as accepting as they should be," she said. A hard look came across her face—and Micah knew, without a single doubt, that she'd fight anyone who threatened or challenged her son. And now, him, too.

It was a gift he'd never expected, but one he couldn't turn away from.

"Yeah, he said."

"Then you know none of us is perfect, with a perfect family," Jolie said firmly. Making it clear she didn't judge him one bit for the fact that his wasn't.

He hugged her one more time. "We should get the rest of the food put away," she said as they headed back into the kitchen. "But you promise me you won't be a stranger, alright? You're part of this family, now."

Micah smiled. "Thanks, Ma. I'll remember that."

"You're adopting him now?" Beck asked, leaning against the island.

"Shows how little you know," Jolie said, pulling out a big stack of Tupperware from a cabinet. "*You're* the one who married him."

Beck flushed. It felt as easy as breathing to walk over to him and tuck himself into Beck's side. Like that was the place he belonged.

What had Jolie said? *You two were so oblivious and so obvious.*

Yeah, looking back at all the times he'd spent in this house, thinking of all the hundreds of times they'd hung out, all the moments they'd been there for each other through thick and thin, they'd all been building to this.

"You alright?" Beck asked and then made a face a second later, like he'd just remembered he wasn't supposed to ask it anymore.

But Micah knew why he'd asked this time, and *this* time, at least, he could appreciate Beck's concern.

"Yeah," he said, nudging his knee with his own. "I'm good."

Jolie was right; her family couldn't replace his own. But a family could expand. The people who cared about you weren't just limited to anyone related to you by blood. Scott had proven that, over the last year, and now, with Beck's family, Micah was just making more room in his circle.

Scott, now that he thought about it, would absolutely love Jolie. They'd get on like a house on fire.

Maybe they'd actually meet, next summer, when he and Beck threw that big wedding reception they kept talking about.

But Beck? Beck would be meeting him sooner.

Next weekend.

When the Piranhas came to town.

Micah could admit he was both looking forward to it—to seeing Scott and his old teammates again—and also dreading it, because the Piranhas were a damn good football team, and he wanted to beat them, no matter how much he still loved them.

CHAPTER 16

"Seems like you guys had a good bye," Jem said to Beck and Micah as the three of them headed out through the tunnel onto the practice field.

Micah laughed, and Jem flushed.

"Not what I meant—though seriously, I really am happy for you guys. I meant the visit to Northwestern. They had something on Sportscenter when I tuned in the other night. I guess you two are the first married couple to ever make it onto a ring of honor in a stadium in *any* sport."

"That's pretty freaking cool," Micah said, and Beck nodded. It *was* cool. He'd have to ask his agent if he'd recorded the segment, because he'd like to see it.

"Bet you two weren't thinking about that though, when you tied the knot," Jem teased.

"You don't wanna know what we were thinking," Beck muttered under his breath.

"But I can guess." Jem grinned. "Hey, it's all good. You two have been married for over a week now. You settlin' in okay with it?"

Beck exchanged glances with Micah.

Micah might have been the one with the painful secret he'd been holding onto, but it wasn't like Beck had been entirely comfortable either, with the accelerated timeline their relationship had taken.

But they were figuring it out, and if he was going to be honest, coming home last night, to his house—to *their* house, because Beck couldn't deny that was how he was beginning to think of it—had felt good. Felt *real* good, and not just because Micah had ended up in bed next to him.

Before, when Micah had been gone, when they hadn't been speaking, everything had felt slightly off. No matter how much Beck tried, nothing had felt right. It was part of why he'd been so goddamn angry; how was he supposed to spend the rest of his life without him, feeling this way all the time?

But now, now that they'd begun to settle into this and get used to the idea and what it meant, nothing had ever felt more right to Beck in his whole life than walking into the bathroom and seeing Micah's toothbrush next to his own, and his laundry piled on the dryer, mixed in with his.

And waking up next to him, with Micah's inevitably grumpy face when he realized they were headed back to practice today?

Perfection.

And not because everything was perfect either.

"We're good," Beck said.

"Better than good," Micah agreed.

"I'm glad to hear it," Jem said, smacking both of them on the back. "You ready to sweat some today? We got a kick-ass Piranhas offense to get ready for. You know somethin' about that, Rose?"

"Yep, they're gonna be a challenge, but at least I've got lots of experience covering Nicholson." Micah's voice rang with confidence—but not *over*confidence, like had sometimes gotten him into trouble at Northwestern.

"He got way better at running a route between last season and this season," Jem observed.

"Yeah, he spent all offseason in LA, working with Chase Riley."

"Fuck," Beck said.

"Yep." Micah paused by the bench on the sideline. Adjusted his gloves. "But I got this."

"*We* got this," Beck said, and Jem nodded in approval.

Coach Kelley jogged onto the field, clapping his hands. He looked slightly more well-rested, but there were still gray-ish circles under his eyes, obvious despite the shade from the visor he wore.

"Come on," he said, "let's gather 'round."

Coach Kelley didn't always give a pep talk pre-practice, but it *was* their first practice in a week, and it made sense to Beck he'd want to check in with his whole team.

"This week," he said, "is a big week for us. Divisional game. Rival game. And the team that sent us packing last year in the playoffs. But more than that, it's a team we've got a lot of connections to—good *and* bad. A team that I think we can all say, without pride or ego, that we wronged." Coach paused. "But just because we respect the hell out of the Piranhas and their coaching staff and their players, that doesn't mean we don't want to pull out a win, especially when very few people are expecting it from us."

Beck knew it was true. The Piranhas were everyone's favorite pick to win the Super Bowl this year. They had started the season undefeated. Last week, they'd beaten the Packers thirty-eight to three. They were on fire, and even though, *yes*, the Condors were playing better than anyone had predicted, it didn't mean they were a match for the Piranhas.

Even though the Condors now had the benefit of Micah's undeniable skills on *their* side.

"But to win," Coach continued, "we're gonna have to work damn hard this week. Extra hard, 'cause we were on bye last week. But now's the time to be done with distractions. Done with doubts. We're lookin' forward, and we're going to be ready for whatever they throw at us." He turned around, taking in all the players and coaches around him. "We ready to fly, Condors?"

Listening to the chorus of cheers and yells of agreement, Beck had a feeling that he wasn't the only one eager to meet this particular challenge.

Normally, they'd have meetings in the morning and practice in the afternoon, but Coach had called for an extra practice today, to make sure everyone's conditioning was top-notch and they were ready for what was to come.

It would be an extra-long day, for everyone.

Practice, then meetings, with lunch squeezed in, and then more practice this afternoon. And then, Beck already knew, they'd be breaking down film long into the night.

But he knew preparation was going to be key for beating the team that nobody thought they could touch. That nobody thought *any* team in the NFL could touch.

Like he'd promised, Coach started out this morning's practice with a long conditioning session.

By the end of the first sprint ladder, Beck was sweating, breath coming in shallow pants, and he wasn't the only one.

He and Micah had lifted, a couple of times, over the break, but they hadn't been running, full out, the way he knew they probably should have.

Glancing over, he saw Micah was suffering just as much as he was—just as much as the rest of the team.

Coach clapped his hands again. "Good work. Now, let's do another one."

Micah groaned under his breath.

"Come on," Beck said, dredging up some kind of enthusiasm for doing the hellish combination of sprints for a *second* time. "We can do this." He shot a smile Micah's way. "Race you?"

But before he could get set, Micah was already taking off, and God, he was *fast*. Fast enough Beck couldn't hope to touch him, and he knew it, shooting a smug look behind him as he ran.

Practice ended, and Beck slumped to the locker room, tearing off his sweat-soaked practice jersey and running a hand through his equally soaked hair. "Ugh," he said, collapsing onto the bench in front of his locker.

Carter grinned at him as he walked by. He looked like he'd barely broken a sweat. The asshole. "You okay there, West?"

"Yeah." He would be, after about a gallon of Gatorade and a cold shower and maybe some lunch, when he thought he might not throw it up again.

"Thought you'd be more used to two-a-days," Carter said. The corner of his mouth quirked up into a knowing smile. "Guess you spent more time on the bye week in bed than in the gym, huh? Though that can be a workout all on its own. I bet Rose . . ."

Beck shot him a warning glance, and Carter threw his hands up. "Okay, okay, point taken. Now that he's all yours, he's *all yours.*"

"He was all mine before that, too," Beck growled.

"Yeah, he kinda was," Carter agreed with a smile that told Beck he hadn't had to get all possessive for Carter to know the truth. He'd already known it. He was poking the bear, just because he could.

That was Carter Maxwell for you.

"So, when are you gonna do this?" Beck asked. Because yes, last year Carter had totally subjected him to a twenty-minute lecture on why marriage wasn't for him. Why monogamy wasn't for him. And maybe it *still* wasn't, but there was also a desperation in Carter's behavior now that hadn't been there even last season.

Like he was so desperate to keep himself on that razor-fine edge, he'd do anything.

And while he and Beck were not necessarily close, Beck had a feeling Carter's version of *anything* was not good.

"Do what? Get in shape?" Carter's grin was sharklike as he crossed his arms over his chest. "Oh, buddy, have I got news for you."

"Find someone you want to fuck for more than one night." Beck said it bluntly. He had a feeling Carter wouldn't understand it any other way.

Carter gaped at him. "Um, *never*?" He waved his arms around. "Not that I haven't had really good sex. I have. Sex probably worth repeating. But . . ." He hesitated, like he didn't want to share, which, this was Carter, so that was odd. But Beck's interest and curiosity were aroused now, and also, this was a good distraction from how much his muscles were currently burning.

"But?" Beck prompted.

"But *what?*" Carter made a face, and Beck knew he wasn't going to get any more answers out of him. He wiped his face off with his equally disgusting jersey and was surprised to see Carter still leering at him.

"Did you need something?" he asked cautiously.

"Why are you so worried about me?" Carter asked, a frown creasing his forehead.

"I'm . . ." He was about to say he wasn't, but he was, wasn't he?

"Because we're friends, Carter." Beck paused. "You know what friends are. They're people you hang out with and care about and don't have sex with."

Carter's sudden smile was wild. "But *you* had sex with *your* friend."

"If this is your way of trying to finagle an invitation into our bed, think again," Beck grumbled.

"Noted." Carter was still grinning. "Not that you'd mind, once I was there."

"I'd mind," Micah said, appearing on the other side of Carter. "Are you gonna shower? Or are you planning on moldering on that bench forever?"

He'd already taken his own shower, and now he was clad in only a pair of black boxer briefs that hugged him in all the best ways. While it was inherently distracting because of how goddamn good Micah looked, he noticed he wasn't the only one whose gaze had snagged on Micah's body.

Carter was totally checking him out.

Annoyed possessiveness streaked through Beck and he got up, throwing his sweaty jersey right in Carter's face as he did.

Carter spluttered but he was laughing as he tailed Beck towards the showers. "I know you're into it," he called out.

Beck shook his head and had a feeling that while Carter might *talk* big, he didn't even mean half the shit he said.

Maybe not even seventy-five percent.

When he got out of the shower, changed, and headed to the defense room for their lunch meeting, he ran right into Deacon.

"Hey, you good after that practice?" Deacon asked as Beck guzzled down half a bottle of Gatorade.

"I'm fine," Beck said. Though he hadn't been fine thirty minutes ago.

"Good. Glad I ran into you." Deacon's forehead creased the same as Carter's had a few minutes ago, but Beck had a feeling it was for very different reasons.

"What's up?"

"I'm gonna pump Micah for more info on the Piranhas offense, and I have a feeling he's not going to like it."

"He knows his job," Beck said slowly.

No, Micah was not going to like it. In fact, Beck could predict that he was absolutely gonna hate it. Understand it, too. But hate it all the same.

"Yeah, he does. But he's gonna need you, I think." Deacon said it very matter-of-factly.

"Would you be asking me this if . . ." Beck hesitated.

"If you weren't married? Uh, *yeah*. You're the guy's best friend. You two deciding to finally do something about your feelings doesn't change that—or the way I run this defense," Deacon said bluntly. "It's gonna hurt him. His loyalties are probably still divided. And I get that. I'm sympathetic to that."

"No, you're not," Beck said, deciding that maybe Deacon could use some bluntness of his own.

"Alright, so I *am* sympathetic, but when he takes the field on Sunday, he needs to know who he's playing for. Who he wants to win."

"He knows," Beck said.

Deacon raised an eyebrow. "You know how tough this is gonna be. We need more than a hundred percent from everyone. And we could use a little extra."

"You think they aren't gonna change everything? They *know* you're gonna pump him for info."

Beck knew what it sounded like, like he was trying to protect Micah from the inevitable. And maybe he was, a little, even though he knew perfectly well Micah needed a partner, not a protector.

"Yeah, but that doesn't mean I won't do it," Deacon said. At least he sounded slightly regretful. "Anything might give just an edge. That's all we need. The tiniest bit of an edge."

Beck nodded, because he knew Deacon was right.

Micah would too, but Deacon was also right there. It wasn't going to be easy for him.

Micah knew it was coming, but somehow, he still wasn't prepared for the moment in the meeting when Deacon turned to him and asked the inevitable question.

He'd both known about and dreaded exactly this from the moment he'd landed in Charleston. Week Six, when the Piranhas came to town, and he'd be expected to turn out his brain and give up every secret he'd ever hoarded about the Piranhas' offense.

Pax and Davis. Tristan and Wade. Logan.

They were friends—that hadn't always been true, but eventually, he'd grown close to them.

It didn't matter that they'd expect him to speak up.

It didn't matter that he wanted to, because it wasn't just the Piranhas he was close to. There was Beck, of course, but Carter and Jem and Deacon had reached out to him. Landry and Riley. The nauseating roll of guilt in the bottom of his stomach existed anyway.

"Is this going to be a problem?" Deacon's voice was neutral as he asked the question, but Micah heard the hardness in it anyway.

"I know what color uniform I'm gonna be wearing Sunday," Micah said, his chin jutting out stubbornly.

He did. He'd *asked* for this.

But that didn't mean that when it came down to it, it didn't absolutely fucking suck.

Beck sat next to him at the table, and his fingers grasped his knee and squeezed reassuringly.

"Good. Now, what can you tell us about Paxton Kelly?" Deacon's voice was still neutral—and he'd used Pax's whole name, not just the abbreviated version all his friends and teammates used.

All of that didn't make it better, necessarily, but it did help.

The Piranhas were just another opponent, he told himself.

The biggest betrayal of all would be to keep quiet now.

He believed it, *finally*, truly believed it, and so he began to speak.

He outlined all the weaknesses of all the players he knew on the Piranhas offensive roster. He talked about what their game plan might be.

Thankfully, it didn't take long.

He was sure, later tonight, he'd be giving similar info to Riley about the Piranhas' defense, but it was not nearly as explosive or as dangerous as the offense was.

"Contain him in the pocket and he'll struggle. Got it." Deacon made notes on his pad. Coach Rufus was nodding along with everything he said.

"That means the backfield's gonna have to cover," Jem pointed out.

"We can do it," Beck said, nodding. "I'll keep an eye on Micah and Nicholson."

"I can handle him," Micah said.

"Yeah, I'm sure you've got more experience than most," Coach Rufus said, "but take Beck's help. Their other receivers aren't nearly as good. He can help you cover him. Make sure he's not gonna break away."

"What about Wade Lewis?" Jem asked. "We gotta make sure he's covered. He might not have Nicholson's speed, but he can be sneaky. He'll sit right there in the middle of the zone and then muscle his way forward for first downs."

"I'll keep an eye on him too," Beck said.

"You can't do it all," Micah complained, shooting him a look. Even though he knew Beck well enough to know that he *did* want to do it all.

"I can help him out," Jaden, one of the other outside linebackers, chimed in.

"Great," Coach Rufus said. "We'll have a game plan set up for tomorrow's practice. This afternoon, we're gonna focus on fundamentals, because damnit, if the Piranhas get first downs because y'all can't tackle, I'm gonna lose my mind." He glanced around the table. "Double practice again tomorrow."

There were a chorus of groans, but Micah wasn't surprised.

The Piranhas were going to be one of the toughest challenges the Condors faced this season.

"Well, I guess you knew that was coming," Beck said to him as the meeting finally broke up, and they went to get ready for the second practice of the day.

"Yeah," Micah said. If he thought too hard about what he'd just done, that nauseating roll would be back, but Beck seemed determined to talk about it.

"And you're alright with it?"

Micah shot him a look as they headed towards the locker room to get changed. "Not *alright*, exactly, but I'm dealing."

"Alright." Beck looked like there was something else he wanted to say, and Micah could absolutely guess what it was.

"Don't you dare ask me if I'm okay," Micah said, without much heat.

Because it *did* feel good that Beck gave a shit about how he was doing.

Especially after how that had felt.

Beck glanced over at him, and then suddenly, his fingers were around Micah's forearm and he was dragging him down the hall, the opposite direction of the locker room, towards a section of the building Micah didn't think he'd been in yet.

Beck opened a door, pulling them both inside, and to Micah's surprise, it turned out that there was an extra bathroom down the hallway. From the fine coating of dust over everything, it was clear it didn't get used much.

Micah raised an eyebrow as Beck settled against the counter, crossing his arms over his chest. "Are you?" he asked.

"I think you forget I *asked* to be traded," Micah reminded him. He'd asked to no longer be part of the Piranhas.

"Not because you were angry at them. Not because they treated you like shit. Not because you wanted to get back at them. If any of those things were true, it would be understandable that you'd be the first in line to go over every single fucking detail of their game plans. But they aren't true. You still talk to their defensive coordinator all the time. You call him *Dad*."

"As a joke," Micah said weakly, but he knew Beck was right. "He look like my *dad* to you?"

"Micah," Beck warned. He had that tough look on his face. The same look Deacon had worn an hour ago when he'd asked all the questions Micah wasn't sure he wanted to answer.

Like he *needed* Micah to face this head-on and stop turning away from it.

"Okay, *fine*. It fucking sucks. That make you happier?"

"I'm not *happy* about any of this," Beck said, and his expression melted into something sweet and protective and loyal. An expression Micah would recognize on his face a hundred years from now.

Beck reached out a hand and grasped him, tugging him closer, until he was leaning right against Beck's big strong body, his arms around him.

"I know," Beck said quietly.

"Like I said before, I know which jersey I'm wearing Sunday, I know how this goes," Micah said after a long silence.

"It's okay to be conflicted. I know that. But we got a chance to win this thing," Beck said. "I don't gotta tell you that."

Micah nodded. He knew—but somehow that didn't make it easier.

"I think Scott . . .that's his name, right?" Beck asked and Micah nodded again. "He'd tell you that you gotta decide which team you belong to. And we *want* you, Micah. We gave up a shit ton of draft capital to get you. Mr. G did that because he knew it was the right call. He knew where you belonged, and it's right here with us." *With me.*

Maybe Beck didn't say the last part, because that made it personal, when Beck was trying to make it just about the Condors, but Micah heard it anyway.

"I know you can't possibly care enough about the other guys yet. I get that."

"I don't. I *want* to, but I don't." Micah sighed. "But us? We're the Wall. We always were. We always will be." Micah heard the promise in his voice.

"But not if we're not playing together. I'm not gonna lie. When we weren't, that was all I wanted. Even if it seemed like it was fucking impossible, a pipe dream that wouldn't ever come true, I still wanted it. More than anything." Beck's eyes had gone soft, and his fingers were gripping Micah's waist a little tighter than he had been before.

It was a good reminder. Not only that Beck loved him—had loved him, long before this, long before he'd even realized that he did—but that they had *this*.

This intangible connection they'd never dreamed they'd get back.

That if he needed a reminder of why he was playing for the Condors, not the Piranhas, he just had to find Beck on the field.

He cared about Deacon and Jem and Carter and Riley, sure, but what he felt for them was a drop in the bucket compared to his feelings for Beck.

"Just remember how that feels, how it feels to play next to me," Beck said softly. "'Cause I know how it feels to play next you, and I've never been happier than when I'm doing it. Win or lose. You're mine."

"And you're *mine*," Micah said. He didn't even try to hide the possessiveness in his voice. He tilted his head and kissed Beck hard.

Beck's hands came up his head, cradling it in his palms, and they kissed long and sweet and slow for another minute.

When they finally broke apart, it wasn't like the nauseated roll was gone—or the guilt, either.

But he unequivocally knew which side he was on.

And which side he wanted to win.

Chapter 17

"My mom's coming to the game this weekend," Beck said as he finished getting dressed.

It had been a brutal week of practice, and now they were finally getting an evening off.

An evening, if Beck had anything to say about it, he was planning on spending with his husband *not* on a football field or in a meeting room or so sore he felt like he could barely gather the energy to touch him the way he *deserved* to be touched.

The way Beck was dying to touch him.

"Really? Why?" Micah's glance over at him was perplexed as he gathered up his bag from the locker in front of him. "Is everything alright?"

"Oh, she just thought she'd fly over. I think she's checking on me. Maybe on us," Beck said with a chuckle. "Making sure we haven't decided marriage is too hard."

"Marriage isn't fucking easy," Micah grumbled, "but you're gonna have to work a lot harder than this to get rid of me."

"Good to know." Beck grinned at him. "You ready to head to dinner?"

He'd spent all week trying to get the two of them some quality time alone—not right before they collapsed, exhausted, into bed, or woke up, the sleep they'd gotten barely making a dent in their exhaustion. His mother had reminded him more than once that being married wasn't just sharing a house or chores and responsibilities but making sure to take the time to value each other.

Beck wanted to take Micah out, just the two of them—not just because they'd never had the chance to really *date,* and he knew they both wanted that—but because he didn't want Micah to ever think he took him for granted.

"Yeah," Micah said, nodding. "You really want to do this? I kinda thought we'd grab takeout and hang out on the porch." He nudged him and lowered his voice, until it was just a rough scrape over all of Beck's nerves. "And maybe some Netflix and chill?"

They could've. But that was something they'd done before, and this was *after.* "But we could do that any night," Beck pointed out, leaning in and brushing a quick kiss across Micah's mouth. "Tonight's special."

"It is?"

"What's so special?" Carter chimed in.

Beck straightened, adjusting his belt and grabbing his own bag. "We're going on a date," he said. "I got us reservations to that hot new place, down by the water? Kieran mentioned going there, when we were at the Pirate's Booty last week, and I figured why not take advantage of our night off."

"Aw, you made us reservations?" Micah smiled at him, looking even more pleased than at the thought of takeout and making out on the couch.

Though if Beck had any say in the matter, there was definitely going to be some of that, too.

"It wasn't that hard," Beck protested. Which was true. He'd only had to call up the restaurant and mention his name, and they were in.

"But it's the thought that counts," Carter pointed out.

"Do we want to ask what *you're* up to?" Micah asked, raising an eyebrow.

"Nope." Carter grinned. "Or maybe you do, 'cause you already need something to spice up your relationship."

"Nope, we're good," Beck said, while Micah shook his head emphatically *no*.

"Dang it," Carter said. "You guys know I like that."

"Sharing? Or being a not-so-secret exhibitionist?" Jem asked, from a few lockers down.

"Both." Carter's expression didn't contain a shred of shame.

"Well, you enjoy that," Micah said, tucking himself into Beck's side. Something Beck would *never* get tired of. "And we're gonna enjoy our nice romantic evening."

It turned out it *was* romantic. Beck had hoped, but he was surprised at just how romantic it was, as he pulled up to the valet stand and the attendant opened the passenger door.

It was dimly lit inside the small restaurant—small enough to be intimate, between the candlelight and the high foliage, that shielded their table from all the other diners.

"Well, you win," Micah said wryly, as they sat down. "Did you expect all this?" He gestured at the walls with their curling vines snaking their way in between the wooden slats, orchids gathered in large clumps with candles scattered throughout.

It looked like the most intimate jungle Beck could imagine.

"No," Beck admitted. "Kieran just said it was nice."

"Well, it is," Micah said, leaning forward. "Almost as nice as Netflix and chilling on the couch."

"Do people still do that?" Beck asked as he perused the menu.

"People have *always* done that, even when it wasn't called that. And whether they call it that or not, they're still doing it," Micah pointed out.

Beck met Micah's gaze over the edge of his menu. "Just saying, I'm not gonna object if that's how the date ends."

"Noted."

The waitress arrived, took their drink orders, and then retreated with a sweet smile that told Beck she knew exactly who they were but wasn't going to mention it unless they did first.

"So are you gonna tell me why your mom is really coming?" Micah asked.

Beck shrugged, telling himself to play it cool. "It's really not that big of a deal. She came to a bunch of my games last year. She's got an empty house, and she's a little bored."

"Ah." Micah didn't say anything else, but there was a wealth of meaning in that one word.

"Thought we could get some dinner, Saturday night before the final walkthrough, if you wanted to join us."

Micah shot him a weird look. "Why wouldn't I?"

"No reason," Beck said. Though there was no denying he *really* want his mom and Micah to become friends. "Just wanted to make sure before I made the arrangements."

"Count me in. I like your mom a lot."

"She likes *you*," Beck said, then changed the subject. "How you feelin' about the game?"

Micah shrugged. "It's going to happen. We're gonna play our goddamn best. I feel like we're prepared. Coach made sure of that."

"Yeah, he did." It had been brutal preparation, but the best kind usually was. "Felt a little like when we geared up to play Ohio State and Michigan each year."

Micah nodded. Toyed with his fork. "Riley came to me today. He said he wanted to wear a different number for the game. Asked my opinion."

"Yeah?"

"He wasn't here last year, right? But he feels . . .he feels like he wants to make a statement about it. About the way the Condors treated Davis. And he asked me, because he knew I knew him."

"You know him pretty well?" Beck was surprised, because Davis Abernathy was the Piranhas' quarterbacks coach, and he'd work most closely with Pax Kelly—not any of the defensive players like Micah.

"Yeah, he was part of this group I was friends with. We weren't close, but I know him." Micah hesitated. "Riley also wanted to make sure what he wanted to do wouldn't distract from the game *we* were playing."

"He's gonna wear number four, isn't he?" Beck asked, even though it was obvious. Pax's tribute to his coach, the ex-Condors quarterback, was famous. Every time he'd scored against them last year—and Beck was ashamed to remember just how many touchdowns there'd been—he'd raised four fingers to the sky.

It had been not only a reminder to the Condors, and to the rest of the NFL, that Davis was standing on the Piranhas' sideline, but an admonition to everyone who'd treated him like shit.

Who'd believed the lies: that he was washed up and *worse*.

"Yeah, that was the idea," Micah said. "I told him he should do it. Maybe it won't take the sting out of the Piranhas losing, but it's a nice tribute. A nice bit of sportsmanship."

"You think we're gonna win, huh?" Beck teased.

Micah's stare was dark and intent. "I intend to do every fucking thing I can to make sure we come out on top," he said.

"Not torn anymore, then?" Beck had kept a close eye on Micah during the last few days, but after that first day of practice, he'd both relaxed and totally committed to preparing for the upcoming game.

"I wasn't ever *torn*," Micah retorted. "I was . . .well, maybe I was. A little. But I just need to look at you, and I *know* exactly what I want. I want us, winning."

"There you go," Beck said with a grin.

"Charleston isn't quite home yet, but it's becoming more of a home for me than Miami ever was." Micah's voice softened, his eyes full of love. "I guess you probably know why that is."

"It wasn't home until you came here," Beck replied. Reached under the table and wasn't surprised to find Micah's hand reaching for his, too. "Love you."

"See?" Micah's lip curled up into a smile. "That's exactly what we're fighting for."

"I think that was . . .was that our *first* date?" Beck asked, as they walked into the house from the garage.

Micah shot him a look. "Beckett, we're *married*."

"Yeah, yeah, but we're . . ." Beck reached out, took Micah's arm, and tugged him close, just as they entered the kitchen. "We're still *dating*."

"Is this your way of tryin' to get lucky?" Micah asked, raising an eyebrow. "Calling it a date?"

"I made reservations at a nice place. I drove us there. We had a nice dinner. I think it's the *least* you can do," Beck teased.

"Oh, you want me to be self-sacrificing, huh?" Micah's voice was rough and his gaze was intent as he leaned in. "I can do that."

Beck was about to point out he wasn't exactly going to be suffering, but before he could, Micah kissed him.

He kept thinking he was used to Micah making the first move, and Micah wanting him just as much as he wanted Micah, but then it would happen, and *God*, it still felt like a fucking miracle.

Like Micah was a miracle.

They staggered backward, Micah's hands everywhere, tugging the shirt out of his pants, reaching up underneath the fabric and pressing against his abs, then his chest.

"Do you know," Micah gasped as Beck's lips coasted down his neck, "just how much I fucking love how you persist in wearing everything a size too small?"

Beck lifted his mouth. "I do?"

"Yeah, and please, don't fucking stop." Micah groaned.

Beck didn't know what specifically Micah was referring too—apparently wearing everything too small, or kissing his neck—but he knew what *he* never wanted to stop doing, so he kept going, fingers popping open the buttons on Micah's shirt, giving him more room to work and so much more skin to kiss.

"You taste so fucking good," he murmured into the top of Micah's pectoral muscle. "I could eat you up."

Micah's hands were working on his belt, his palm brushing his cock every few moments, and between those lightning-quick flashes of pleasure and the taste of Micah's skin on his tongue, he felt lightheaded.

"Come on, come on, *come on*," Micah chanted, finally shoving his pants down around his ankles. "Couch, *now*."

Yes, they could end up grinding together on the couch. That would be undeniably good. Beck knew because they'd done it twice this week already.

But he'd had a little more in mind for tonight.

"No," he said, yanking back on his control. It was hard—*very hard*, his mind supplied—but he did it anyway. "I wanna watch."

Micah's eyes were wide and blown, confused.

Beck leaned in. "You told me, that first day, you liked to stuff yourself full of your fingers and come on them, thinking about me fucking you. So yeah, I wanna watch."

He heard Micah's sharp intake of breath when he finally understood what he was asking for.

"That's what…" Micah groaned. "You gotta stop saying stuff like that."

"Why should I when you like it so much?" Beck knew his grin was cocky and smug, but goddamn it, they'd earned at least a little smugness, hadn't they? They'd found each other in the first place, and now they were actually, *finally*, really enjoying each other.

If he couldn't feel damn good about that, then he couldn't feel good about anything.

"Yeah, don't stop," Micah corrected.

It wasn't easy to drag the two of them upstairs with his pants around his ankles, and he lost them halfway up the stairs, but he didn't give a shit.

He just wanted him and Micah, naked, in his bed.

In *their* bed.

"Take it all off, baby," Beck ordered, settling on the edge of the bed.

Micah gazed at him. "You want me to strip for you?"

"Oh yeah. And a whole lot more." Micah was a work of art—he was so tall and chiseled, his muscles in perfect proportion to the long lines of his body. Just watching him like this, as he slowly began to unbutton his shirt the rest of the way, shrugging it off his shoulders, made Beck so hot he had to bite his lip and dig his fingers into the coverlet so he didn't reach out and touch.

He'd said he wanted to watch, so that was what he was gonna do.

"Like this?" Micah asked, a shadow of uncertainty passing across his face. Like he didn't know just how good he looked. How desperate Beck was to touch him.

"God, yes, sweetheart. You're so fucking gorgeous." Beck knew he could run his mouth when he was lost in a haze of arousal, but nobody had ever made him lose himself the way Micah did.

It made sense, because he'd never wanted anyone like he wanted Micah. Never loved anyone he'd ever gone to bed with.

Only Micah.

Micah chuckled under his breath, his fingers working on his pants, shoving them down over his thighs. He kept talking about Beck's thighs, but his were glorious, every inch of them a masterpiece Beck wanted to worship.

He shed the last of his clothing, working his briefs down those thighs, until he was standing right in front of Beck without a stitch on.

"Goddamn it," Beck growled.

"You're the one who was stupid enough to say he only wanted to *watch*," Micah teased, reaching for the drawer they kept the lube in.

"Yeah, make me crazy, sweetheart. Make me wish I'd never said any of that."

Beck tugged off his shirt, and let it fall to the floor next to Micah. He palmed his cock, hard and straining against the fabric of his boxer briefs, and watched as Micah's gaze darkened even further.

Maybe both of them could play this game.

"God, you can't do that," Micah complained, even as he slicked up his own fingers with an expert kind of movement that made Beck's heartbeat accelerate.

Sure, he'd said he'd done this to himself, but there'd been a part of Beck that had wondered if he'd been exaggerating.

But clearly, that was not the case.

"I can do anything I want," Beck said softly, watching as Micah climbed on the bed and, in a move that made his breath literally catch in his chest, curled his fingers between his legs.

He knew the moment Micah tucked his thumb inside himself, because of the sharp intake of his breath.

"Feels good?"

"Yeah, yeah," Micah babbled, arching into the movement of his own hand. "Not as good as you do, though."

"What feels good?" Beck asked sternly—more roughly than he'd intended, because he was right there, on the edge of his self-control.

"Your cock. God, your cock." Micah ground against his fingers. "You gotta give it to me. I'm gonna . . ."

"No, you're not," Beck ordered. "Give yourself another."

Micah writhed against the pressure, pushing into it and away from it at the same time. Not because he didn't love it, Beck realized, but because he loved it too goddamn much.

Fuck.

Whatever fight he'd been having with his self-control he lost then. He grabbed for the lube and then for Micah, sliding a finger between his thighs, right alongside Micah's own.

He could feel where they were pressed into his hole, slippery with lube, and Micah groaned loudly as Beck pressed in lightly with his thumb.

"God, *please*," Micah said.

"You gonna ask me real nice?"

Micah's look was so hot it resembled a flamethrower.

Beck wiggled his thumb, driving Micah's fingers deeper. Micah huffed out a breath and then another, and he knew he'd pushed him just about as far as he could go.

Not that Micah couldn't possibly take more, but that *he* couldn't bear to not give him exactly what he wanted.

Exactly what they *both* wanted.

He pulled back, and Micah moaned in approval, his eyes fluttering shut as he fucked himself with his fingers in anticipation of what was going to be fucking him next.

"Shit, next time, it's my turn," Beck said, his own breath not quite steady as he scrambled for a condom. "You just . . .*God*. You just love it so much it's hard to deny you."

"It's 'cause I'm irresistible," Micah said, panting.

"And I love you." Beck's trembling fingers ripped open the condom packet and rolled it on, being generous with the lube after.

He had every intention of bending Micah over the edge of this bed and giving him the fucking he'd been dreaming about all week.

He wasn't going to be slow or gentle about it, because both of them were way past that, the handjobs and quick, hurried orgasms they'd shared this week gratifying at the moment, but not enough to satisfy their craving for each other.

"Yeah, yeah, you do." Micah's voice was dreamy and sweet as Beck smoothed a hand down his back, laying him out exactly like he wanted him.

"So fucking much," Beck agreed. His voice wasn't as steady as it could have been, his control hanging on by a thread as he finally slid home.

He gave Micah a moment to adjust, but before he even said he was ready, Micah set his feet and thrust backward.

"That's what I *wanted*," Micah said, gasping for breath as his hips flailed against Beck's.

Micah was strong as hell, and it was hard to stop his bucking body as he chased after the pleasure he was so desperate for, but Beck was strong too, and he set his hands at his hips and stopped him, mid-thrust.

There'd probably be bruises there, from the way his fingertips were digging into Micah's flesh, but he'd kiss each and every one later.

"God, you're such a fucking sadist," Micah whined in a high squeaky voice.

"If you let me do this," Beck ground out, "you'll enjoy it. Trust me."

Micah glanced at him, and there was an infinite amount of love and trust in his gaze. "Yeah, *yeah*," he groaned.

Beck took a hand and placed it on his back, easing him down to the bed, Micah shuddering as his over-sensitive cock brushed the comforter.

"That's right," Beck murmured, leaning down and pressing his mouth against Micah's shoulder blade. "Yes, sweetheart, just like that."

"Anytime now," Micah said, then hissed, the end of his admonition lost in a sigh as Beck finally began to move again. His hips snapped back and forth with a strict control he wasn't sure would last, not with how tight and hot and welcoming Micah's body was as he fucked him.

Underneath him, Micah was almost immediately lost to the pleasure of it, and Beck couldn't help but chase after it too, thrusting harder and faster.

Micah was making garbled noises against the bed, and Beck wasn't sure he was any better. The *only* coherent thought running through his head was *yes, more, always, please, forever*, and finally, *God, I'm not gonna last.* The latter had him reaching down and around Micah's hip, hoping to give him the last little bit of pleasure he needed to fly off the edge.

But before he could, Micah gave a desperate thrust of his own, and then he was shaking and squeezing Beck's cock so tightly in his body Beck was helpless to do anything else but follow after him.

A few long moments later, they collapsed onto the bed, Beck half-aware of what a mess they'd made of the comforter, and not giving a single shit.

Micah was laughing again, his whole face crinkling up as he turned towards Beck.

It filled his heart with joy—and love—to see him like this. So free, so open, so ready and willing to embrace everything that was true about himself.

It wasn't just the sex, though that was undeniably awesome.

It was everything else.

"Wasn't too rough, was I?" Beck asked softly, reaching up and, with a semi-clean finger, tracing the laugh lines around Micah's eyes.

"Not even close. Besides, I loved it." Micah hesitated. "I love *you.*"

"Especially when I fuck you into the mattress, apparently." It was Beck's turn to chuckle. He'd never laughed this much with anyone else in his whole life, especially not during or directly after sex. It was a revelation, but then everything about Micah seemed to be. How well they'd fit as friends, first off, and then how easily they'd become something more.

"Hey, I said I wasn't the type of husband who was interested in separate beds, and I meant it." Micah's voice was light and happy.

Beck would do everything in his power to make sure he *always* looked that way.

Even during the inevitable bad days.

Especially, Beck realized, *during those bad days.*

It was easy enough to make Micah happy when he was already happy, but it was something so much more precious and magical if he could do it when he *wasn't.*

Chapter 18

"Are you going to tell me what has you so jumpy?" Micah asked as they walked down the hotel hallway towards the elevator. They were meeting Beck's mom in the lobby and heading to dinner before they had to be back for the final pre-game walkthrough.

"Nothing. It's nothing," Beck said, waving a hand as Micah hit the button.

"Somehow, not convincing."

"Maybe I'm nervous about the game."

Micah shot him a look as they headed downstairs. "You've never been nervous about a game in your whole damn life."

Beck glanced over at him, gaze skimming over his body, from the top of his head, down his chest and then his stomach, and stopping on his thighs. For a moment, the worry that had lingered in the back of his mind all day that Beck had seemed both edgy and quiet at the exact same time faded into the background. What replaced it was a white-hot spike of desire.

"Yeah, but *you're* nervous about the game," Beck pointed out.

It was true. He *was* nervous about it. Facing the Piranhas wasn't like facing anyone else.

"I'm probably more worried about it for you, than for me, or," Beck added with a chuckle, "maybe I'm thinkin' of something else."

Micah groaned. "We're just about to go see your freaking *mother*. I don't want to even begin to think about sex."

"Fine, fine." Beck grinned at him. "*I'll* just think about it, instead."

"God, you're the worst," Micah complained. The elevator doors dinged open and he and Beck strode across the room towards a grouping of couches near the set of front doors.

They were halfway there when he saw Beck's mother's head, with its distinctive dark hair, and heard her laugh carrying across the lobby.

And she wasn't alone.

Micah instantly recognized the woman who was sitting next to her, even though all he could see was the back of her head, her braids resting over one shoulder.

He stopped in his tracks. Just plain fucking froze.

Beck put a hand on his back, and Micah reacted before he could stop himself—he threw it off and shot his husband a glare. The most heated one he'd ever given him, that was for sure, in all their years of friendship and now this, their new relationship.

"What's she doing here?" Beck exclaimed, and Micah realized, hearing the shock in his voice, that he hadn't known she was coming either.

He was just as surprised as Micah was that his mother hadn't just brought herself but Sheila, too.

"You could ask your mother that question," Micah said in a hard voice.

"Micah—" Beck started to say quietly, but Micah didn't want to hear it.

"No, you don't get to do this interfering shit," Micah retorted.

"*I'm* not doing it," Beck reminded him. But he was still looking over, every few seconds, to where his mother and Sheila sat together.

"But you still think I should go over to her," Micah said.

"Yeah, *yeah*, okay, I *do* think you should. She came here to talk to you. I know she's hurt you, and *God*, that sucks. I wish I could change it, more than anything. And if she hurts you again, believe me, it won't just be you pissed at her. But I do think you should let her say whatever she came to say. I know my mom. She wouldn't have helped if she thought it was going to be bad."

Micah didn't say anything.

What *was* there to say?

Maybe someone else, someone who wasn't Micah, would be appreciative that Beck was trying to help mend his family. But Micah wasn't. He didn't *want* it to be fixed. He was so fucking tired of people, including his mother, who was currently sitting over on the couch with Jolie West, expecting him to settle and give in and be *rational* and *reasonable* and swallow whatever fucking bullshit they'd done to him.

He turned and walked off.

He was nearly back to the elevator and the safety of his room when Beck caught up to him. "Wait, *wait*, goddamn it," Beck said, exhaling sharply and catching his arm.

"I just asked her, because I had to know. For *you*," Beck said. "My mom told me she'd reached out, but that in the end, coming here together was all Sheila's idea. Apparently your mom's been wanting to apologize and fix things with you for awhile, but you wouldn't listen. Wouldn't let her in. So my mom thought, she'd give her a chance. That's all this is, Micah, a *chance*. If she chooses your uncle over you again, I will be the first one to tell her to get the fuck away from you. And I *know* my mom will be the second."

He'd shut his mother out of his life because all she'd wanted to do was talk. Placate him. Reason with him. Until he was okay being in the same room as someone who'd called him . . .

Micah swallowed hard.

No. No, he wouldn't do it. Not again.

Not ever again.

But Beck kept going, like he'd seen his resolve weakening. "I know how you can be," he said, and *God*, he hated how much sense Beck made. How the love in his eyes was shining so clearly he couldn't fucking miss it. It didn't really change anything, but then it *did*, also. "I know how you can shut people out when you're angry with them. When they've hurt you. When you're afraid of the power they have over you. You did it for me, and yeah, I could've reached out more, when we weren't talking, but I don't think it would've mattered, Micah. You *do* that. And you were doing it to her. She just wants to fix things—"

"You mean, somehow convince me to accept my uncle in my life, after he said . . ."

He couldn't say it again. Couldn't even think it.

It was unreal that less than two years ago, he'd said the word himself. Called someone else that.

He didn't even feel like the same person he'd been on that day. All the anger and hate and fear had leaked right out of him, in dribbles and drabs, and then after it had gone, he still hadn't quite known who he was. He'd felt like an empty box, wanting to be filled up with something else, *anything else.* But over the season in Miami, he'd discovered a new purpose, new friends, new interests. Then, when he'd come here, he'd continued to fill it, with things that mattered.

With people who mattered.

Beck had gone in, of course, because he'd been helpless to keep him out.

Because he *belonged*.

"No, *no*," Beck said. "I don't know exactly what went down, because that's between you and her. She should tell you what happened. What's changed for her. But if I thought for even a single fucking minute that was what she wanted, she would *not* be here, and she definitely would not be here with my mother. I can guarantee that."

Micah stared at him.

"You knew something was up."

Beck flinched. "Yeah, I'll admit, something about my mom coming didn't seem right, but I had no fucking clue it was this. I need you to believe me. To *trust* me."

Micah did. Not only with his life, but with his whole fucking heart.

That was the problem.

"I want to," Micah said stubbornly.

"I love you," Beck said and reached for his hands, squeezing them, even as Micah tried to pull them away. "You come *first*, always. I'm only encouraging you to go talk to her and take advantage of this opportunity, because I think there's a chance this is the best thing for you. But if it's not, it's not. We'll leave, and I'll respect your wishes on this forever."

"You mean it, don't you?" Micah hated that his voice cracked, but he didn't flinch away from it.

Beck nodded emphatically. "If even for a *second* she makes you question what you did or how you did it or wants you to make good with him, I will be there for you. No questions asked."

Micah didn't say anything for a long moment. "I don't want to do this," he finally admitted in a low, wrecked voice. "It *hurts*. I didn't tell you about it, because it hurt too much to even *think* about, so I didn't. I . . .I blocked it out. I pretended."

"To lose someone you care about? Yeah, I know. I don't have to imagine how much it hurts, because I *know* how much it hurts."

Micah knew what Beck meant. And yeah, he'd done the same thing to Beck, because he'd been terrified out of his goddamn mind, and hiding from it had felt easier than facing it.

Just the same as today.

Maybe Beck was right. Maybe he should at least give his mother a chance to say her piece. If he didn't like it, then yes, that would suck, it would enormously suck and it would hurt, but at least he would *know*.

"I'm sorry I did that to you," Micah said quietly.

"I know." Beck squeezed his hands again. "And it's okay."

"If I want to go back upstairs and not see her . . ."

Beck exhaled. "Then that's what we'll do."

"No questions?"

"No questions."

"Even though you disagree with me?"

"Micah, I never want you to do something you don't want to do. Sometimes, yeah, we need a little push. Maybe you need one right now. Maybe not. But if you absolutely do not want to see her, we go back upstairs, and that's the end of it."

"I need a minute." Micah knew what he *should* do. How was it that he'd done so many of those things—*hard* things that hadn't come easily at all—over the years, but somehow this one felt insurmountable, like he could barely face it?

Because it mattered.

And because it mattered, he should give it serious consideration before he rejected it out of hand.

"Take all the time you need." Beck waved over by the couches, where Jolie sat with his mother. They'd seen them, and Jolie was patting Sheila on the shoulder, comforting her, it looked like.

Much like she'd comforted Micah when they'd been in Chicago.

Maybe it should feel like a betrayal that Jolie was doing it now, but Micah had a feeling she wasn't on anybody's side in particular; she just had an enormous capacity to empathize with and love everyone she believed deserved it.

So that meant she believed there was something in his mother worth listening to.

She wouldn't have done this otherwise. Beck seemed completely convinced of it, and Micah wanted to believe it too.

"And if I need you?" Micah couldn't swallow the words back once they were out of his mouth, but they were real. True.

He'd always need Beck, even when he didn't want to admit it. Even when he felt lesser for admitting it.

But Beck didn't judge. Instead, his gaze softened. "I'm always here for you, Micah. Always. That's what we promised each other that night in Vegas, and I mean it, every single day."

"I meant it too," Micah said. Maybe he hadn't always been strong enough to mean it, but he did now.

"I know," Beck said. Brushed a kiss across his lips, tender and sweet and loving. Saying everything he wasn't saying. "I'll be just over there, okay?"

"Okay."

After Beck walked over to their mothers and sat down with them, Micah turned the corner towards the elevator bank, but instead of hitting the button to take him up to his room, he leaned back against the far wall.

For a minute, he just stood there and let himself think about it.

What if she was here to continue brokering peace?

What if that was all she wanted? To stay in her house—which, he might add, he'd never even threatened to take away, even though he'd been so angry when she'd let Josiah move in. Even after they'd stopped speaking.

Then . . .he supposed that was the truth, and he'd learn to live with it, the way he'd learned to live with all the other truths that were at first too difficult to face.

But, a voice inside him said, *you never faced them alone. You always fought them together, with Scott. And then with Beck. And Carter. And Deacon. Jem. Riley and Landry.*

You were never alone.

He pulled out his phone. It was too much to ask that tonight, of all nights, the evening before one of the biggest games of the season, when they were actually facing each other, that Scott would answer.

But he did. On the second ring.

"Micah," he said, his voice even warm. Welcoming. Like he was actually the son he'd never had. "Good to hear from you."

Micah squeezed his eyes shut. Let the warmth of that drawl of Scott's fill him up in all those places he'd felt alone.

It wasn't weak to admit you were weak. It was only weakness if you bent to it. Let it consume you.

He didn't say anything. Couldn't force the words past the sudden lump in his throat.

"Micah?" Scott questioned. "You alright?"

"No," he said, squeezing the single syllable out.

"No? Where are you at? Are you at the Condors' hotel? We're just down the street . . ." Micah could hear him getting up, hear his voice as he murmured to someone next to him—Coach Dawson, maybe?

"Yeah." His voice continued to come out resembling a croak. He cleared his throat. "My mom's here. She wants to talk to me, but I don't know . . . I don't know if I can *let* her. Beck thinks I should but Beck—"

Scott interrupted. "Because he thinks it's so easy to fix that rift between you?" he asked, and there was a deep frustrated anger in his voice. Micah could hear it. Micah *understood* it, even if it wasn't right.

"No. No. Actually no. Because I wouldn't . . . because I wouldn't listen to her. And he thinks maybe if I did . . ."

"Has she been trying to talk to you?"

"Probably. I don't know. Yeah. I guess." Micah stumbled over the options. He didn't know which was actually true. He did know he'd deleted probably a hundred texts from her and voicemails and emails. She'd clearly been trying to tell him *something*. The only question was if it was something he wanted to hear.

"You want to hear what she has to say?" Scott asked.

He did. Desperately.

And he also, just as desperately, wanted to take the elevator back to his room and try to forget she'd ever come here to Charleston.

"I get that it's hard," Scott continued when he stayed quiet. "It's probably way harder than Beck realizes. He means well—"

"It's more than that. He loves me," Micah said, interrupting.

"Yeah, yeah, he does," Scott agreed, voice softening. "So you gonna do it? If you don't want to, that's okay, too. I can come over there, sit with you, if you want."

"But we're—"

This time Scott didn't let *him* finish. "But we're playing against each other tomorrow? Yeah, so what? You're still Micah Rose. You're still a guy I care a lot about. It doesn't matter what color uniform you wear tomorrow. Which sideline you jog back to. You still got a place with me. I keep tellin' you that."

"Even though . . ." Micah could barely choke it out. "Even though I . . ."

"Even though you probably told the Condors everything you could about us? Son, you don't think we haven't spent the whole week going over your last season of tape, those last few games when you really came into your own, figuring out how we can get Tristan loose when you cover him? That's football; this is something more."

"Yeah. Yeah, it is." And for the first time, Micah truly believed it. Scott wasn't just talking out of his ass when he called him *son*. When he promised him that it didn't matter which side he was on.

Because it didn't.

They had something special. They understood something in each other. When Scott had come to Miami, Micah certainly hadn't wanted a father. He'd long accepted that he wasn't going to have one. His own had died too young to leave much of an impression and Josiah certainly hadn't filled his shoes. So when Scott had arrived and he'd begun to reach out, Micah had tried to fight it at first. But Scott had made sure he'd known he wasn't alone. Not then. Not ever.

Same as Beck had done.

"I'm going to talk to her," Micah said, finally making up his mind.

"Offer stands," Scott said. "I'm here if it goes badly. Even if it goes well, and you need an ear or a friendly face."

"Thanks." Micah squeezed the phone case in his hand. "That means . . .that means more than you know."

"Son, I know *exactly* what it means." And he probably did, Micah realized. "Otherwise, I'll see you tomorrow, okay?"

"Yep, you won't be able to keep me away," Micah said, and he was laughing. His eyes were wet but he was *laughing*.

"I'm countin' on it," Scott said and hung up.

Micah approached where his mother, Jolie, and Beck were sitting, cautiously.

His mother's eyes were also wet, but they were also undeniably filled with joy when she glanced up and saw him standing there.

"Oh, Micah," Jolie said when she noticed he'd arrived. "I'm so glad you decided to join us."

There was an unspoken apology in her gaze. So similar to her son's. *I'm sorry if I overstepped*, it said, *but I think you are going to be glad you did this.*

Micah hoped he was, too.

"Micah," Sheila said softly. "It's so good to see you again."

"It's good to see you too." He wasn't sure that was true, but as he settled on the couch, next to Beck, he *wanted* it to be true so badly it ached.

"Jolie here friended me on Facebook, after the wedding," she said slowly, nervously. "And then I thought, we should be friends, right? Our sons are married. I didn't think you'd told her, but when we started talking . . ." Sheila hesitated. "You had. You'd told her everything."

"She deserved to know," Micah said unapologetically.

"She did," Sheila said, nodding. To his utter shock. "And I thought maybe it might be a chance to get you to listen when I tell you how sorry I am. How much I screwed all of this up. I should have . . .God, Micah, you're the best son. You worked so hard. You did everything you ever promised you'd do. And you just wanted this one thing. For me to get rid of Josiah, and I knew he was no good, I just thought . . .I don't even know what I thought. That I owed him, maybe, for how he helped me when Michael died. But I figured out later, he didn't stick around for me, he was there for *you*. What you could bring him." Her voice went bitter.

"You should have listened to me when I told you what he was about," Micah said. Not letting her off the hook. Not for a moment. She deserved it, after how much she'd hurt him.

"I should have." Sheila wiped her eyes. "And I paid for it. By losing you. It was the worst trade I'd ever made, and I realized as soon as I made it, as soon as you wouldn't listen, that it was a huge mistake and how sorry I was. But then you wouldn't relent. You hid yourself away, put up all those walls and wouldn't let me apologize. Wouldn't let me tell you . . ."

"Tell me what?" To Micah's surprise, his own voice was steady.

"Josiah is gone," Sheila said, her own voice firming up. Growing more confident. "I kicked him out. He's not welcome around anymore. Not after everything he said about you, not when you're so . . .he wanted to use you and disrespect you, I don't understand that, but he did."

"Micah doesn't deserve either of those things," Beck said, speaking up.

"No, no, he does not, and I'm so glad you see it. That you love him. That you want to make him happy." Sheila threw Beck a grateful glance. "I'll never really forgive myself for letting it go on so long. For not listening." Her eyes met Micah's. "Will you forgive me?"

Up until this moment, even if he'd heard all the right things from her—and she'd certainly said them—Micah hadn't been sure he could.

But now, it seemed like the easiest thing in the world to nod and say, "Yeah, Momma. Absolutely. But you gotta do one thing for me, first."

"What is it? Anything. I'd do anything," she pleaded with him. She seemed to mean it, too, and undeniable relief flooded Micah. It was over. He'd faced her, and faced the potential pain and it hadn't been nearly as horrible as he'd expected it would be.

Just the same as when he'd finally faced his sexuality.

And Beck, after ghosting him for so long.

And Beck's family, when he'd been so sure they wouldn't accept the color of his skin or who he was deep inside.

He'd been wrong every single fucking time.

Maybe what he'd learned from all that shit and all that doubt was to extend the same grace to others that had been extended to him.

"I just want you to forgive yourself," he said, standing and crossing over to her. She was up and in his arms in a minute and as they held each other, he realized one very important thing: there was love everywhere, and if you looked, even in the most unexpected places, you'd find it.

CHAPTER 19

Beck knew the moment Micah spotted Scott Callaway on the opposing sideline.

They'd come out early to do their warmup, Beck following Micah without him even having to ask, because he knew how important this was to him.

Yesterday, *thank God*, had turned out well. As soon as he'd realized Sheila Rose was seated next to his mother, he'd been terrified that it wouldn't.

When his mother had explained to him that Sheila had been talking to her about how Micah wouldn't give her a chance to apologize and explain how the situation had changed—how she'd *forced* it to change—he'd hoped so much that Micah would be willing to take a chance and listen.

He'd wanted the same thing for himself, so badly, and Micah had shut him out.

But he'd listened. Not only that, but he'd accepted her apology, and then, after they'd finally gotten back to the room after an emotional and happy dinner and then the Condors' final walkthrough, Micah had turned to him and hadn't said a word, just hugged him.

But the words were there all the same. Beck heard them as loudly as if Micah had yelled them.

Thank you. I'm sorry. I love you.

But he wasn't stupid enough to think it was *just* him who'd helped Micah. He'd said as much himself, mentioning that he'd talked to Scott—and saying he needed to text him to let him know it had turned out okay.

Beck was just beginning to realize how important Scott and Micah were to each other, and every time he found out more, he was more grateful that *someone* had been there to help Micah when he'd needed it.

Still, today they weren't facing him as a father figure Micah had needed during a tough part of his life. Or someone who Beck was grateful he'd had. Today they were facing him in a bit of a slightly different capacity.

As an opponent.

Beck had looked up Scott Callaway on the internet when Micah had told him how instrumental he'd been to his surging career with the Piranhas—and with his acceptance of his true self.

He was a big man, with a rough but handsome face, penetrating dark eyes, and a perpetual golden-brown tan from too many years spent on too many sidelines.

But what the pictures on the internet hadn't prepared him for was the way he smiled when he saw Micah.

And the way Micah smiled back.

"Micah," Scott exclaimed as they clasped hands and then tugged each other into a tight hug.

They pulled back, grinning at each other. "Been too long," Micah said. He turned to where Beck stood, a few feet away, not wanting to intrude on their reunion.

He'd known it would be heartfelt, but he hadn't expected this.

"Scott," Micah said, "this is my husband, Beck."

The way his chest puffed out as he said it, like even though they'd suddenly, unexpectedly gotten married in a haze of booze and adoration, it was the best thing he'd ever done, filled Beck with love—and hope.

Hope that they might actually make this crazy thing work out long-term.

He was committed, of course, and Micah had said he was too, but here was undisputable evidence of it.

"It's wonderful to meet you," Scott said, extending a hand. They shook. He had a firm grip, and Beck had a sudden feeling he was being examined by that intense dark stare. "And congratulations, by the way."

"Thanks." Beck met his stare. Hoped that Scott liked what he saw there, because even though he'd just met the guy, his reputation preceded him, plus there was how clearly important he and Micah were to each other. He didn't want to ever give Scott a reason to not think he'd always put Micah first. Or that he wouldn't love him forever, no strings and no excuses.

"You two have some time for a honeymoon?" Scott asked, shading his eyes from the sun.

"Scott!" Micah exclaimed, horrified.

God, they really were kind of father and son, weren't they?

Scott just grinned. "It's important," he said. "Takin' some time for yourselves."

"We went back to Chicago. To Northwestern," Beck explained. He wondered if Micah had been this nervous meeting *his* family. It was entirely possible, and Beck belatedly wished he'd asked how Micah had *really* felt about it.

Because suddenly, Beck was way too aware of how important this was.

How much he wanted Scott to like him. Not just like him, but *respect* him. Believe that he was the best man for Micah.

The kind of man Micah deserved.

"Asa and I saw you were both given some kind of ceremony."

"The Ring of Honor, sir," Beck said.

Scott's expression softened as he turned towards Micah. "You didn't tell me that. That's great. I'm proud of you. Both of you," he added.

Micah made a face. "It wasn't . . ."

Beck smacked him. "Don't say it wasn't a big deal, because we both know it was."

"It was, for lots of reasons," Scott said reasonably. "And that's okay. It's not easy being different in this league. But you'll get more comfortable with it. Your new owner seems solid. Asa really likes him."

Beck was beginning to see why Micah liked this guy so much. He had an easy manner, and also a bone-deep sincerity that made him incredibly easy to not only talk to but *believe*.

And Beck could absolutely see Micah, in the worst of his identity crisis, latching onto that belief and unconditional support like a lifeline.

"Yeah, he's great," Beck agreed.

"Hey, look at who it is, the happy couple." A guy with a shaved head and a gorgeous face that looked like it had been carved from marble by a master sculptor approached.

"Sebastian," Micah said, turning his way with a welcoming smile.

And oh God, this was Sebastian Howard. Of course it was. Beck knew him by sight, now that he was thinking about it.

The guy Micah had found so attractive.

The one who'd caused his final spiral.

Beck didn't find himself annoyed at the guy, because he hardly could help the way he looked, but he *was* a little jealous.

He'd tried so hard to not be, when Micah had told him about Sebastian.

You're married to him. It's you he loves. It's you he waited for. It's only you he wants.

"I told Micah I was surprised by what happened," Scott said quietly, and Beck looked up to see that he'd drifted a lot closer, "but I don't think I was, when I really thought about it."

Beck looked over at him. "Really?"

"I didn't know him over the summer, in camp, or at the beginning of the season, but everyone told me how much he lashed out. How deeply unhappy he was. I thought it was maybe his identity crisis, but it was more than that. He was missin' you."

"I missed him too," Beck confessed. Even though it wasn't really much of a confession, was it? "Listen, as much as it sucked to have him push me away when he needed me . . . I *let* him do it, too."

"You were hurt, just as much as he was," Scott said very reasonably.

"But regardless . . .I'm glad he had you. Found you. He needed someone."

Scott raised an eyebrow. "Past tense, huh?"

"No, no," Beck said, surprisingly flustered. But maybe it wasn't all that surprising, considering how much Scott meant to Micah. How important he'd become in his life.

"Good." Scott sounded satisfied. "'Cause I'm not goin' anywhere."

"I hope not," Beck said.

A moment later, Micah and Sebastian joined them.

"So this is the safety you deserted me for?" Sebastian asked, holding out his hand. Beck shook it, and to his surprise, Sebastian pulled him into quick hug.

"Any husband of Micah's is a friend of ours," Sebastian said firmly.

"Thanks," Beck said.

Micah was grinning still, like this was the two best parts of his life colliding, and Beck felt a surge of love.

Of course, in an hour, things would be different.

They'd be facing off against each other.

But for right now, everything was golden.

And, Beck realized, as they headed back towards the Condors sideline after saying goodbye to Scott and Sebastian, they would be golden again.

This game wasn't going to make or break either team. It was *just* a game.

The game itself, just as Micah had expected, turned out to be something of a chess match. Coach K versus Coach Dawson.

He'd warned Coach Kelley, who probably hadn't needed it, that Coach Dawson was not only crafty, he was basically a strategic genius.

But Coach K had lived up to that too. To start the game, instead of kicking off in the traditional way, he'd chosen to be aggressive and had onside kicked the ball, to give Riley and the offense a better chance of moving the ball early.

As Riley dropped back, scrambling to his right, several Piranhas defensive players in hot pursuit, Micah headed over to where Beck stood, at what was now their spot on *this* sideline.

"Hey," Beck said, turning towards him.

"I didn't forget," Micah said.

"Didn't think you would."

"I *do* want us to win," Micah admitted. "More than I thought I did."

He put out his hand. Beck clasped it immediately, and it was just the same as they'd started so many games at Northwestern—and the handful they'd played together in Charleston too—except it was also different. There was a strength in Beck's grip, like he didn't ever want to let go, and a soft love in his eyes as he gazed at Micah.

"Sixty minutes," Beck said.

"No more, no less," Micah chanted back.

They were still holding onto each other when Deacon and Jem approached.

"You guys ready?" Deacon asked. He gestured out towards the field. Carter had just caught one of Riley's passes. But it was short for the first down, and in a minute Ethan, the Condors' kicker, would be heading out onto the field to take their first three points of the game.

It wasn't the touchdown Micah knew everyone had hoped for, to kick off this game, but it was something.

"Aw, look at their cute secret handshake," Jem crooned.

"We're not cute, we're the Wall," Micah retorted.

"I don't know." Beck was grinning as he finally let go of Micah and reached for his helmet. "Maybe we can be both."

Micah had faced Pax and the Piranhas offense plenty of times in practice, but he'd never imagined that he'd be doing it on the game field.

Pax nodded to him, respect brimming in his gaze, and it was mirrored too, in Tristan's gaze as Micah took his position opposite him.

Win or lose, he had the most important thing, Micah realized.

He had himself. He had Beck. And not only that, but he had not only the kind of life he'd dreamed of, that he honestly had never believed would ever be possible, but a future, too, and it was so fucking bright.

"Come on," Micah said, grinning across the line at Tristan. "Bring it, baby."

Tristan grinned right back, and for the first time, Micah realized this could actually be *fun*.

What had Scott said yesterday? *That's football; this is something more.*

Micah felt it now. And not just *felt* it, but *believed it.*

He dug in his back cleat, eyes intent on the ball, resting in Logan's hands. Pax leaned over and Logan snapped the ball, and Micah took off like a shot, tracking Tristan across the field.

He was not only fucking fast, the way he'd been last year, when they were both rookies, but he was way better as a receiver than he'd been.

Trickier. Sneakier.

Exactly the kind of shit Tristan Nicholson hadn't needed to add to his already impressive resume.

Out of the corner of his eye, Micah watched as Beck jogged up in the zone, shifting to cover Wade across the middle.

Everything was covered. One beat. Two beats. Jem pushed through the line, and Pax tossed the ball away.

First down done.

Now just a million to go.

By halftime, the score was ten to ten, and Micah was dialed in a way he hadn't remembered ever being before.

"You're playing fucking lights out," Jem said to him on the sideline as the last minute ticked down in the half.

They were on the sideline watching as the Condors offense ran a two-minute drill, trying desperately to break through the Piranhas' defense and score a few more points to go into the locker room up.

The Piranhas had been double-teaming Carter all afternoon, Sebastian's history as a corner paying off as he had an uncanny knack for predicting exactly the way Carter would break and he was already there, ready to defend the ball.

Carter was usually relaxed and easy on the sideline, between series, but as the game had gone on, he'd gotten increasingly silent and taciturn, barely barking out responses to Riley as they'd sat on the bench with Landry and gone over the prior series, trying to find a way to break the stalemate.

Micah could tell Carter wanted this bad.

He was pulling out all the stops, but he was equally matched in Sebastian, who was clearly determined not to let him win and catch the ball.

Third down and six.

Micah watched as Carter gestured to himself in the huddle. Riley nodded and clapped, breaking the group up.

A few moments later, Carter was racing along the sideline, fighting tooth and nail against both Sebastian and one of the Piranhas' corners—the one who'd replaced him.

Together they were very good.

Maybe not quite as good as Sebastian and Micah had been, but he could see Carter struggling and Riley, just as desperately wanting to make something happen as time expired, tossed the ball anyway, even though there was no way Carter wasn't completely covered.

Micah sucked in a hard breath as Carter went up, jumping up just as Sebastian did, and in the air, they fought for the ball.

But it wasn't Carter who came down with it, but Sebastian, grinning wildly as he took a knee, the clock ticking down to zero.

"Fuck," Carter screamed as he jogged over to the sideline. He kicked a stand full of equipment, sending a bunch of water bottles and cups to the turf.

"Carter, hey, it's all good," Riley said, appearing before Micah and Beck could intercept him and try to calm him down.

"It's not fucking good," Carter yelled. He grabbed a tablet and snapped it in half by smacking it right over his thigh.

Shit.

Since he'd gotten to Charleston, he'd heard other players and coaches obliquely refer to Carter's temper problem, but he'd begun to think they must be exaggerating, because he'd never witnessed anything other than affable, laid-back, easygoing Carter Maxwell.

But this Carter was none of those things.

Fire was burning in his eyes, his face hard, and he was on the fucking warpath.

"Carter," Riley tried again, reaching out to catch his arm, but Carter flung it away like it was nothing. And Riley, while not exactly tall for a quarterback, was undeniably stacked with muscle, so that was saying something.

Micah saw as Riley looked over at Landry and Deacon, who'd come over, too.

The two of them were big enough to restrain him, if it came to that.

And Micah knew he wasn't the only one who didn't want it to come to that.

"Hey, hey, it's all good," Landry spoke up, in a soothing voice. "We got two quarters left. A whole half. And the defense is holdin' them. We'll find a way through. It's hard. We knew it would be hard."

"Not this fucking hard," Carter spat out. He stormed off, and Micah and everyone else followed as he rampaged into the locker room.

There went another tablet.

His helmet got kicked into the corner.

Riley finally got another hand on him. Shooting everyone else a glare and a message that screamed, *I got this.*

"Carter," he tried again. "God, I don't blame you for that at all, okay? You did your best. I knew you would. That's why I threw it."

Carter's eyes were wild as he finally looked down at Riley.

But he didn't say anything.

And he certainly didn't look any less angry.

"We gonna have a problem here?" It was Coach Kelley and he was approaching with a frown creasing his forehead. "'Cause if we do, I *will* bench you, Maxwell. We need you to win but I don't need you having a fucking meltdown either. Riley's right. He knew the risk when he threw that pass."

Carter stared at both of them with a complete lack of comprehension. Like their words couldn't even penetrate the haze of anger consuming him.

"Shit," Beck said, coming up to stand next to Micah, arms crossed over his chest. "What are we gonna do about that?"

"Nothing, we're going to do nothing. Not until he calms down." Deacon's voice was harsh, cutting through the hushed worry in the locker room.

"Really?" Landry's tone was skeptical.

"He can throw a hissy fit all he wants to," Deacon said dismissively, and no doubt it was that edge in his voice that made Carter's gaze narrow and harden. That was hardly going to calm him down, Micah thought, and then he realized that Deacon didn't give a shit. He didn't want to spend any more minutes of their precious time dealing with Carter, and fuck, as much as Micah hated it, he was *right*.

"We got another two quarters of football to strategize for," Deacon continued. "'Cause I want to win this game, goddamn it."

Micah stared at Carter, who stood in the center of the room, chest rising and falling with his breath, hair falling around his eyes, hands squeezed into fists.

"Come on," Deacon said to Micah and Beck. "Let's go over the containment, okay?"

"Sure thing, boss," Beck said.

When they jogged back onto the field ten minutes later, Micah saw Carter sitting on the sideline by himself. He nearly went over, because if it had been him—and goddamn it, it *had* been him, not nearly this bad, but close enough—he'd have wanted someone to reach out. To reassure him that it was alright.

But before he could, Deacon called out sharply, "Rose, over here."

Deacon was unquestionably the leader of the defense, and he was their captain too, and Micah was too new to question anything he said.

Because as much as it sucked, Deacon was right; they needed to be a team if they were gonna win this game.

"Alright," he said, turning away from Carter.

The first Piranhas drive of the second half was a fucking awful time.

They had this new bruiser of a running back—who had a gear he could shift down into that made containment way too fucking hard. Like the Piranhas needed another reason to be fucking amazing, Micah thought as he watched it take both Jem *and* Beck to bring the guy down after he'd gained over twenty yards on just his first carry.

"Shit," Beck said, breathing hard as he returned to the line for the next play.

Micah could agree.

Especially when he realized Jem was still on the ground. He got up, eventually, with Deacon helping him, but he went right over the sideline.

Double shit.

They could not do this without Jem.

Deacon returned to the huddle.

"He gonna be okay?" Micah asked.

Deacon just shrugged, but they could all see the worry in his eyes. Not just for his best friend, but for one of the best defensive players on this team.

"You need me to handle Nicholson on my own?" Micah asked.

Micah wasn't stupid or blind. He knew just how much Beck was holding back on covering the run just in case Micah needed additional help with Tristan.

But Beck shook his head. Being fucking stubborn, Micah knew.

"Stick to the plan," Deacon said, just as Beck shook his head.

"And if they keep laying more runs like that on us?" Micah retorted.

"We'll deal with it." Micah had been here only a few weeks now, but he'd still never heard Deacon sound so intense. So determined.

It wasn't just him who wanted to win this game so badly.

"Yeah, stick to the plan," Beck agreed. "We just need to pick up better when Pax goes into that run-pass option. He's callin' shit at the line."

Micah didn't need to say that Pax hadn't had that ability a year ago. It felt like only a few weeks, he hadn't been able to do that.

But there was a confidence radiating from the Piranhas quarterback these days.

Whatever he was doing—whatever he and Asa and Davis had cooked up, it was something else.

Something they couldn't stop, no matter how they tried.

Inexorably, by running the ball right at their line, the Piranhas went right down the field, notching first down after first down, and there was nothing Micah could do to stop it.

Beck continued to hold himself back, but the truth was, they barely threw the ball.

Whatever adjustment they'd made at halftime had worked. The Piranhas scored a touchdown.

Jem hadn't come back to the game, and he was nowhere to be found. The panic in Micah's stomach grew, even as he tried to force it down.

They'd be okay, even without Jem.

Beck collapsed to the bench next to him as they watched the extra point sail through the uprights, kicked by Dylan Leonard.

"That didn't fucking work at all," Beck grumbled.

"No shit." Micah wanted to say Asa had figured out that the only way they were stopping them was through the air, by holding Beck's coverage in reserve, and once he'd seen that, it was easy enough to shift their focus to the run game.

Now *they* needed to adjust their own focus in response. Normally, they might've been able to, but without Jem?

Not likely.

Still, crazier things had happened in the NFL.

Deacon stopped in front of them, frowning. "West," he barked. "I need you to come up more. Try to help stop this dude from bowling us all down." He shifted his gaze to Micah. "You got Nicholson on your own, okay?"

Micah nodded. It was the only choice they could make.

Sometimes teams just had too many weapons to appropriately stop them.

You couldn't cover everyone.

An hour later, Micah regretted even letting that thought cross his mind as he stood on the sideline and watched as the clock ticked down, Riley and the offense trying to make one last ditch attempt to go down the field and cut their deficit by half.

But he knew that even if they did, there wouldn't be enough time to score again and send the game into overtime.

They were going to lose.

It was painful, there was no question of that.

But it hadn't hurt as much as he'd thought it might. There'd been a part of him that had known, deep down, that winning this game was probably impossible. Micah, more than anyone else, knew just how good the Piranhas were. How stacked with talent and poised they were to make the leap from a very good team to a *great* team.

What else helped?

Watching as Riley ran into the end zone for their last touchdown. Ultimately it was meaningless, because it wouldn't change the game's result, but then Riley lifted his face and four fingers of his right hand towards the sky. Making the last touchdown count for something bigger than just a number on the scoreboard.

He'd worn the number four jersey too—Davis Abernathy's old number, when he'd played for the Condors, before they'd shunned and blacklisted him.

The clock ticked down and hit zero as Pax took a knee and ended the game.

"Hey, great effort," Coach K said, reaching over to pat his shoulder. "You did everything you could. All of you did."

Micah nodded.

It *did* hurt, but like he'd thought earlier, not nearly as bad as he'd imagined it would.

"Yeah," Micah agreed. He looked over at Beck as they walked back onto the field.

Next to them, Pax was greeting Riley with a hug and a smile.

"You'll get us next time," he heard Pax say, and then Pax's gaze fell to the number on Riley's chest. The number he'd worn proudly today.

"We sure will. And thanks for letting me borrow your gesture," Riley said, and Pax's smile widened.

"Thanks for thinking of him. It's not easy for him, not when we play you guys. Though easier now than it was last year," Pax said.

"Hope it gets easier still," Riley replied earnestly.

Pax turned to Micah, and to his surprise Pax hugged him too. "Good to see you, man," he said. "You're fitting in well here."

He was, Micah realized. Better than he'd ever imagined.

And not just because of Beck.

Though, undeniably, that *was* part of it.

Scott reached them next. "Great game," he said, pulling Micah into his big, warm embrace. "I thought Asa was gonna have an aneurysm at halftime."

"But he didn't, and he pulled it out."

"But the more we win, the more pressure we've got," Scott said ruefully. "So there's also that."

"You'll keep him together. You're the only one who can."

"Well, me and Beau," Scott pointed out dryly. "But yeah. We've got this. And you know what? You guys came out and fought harder, played better, than we ever imagined. That was part of Asa's panic. He didn't think we could pull it out."

"Wasn't sure you could either," Micah retorted.

"Next time," Scott said.

"Yep," Micah agreed.

CHAPTER 20

"I'M NOT SURE WHAT we should do about this," Beck said, holding his phone out towards Micah as they sat on the couch, relaxing after sleeping in and then joining their mothers for brunch before they left for the airport. Half an hour later they'd come back to the house, and Beck was still internally debating whether he'd take a nap or actually try to do something productive. Before he'd decided, this text from Carter had come in.

He'd hoped it was about Jem, but so far everyone had been close-lipped on what was going on with their favorite linebacker.

Party tonight for Disco Night. The Pirate's Booty.

Micah just shrugged. "I already told Carter we'd be there."

"You did *what*?" Beck exclaimed, reaching for the remote and muting the TV.

He hadn't been convinced he wanted to go. Not only because he was still bummed that in the end, they hadn't won the game, but because he didn't know if he thought it was a good idea Carter was still going to be partying, even though they'd lost.

Even though he'd clearly been struggling with his temper during the game.

Maybe the best thing for him wouldn't be another load of shiny distractions.

But he wasn't Carter.

He wasn't responsible for Carter.

Maybe the best thing they could do was to just support him. Be there for him. Be his friend.

Beck realized, as he stared at Micah, that was exactly the conclusion he'd come to. Long before Beck even had.

"Things weren't always perfect in Miami. But even when they sucked, we learned pretty goddamn fast the only way to deal with them was to stick together," Micah explained. "That's what going tonight is about—sticking together."

"Yeah. Yeah, I can see that." The Condors hadn't had a team-first mentality last year. There'd been a handful of players who'd stuck together, of course, but it wasn't the same.

"If you want something, I learned you gotta build it. Even when it's hard. *Especially* when it's hard."

"It just . . . *ugh*," Beck said. "I hate that we lost *that* game. We're gonna lose, I know that. But *that* game."

"Trust me, I know. I wanted it too," Micah said wryly. He leaned over, resting his head on Beck's shoulder.

"I thought we had it too, 'til Dawson figured out a way to spread us too thin."

"You're just one man. One player," Micah said reassuringly, which galled Beck even more. Shouldn't he be the one comforting Micah? Surely, that game meant even more to Micah than it had meant to Beck?

But even after the game, on their way back home, and after they'd gotten home, Micah hadn't said a word about it.

He hadn't been particularly quiet either, which Beck had worried about. Nope—he'd acted like everything was normal. Fine and normal.

Like losing was not okay but . . .well, like it was okay.

Beck turned towards him. "You're not upset we lost." Maybe all the shit he'd said about being torn between the Condors and the Piranhas was really Micah saying that he'd been on the Piranhas' side this whole time.

Micah smiled, which wasn't something he'd be doing if he was upset—or if he wanted to tell Beck he'd actually been rooting for the Condors to lose.

It reassured Beck a little.

"I'm not happy we lost. Don't get me wrong. I wanted the win, too. I wanted it bad. I wanted it because . . ." Micah hesitated. "Part of me wanted to prove something. Look at what a good decision I made. Look how happy I am. Look at me with my . . ." He cleared his throat. "But then I realized when we were standing there, and Davis and Riley were hugging, that it was about so much more than that. This is all about way more than just me and some petty feelings. And you know what else I realized? We'll get where they are. But we gotta put the time in. Become a team, first."

"Thus, going to Carter's party," Beck said after a long moment considering this.

Micah nodded.

"There was no way we were going to win. They had too many weapons, and they're too clever with them. They knew just how to use them so we couldn't cover. You know it. I know it. Coach Rufus knew it. So did Coach K. It's why they pushed us so hard. And yeah, we got damn close."

"Closer than a lot of other teams the Piranhas played this year," Beck acknowledged. It still sucked. He still wanted to sit on this couch with Micah and lick his wounds.

Maybe lick Micah a little.

Or more than a little.

But instead, Micah was annoyingly right, that if they all did that, sitting alone in their houses, licking their wounds and *not* going to Carter's party, nothing would really change.

"And we get to play them again," Micah said. "Week fifteen, and I think we're gonna be a hell of a lot more ready for them then than we were this week."

"So this isn't . . ." Beck hesitated. "You giving up? Resigning yourself to losing?"

"No way. No fucking way." Micah grinned at him.

Beck relaxed.

"Is that really what you thought? That I wasn't pissed off? That I didn't want it?" Micah's gaze was intent. "I *wanted* it. But you know what? Now I want the next one even more. And the next one. And the one after that."

"Yeah. Me too." Something unwound inside Beck.

"So are you gonna stay home then?"

Beck leaned over and kissed him. Long and slow and intent. When he pulled back, Micah looked just like he felt: deeply, madly, completely in love.

"And miss Disco Night with you? Not likely," he said.

Disco Night was in full swing by the time their Uber pulled up to the curb in front of the Pirate's Booty.

Beck shoved his phone in his pocket as he got out of the car, following Micah through the front door of the bar.

He could already hear the faint strains of Donna Summer from the dance floor as they walked in to see Kieran pouring drinks on the long bar.

Carter was leaning against it, along with Jem and Deacon.

"You guys came," Carter said excitedly, waving them over.

"We said we would," Micah said, giving him a quick embrace. "Sorry we're late-ish."

"Do we want to know why?" Deacon asked, raising an eyebrow as he sipped his beer.

"Honestly, we fell asleep," Beck said. Though he didn't say what they'd been doing before that.

And *before* that.

"Right." Jem grinned. "Totally innocent."

"How are you doin', man?" Beck asked Jem, who just shrugged.

"I'm alright, but . . .it's definitely a torn pectoral. Goin' in for surgery next week. I'm out for at least a couple months. Maybe more." Jem grimaced at the thought, and Beck felt that.

He loved playing with Jem, and he didn't want to win games without him—or *lose* games, if they couldn't handle their shit without his assistance—but that was the reality of the NFL. Injuries happened.

"That really sucks," Micah said.

"Yeah, it's not great. But I'll be around," Jem said. "At least most of the time. Family's been buggin' me to go home, so I may do that for a bit. Not sure yet."

"Jem's from this crazy ass town in Illinois that's famous for Christmas," Deacon said.

"Famous for Christmas?" Beck actually thought he'd heard of it. His mother was always talking about it. "You mean Christmas Falls?"

"Yep, that's the one. Always miss the big to-do because of the season, but I guess . . .not this year." Jem sounded tired.

Beck couldn't help but be worried about him. He'd been his friend, when friends hadn't been very thick on the ground.

"You're gonna be solid, man. There's always next year."

"Yeah," Jem echoed but Beck wasn't stupid enough to hear the reluctance in his voice. Jem was in his thirties—younger than Deacon, but still not *young*, not anymore. Maybe there wouldn't be a next year.

"Anyone else here yet?" Beck asked, changing the subject.

Micah nudged him and then glanced over at Kieran, and he nodded in response.

"Wait—" Jem said, before Carter could answer his question, "did you two just do a whole psychic communication thing?"

"Maybe it's the wedding vows; maybe they give you secret powers," Deacon teased.

Carter looked suddenly more interested in the institution of marriage.

"Sorry to burst your bubble," Beck said, chuckling, "but it's 'cause we've been friends forever and Micah knows just what I like."

"Oh, I bet he does," Carter teased.

"Actually," Micah said, coming back up to them, an impudent smile on his face, "I *do* know just what he likes."

"It's mutual," Beck insisted.

It definitely hadn't been only him falling to pieces on the couch just a few hours earlier—and then again, after.

"You two are adorable," Carter said. "Sickeningly sweet and adorable. And to answer your question, the *other* cavity-inducing couple we've got is already out on the dance floor. You two gonna join them?"

"Yeah, I think we should." Micah turned to Beck, the corner of his mouth quirking up. "You wanna dance with me?"

It was not very hard to answer that question, but before they did, Beck wanted to do one other thing.

"Yeah. Just . . ." He turned to Carter and lowered his voice. "Are you okay?"

Carter looked surprised. That he'd been the one to bring up the elephant in the room? Or that someone had at all?

None of them were perfect.

They'd all had bad practices. Bad games. Bad *stretches* of games.

There were times Beck hadn't wanted to get up in the morning and go into the practice facility last year because seeing Tom Taylor's smug face had been almost too much for him to bear, not when it was coupled with his own pain at his broken friendship with Micah.

He'd wanted to hide away. Not go in. Pull the covers over his head and pretend that his life hadn't turned out as shitty as it had.

But Deacon and Jem had been there too, pulling him along, making him believe, despite all the evidence to the contrary, that good guys existed.

He wasn't going to let Carter just pretend that everything was okay.

Wasn't going to let him drown out the noise in booze and sex and music.

"I'm . . ." Carter wet his lips. "I'm alright."

Beck put a hand on Carter's arm. Squeezed it. "If you need to talk about it, we're here, okay?"

"Yeah," Micah agreed. "Losing that game, that was rough."

"Rougher even because I feel like give us another two quarters and we could've gotten there," Deacon said wryly.

"Yeah, we could've," Jem agreed.

Beck and Micah exchanged glances. They famously promised each other sixty minutes of full-out effort and drive at the beginning of every game they played in together.

But maybe, Beck realized, they should be promising themselves more than that. Promising the whole *team* more than that.

"That's the next game," Beck said. "The next two quarters? That's our next game."

Deacon nodded slowly.

"The season's not over," Jem agreed.

But Carter hadn't really said much.

He didn't *look* okay, Beck realized. Like he was hiding all that pain behind an easy, uncomplicated front.

But he burned—Beck could see it in his eyes, now that he was looking for it.

"Carter," he tried again, "we're here for you, okay?"

"Even after I—" Carter stopped abruptly.

"Even after that," Deacon said gently.

"Especially after that," Micah added.

"We've all been there," Beck said. He knew it. He'd been deep in it. Drowning in it. And yeah, Micah's hand had appeared at the perfect time, but he'd had to be receptive to it too. He'd had to see it for what it was. That wasn't on Micah; that was on *him*.

"I'm thinking . . .maybe making a big change." Carter looked hesitantly from one of them to the next, taking in the whole loose circle around him. Beck hoped he could see that they were friends—that they were *his* friends. They weren't just here because they wanted to win games, though they did; they were here because it was no good to win games if you couldn't stand each other. If you weren't something bigger than the sum of your parts.

Micah was one hundred percent fucking right about that.

"What kind of change?" Deacon asked. "You're not thinking of leaving us, are you?" He sounded concerned.

But Carter just laughed. Socked him in the shoulder. "No way, dude," he said, "you're all stuck with me forever, I hope. Y'all know Alec Mitchell, right?"

"'Course we do." Beck had seriously considered using him when he'd signed with an agent right out of college. He'd ended up going in a different direction, but every interaction he'd ever had with Alec had been fantastic.

"He . . .he kinda specializes in my sort of shit. He got Chase Riley to clean up his act, big-time." Carter said. "I was thinking I might ask him to take me on. See what he can do to help me out of this situation. Improve it for the future."

"That's a great call," Deacon said. "And if you need our help, you know, all you have to do is ask."

"Yeah," Carter agreed—but he didn't look one hundred percent convinced.

From what Beck knew of Alec Mitchell though, he was one of those kind of guys who *would* do whatever it took to make sure that you were convinced. That you weren't a stranger in your own goddamn skin.

Carter could use that certainty.

Micah nudged him. "You ready to dance?" he asked softly.

"You ready to tolerate my shit dancing?" Beck teased back.

"I don't know, is it that shitty?" Micah asked as they set their beers down and headed out towards the open-air dance floor situated in the courtyard.

Beck rolled his eyes. "You *know* it's shitty."

"Maybe. Maybe not. Or maybe . . .maybe I can help you." Micah flashed him a quick charming grin. The same one that had lit up his insides for years now. For so long he hadn't even realized what the feeling was, but now he was sure.

It was friendship. It was *also* love.

It had been love this whole goddamn time. But instead of feeling like he'd missed out or like he was still trying to catch up to that realization, instead now, he just . . .embraced it.

"Love you," Beck said, tucking an arm around him.

"You just sayin' that so I teach you to dance?" Micah wiggled his hips.

Beck couldn't help the uncertainty. "I don't think you can," he said.

"Oh, baby, I got you," Micah said and, taking Beck's hands, tugged him closer to the middle of the dance floor.

There, under the flashing neon lights, were Riley and Landry, Riley's body tucked firmly against Landry's, the two of them grinding together to the music, pure joy written across their faces.

We do look like that, Beck realized.

"Just like that. See, you can move your hips," Micah teased, leaning in. "You were movin' them pretty damn well earlier. I knew you could."

Earlier had been when they'd been fucking on the couch, Beck riding Micah, sweat dripping down his head, mixing with Micah's, as they'd gasped into each other's mouths.

Beck's hips stuttered at the memory.

"And here you were doing so much better," Micah pointed out. But then, he didn't seem to care much, because he pulled Beck tightly against him, his hands over Beck's hips, moving them both flawlessly to the rhythm of the Bee Gees.

"God, I love you," Beck said. Couldn't think of any other words at the moment. His brain was empty of anything other than just *Micah* and *love* and *forever*.

"Good thing you do," Micah murmured, pressing a kiss to his neck, right by his ear. Nuzzling him. "That means one of us is *always* gonna know how to dance."

EPILOGUE

Micah was running behind.

He'd been gone nearly all day, running one errand after another, and just when he thought he'd finished them all, that he could head home—because in the eight months since they'd been married, Beck's house *had* become his home—and enjoy one last relaxing evening with his husband before they left for Chicago and the belated wedding celebration they were throwing, Beck kept texting him, asking him to do just one more thing.

But it wasn't just once. Beck had sent *three* texts just like that. Pick up the dry cleaning, he'd asked, and when Micah reluctantly agreed, there was another message, half an hour later, asking him to grab a new pair of AirPods from Best Buy, because Beck had lost his. Then finally, Beck had texted, asking him to pick up something for dinner, *because I just threw out everything in the fridge, whoops.*

But it was okay, Micah reasoned, taking a deep breath as he balanced everything in his arms, all the things Beck had asked him to take care of, because he was home now.

He shoved open the door with his hip after managing to type in the front door code correctly with a third of a functioning hand.

Barely making it to the kitchen, he dropped everything on the central island.

Beck was standing there, shirtless, only in a pair of loose athletic shorts, scrolling through his phone as he bent over the other counter.

"You got everything?" Beck asked, raising an eyebrow as he took in all the stuff Micah kept unloading. The AirPods, the pizza. The dry cleaning.

"I don't see how I could have possibly missed *anything*," Micah said dryly. "I think I got the whole fucking city something."

"Aw," Beck said, rising, and suddenly, there was something there Micah didn't recognize, plastered right there to his chest, right over Beck's heart. A square of white plastic, taped to his chest.

"What's that?" Micah asked slowly, heading around the island and stopping in front of his husband.

His grinning-like-crazy husband, who absolutely one hundred percent had been up to *something*, while Micah had run all these goddamn errands.

The one who'd kept insisting he stay out longer and longer and *longer*.

He pressed a finger against it and yep, Beck flinched.

The asshole had been getting a tattoo! Without Micah!

"You know," Micah said, conversationally, not giving Beck a chance to answer as he tugged at the corner of the wrap, "if *I* was planning on putting something permanent on my body, the body you're gonna have to look at *forever*, then I'd sure as hell want you to have input first."

"Oh?" Beck questioned. But he was still grinning that wild, charming, insane grin. Like he knew whatever Micah found under there wasn't just something he was going to like; it was something he was going to *love*.

And that, well, that was both a tiny bit worrying and also incredibly exciting.

Nobody knew him as well as Beck did, and if Beck thought he'd love it, then chances were, he would.

"Ouch," Beck murmured as Micah tugged more insistently on the wrap. "Be careful. I think you're pulling out some hair."

"Doubt it," Micah said resolutely, still carefully unwinding the wrap that covered the tattoo. "And damn you, for doing this first."

"Were you gonna get one too?" Beck asked, his smile impossibly widening.

"I was thinking about it," Micah grumbled. He hadn't come up with a good design yet, but he'd been considering it. Of course Beck had beaten him to it.

He'd never suspected, when they'd just been friends, how swoony of a romantic Beck was. But now that they were married, he got a front row seat, a *fully engaged* seat, to just how sweet and charming Beck could be when he chose.

And with Micah, he *always* chose to be.

"Well, nobody's stopping you," Beck teased.

Except, Micah realized, Beck himself, as he finally tugged the last corner of the wrap off Beck's chest, and there was the tattoo, beautifully articulated in stark black and red lines.

The design was simple: four spokes of a compass, fanning out across Beck's pectoral muscle, and intertwined among them were roses, circling the entire compass, done in a dozen or so different shades of red and pink.

But there was only one spoke they climbed across, and only one they rested on, and that was the spoke that pointed directly towards him now.

The spoke that pointed west.

Micah swallowed hard.

It was good he'd never gotten around to making a decision about his tattoo because nothing else was ever going to top this one.

"We got married so fast," Beck said quietly as Micah speechlessly and gently traced each fresh line of the tattoo with a single finger, "and I don't regret it, not for a second. I can't regret anything we've ever done together, but I wanted something . . .I don't know . . .something that didn't feel so rushed, so impermanent. Like we couldn't just undo it, if it got too hard."

"And," Beck added when Micah still didn't say anything, "I wanted to do it before this weekend, before we went back to Chicago. Yeah, we're already married, but we're taking our vows again, in front of our whole family and your old teammates and practically everyone we fucking know—"

Micah didn't let him get another word out. Not one single additional word.

He reached up and kissed Beck, dragging his head down to meet his own.

Beckett West. His husband and the love of his life. The man he was going to spend the rest of his life with, who'd just permanently etched their promises to each other on his skin.

Beck groaned low and deep in his mouth and they kissed and kissed, Micah finally turning them so Beck was pushed against the edge of the counter.

When he finally pulled back, ready to suggest they go upstairs so Micah could ride him, and never take his eyes off this tattoo for a single moment, Beck was dreamy-eyed, gazing at him like he'd won the world.

Like Micah was a prize he'd fight for, any day of the week.

Like he was a prize he'd fight for, every day for the rest of their lives.

Was it any wonder he loved this man?

For so long Micah had wondered why it had *always* had to be Beck or nobody.

But now he knew.

Because nobody else could make him feel safe and treasured and also completely, utterly free to be himself at the exact same time.

"I love you, too," Micah said, because he knew, without Beck saying it, exactly what he'd meant. "Love you *forever*."

Beck grinned. "After that tattoo, that's all I'm getting? Just a kiss and a few words?"

"You're getting me," Micah said confidently.

He'd never thought before he was a prize worth valuing, worth *keeping*, but now, miraculously, after all this admittedly shitty work he'd put in, he saw it now.

"If I get you?" Beck raised an eyebrow. "Then I'm getting everything. Everything I've ever wanted."

And it was everything Micah had ever wanted, too.

Carter's book is next! Preorder *The Score*, out in Fall 2023, here!

Make sure you don't miss the bonus scene – Deacon and Mr. G discuss what on earth they're gonna do about the Wall (and no, they've not got a clue how to deal with their own growing attraction).

And curious about Jem and his future? What about that town of Christmas Falls he's going back to? *Silent Knight* is book four in the Christmas Falls multi-author series, coming this holiday season!

INTERESTED IN READING MORE OF
BETH'S BOOKS?

CHECK OUT A FULL LIST OF TILES
BY SCANNING THE QR CODE
OR VISITING HER WEBSITE

WWW.BETHBOLDEN.COM/BOOKLIST

WANT TO FOLLOW BETH?

MAKE SURE YOU NEVER
MISS A RELEASE?

SCAN THE QR CODE BELOW
OR VISIT HER WEBSITE
FOR A SOCIAL MEDIA LIST,
NEWSLETTER SIGNUP,
AND SO MUCH MORE!

WWW.BETHBOLDEN.COM/ABOUT

www.ingramcontent.com/pod-product-compliance
Lightning Source LLC
Chambersburg PA
CBHW060424310726
48977CB00001B/42